The Festival C[illegible] on sun, the funf[illegible]am-ouring to try o[illegible], the girls shrieking on the roundabouts and swings. In the sunshine Clare Roper, a young lady of initiative, looking a treat in a polka-dot dress, her auburn hair full of sunlit tints, was bent on securing the interest of Jimmy Adams.

Clare caught sight of Jimmy, and she saw the girl with him. I don't believe it, she told herself. The girl was pretty enough, but real skinny – no more than a schoolgirl. 'Meet my cousin Linda,' said Jimmy, and Clare experienced enormous relief. 'Come on,' said Jimmy, and put his arms round both their shoulders. Clare positively tingled at his touch. Oh Lor', she thought, I can't hardly believe I've got it this bad already.

By Mary Jane Staples

The Adams Books

DOWN LAMBETH WAY
OUR EMILY
KING OF CAMBERWELL
ON MOTHER BROWN'S DOORSTEP
A FAMILY AFFAIR
MISSING PERSON
PRIDE OF WALWORTH
ECHOES OF YESTERDAY
THE YOUNG ONES
THE CAMBERWELL RAID
THE LAST SUMMER
THE FAMILY AT WAR
FIRE OVER LONDON
CHURCHILL'S PEOPLE
BRIGHT DAY, DARK NIGHT
TOMORROW IS ANOTHER DAY
THE WAY AHEAD
YEAR OF VICTORY
THE HOMECOMING
SONS AND DAUGHTERS
APPOINTMENT AT THE PALACE
CHANGING TIMES

Other titles in order of publication

TWO FOR THREE FARTHINGS
THE LODGER
RISING SUMMER
THE PEARLY QUEEN
SERGEANT JOE
THE TRAP
THE GHOST OF WHITECHAPEL

CHANGING TIMES

Mary Jane Staples

CORGI BOOKS

CHANGING TIMES
A CORGI BOOK : 0 552 15046 0

First publication in Great Britain

PRINTING HISTORY
Corgi edition published 2003

3 5 7 9 10 8 6 4 2

Set in 11/12pt New Baskerville by
Phoenix Typesetting, Burley-in-Wharfedale, West Yorkshire.

Corgi Books are published by Transworld Publishers,
61–63 Uxbridge Road, London W5 5SA,
a division of The Random House Group Ltd,
in Australia by Random House Australia (Pty) Ltd,
20 Alfred Street, Milsons Point, Sydney, NSW 2061, Australia,
in New Zealand by Random House New Zealand Ltd,
18 Poland Road, Glenfield, Auckland 10, New Zealand
and in South Africa by Random House (Pty) Ltd,
Endulini, 5a Jubilee Road, Parktown 2193, South Africa.

Printed and bound in Germany by
GGP Media GmbH, Pößneck.

To
Adam, Catherine, and Amelia Rose

THE ADAMS FAMILY

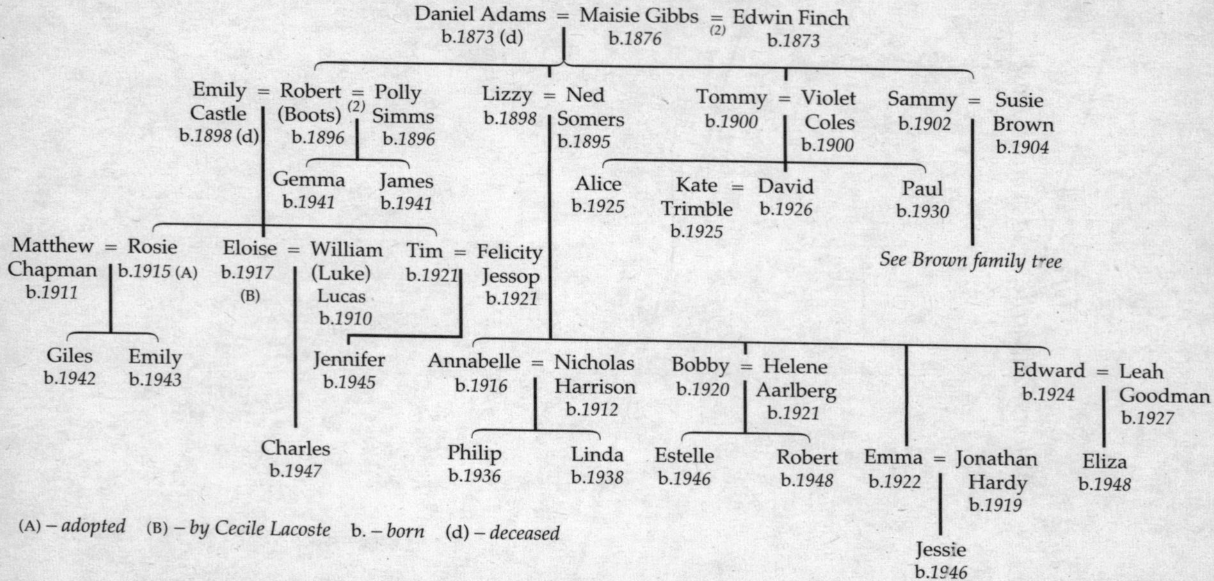

THE BROWN FAMILY

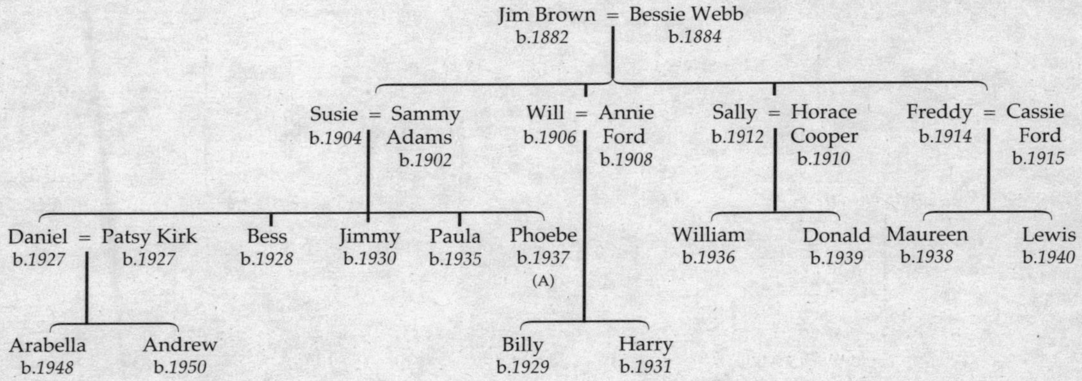

Chapter One

London had known a winter of deadly smog that proved fatal to many hundreds of people. It had lasted from November 1952 right through to March 1953, forcing Parliament to vote at last in favour of that which had known many debates but no positive action, a much-mooted Clean Air Act. The installation of central heating in some factories and some new blocks of flats had only touched a small part of the problem. Aside from all that, the country was looking forward to the coronation in June of the young Queen Elizabeth, following the tragic death last year of her admired father, King George VI.

Now, on a day in early May, midnight came beneath a dark but clear sky. A furtive character, using care and expertise, prised open the kitchen window of a handsome house on Red Post Hill, off Denmark Hill. He climbed silently in, his rubber-soled shoes soundless as he reached the floor.

He stayed quite still for a few moments, listening, then switched on his torch. The beam of light traversed the kitchen. He went through to the hall and entered what was obviously a study. His torch examined its contents, revealing a silver inkwell on the desk. Without compunction, he emptied it over the desk and placed it in a carpet bag. He followed that with a silver paperknife, then, finding nothing else that took his fancy, crossed the hall to the parlour. There, by the light of his torch, he was at once aware of family photographs in silver frames.

Upstairs, a woman came awake. She listened, then slipped out of bed without disturbing her elderly husband. Being no kind of a fearful woman, she wrapped herself in her dressing gown and, in her bare feet, made a silent way down the carpeted stairs to the hall. She came to a halt, listening to little sounds emanating from behind the closed door of the parlour.

The intruder was busy. He turned as the door suddenly opened, and fingers pressed the electric switch. Light flooded the room, and at the open door stood a slim but firm-bodied woman, greying brown hair loose, face and eyes expressive of outrage. She held a stout walking stick, taken from the hallstand.

'Well, I never did,' she breathed, 'you're robbing my house, you hooligan.'

'Out of my way, you old cow,' spat the burglar, and made a dart. The walking stick swung high and swiftly descended, striking his cap-covered head with a heavy thump. The blow savaged his scalp and staggered him. The stick followed up by poking him hard in the stomach. He bent double with pain. A hand extracted the key from the inside of the door and pulled the door to. The key was inserted and turned, locking him in, and leaving him alone with a thumping headache and a sore stomach.

The woman went back upstairs, entered the bedroom and gently shook her husband awake.

'What's wrong?' he asked.

'There's a blessed burglar in the house, and I've locked him in the parlour,' she said.

Her husband, despite his age, was out of bed then with surprising agility. Down he went, reaching the parlour and unlocking its door just as the pained burglar was climbing out of the window. Unfortunately for his suffering body, he dropped into a dark-shrouded bed of clustering rose bushes in sumptuous bloom. The thorny jungle received him, enclosed him and inflicted more suffering, that of a tearing kind. Broken blooms showered him. Torture quickly induced him to stop struggling. He opened his mouth and shouted for help.

Out came the woman's husband with a torch of his own. Its light picked out the thorn-trapped miscreant. Out came the woman, the May night warm.

'Maisie, phone the police,' said Sir Edwin Finch, knighted three years ago.

'Oh, Lor', I better had, Edwin,' said cockney-born Lady Finch, having acquired her title on the day of her husband's investiture, but still affectionately known to her family as Chinese Lady.

Her eldest son Robert, called Boots, dropped in on his way to work the following morning, after being apprised of the incident over the phone. He brought his wife Polly with him, at her insistence. Boots, now close to fifty-seven, wore his years in the easy fashion of a man whose tolerance and whimsical nature enabled him still to find life and people amusing rather than troublesome. Polly, approaching fifty-seven herself, took great care of her being, since she had an enduring horror of wrinkles and everything else that would place her in the ranks of women whose best looks were long past. Result, she still had an air of elegance and a hint of the 1920s flapper.

The parts played by Boots's mother and stepfather in dealing with the burglar astonished, impressed and even, to some extent, amused him. Polly's reactions were similar.

'You're telling me, old lady,' Boots said to his mother, 'that you came down by yourself and hit the bugger with the walking stick?'

'D'you have to call me old lady, and use that kind of unrespectable language?' she said, with a touch of indignation. 'Hit him? Well, of course I did. I had to, before he hit me. You never know how people like that were brought up, and what they might do. Your stepdad will tell you so.'

'So would I, Boots old soldier,' said Polly.

'Certainly, no-one could deny that the wrong kind of upbringing will turn such people into unprincipled reprobates,' murmured Sir Edwin. 'This one was graceless enough to empty my inkwell all over my desk.'

'There you are,' said Chinese Lady severely to Boots, 'I told you so.'

'Mother,' said Boots, 'I congratulate you on your

courage and nerve in downing that kind of social misfit.'

'I don't know about that,' said Chinese Lady, 'I only know I don't like shifty men coming into my house without being invited. Yes, and making off with what don't belong to them. It's outright thievery.'

'Do I understand the shifty character fell into your front rose bed when climbing out of the window?' asked Boots.

'Indeed he did,' said Sir Edwin.

'And you went out and kept him there?' said Boots.

'Well, if I'd helped to free him,' said Sir Edwin, 'he'd have quickly disappeared, along with his loot. So since he couldn't move without taking – um – a thousand sword cuts, as it were, I did nothing. It was the police who freed him when they arrived. He's now in a cell, awaiting a magistrates' hearing.'

Boots regarded his mother and stepfather with a smile. There they were, in their seventies, and neither looked as if their encounter with a midnight burglar had left them nervous wrecks. Far from it. His mother, of course, was as resilient and resolute now as she had been throughout two world wars, and his stepfather had always been a man of cool daring allied to self-control.

'The loot, what happened to it, Edwin?'

'The police are keeping it as evidence,' said Sir Edwin. 'We'll get it back in time. My inkwell, my paperknife and silver frames containing family photographs.'

'I don't know why that thieving man didn't take

the photographs out and leave them,' grumbled Chinese Lady.

'Perhaps he liked the looks of your family,' smiled Polly. 'Perhaps his own family are fairly repulsive.'

'H'm,' said Chinese Lady.

'Everything will come back to us, Maisie,' said Sir Edwin.

'You realize the two of you will have to attend the court hearing?' said Boots.

'Oh, Lor', I never did like the idea of attending any court,' said Chinese Lady. 'You get talked about.'

'Would you like us to go with you?' asked Polly. Married to Boots for twelve years following the death of his first wife, Emily, she had become deeply fond of his mother and stepfather, two people devoted to each other, even though they were totally different in character and background.

'Well, I'm sure Edwin and me would be very pleased,' said Chinese Lady.

'Boots will hold your hand, Maisie,' said Sir Edwin, 'and –' He smiled. 'And I daresay Polly will hold mine.'

By the time certain husbands arrived home from their work that day, their wives were in possession of the latest family news, news that was both startling and entertaining.

'*Chéri*, what do you think!' exclaimed Helene, the volatile French wife of Bobby Somers, eldest grandson of Chinese Lady.

'What should I think?' asked Bobby, applying

affectionate hugs to his children, six-year-old Estelle and four-year-old Robert.

'Your grandparents caught a burglar in their house last night,' said Helene, her excellent English touched with an engaging French accent, 'and your grandmama hit him with a walking stick and knocked him out.'

'She did what?'

'Yes, knocked him out – *voilà!* – just like that. And your grandpapa kept him trapped until the police arrived.' Helene gave other details, while their children scampered around them.

'Jesus,' said Bobby, 'what a priceless pair of old warriors. Trot round to their house tomorrow with a large bunch of roses and our compliments.'

'Ah, that is an order?'

'Consider it a request,' said Bobby, 'I put the words the wrong way round. Would you include the gift of a tin of metal polish for their chain mail?'

'Chain mail? Chain mail?' said Helene. 'What an idiot.'

'By the way, who told you about what happened?'

'Your mama,' said Helene.

Lizzy had also told her daughters Annabelle and Emma. Annabelle acquainted husband Nick and daughter Linda with the news that evening. Nick, forty, and an ex-RAF pilot officer, collapsed over his supper in a manner of speaking, and fifteen-year-old Linda regarded him as if he'd suddenly turned into a sad case of retarded fatherhood.

'Daddy, it's not as funny as that,' she said.

'No, it isn't,' said Annabelle, now thirty-six and very much like her mother with her chestnut hair and brown eyes, but beginning to fight what post-war calories were doing to her figure. In other words, she was getting plump. 'Grandma could have been badly hurt.'

'Let's be joyful that it was the burglar who got thumped,' said Nick, laughing himself weak at the mental picture of Granny Finch bashing the bloke. Linda joined in then, so did Annabelle. Linda's brother Philip would certainly have joined in too, but as a seventeen-year-old cadet he was attending an RAF training establishment in Wiltshire.

At their poultry farm near Woldingham in Surrey, Emma expressed astonishment at her mother's news, which she at once passed on to husband Jonathan and their partners, Rosie and Matthew Chapman. All four, after letting the news sink in, experienced the same mental picture as Nick, that of Grandma setting about the burglar with a walking stick, and forthwith fell about. The chickens, eavesdropping, must have wondered what was going to happen to them, for they fled squawking.

The family grapevine, buzzing most of the day, reached Susie's ears through sister-in-law Vi, wife of Sammy's brother Tommy.

'Sammy,' she said, as soon as her other half entered their house at the end of his day's work, 'did you know—'

'About my dear old ma and pa?' said Sammy. 'You bet I know. Boots told me when he reached the office a bit late this morning. It made my day, hearing that some thieving geezer got done in by my dear old ma. Talk about who was on the floor when the lights went up. Not Ma. I'm still tickled.'

'Did Boots tell you the burglar fell into the rose bushes and couldn't get out?' asked Susie. 'And that your stepdad kept him there until the police arrived?'

'Well, you know Boots,' grinned Sammy, 'he wasn't going to leave out our stepdad's part in the free-for-all.'

'And that tickled you a bit more, did it, Sammy?'

'Not half,' said Sammy, 'I've been rolling in the aisles all day.'

His elder son Daniel didn't do any rolling until he received the news from his American wife Patsy on his arrival home.

'Daniel, Granny's hit a home run!'

'Well, good old Granny, she's taken up baseball?' said Daniel. Patsy was a fan of the Boston Red Sox. She hailed from Boston.

'You get cuter,' said Patsy, a very animated edition of an all-American female. 'Forget baseball.' She recounted the news that was travelling around the family.

'Granny did what?' said Daniel, presently making a promising career for himself in the firm's property company. 'She and Grandpa did what?' That was an echo of his cousin Bobby's reaction.

'Daniel, are you getting deaf?'

'No, it's my sense of belief that's cracking up. You say Granny knocked a burglar out at dead of night and Grandpa dumped him in the blackberry bushes?'

'Sure thing,' said Patsy.

'They don't have any blackberry bushes. Who told you this fairy story?'

'Aunt Polly. I phoned to ask if she'd give a talk to our local Girl Scouts –'

'Girl Scouts?'

'OK, Girl Guides. About her experiences as an ambulance driver in the Great War. She said not bloody likely—'

'Patsy, not in front of the children.'

Their children were five-year-old Arabella and three-year-old Andrew.

'They're in the backyard, waiting for you to have games with them,' said Patsy. Occasionally, she used the American term for a garden. 'And Polly did say not bloody likely, that it would tell her audience just how old she was, and I said she didn't look a bit old – oh, then she told me about how Granny Finch had caught up with a burglar, busted his head open with a poker or something, and how your grandpa then—'

'Don't go on, Patsy, I got the drift the first time. Aunt Polly must be off her chump.'

'Not Aunt Polly. Aunt Polly's cool.'

'You're telling me this is true?' said Daniel.

'Sure is,' said Patsy. 'I called Granny and she confirmed it. Daniel, aren't you proud of your old-timers?'

Daniel laughed.

'Well, I've been out of the office all day,' he said, 'or I daresay Dad would've told me the news. But I still wouldn't have believed it. All right, so it's true, so they're great old-timers. One or both must be related to Buffalo Bill or Geronimo.'

'We'll make enquiries when we get to Boston in September,' said Patsy. Daniel had long promised to take her and the children to her home town one day, and as a well-paid director of the property company, he was now able to afford the trip. Patsy was dying to show him Boston, the cradle from which sprang the lusty child of the American Revolution. 'Daniel, you can call Granny this evening and tell her we sure are proud of the way she played Geronimo.'

'No, we'll cut Geronimo,' said Daniel. 'She'll think he's an Italian ice-cream bloke.'

Before the day was over, the grapevine had carried the news to almost everyone in the family, including Vi and Tommy's son David and his wife Kate at their dairy farm in Kent.

There were two exceptions. Sammy and Susie's elder daughter Bess was in Chicago with her American husband, Jeremy Passmore, while Boots's French-born daughter Eloise and her husband, Colonel 'Luke' Lucas, were presently in West Germany. The Four Powers, America, France, Britain and the Soviet Union, were still in occupation of West Germany, and Colonel Lucas had taken command of a British Army surveillance unit for the purpose of helping to police the British zone, reputed to be thick with Soviet agents.

The Iron Curtain, foretold by Winston Churchill, had come down with an almighty thud on Russia's border with democratic Europe. Stalin, the architect, designed it to protect his vast post-war Communist empire from the corrupting capitalist influences of the decadent West. Alas for this son of Georgia who hoped to live for ever, he had collapsed and died in March at the age of seventy-three. The West heaved a sigh of relief, and Chinese Lady said she'd been waiting nearly a lifetime for that Bolshevik to be done away with for the good of the people. However, as Sir Edwin said to Boots a month later, the Iron Curtain was still solidly in place, and nothing much had changed. In fact, there had been a war of ideology in Korea, when the North Koreans, with the backing of Red China, had attempted a Communist takeover of the South Koreans who, supported in the field by troops of the United Nations, successfully resisted.

Elsewhere, Communist rebels in French Indo-China were fighting savagely to drive out the colonialist French, and a force of British National Servicemen was at loggerheads with Communist-backed rebels in Malaya. If that wasn't enough, Communist revolutionaries like Fidel Castro and Che Guevara were trying to oust a capitalist regime in Cuba.

Talk about the world at peace, I don't think, said Sammy Adams to all and sundry. Even so, the various elements of the Adams family, busy making the most of post-war life, were enjoying a moment of great amusement over the achievement of Chinese Lady and Sir Edwin in landing a burglar in the rose bushes, even if there were a few reservations about the risks Chinese Lady had taken in confronting the geezer.

As to the Cold War, only Bobby, working at the Foreign Office, was fully aware that agents and double agents of the West and the Soviets were beavering away on both sides of the abominable curtain. On top of that, elusive Nazi war criminals were still being hunted.

Chapter Two

The magistrates' court hearing took place the following day. The accused, one Fred Summersby of Wandsworth, looked a bit of a smoothie, wearing without difficulty an innocent and slightly hurt expression. He pleaded not guilty, and said he would accept the verdict of the magistrates instead of going for trial before a judge and jury.

A police sergeant, referring to his notes, described how the arrest had been made following a phone call from Lady Finch, who grimaced at this public mention of her title. Polly and Boots, present in court, smiled at the sergeant's description of how he and a constable freed the defendant from his bed of thorny rose bushes. The bench made an inspection of the silver and a carpet bag found in his possession.

Sir Edwin and Chinese Lady, in turn, recounted their distinctive parts in frustrating what Chinese Lady declared to be a downright liberty on the part of the burglar. Sir Edwin looked distinguished on the stand. Chinese Lady, in a sober dress and her second-best hat, looked stiff and upright. The bench commended them on their bravery.

The accused was conducting his own defence on account, he said, of being able to speak up for himself better than any lawyer who was only in it for the money. He insisted he was innocent, that he'd been walking in his sleep, which had come about because of being unfortunately unemployed and having his hard-up wife and children on his mind. He couldn't remember nothing about going into any house to commit a burglary, he said. Nor could he remember ending up in no rose bed, only that when he finally woke up his loaf of bread didn't half hurt.

'Loaf of bread?' enquired the chairman of the bench.

'Me head, Yer Lordship, me napper,' said Fred, 'but I don't remember why.' Further, he said, he was scratched and painful all over, and a couple of coppers were manhandling him, which was an offence against his person considering he'd been sleepwalking and was accordingly as innocent as a baby. Also, he'd never done nothing wrong in all his life. 'So can I go now, Yer Worships?'

He was advised by the bench that his claim to have been sleepwalking was dismissed as an invention, and that the evidence justified a verdict of guilty. He was sentenced to fourteen days in prison.

'Here, 'alf a mo,' said the offended defendant, 'what about me wife and kids?'

'They'll be referred to the probation service. Take him down, constable.'

Outside the court a little later with Boots, Polly and Sir Edwin, Chinese Lady said the burglar had received lawful justice, except it would have been more to her liking if no-one had used her title. She wasn't fond of it being mentioned in public, because if her old friends in Walworth got to hear about it, they'd think she was showing off and getting above herself. Still, she said, predictably, that needn't stop us all going home and enjoying a nice pot of tea.

'Could anything stop us?' murmured Boots.

'Only an earthquake,' said Polly.

'Not even an earthquake, unless it swallowed the teapot,' smiled Sir Edwin.

'I don't know why we're standing here on the pavement trying to be comical, Edwin,' said Chinese Lady, 'unless you and Polly have caught it from Boots.'

'Well, the happy fact, Maisie, is that the unpleasant aspect of the incident is all over now,' said Sir Edwin.

Unfortunately, it wasn't all over.

When the weekly local paper was delivered the following day, its front-page headline upset Chinese Lady considerably:

BURGLAR DOWNED BY THE NOBILITY

'Oh, Lor',' she said, 'look at that, Edwin, it's spoiling my breakfast.'

'I've seen it,' said Sir Edwin, at seventy-nine as silver-haired as Polly's father at seventy-eight. Both gentlemen, however, were commendably distinguished in appearance. 'I shan't allow it to spoil my breakfast. One must rise above newspaper headlines.'

'But, Edwin, it's more than that, there's a story all about our time in court.'

'Written, of course, by the paper's court reporter, and no doubt in exaggerated fashion.'

'Edwin, listen to what it says.' Chinese Lady quoted from the front-page report. ' "Despite their advanced ages, Sir Edwin and Lady Finch opposed the intrusion of their mansion with the same blue-blooded spirit the knights of old showed in defence of their castles." Oh, Lord above, suppose some of our friends and neighbours read all that?'

'I hope they'll find it entertaining,' said Sir Edwin.

'I always felt that going into that court was going to be upsetting, not entertaining,' grumbled Chinese Lady. 'I don't know what our friends and neighbours will think, nor our family, especially about castles. None of my family ever lived in a castle, and I'm sure none of yours did, either.' She went muttering on, thus saving Sir Edwin from having to comment on his family background. He had only ever told her he was his parents' sole child, which was true, and that they had died many years ago while abroad. This was also true if one could pass over the fact that abroad meant their native Germany. Boots was still the only person in the family who knew he was German-born, and Boots had kept the secret close to his chest. In response to Chinese Lady's curiosity when he married her, Sir Edwin had shown her a small sepia photograph of his mother and father. Without saying so, she had thought what a stern, stiff-looking couple they were.

She had never delved into his time as a young man, but she had sometimes made an unexpected comment, such as, 'You're ever so well educated, Edwin, you must have gone to a very good school.'

'Good enough, Maisie.' He could have said a boarding academy, prior to university.

'Which one was it?'

'Oh, a boarding school in the country, Maisie.'

'Well, it made a gentleman of you, Edwin.'

'Thank you, Maisie. Um, on a par with Boots, would you say? If so, you're paying me a very acceptable compliment.'

'Oh, I don't know I've ever thought of my only oldest son as a gentleman. More of a music-hall comedian at times. Still, I have had people tell me he's turned out very distinguished.'

'Boots is a born gentleman. Maisie, you have three remarkable sons and, in Lizzy, a splendid daughter.'

'How kind you are, Edwin.'

Now, she finished her grumble about what was in the local paper, and tried to forget it.

But when the phone rang ten minutes later, Lizzy was on the line and bringing it back to her attention.

'Mum, have you seen the local paper?'

'Yes, I have, and it spoiled my breakfast,' said Chinese Lady.

'But it says really nice things about you and Dad,' said Lizzy.

'We don't want nice things said about us, not in any newspaper, Lizzy, it's like being shown off in public.'

'Ned said it's made him feel proud of you.'

'You can tell Ned we don't want him feeling proud of us for being in a newspaper,' said Chinese Lady. 'Yes, and on the front page and all. I don't know I've ever felt more embarrassed.'

'Well, I thought I'd phone and tell you me and Ned like what the paper said about you and Dad,' said Lizzy.

'Yes, all right, Lizzy,' said Chinese Lady, 'but I've got to go now. There's a knock on the door and your dad's upstairs.'

She said goodbye, put the phone down and answered the knock. On the doorstep stood a breezy-looking young man, tipping his hat.

'Oh, hello, good morning, madam,' he said.

'Good morning,' said Chinese Lady, then added suspiciously, 'are you selling something I don't want?'

'Perish the thought,' said the young man. 'Would you be Lady Finch?'

'Well?' Chinese Lady was primly non-committal, which the young man took as an affirmative.

'My card, Your Ladyship.' He showed her his card. She picked out the salient details, Barney Waterford, Journalist. 'I'm representing your local paper, and would like to interview you and your husband, Sir Edwin Finch.'

Chinese Lady stiffened.

'Was it you that wrote about us in the paper that spoiled our breakfast?'

'No, that was a colleague, our crime reporter.'

'Oh, it was, was it? Well, tell him me and my husband don't happen to like crime reporters when they write about us. We don't interfere with their private lives, so they shouldn't interfere with ours.'

'But you're news, Lady Finch, uplifting news. May I come in and talk to you and Sir Edwin?'

'I've never had no-one from any newspaper in my house, and I'm not having one now. They write scandal-mongering things about people.'

'I assure you, Lady Finch, that—'

'Kindly take your feet off my doorstep and go away,' said Chinese Lady, and banged the door shut.

Sir Edwin came down to the hall then, and asked what had been going on. Chinese Lady spoke with umbrage about the reporter who'd tried to get himself into the house without being asked.

'Ah, the price of fame, Maisie,' smiled Sir Edwin.

'Fame? What fame?'

'Ours, Maisie, for trapping Mr Fred Summersby.'

'Well, I don't know I ever wanted anything to do with fame, Edwin, especially when it brings newspaper reporters to our front door. It's always seemed to me that fame's unrespectable.'

'Certainly, it can bring notoriety,' said Sir Edwin.

'Edwin, I never heard a word more unrespectable than that one,' said Chinese Lady. 'I just hope that reporter doesn't call again.'

But he did, during the afternoon, bringing a photographer with him. Sir Edwin dealt with him in his own way. Quietly but firmly, he made it clear that neither he nor his wife wished to be interviewed or photographed.

'So sorry, young man. Goodbye now.'

'But wouldn't you like to see your photographs in—'

'Goodbye.' Sir Edwin closed the door gently. That had nothing in common with the way Chinese Lady had made it rattle earlier.

Worse was to follow. Two gentlemen of the press phoned during the evening. The first represented a national daily, the second, horror of horrors, the *News of the World*, a Sunday paper which Chinese Lady declared ought never to have been invented, especially not on a Sunday. Both journalists insisted that the nation should know about the act of courage of Sir Edwin and Lady Finch, and earnestly requested an interview. Sir Edwin asked each man to respect the privacy of himself and his wife. In vain did the journalists press their case.

'Edwin,' said Chinese Lady, after he'd dealt with the phone calls, 'we'd better keep all our doors locked and bolted.'

'Against the press?' said Sir Edwin.

'Well, suppose we woke up one morning and found the *News of the World* man in the house? I can't hardly bear thinking about it.' Chinese Lady quivered. 'Where's my smelling salts?'

'Be assured, Maisie, the enemy will be kept without, and your smelling salts within,' said Sir Edwin, who, like his stepson Boots, had a gift for remaining unruffled in the face of the unwanted. 'Those I shall guard with my life.'

'I don't know about within and without,' said Chinese Lady, 'I just know I can't wait to get away for our summer holiday.'

They were due to spend a quiet fortnight in the

Devon countryside with Polly's parents, Sir Henry and Lady Simms. The invitation had come from Sir Henry, who found Sir Edwin a man much to his liking. His charming wife, still involved with charities, had no affected airs or graces, and had long regarded Chinese Lady as an unworldly but stimulating woman.

Sir Edwin took a phone call from his stepdaughter Lizzy the following morning. She asked if he'd seen what was in one of the daily newspapers, because in hers there was a story about him and her mother, how they'd tackled a burglar and knocked him out, and how their bravery had been commended by the presiding magistrate at the trial. Sir Edwin guessed that the story was the work of the reporter who had phoned on behalf of the daily.

'Then there's some stuff about you and Mum, as members of the nobility – nobility, Dad, would you believe – setting an example to the country on how to deal with dangerous burglars.'

Sir Edwin smiled to himself. If the reporter in question had gained access to Maisie he would have quickly realized she had cockney roots, not aristocratic.

'Fortunately, Lizzy, we don't read that particular paper,' he said, 'and I've no intention of buying a copy. It would only upset your mother.'

'Oh, well, I know she never did like the idea of being read about in any newspaper,' said Lizzy. 'Mind, not that she's got anything to be ashamed of, she's never done wrong all her life.'

'Your mother, Lizzy, is a remarkably upright woman,' said Sir Edwin.

'Bless her,' said Lizzy.

The worst happened on Sunday. A newspaper that had never found favour with Chinese Lady ran a story on Sir Edwin and herself. It contained a great deal of flowery exaggeration, as well as some admiring comments garnered from interviews with neighbours. The story romanticized the incident for the benefit of readers.

It was a neighbour who phoned during the morning, and it was Chinese Lady who answered the call.

'Oh, good morning, Maisie,' said Mrs Freda Rogers, a friend of many years' standing.

'Good morning,' said Chinese Lady.

'I simply had to phone and ask if you've seen one of today's papers.'

'If it's one of those that print scandals, we don't take it, nor any other unrespectable paper,' said Chinese Lady tartly.

'Oh, the report's a very complimentary one,' said Mrs Rogers.

Chinese Lady was unimpressed.

'All my life I never wanted to be read about in that kind of paper,' she said, 'and it's giving me a nasty turn now it's happened. It'll ruin my good name, and my husband's too. I'll have to go and lie down to get over the shock.'

'Maisie, I'm sure—'

'Some papers ought never to be allowed in

respectable houses,' said Chinese Lady, and put the phone down. Off she went to talk to her husband and let him know that disaster had struck.

Sir Edwin refused to panic.

'Well, it's done now, Maisie my dear,' he said, 'and the best thing we can do is turn our backs on it and forget it.'

'I don't know how anyone can forget being in a scandal-mongering paper,' said Chinese Lady, 'it's like being mixed up with the kind of sinful people that some of my old friends, like Susie's mother, have told me you can read about every Sunday.'

'You mean some old friends like to relay – um – scandalous titbits from the paper?' enquired Sir Edwin.

'It's not what I like to listen to. Lor', Edwin, I don't know I can face going to church this morning, not with everyone looking at us.'

'Not everyone will have read the paper, Maisie, but we'll give church a miss, if you like.'

'Don't you remember how everyone looked at us just after you'd been knighted?'

'That, I'm sure, was a different kind of look from the one you anticipate now, my dear.'

'Well, we'll go, Edwin, just like usual,' said Chinese Lady with courageous firmness, 'and we'll just have to take no notice of any looks.'

'Yes, certainly let us go, Maisie, and with stout hearts,' said Sir Edwin, hiding a smile. After all, if she could stand up to a burglar, and down him as well, she could stand up to looks.

So they went.

Not everyone in the church looked. And those

that did, didn't seem scandalized. Sir Edwin Finch, although leaner of body in his old age, was still unbowed and highly respected. And his lady wife, never less than firm and upright of figure, was a woman of respectability who had bravely put paid to a very unrespectable intruder.

Smiles appeared.

All the same, Chinese Lady decided that if she ever had to deal another burglar a knockout blow, she'd phone Boots, get him to come over, whatever time of night it was, drag the hooligan out and dump him on the pavement well away from the house. On no account was she ever going to appear in a court again, and get herself and Edwin read about in newspapers.

Chapter Three

Monday morning in the West End.

New Bond Street, famous for the elegance of its shops and its equally elegant clientele, had recovered from the limitations of the war and the subsequent years of austerity. Its ladies' wear once more carried the labels of Paris's most creative designers, which meant that only the rich could contemplate entering a Bond Street dress shop with a purchase in mind.

A bulky, square-faced man was inspecting the window display of one such shop. He wore a grey trilby and a dark grey suit that, while a fairly good fit, would have been considered an example of mediocrity by any Savile Row tailor. But then, Lieutenant Colonel Boris Alexandrov, Deputy Head of KGB Political Intelligence in Britain, but posing as a senior member of the Soviet Press Bureau, bought all his clothes from a Moscow department store which, although exclusive to privileged Party members, did not offer the excellent tailoring available in London.

He was musing at the shop window as a tall and stylish woman, in a silver-grey costume and a fetching black and white hat, stopped in her languid walk and joined him. Together they regarded the delicate creations on display. They began to talk in discreet murmurs.

'This is a faulty meeting place,' she said.

'Why?'

'Men don't window-shop for ladies' fashions.'

'Some men do. Those who have their mistresses in mind.'

'But you would not make purchases yourself, would you?' she said.

'No, only recommendations, but that's enough to justify my presence at this window. What do you have to tell me?'

'That I do know the gentleman,' she said, her Slavonic looks still striking despite the fact that she was fifty-four. 'Fourteen years have made no difference. I recognized him at once when he was tending his front garden. He's the same man who came to Poland to observe our army's manoeuvres in 1939, not long before Hitler and his barbarians invaded and you followed to complete the conquest.' Her accented English was charming, her face smooth and unlined, her lightly carmined lips firm and resolute.

'The Soviet arrival proved fortunate for Poland in the long term.' His accent had a brutal edge. 'It now has full protection from threats by the West.'

'For which, of course, Poland is grateful,' she said.

'Comrade Galicia, your own gratitude makes you a helpful woman.'

'I'm touched,' said Katje Galicia drily. She had been a major in the pre-war Polish army.

'I'm instructed to tell you that now you have found the man, yours will be the privilege of bringing him to us.'

'The English press found him for us with their reports of a court case,' she said. 'I only followed up.'

'It's unlike you to be modest. Shall we walk a little?'

'I've seen enough of this shop's window display of outfits that could only be worn at Ascot,' she said. 'I'm a lover of horses, but not of Englishwomen dressed in frills and flounces, and absurd hats.'

They began to walk. Her gait was long-legged and graceful, his heavy and ponderous. He spoke again.

'His file is interesting. He was given a title for his work with British Intelligence. But did you know that well before the war, an unsuccessful attempt was made by Gestapo agents to either transport him to Berlin or to secure his services as a double agent?'

'No, he didn't inform me of that during the few days we were together in Poland,' she said. Her dark eyes showed amusement, and a little smile of reminiscence flickered. 'He was a guarded man who performed a quiet act of disappearance before I could get him into my bed.'

'He's too old for a woman now.'

'Some men are never too old,' she said.

'Well, however you entice him is your privilege. He must have a great deal of information useful to us. We need to extract his Intelligence secrets.'

'But is his knowledge up to date?' asked Katje. 'Are old secrets valuable?'

'Comrade Bukov will decide that.'

'Ah, Bukov,' said Katje. Gregori Bukov, a KGB colonel, was head of the KGB section operating in London. 'What a nest of eagles you have in the embassy.'

'In offices, not the embassy. Arrange, if you can, a meeting.'

'With Bukov?'

'With me. Say in Hyde Park.'

'You're confident I can persuade our man to visit Hyde Park for the purpose of meeting a Soviet – ah, diplomat?' said Katje.

'His years as a German agent, and subsequently as a British agent, will have left him with a lasting interest in diplomatic affairs of a certain kind.'

'A cloak-and-dagger kind?' she suggested, using the now popular English term for espionage adventurism. A red bus passed by. The colour was as brazen as the Red Flag. 'I had a moment of astonishment when you informed me he was born a German, since I can't think of any man more English than he seemed to be. However, I agree, his interest in diplomacy when it's another name for espionage will still be with him.'

'We don't expect an immediate meeting, since it will probably take you some time to effect your act of persuasion. Use, if necessary, the same element as the two Gestapo agents used before the war, the fact that unknown to his family here, the man Edwin Finch was a German agent prior to defecting to the British.'

'How do you know this?' asked Katje.

'We do know. Certain Gestapo agents defected to the Soviets towards the end of the war and supplied us with a mine of information about British agents.'

'You are talking of information that indicated one of those agents, Edwin Finch, was once threatened with blackmail?' she said. 'But by now, can we be sure his English family still doesn't know his full history?'

'No, we aren't sure, Comrade Galicia, and must leave it to you to find out, as I'm confident you will. But, I repeat, you may take your time.'

'I never like working under pressure, so yes, allow me reasonable time,' she said.

'Maintain contact.'

'Fortunately,' she said, 'public telephones work here.'

'Moscow is currently replacing some public service engineers, Comrade Galicia.'

'That is so?' said Katje, who could picture what was happening to the inefficient engineers. They would be tried as criminal saboteurs, and a verdict of guilty would be decided in advance. Some, probably, had already been executed. But that was the price one had to pay for inefficiency in the Soviet Union and the People's Republic of Poland. 'We can look forward to major improvements?' Her slightly caustic tone implied scepticism.

'Moscow is always searching for industrial perfection. Goodbye now, comrade. I look forward to hearing regularly from you.'

They parted at a junction. Boris Alexandrov let

himself merge with pedestrian traffic, and Katje Galicia hailed a taxi to take her to her modest flat in Bloomsbury.

'What's going on?' asked Sammy Adams at supper that evening. His attendant family at this moment consisted of his wife Susie, his younger son Jimmy, and his daughters Paula and Phoebe. His elder son Daniel and daughter-in-law Patsy lived close by. And his eldest daughter Bess, with her American husband, Jeremy Passmore, lived in Kent. At present, however, they were on holiday in Chicago, staying with Jeremy's mother. 'That's what I'm asking, what's going on?'

'Nothing you don't know about,' said Susie, forty-eight and very nicely preserved, thank you.

'Listen,' said Sammy, fifty-one and still sharp enough in business to see off any of the country's unhallowed spivs. 'What I mean is which geezer was responsible for getting my dear old ma and stepdad mentioned in newspapers? It's upsetting them.'

'It wasn't me, word of honour,' said twenty-three-year-old Jimmy, a chip off the old block.

'Nor me,' said Paula, eighteen. As one of the multitude of young blondes inhabiting the Western world, she could claim to be more fashionable than a brunette or redhead. But, of course, fads and fancies of the West came and went like coughs and colds, and it was enough to say Paula's happy personality was more endearing to her family and friends than the colour of her hair. She worked for the family business in its Camberwell offices, and spent most of her weekends on the farm run by cousin David and his wife Kate. Her young man, an Italian, laboured there as an invaluable farmhand. 'Yes,' she went on, 'none of us are geezers, Dad.'

'I wouldn't know how to recognize a geezer,' said Phoebe, Sammy and Susie's adopted daughter. She was sixteen, slim, and deliciously pretty.

'Oh, they're shifty-eyed and kind of furtive,' said Jimmy.

'I grant that,' said Sammy.

'Daddy,' said Phoebe, 'd'you mean like Bill Sikes in *Oliver Twist*?'

'I also grant that,' said Sammy, 'so someone find out which one was responsible for upsetting your grandparents, and knock his block off or break his legs.'

'Over to you, Jimmy,' said Paula.

'Oh no you don't,' said Susie. 'No-one in this family is to take any notice of your dad when he's talking daft.'

'I ain't granting that,' said Sammy. 'What's daft about Jimmy knocking several holes in the bloke that aggravated my old ma?'

'Well, Dad,' said Paula, 'it could mean Jimmy being arrested for committing grievous bodily harm, and you wouldn't call that clever, would you?'

'Well, my intentions are honest,' said Sammy, 'but seeing your mum would feel aggravated herself if some flatfoot took Jimmy by his collar, I give up.'

'Good,' said Susie, 'that'll save you getting a nasty blow from my egg saucepan.'

'Take note, you young 'uns,' said Sammy, 'that your mum can still make funny jokes.'

'Mum's egg saucepan, Dad, is no joke,' said Jimmy.

On Friday morning, Bert and Gertie Roper, stalwarts for many years as factory maintenance man and chargehand respectively for Adams Fashions Ltd, were at breakfast in their homely old Victorian terraced house by Victoria Park, Bow. The street had miraculously escaped wartime air raids, and the house was their own. With Sammy's advice, help and guidance, it had been bought and paid for by their combined monthly earnings, thus releasing them from the curse that afflicted most East End people, that of forking out rent all their lives.

Breakfast was a leisurely meal, for the day was special, the occasion of their retirement from the firm, and they did not have to reach the Bethnal Green factory until ten thirty. They were both in their sixties, both grey-haired, but Bert was still hale and hearty, and Gertie was still active and lively.

'Gertie gal,' said Bert, eyeing his wife's new plum-coloured dress, 'might I be so bold as to say yer glad rags make you look like the Duchess of Petticoat Lane?'

'Well, I couldn't go to no retirement party in me old blouse and skirt,' said Gertie, refilling their large breakfast cups from her glazed brown teapot which, like Chinese Lady's, had lived through Kaiser Bill's unfriendly Zeppelins and Goering's blasting bombers. 'And I must say you're fine and 'andsome in yer new brown Sunday suit.'

'Well, special day, y'know, me old Dutch,' said Bert. 'Mind, I still ain't sure that when I wake up tomorrow I'll know what to do with meself.'

'You'll know, love,' said Gertie, 'you wasn't ever lost for something to do in yer spare time, and you can work longer hours on your allotment after today. We'll buy a nice new garden shed for it, with a table and a couple of chairs, where you can drink yer flask of tea in comfort, like, and I'll come down and join you sometimes and see 'ow yer carrots and onions are doing.'

'Buy a couple of foldin' deckchairs too, and I'll use one for sitting in the sun in me short pants, eh?' grinned Bert.

'Bert Roper,' said Gertie, 'don't you ever let me catch you down at that there allotment with yer trousers off and Mrs Gates gawping at yer.'

Mrs Gates, a sturdy war widow of forty, also worked an allotment in her spare time.

'Now don't you worry,' said Bert, 'I ain't nothing special to look at in me short pants. Well, nothing that 'ud give Connie Gates funny ideas.'

'Don't be too sure,' said Gertie, 'widow women can get ideas that ain't a bit funny. Bert, wasn't it nice of Tommy Adams to tell us our family can join the celebrations?'

'There ain't many nicer blokes than Tommy Adams,' said Bert. 'Or Boots and Sammy. You'd 'ave to go a long way to—'

‘Here, I remember now,’ said Gertie.

‘Remember what?’

‘I remember meeting Mrs Gates last Saturday and her asking after you and saying what an ’andsome figure you’d got for a man of fifty.’

‘Eh?’ said Bert.

‘So I asked her where she got fifty from, ’ad she seen your birth certificate? And she said no, she’d just guessed your age, so I said she’d better guess again. I mean, what did it make me look like at me own age, that I’d snatched you out of yer cradle when I married you?’

‘I don’t remember no cradle-snatching,’ said Bert, ‘only yer dad trying it on with one of the bridesmaids, and ’aving her pour a glass of port and lemon down his trousers. Shock to ’im, that was, seeing the port and lemon had been iced by the caterers. Gertie, you sure Connie Gates thought I was only fifty?’

Gertie gave a little chuckle.

‘Only teasing you, love,’ she said. ‘Well, it’s a happy day for us and no cause for being serious. We might miss going to work for a bit, but it’ll be nice not ’aving to get up early every morning. Mind, what I said about Mrs Gates, it was still a warning to you to keep yer trousers on when she’s around.’

‘Much obliged for the reminder,’ said Bert. ‘By the way, what d’you think of young Jimmy Adams now he’s been working at the fact’ry for nigh on three year?’

‘What a nice young man, and a proper young gent to the machinists,’ said Gertie. ‘I can’t think why he don't 'ave a steady girl. His Uncle Tommy told me he did 'ave one once, but she went off to America and he hasn't found anyone else since, which is a bit sad, seeing there's any number of young ladies going short on account of all them thousands of young men killed in the war. They'd 'ave been a fine marrying age by now.'

'I ain't too fond of remembering how many we lost,' said Bert soberly.

'Well, love,' said Gertie, 'let's be thankful you come out of the Kaiser's war alive and kicking. I wouldn't 'ave no family if you hadn't.'

Her family was her husband, her two sons and daughters-in-law, two grandsons and three granddaughters. And they were all going to be at the factory for the retirement party.

'I'll see you later, then,' said Boots to Polly at their open front door. He was about to depart for his office.

'I must pay my respects,' said Polly. 'I do have memories of Bert and Gertie when your fashions offshoot was in its infancy, and Rachel Goodman and I were persuaded by Sammy to model Lilian Hyam's flapper designs. Ye gods, did we dotty damsels really do that?'

'Memorably,' said Boots.

'How memorably?'

'With any amount of courage and flair,' said Boots, 'and a minimum amount of dress.'

Polly laughed.

'Off you go, old lad,' she said. 'I'll be at your office at two thirty and travel up to Bethnal Green with you. Flossie will take care of our racketing twins.'

Twins Gemma and James, now eleven and on mid-term holiday from school, were a handful, but Flossie the housemaid had her own way of making sure the house and furniture remained intact.

'See you, then, Polly old girl,' said Boots. He kissed her and departed, leaving her to reflect on relentless time and how fast their years of marriage had flown. On that basis, the age of sixty would simply rush up on both of them.

Polly, closing the door, made a face at the thought of being as old as that.

'Mummy, you're looking sad.' Gemma was there, gazing up at her.

'Oh, I'm not sad, darling,' she said. 'I've too many blessings to ever be sad.'

'Oh, that's good,' said Gemma, so much like her mother with her dark sienna hair and her piquant looks. Up came James, a reflection of his dad, his hair dark brown, his grey eyes with a hint of blue, and his features already firm. You, young man, thought Polly with an inward smile, are going to be very much like your father when you're older, a danger to young ladies.

'Listen, Mum,' he said, 'can you buy jeans for me and Gemma?'

Polly demurred.

'Not without giving heartburn to your Uncle Sammy,' she said.

'Why?' asked Gemma.

'He doesn't favour them,' said Polly.

'But he makes them at the factory,' said James.

'Only as a matter of business,' said Polly. And profit, she thought, with another inward smile. 'Still, we'll ask Daddy, shall we?'

'I will,' said Gemma at once.

Boots rarely said no to any request from his daughter, and Gemma knew it. She already had the instincts on which the female of the species could capitalize when dealing with the opposite sex, especially fathers.

Some fathers were a pushover to some daughters.

It was true that Sammy didn't think American jeans were the best thing to have ever hit the fashion industry. He still considered them fit only for cowboys. But growing demand had compelled him to put business before prejudice, and Adams Fashions Ltd, having secured an import licence for denim, was now manufacturing them in quantity for customers such as Coates, the West End store with branches all over the South of England, as well as for the Adams retail shops. A healthy profit was resulting, a happy outcome for Sammy, especially as an even healthier profit was the consequence of manufacturing what he saw as fashions that made girls and women look like true feminine females. Fashions such as flared skirts worn over layers of frilly net, with pretty blouses or tops. Such outfits said a flouncy goodbye to the unflattering utility stuff that had prevailed during the war and the several years that had followed. The import licence brought in all the necessary raw materials, and the Bethnal Green factory was working full-time.

Well, Winston Churchill and his Conservatives were back in office, and that made a difference to business and private enterprise. The old boy was still a major figure in politics, if not quite as lively as of yore. His Foreign Secretary, Sir Anthony Eden, was in line to succeed him, for the country's indomitable wartime leader was now approaching eighty.

That horrendous war, which saw the extermination of millions of Europe's innocent Jews, was well and truly over now, and, with business up and running, Sammy considered life for himself and his family offered a bright new future. Only meat and one or two other consumables were still rationed, and if Susie did happen to sigh for a large sirloin of Sunday beef at times, well, he knew a spiv or two. He was always able to tell her a business friend dropped it into his office while passing, which, if not exactly true, was as near to it as he could get. If Susie gave him a funny look, well, he'd received a bucketful of those in his time and survived them all.

Reaching his desk this morning, he noted the day was a Friday and a special one. Special for good old Gertie and Bert Roper at the factory. It was their retirement day, and a party had been arranged to celebrate the occasion. All the staff would finish work at four, when the party would begin.

Chapter Four

The firm's factory at Bethnal Green, built three years ago, was a model of its kind. Commodious, airy, with full amenities and a large canteen, it provided conditions of work for the machinists and seamstresses that were totally civilized compared to those that obtained in the grimy pre-war East End factories and sweatshops. It was the kind of workplace Sammy had always dreamt about, for above all it was obviously the citadel of a prosperous and highly reputable business. And Sammy knew that that had a very positive effect on potential new customers.

The factory now employed a hundred and sixty machinists and seamstresses, together with several men who did the heavy work, such as loading, unloading and driving the firm's trucks. Sammy's elder brother Tommy was the manager, son Jimmy personnel manager and a versatile dogsbody. Sammy himself was the inspiration operating from his old and cherished Camberwell offices, from where his visits to the factory were frequent, as were his visits to the firm's retail shops. He also kept an eye on the progress of his elder son

Daniel and Boots's son Tim, joint managers of the property company. Boots, the old reliable, was the ever-present and unflappable general manager of the whole enterprise.

'I've got a feeling,' Sammy said to him once, 'that when the time comes for me to be suffering ulcers on account of all me business worries, you'll still be looking as if Father Christmas has just dropped a crate of Scotch down your chimney.'

'Sammy old lad,' said Boots, 'we're all born to worry about something. Fortunately, your worries are meat and drink to you. You won't get ulcers, but if you do, cut out the drink. Apart from Scotch, taken with water, wine and spirits contain too much acid.'

'I regard that kind of advice as a load of old cobblers,' said Sammy.

'Given with a good heart, Sammy,' said Boots, 'but certainly, don't let it worry you.'

'I give up,' said Sammy, but with a grin.

At four thirty, the retirement party for Bert and Gertie was in full swing in the factory canteen, with soft drinks and sherry laid on for staff and guests alike. Bert and Gertie were the centre of attention, Gertie's homely face flushed with pleasure as she talked to Boots and Polly. Bert was all amiable grins in company with Tommy and Vi. Sammy and Susie were going the rounds of the machinists and seamstresses, the spacious canteen packed out. Among the throng were Rachel Goodman, an invaluable asset to Sammy as company secretary, and old Eli Greenberg, who, for many years, had done Sammy favours, all of which, he often said, had taken the financial shirt off his back.

Jimmy, looking after the needs of guests, attracted the attention of three girls.

'Crikey, who's he?' whispered sixteen-year-old Jane Roper to her fourteen-year-old sister Maggie.

'I dunno,' said Maggie, 'ask Clare.'

'Clare, who's he?' asked Jane of her eighteen-year-old cousin, Clare Roper. All three were Gertie and Bert's granddaughters.

'I'm sure I don't know,' said Clare.

''Elp, he's coming over,' said Maggie.

Jimmy arrived with a tray containing glasses of soft drinks and sherry.

'Hello, young maidens,' he smiled, 'wherefore art thou?'

'Oh, me gosh,' said Maggie, 'what's that mean?'

'Oh, just how's your father and where d'you come from?' said Jimmy. He caught the eye of Clare. My word, he thought, she's something. She had big brown eyes and dark auburn hair in clustering curls, and looked altogether engaging in an embroidered blouse, flared skirt and shining nylon stockings. He smiled at her. Clare tingled. 'Half a mo, could you be the granddaughters of Gertie and Bert?'

'Yes, that's us,' said Jane. 'I'm Jane, she's Maggie and she's Clare.'

'Jane, Maggie and Clare, right,' said Jimmy. 'It's my lucky day, meeting all three of you at one go.'

'Why's it lucky?' asked young Maggie.

'Well, from where I'm standing, you're all pretty,' said Jimmy. That was more gallant than true, for Maggie was a little plain and Jane merely pleasant-looking. However, they both had a kind of girlish sparkle.

'Oh, we know we're pretty,' said Jane blithely.

'Well, I didn't until now,' said Jimmy. He caught the eye of Clare again. She pinked a little. 'Now I'm convinced.'

'Oh, pleasured, I'm sure,' said Clare.

'Ever so,' said Jane.

'You ain't said who you are,' piped Maggie.

'General dogsbody,' said Jimmy, tall, manly and born, like his Uncle Boots, to be a friend to all except uncivilized villains. He was also as self-assured now as cousin Bobby and brother Daniel. He eyed Gertie's three cockney granddaughters encouragingly. 'Come on, help yourselves to the drinks.'

'Could we 'ave sherry?' asked Jane.

'If you're old enough,' said Jimmy. 'If you're not, well, as it's your grandparents' special day, I'll turn a blind eye.'

'Course we're old enough,' said Maggie.

'If it makes you squiffy, it means you're not,' said Jimmy, 'and as I'll be responsible, I'll have to carry you all home.'

'Crikey, all of us?' said Jane.

'So watch out,' said Jimmy, and winked at Clare, obviously the eldest. Clare tingled again. Crikey, she thought, if he's trying to get off with me, I think I might forget about Harry Dallimore. Harry Dallimore, the son of a neighbour, was her current young man. He'd succeeded Frankie Wells, and Frankie had succeeded someone else. Clare looked for more than the ordinary in fellers. These days life was more open for girls. Before the war, most of them lived the same old-fashioned lives as their mothers, counting themselves favoured if the first blokes they got to know offered them marriage. Well, that was what Clare had come to believe, and she was right. 'Come on,' said Jimmy again, 'help yourselves.'

Clare said, 'Oh, ta,' and took a glass of sherry. Jane and Maggie were quick to follow. All three girls sipped the wine, and there were immediate comments from Jane and Maggie about it making them tiddly.

'Well, make it last,' smiled Jimmy, 'one glass is enough for young girls.'

'Beg your pardon?' said Clare.

'Clare's eighteen,' said Maggie. 'She's a young lady, she'd 'ave you know.'

'Don't worry, I've got the picture,' said Jimmy. 'So long, must go the rounds now.'

'But you 'aven't told us your name,' said Jane.

'I'm Jimmy Adams. Sammy Adams is my dad. He employs me to look after the welfare of the seamstresses. I'll look after yours if you do get squiffy.' And Jimmy took himself away to offer the drinks to other guests.

'Crikey,' said Jane, 'ain't he a dishy bloke?'

'Not half,' said Maggie, 'but Clare ain't saying much.'

'I'm reserving me judgement,' said Clare, and took another sip of sherry. Jane and Maggie followed suit.

'If Clare gets squiffy,' said Jane, 'we'll let her be carried home by herself.'

'In the arms of Jimmy Adams?' said Maggie, giggling.

'Well, it can't be Frankie Sinatra,' said Jane, 'he ain't here.'

Frank Sinatra, an American vocalist and an up-and-coming Hollywood film star, was now rivalling Bing Crosby. American girls went hysterical at his concerts or swooned all over their seats, and English girls sent him passionate fan mail.

The retirement party became festive and noisy, the machinists and seamstresses shouting for 'Knees Up, Mother Brown'. Jimmy did his stuff by putting the record on a radiogram. The canteen floor trembled as most of the staff and guests began to perform this cockney ritual, singing to the refrain. Clare, Jane and Maggie joined in, knees high, skirts and frilly net flying, voices exuberant.

Jimmy reappeared, making himself heard above the racket.

'Thought as much, you're all squiffy.'

'Oh, come on, join in!' panted Jane.

Jimmy laughed. Along with the factory girls, Gertie and Bert's granddaughters were a collective eyeful.

'Can't stop,' he called, and went on his way, down to the office where the switchboard girl had stayed at her post to receive calls and take messages. 'Come on, Dodie,' he said, 'it's five o'clock and you can pack up now. There's still some sherry left, and you'll be in time to listen to Dad proposing a toast to Gertie and Bert. So come on.'

'Love to,' said Dodie Woods. She closed the switchboard down and went up to the canteen with him. He gave her a glass of sherry. Mother Brown's knees had finished galloping, and Sammy was about to make a speech.

'Ladies and gents, might I have your attention?'

'Course yer can, Mister Sammy, if it don't cost us,' called a machinist.

'Promise,' said Sammy. 'Ladies and gents, we're gathered here together on this special occasion for Gertie and Bert to—'

'Blimey, Mister Sammy,' called another machinist, 'you ain't going to marry 'em, are yer? Ain't Bert made an honest woman of Gertie yet?'

Yells of laughter.

'Take 'er name!' Gertie made herself heard.

'It's Queenie,' called Lilian Chambers, the fashion designer.

'Well, you tell Queenie any more interruptions and I'll start docking wages,' said Sammy. Tommy, beside him, let his handsome face crease in a wide and amiable grin.

'Here,' said one seamstress to another, 'I wouldn't mind Mister Tommy docking me in private, like.'

'You'll be lucky,' said her workmate.

'Kindly listen,' said Sammy. 'On behalf of self and everyone else here, let me say people don't come more genuine than Gertie and Bert. I should know, seeing it's been me pleasure and privilege to have had them doing their bit for the firm since – um –'

'Waterloo?' suggested Boots.

'Battle of Hastings, more like,' said Sammy.

'I go for Waterloo,' said Tommy. 'According to me schooling, the Battle of Hastings is a bit over the top. It would make Gertie and Bert about – let's see –'

'About nine hundred?' said Boots.

More yells of laughter.

'Boots is alvays himself, ain't he?' said Mr Greenberg to Rachel. 'Other people make trouble, ain't it so? Boots only makes jokes.'

'I should dispute that?' said Rachel, still a fine figure of a woman at fifty. 'Eli, if all men were like Boots and Sammy, the world would be a sweeter place for women.'

'Ah, vhen vas there a sharper vun than Sammy?' said Mr Greenberg. 'But vith a heart of gold.' He glanced at Rachel. She was looking at Sammy. Her expression was almost wistful. He sighed for her. He was, perhaps, the only person apart from Polly who knew Rachel had been in love with Sammy since their young days.

'To my mind, ladies and gents,' said Sammy, claiming attention again, 'Gertie and Bert are a prime advertisement for how to keep young and healthy, and lively as well. I can't recollect any time when Bert wasn't keeping our factories in first-class condition, and Gertie wasn't keeping order in the workrooms. Talk about Peter Pan and his missus, and who could say fairer?'

'Hold 'em down, then,' said Tommy, 'we don't want 'em flying through a window till this show's over.'

Bert laughed, Gertie giggled.

'Ladies and gents,' said Sammy, 'I ain't set on making a long speech –'

'Good on yer, Mister Sammy!'

'But I am set on all of us showing proper appreciation of Gertie and Bert's long and valuable years with the firm, so first it's my pleasure on behalf of the staff to invite them to unveil the object now standing on the canteen serving counter.'

All eyes took in the object, square and large, that was covered by a tablecloth. In front of it stood a high and wide made-up card with a painted gold border, on which were the words, 'TO GERTIE AND BERT – A PRESENT FOR YOUR PARLOUR – GOOD LUCK AND BEST WISHES FOR A LONG AND HAPPY RETIREMENT FROM ALL YOUR WORKMATES.'

'Oh, Lor',' said Gertie, and drew a breath. 'Oh, Lor',' she said again, 'I ain't ever unveiled anything in me whole life.'

'Oh, kept it in the dark, 'ave yer, Gertie?' called a seamstress. ''Ard luck, Bert!'

Shrieks ran around the canteen, naturally.

'Cockney quips,' whispered Polly to Boots, 'are never-ending, old lad.'

'They've been following me about all my life,' murmured Boots.

'Well, come on, Gertie,' said Bert, 'let's do the honours.'

They made their way to the counter amid yells of encouragement, and together they pulled off the tablecloth to reveal a handsome and shining television set, brand new, paid for by contributions from every staff member.

'Oh, me Gawd,' breathed Gertie in delight.

'You know what, Gertie?' said Bert. 'I ain't going to spend as much time on me allotment as I thought.'

'Bert, speak your thanking piece,' said Gertie.

'Well, so I will,' said Bert, and turned to face the festive gathering. 'I'm no speechifier, but that don't stop me from thanking all of you from the bottom of me heart, and from Gertie's as well. There ain't been no time when it wasn't a pleasure for us to be one of you. No, two of you, and that's a fact, brothers and sisters. Thank you kindly.'

Loud claps and rousing cheers.

'Now, second,' said Sammy. 'Gertie and Bert, kindly step forward so that I can hand you a retirement gift from the directors. Good. There we are, then.' He gave Bert a folded cheque. Bert opened it. It was for a thousand pounds, payable to himself, the amount made up by equal contributions from Boots, Tommy and Sammy. Bert blinked, then showed the cheque to Gertie.

'Oh, me Sunday elastic,' gasped Gertie, 'all that's for us?'

'That and yer Sunday elastic,' said Bert, touched to the quick. He coughed, cleared his throat and did his best to thank the three brothers.

'Think nothing of it, every penny deserved,' said Sammy, and addressed the staff and guests again. 'Now, finally, might I ask all and sundry to raise your glasses in a toast to their happy retirement. Right, to Gertie and Bert, bless 'em.'

'To Gertie and Bert!' exclaimed all and sundry.

Gertie went a happy pink in company with her family, and Tommy led everyone into the finale.

'For they are jolly good fellows . . .'

It was sung with gusto. After which, with people preparing to leave, Clare asked a whispered question of Gertie. 'Grandma, who's that girl with Jimmy Adams?'

'Oh, you've met Jimmy, 'ave you?' said Gertie. 'What girl d'you mean?' She took a look. 'Oh, that's Dodie Woods, what works the switchboard, like you do at Parsons Engineering.'

'Is she his girlfriend?' asked Clare.

'Well, 'ardly, seeing she's leaving in four weeks to get married,' said Gertie. 'Jimmy Adams doesn't have a girlfriend. Well, not a steady one. That's what Mister Tommy told me.'

'Crikey, a lovely feller like 'im with no girlfriend?' said Clare.

'Hold on, 'ave you got your eye on him?' asked Gertie.

'Me?' said Clare with big-eyed innocence, at which point her grandmother became the target of well-wishers wanting to say a few words to her before they left. Clare gave way.

A little later, with more people leaving, she bumped into Jimmy. She made it look accidental.

'Oh, sorry,' she said. Then, 'Oh, it's you.'

'Hello again,' said Jimmy, 'are you off now?'

'Yes, I'm departing with me mum and dad in a few minutes,' she said.

'In a few minutes, then, it's goodbye, is it?' said Jimmy. 'What a wrench.'

'Beg pardon?' said Clare.

'Just a comment,' said Jimmy.

'Oh, well,' said Clare, 'I just want to say me and Jane and Maggie liked meeting you.'

'My pleasure,' said Jimmy. 'First time I've ever met three pretty maidens all at once and at the same time.'

'Pretty maidens?' Clare laughed and showed well-kept teeth. 'Are you real? I mean, what year you living in?'

'Same year as you,' said Jimmy.

'Pretty maidens don't sound like it,' said Clare. 'More like the time of King Arthur?'

'Who's he? Oh, you mean King Arthur and his Knights of the Round Table. That's daft.'

'Well, it's not correct, I agree,' said Jimmy, as the catering staff began a clear-up. Being a typical Adams, he could chat a bit. 'It was fair damsels in distress then, and they weren't round any table, they were frantic to escape from a foul knight's locked-up castle before he came back from some evil enterprise to make life frightful for them. Pretty maidens happened later, about the same time as George Washington.'

Clare gave him a funny look. Was he all there? He seemed to be. Well, he wasn't twitching or anything like that.

'You're having me on,' she said.

'No, seriously,' said Jimmy, 'pretty maidens did come after fair damsels.'

'And that's serious?' said Clare. 'Crikey, what're you like when you're being funny, then?'

'I make faces,' said Jimmy.

Clare gave him another look. Jimmy gave her a wink.

'I just know you're having me on,' she said.

'No, I'm just happy for Gertie and Bert,' said Jimmy. 'They deserved their send-off. Did you see them going it in the knees-up? What a performance.'

'I didn't see you doing it,' said Clare.

'I've got a problem with my feet,' said Jimmy, 'I fall over when they're both off the ground.'

Clare laughed again.

'Crikey, ain't you droll?' she said.

'What's that mean?' asked Jimmy.

'Well, we'd all fall over, wouldn't we, if we did the knees-up with both feet off the ground,' said Clare. Oh, my pulses, she thought. I don't get Harry talking with me like this, he's always on about John Wayne films. 'I'm not simple, y'know,' she said.

'No, you're a very pretty maiden,' smiled Jimmy, and Clare was sure she'd never met a more entertaining bloke.

'Not that again,' she said.

Her dad called then.

'Come on, Clare, we're going now.'

'Coming,' she called. 'Well, goodbye,' she said to Jimmy.

'So long, Clare, good luck,' said Jimmy.

'Thanks,' said Clare. She left to join her departing family.

What a doll, thought Jimmy. He'd been told ten minutes ago that she had a fancy bloke called Harry Ballymore, the informant being her cousin

Jane. Could anyone be called that? Ballymore? Perhaps he hadn't heard right. If he had, then Ballymore was possible. If he was Irish.

Gertie and Bert were the last to leave, and the last to see them off were Sammy and Susie, Tommy and Vi, and Boots and Polly. That made it a farewell from the family, and that, in turn, made it a very touching one for Gertie and Bert. Gertie, a tough old bird, couldn't help being wet-eyed, and Bert, a brick monument, had to blow his nose more than once.

When the retired couple had gone, Sammy said, 'It won't be the same without 'em.'

'We couldn't expect them to work for ever,' said Tommy.

'Granted,' said Sammy, 'but today's like you get in books, it's the end of a chapter.'

'A sad one, Sammy?' said Polly.

'Not the chapter,' said Sammy. 'The chapter was lively all the way, and you could read profit for the firm in it. Well, indirectly, you could. It's just the ending that's giving me a bit of heartburn.'

'Sammy, you're a softie,' said Susie.

The end of a chapter. The three brothers and their wives mused on that. Their own lives had been a series of chapters, each with its beginning and ending.

Chapter Five

Saturday evening.

In her Kennington flat, Miss Lulu Saunders, daughter of Honest John Saunders, Labour MP, was preparing supper for herself and her expected visitor. She wasn't sure it was right to be enjoying this kind of domestic chore. A modern free-thinking young lady with political ambitions, she considered attachment to a kitchen and its cooker could lead a woman into a state of confusion about her priorities. But, much against her determination not to allow a human relationship to get in the way of her independence and her ambitions, she was in love.

It had been a quite ghastly moment when she realized she was the victim of a woman's biological weakness, that suddenly a young man meant more to her than her independence. God, how humiliating. Imagine wanting to be touched and kissed in preference to enjoying a good book, like the biography of Keir Hardie, the first Socialist MP and renowned for pioneering the rise of the Party. Of course, she had fought the rising levels of her disastrous feelings for many weeks, but the young man in question played havoc with her emotions, and one day she simply fell into his arms. Love arrived like an electric shock, and everything else flew out of the window.

He talked about marriage.

Marriage? Marriage? That was death to a woman's independence and her worldly ambitions.

'Marriage?' she said.

'I'm not settling for less,' he said.

Weakness went crazy, making her say, 'Well, if that's what you'd really like.'

'Not immediately,' he said. 'In time, when I'm earning enough to keep us off the breadline.'

She wasn't sure if that was a reprieve or a disappointment. It had all happened a couple of years ago, and he was still set on waiting until he felt he could afford the financial responsibilities of marriage. Her situation now had nothing to do with reprieve or disappointment, but frustration. Should she call it off, chuck it up, and revert single-mindedly to a political career? After all, it was a fact that the Labour Party needed some fiery new blood to be certain of turning Winston Churchill and his Conservatives out of office at the next election. She could see herself qualifying as a candidate for a seat by '56 or '57. She was still an incurable Socialist, still a champion of the working classes and the poor and oppressed, particularly oppressed women.

Because of the effect of love, she had taught herself to cook, even though that represented another step in what she considered the wrong direction. However, it need not happen. Being a modern wife didn't mean accepting a menial role. Serious magazines were encouraging wives to come out of their kitchens and make a name for themselves. That, of course, got up the noses of hidebound men. But, one day, a women's movement would really take off. Meanwhile, someone had to do the cooking, and if she taught herself, she could also teach her husband. If, that is, she didn't call it off.

A knock sounded on the door of her flat. She jumped, and despite her mood little excitements rushed. She took her apron off, dumped it and answered the knock.

'Hello, good evening, and how's your father?' said Paul Adams, younger son of Tommy and Vi Adams. Lulu approved of his parents. They were cockneys with honest working-class roots, even if they did live in a middle-class house.

'Hello yourself,' said Lulu, 'and what's that you're holding behind your back?'

'Some of my dad's garden foliage,' said Paul, now well into his twenty-third year and wearing a sports shirt and casual brown slacks on this summer evening. While not as handsome as his dad, his looks were passable enough to please most girls, and, like his dad, he had fine shoulders and a firm chest. He eyed Lulu with a smile. What a change from when he had first known her, straight hair hanging like lank black curtains on either side of her face, horn-rimmed spectacles heavy-looking, apparel pretty junky and more masculine than feminine. Now her hair was attractively styled, her spectacles gold-rimmed, her dress of salmon pink very feminine. 'There we are, Lulu, sweet peas with the compliments of my dad.'

He brought a large bouquet of the colourful flowers into view, handed it to her and bent to kiss her. Lulu thought about avoiding it as a warning to him that she was rethinking her situation. Too late. A warm smacker arrived on her lips, which sent a major part of her dissatisfaction flying into limbo. Then, of course, she thought how traitorous a woman's weakness could be.

'Sweet peas? Oh, thanks,' she said. 'Come in, supper's ready.'

Paul entered.

'Had a happy cooking time?' he said, closing the door.

'Up to a point. Well, you know me.' Lulu regularly spoke in staccato fashion. It reflected a mind that raced. 'Don't want to get too attached to my cooker and sink. It's not my idea of what women are made for.'

'I can't count the number of times you've told me that, or something like it,' said Paul, a good-humoured smile appearing.

'Well, one more time won't hurt,' said Lulu.

'Your cooking could be a labour of love,' said Paul.

'Oh, yes?' smiled Lulu. 'That comment's typical of men. Is that a new shirt? I like it.'

'I like your dress and the supper aroma,' said Paul.

'Come and sit down, and I'll serve it,' said Lulu.

She put the flowers in a vase first, and placed it on the kitchen table as a decoration.

She used the kitchen for all her meals. Paul, seated at the table, watched as she served a supper of lamb chops of a modest size because of continued meat rationing. With the chops came onion sauce, new potatoes glistening with melting butter – a sacrifice of part of her weekly ration – and dark green broccoli. To Paul it looked as if Lulu's cooking was coming on a treat.

There was also a bottle of Sauternes, a white wine that was cheap. People were taking to wine. At least, middle-class people were. The labouring classes stuck to beer. Lulu, who considered herself one of them, was nevertheless not insensible to the merits of wine, and could always point out it was the daily tipple of the French working classes.

'Lulu, this is great,' said Paul. The onion sauce was creamy and flavoursome, his chop grilled to tenderness.

'I do my best to show that my distrust of kitchen chores doesn't get in the way of my hospitality,' said Lulu. She swallowed wine, took a breath and went on. 'Paul, I have to talk to you.'

'Good-oh,' said Paul, 'a supper like this deserves some entertaining chat.'

'I don't think it's going to be entertaining,' said Lulu. 'It's about our situation. Our situation is stuck in a groove.'

'That's got to be something to do with our circumstances,' said Paul. 'They need changing. That is, mine do – no, wait, what was it you were going to say?'

'It's all right, you go ahead,' said Lulu.

'No, you had the floor,' said Paul.

'No, I'll let you have it,' said Lulu, who thought he might be going to make it easier for her to drop her brick.

'Right,' said Paul, blithe of spirit and enjoying his meal. 'Lately, I've given a lot of thought to improving my earnings. I can't marry on what I get now.'

'But there's mine as well,' said Lulu. 'I've told you that.'

'Mortgage companies won't lend on the combined earnings of a husband and wife,' said Paul. 'They don't regard a wife's earnings as permanent.'

'Typical,' said Lulu. 'It's done to make a wife feel inferior. That she can't hold down a job.'

'Um, not really,' said Paul. 'The fact is, you never know what might happen in a marriage.'

'Happen?' Lulu eyed him suspiciously. The penny dropped. Great balls of fire, she thought, he's talking about babies. Babies? They'll sabotage my ambitions. Further, such talk embarrassed her. She gulped wine and refrained from making any comment.

'So I want to be sure I can increase my earnings,' said Paul.

'Oh?' said Lulu. She and Paul now worked as joint assistants to the constituency's agent. 'D'you mean you're going to ask for a rise?'

'Some hopes,' said Paul. 'Money for activist workers has to be fished out through a small slit in a tight drum. I'll never earn as much at Party headquarters as I need. Party work is a real labour of love, but I've decided it's not for me.'

'You can say that about our work for Socialism?' said Lulu, shocked. 'Socialism is the only system that can free the workers from the bosses. And from poverty. If we win the next election, I hope I'll secure a seat myself. Then I'll propose we nationalize everything.'

'Lulu, you dope, that's not Socialism, that's Communism.' Paul shook his head at his fiancée. A faithful Labour supporter, he said, 'I'll wish joy to our activists when I leave. But for now, listen, I had a chat with Dad last night, and a talk with my Uncle Sammy this afternoon. Of course, they were surprised, they both thought I intended to spend all my working life with Labour's grass roots. Lulu, it's over two years since we became engaged, and it's time we tied the knot and made a pretty bow of it. We'll use pink ribbon.'

'Oh, get you,' said Lulu. 'But you've come to, have you?'

Paul said he'd been held back by being underpaid, and now had the chance of being well paid. With his dad's support, his Uncle Sammy had offered him a job at the family firm's offices in Camberwell, as an assistant to his cousins Tim and Daniel, who jointly managed the property company.

'I'm to start Monday week, after I've given notice,' he said. 'And at six pounds a week, twice my present wage. In this day and age, how can a bloke keep a wife on three quid a week? Especially when she's good at cooking, and accordingly deserves a new outfit from time to time.'

'But a property company?' said Lulu. 'That's the worst kind of capitalism.'

'Yes, it does look like betrayal of my Socialist principles,' said Paul, and forked a luscious piece of lamb chop into his receptive mouth. Chewing, he said, 'Still, under the circs –'

'Don't talk with your mouth full,' said Lulu. The prospect of a radical change in the situation having its dizzy effect, it was all she could think of saying.

'You sound like someone's mother,' said Paul. 'Lulu, I'm not after the comfort of a motherly bosom, I'm after a good cook who looks like you do in your Sunday frock.'

'Sunday frock my eye,' said Lulu. 'Don't be archaic. And stop thinking I'll let you marry me for my cooking. It'll be a modern marriage, one of equality.'

'I've got my suspicions about that kind of equality,' said Paul. 'I know you all too well. You'll end up more equal. What'll that do to my trousers? You'll wear 'em. Anyway, can you shut your eyes to my working for my family's capitalists?'

Behind her spectacles, Lulu's eyes looked reproachful.

'I'll never live it down, not as the daughter of a Labour MP,' she said. However, reproach took a back seat and a little smile flickered. 'Still, if you can't live without me, what can I do? I'll have to marry you, you poor bloke.'

'Half a mo,' said Paul, 'does that mean out of pity?'

'I wouldn't marry any man out of pity,' said Lulu.

'I'd send him on a course through life's barbed wire that would cure his feebleness.' A prickly thought struck her. If Paul began this job at Camberwell while she remained at Party headquarters in Walworth, that would be the end of seeing him every day, unless they were married. 'Well, look here,' she said, 'when do we tie the old-fashioned knot? In another couple of years? If so, let me tell you –'

'I thought in a few months, say September, when I'm well into my new job and running a bank account,' said Paul.

Woman's weakness enjoyed a moment of old-fashioned pleasure that knocked a temporary hole in political ambition.

'Oh,' she said. 'Oh, all right, then. September.' If she sounded almost casual, a definite smile gave it the lie. 'Paul?'

'Well, Lulu?'

'Thanks.'

'You're thanking me?' said Paul. 'I'm the privileged one, you're the angel.' He refilled their glasses and they drank to each other. 'Happy days, Lulu.'

'Happy days, Paul. Do I have to wear white?'

'If you don't, my grandmother will think the service isn't legal.'

'Well, all right. I'll go along with what your granny expects. But I don't usually conform to customs initiated by patriarchal societies.'

'That's my girl, make a sacrifice. Now, what was it you wanted to talk to me about?'

'Oh, nothing much, nothing important. I've forgotten, in fact. Incidentally, a September wedding could be great. It could coincide with the Labour Party conference.'

'So?' said Paul.

'We could spend our first married week in Blackpool, and attend the conference.'

'Eh?'

'Would you like that?'

'Only if I were cock-eyed. Lulu, for that particular week, politics are out. Out, out, out. So's Blackpool and its tower. I fancy renting a little country cottage for two far from anything higher than a haystack.'

'But what about activities?'

'That's not a serious question, is it, Lulu?'

Lulu preferred to ignore that.

'Look,' she said, 'about this mortgage you mentioned. Does it mean you've got a semi-detached suburban house in mind? If so, we'll be taking our first step towards becoming middle class. It'll be like dying a death. Our friends in Walworth won't even come to the funeral.'

'I know, it'll be hard to bear and a bit depressing, but we'll just have to grit our teeth.' Paul sipped wine and thought. Then he came up with, 'I wonder if some estate agent could point us at a semi-detached hovel at the back end of Peckham?'

'Oh, very funny,' said Lulu.

'I think I'm a bit light-headed because of all the happy aspects, and that includes the supper,' said Paul. 'By the way, any afters in the offing?'

'Strawberry jam tart,' said Lulu.

'I'll have some of that, then help you with the washing-up,' said Paul. 'Love you, Lulu.'

Lulu felt a rush of warmth.

'Oh, you can have two helpings of tart for that,' she said.

There were moments when a woman's weakness was quite bearable.

On arrival home that night, Paul found his parents watching an Arthur Askey comedy show on the television. They were seated together on a settee upholstered in soft brown leather. They looked so relaxed, so comfortable, and so content with each other's company, that Paul thought them an example of how to be happy though married.

As soon as he made his entrance known, the television was switched off, and the first thing he did was to inform them that he and Lulu were going to get churched the first Saturday in September.

Vi looked startled but pleased.

'Oh, that's nice,' she said.

'But not before time,' said Tommy.

'Yes, your dad and me wondered when it was going to happen,' said Vi.

'If ever,' murmured Tommy.

'Well, of course, you both know my new job is going to provide me with the kind of bread money I need as a married bloke,' said Paul. 'Good on you, Dad, for having a word with Uncle Sammy, and good on Uncle Sammy for taking me on.'

'Don't mention it,' said Tommy. 'I congratulate

you for seeing sense, considering your mum and me were thinking you didn't have any.'

'Now, Tommy,' said Vi, 'I never thought Paul was short of sense.'

'Personally,' said Tommy, 'I thought he'd end up marrying the Labour Party.'

'I will be, when I marry Lulu,' said Paul. 'Well, good as.'

'Paul, you and your dad, making jokes like that about your future wife, it's not nice,' said Vi.

'Don't panic, Mum,' said Paul, 'I'll work on Lulu once we're married. Perhaps I'll get her to settle for being just a voter.'

'Conservative?' said Tommy.

'Could I perform a miracle?' said Paul. 'Not much. And a change of jobs won't mean I'll ditch Labour.' He might have been elected to the Walworth council if he had been prepared to move into the area, but he liked his family home too much. 'I've got to be frank, Dad, I still believe a Labour government's the best bet for the country.'

'That'll be worth watching, a young capitalist trying to stick to Socialism,' said Tommy.

'Now you two,' said Vi, always a peacemaker, 'we ought to be talking about the wedding, not politics. Politics just cause arguments.'

'Well, about the wedding, Mum, I can tell you one thing that won't cause an argument,' said Paul. 'Lulu's consented to wear white.'

'Consented?' said Vi, who had come to like Lulu enough to overlook the young lady's odd Socialist ideas, such as turning Buckingham Palace into a home for old retired workers. 'Consented? Well, I hope she wasn't against it, it wouldn't be a proper wedding if she didn't wear white.'

'She's promised, so she will,' said Paul, 'but I'm not sure if she's going to include "obey" in her vows.'

'Bless me, what a funny girl she is,' said Vi.

'Barmy,' said Tommy. 'Still, there's more like her these days. Like your grandma says, me lad, it's come about through putting women in the army during the war.'

'Lucky Lulu wasn't old enough to be conscripted,' said Paul, 'or I'd be marrying a female sergeant major.'

Chapter Six

Sunday morning.

The weather was fine and warm, the London sky blue, the air clear. The capital's people were hoping to benefit from the increasing use of smokeless fuel and the rising popularity of central heating, particularly in the blocks of post-war council flats, even if many tenants still hankered after their old Victorian terraced houses, which either bombs or development had razed to the ground. Not everyone, however, used smokeless fuel or had central heating, not by any means, and during the winter London still suffered yellow fogs. These were caused by domestic and factory chimneys exuding fumes when untreated coal was burnt. Parliament, however, had just introduced a Clean Air Act that would compel the use of smokeless fuels.

But this was May and very few domestic fires were burning. Katje Galicia left her Bloomsbury flat and walked to a bus stop. Only a few people were about, and only two were waiting at the stop. When the bus arrived, she boarded it with them. Moments later, as it moved off, a man hastened up and jumped on.

At Hyde Park, Katje alighted along with other passengers and headed for the park. The late-boarder at the Bloomsbury stop got off last, again making his move just as the bus resumed its journey. He followed people into the park. Katje, instinctively alert in the way of a person who lived a cloak-and-dagger existence, had no doubt she was under observation.

She smiled to herself. So, they didn't trust her. But they didn't trust any agent who wasn't inside their closely integrated circle, however efficient he or she proved. The man, at a distance behind her, was probably under instruction to find out if she was in the park to meet Sir Edwin Finch, whom she always thought of as a typically well-mannered English gentleman, but whose defection from German to British Intelligence made him a figure of interest to the KGB. Since the end of the war with Nazi Germany, and more so since the beginning of the Cold War, the KGB, with the aid of Poland's security services, had been scouring Europe for men and women who had something to offer in the way of information, or owned the potential for becoming double agents, known as moles.

Well, she was not in the park to meet Sir Edwin Finch. Katje smiled to herself again, and pursued her true intention, to simply enjoy the green oasis and its Sunday atmosphere. She liked Hyde Park and she liked London, now recovering from the devastation of war, and offering much more than gloomy Warsaw or any city in the East German Democratic Republic. However much support she gave to the ideology of Communism in preference to the exploitative nature of capitalism, her former political choice, she was a woman with a weakness for bright lights, not dark corridors. All the same, she was considered a conscientious worker for a regime that promised a system of plenty for ordinary people, although she sometimes wondered how much longer the ordinary people of Soviet Russia would have to wait for it. The original promise had been made by Lenin and Stalin as far back as the 1920s. A workers' Utopia. Whether Communist or capitalist, some kinds of ideology, she thought wryly, take a great deal of time to create even the simplest Utopia.

She sauntered through the park, taking note of vibrant young men and women looking as free as the air itself. In Moscow, the air was just as free in that the Central Committee could not control it, but the atmosphere was heavy.

She walked on, indifferent to her shadower.

Tomorrow she would think about making contact with Sir Edwin Finch.

Sunday afternoon.

Annabelle and Nick's son, Philip, having arrived home on Saturday for a week's leave from his RAF cadets' training unit, began to make family calls.

'Yes, you ought to,' his mum had said, 'you haven't seen your cousins for a year.'

'Some won't even recognize you,' said his dad, 'you've shot up like a bamboo sapling.'

Which was true. In a year, Philip had put on the kind of inches that made him long and lanky.

Bloody hell, his RAF sergeant-instructor had said to him only a few days ago, if you don't stop growing upwards, Cadet Harrison, you'll hit the sky before you leave the ground. While you're on leave, get your mother to give you something that'll make you shrink a yard or two.

The Sabbath afternoon was cloudless and sunny, bestowing the kind of early summer warmth that was making elderly people think of casting a clout. Philip, having walked from his parents' house in an avenue off Denmark Hill, knocked on the door of his Uncle Sammy's residence a little way up the hill. The knock was answered by a dark-haired girl in a very attractive patterned dress with a flared hem.

They looked at each other. Philip saw a girl distinctively pretty. She saw a very lanky young man in a check shirt and blue jeans. Young men no longer wore their best suits on Sundays. Casual clobber was the thing for young men and young women too at weekends.

'Crikey,' said Phoebe Adams, 'I think I know you.'

'I'm not sure I know you,' said Philip. He had homely features, but fine clear eyes. His fair hair showed glints of gold in the sunshine, and his grin was engaging. 'You can't be Cousin Phoebe, can you?'

'Well, yes, I can be if you're actually Cousin Philip.' Phoebe was not only pretty, she was a quicksilver girl who herself had put on inches during this last year. 'Are you?'

'Yes, that's me,' said Philip.

'You sure?' said Phoebe. 'Only you're twice as long since you last called.'

'So are you,' said Philip. 'Well, nearly.' Remembering he had once called her a titch, he added, 'Talk about short little girls turning into five-feet-sixers almost overnight.'

'Overnight?' said Phoebe. 'Over a year, more like, and yes, what d'you mean by never coming to see us in all that time? Mum and Dad started to wonder if you'd flown off to Australia in one of your training planes without sending us a postcard. Do you fly them yet?'

'No, not yet,' said Philip, 'and listen, cheeky, are you going to invite me in or not?'

'Well, now you're here you'd better come in and let my mum and dad see that you're not in Australia,' said Phoebe. She smiled then. It reached her eyes and made them light up. Blind Harry, thought Philip, I didn't know I had a cousin like this one. How old was she now? Sixteen? Yes, sixteen. What a sweetheart.

He stepped into the hall, following Phoebe through to the kitchen and out of the back door into the garden, where the newly shaved lawn was a summer green, and shrubs and bushes were coming into flower. At the top, behind a hedge, was a vegetable plot, mainly tended by Jimmy, who had the same liking for that kind of gardening as his Aunt Polly. Around a white-painted wrought-iron table sat Susie and Sammy, Vi and Tommy, and Lizzy and Ned. Paula was at David and Kate's farm, and Jimmy was out with friends.

'Hi there, uncles and aunts,' said Philip.

All heads turned.

'Well, my goodness,' said Vi, 'who's this, Phoebe?'

'He says he's Cousin Philip,' smiled Phoebe.

'The young chap who belongs to your Aunt Annabelle and Uncle Nick?' said Tommy.

'Lovely to see you, Philip,' said Susie.

'Is he on stilts?' asked Sammy.

'Sammy Adams,' said Lizzy, 'you're speaking sarky of my grandson.'

'And if he's on stilts,' said Ned, 'I'm on a flying carpet.'

'You've grown up very nice, Philip,' said Lizzy, 'and I've been telling that to all the family.'

Philip had called on her and Ned last night. Now he gave her a kiss, and treated Vi and Susie likewise before shaking hands with Tommy and Sammy, and giving Granddad Ned an affectionate pat on the shoulder. He thought his granddad looked grey. He knew he had heart trouble, and had retired from his job because of that. He gave him another little pat.

'How's everyone?' he asked. 'No, don't tell me, you're all in the pink, as usual.' Except for Granddad Ned, he thought.

Sammy took a look at his nephew's American jeans.

'Dear oh Lor',' he said, 'might I ask if you've parked your gee-gee in the drive?'

'Gee-gee?' said Philip, and Phoebe showed an impish smile, knowing what was coming next.

'Horse,' said Sammy.

'Why a horse?' asked Philip.

'Why?' said Sammy. 'Well, in that cowboy gear you ride a nag, don't you, me lad?'

'I would if I had one, Uncle Sammy,' said Philip, 'but I haven't, so I don't.'

'Beats me,' said Sammy. 'I mean, what's the point of wearing riding reach-me-downs if you don't have a horse?'

'Take no notice, Philip,' smiled Susie, 'your Uncle Sammy's having one of his comical turns.'

'Anyway, Sammy,' said Vi the peacemaker, 'you've got to admit jeans look a lot better than what the Teddy boys wear.'

'Teddy boys,' gloomed Tommy, 'what a collection of freaks.'

It was the rage among tearaway youths to give anything associated with conformist wear the order of the boot, and to adopt a neo-Edwardian outfit of drainpipe trousers and frock coats, along with a high hairstyle that gleamed with brilliantine and ended in a quiff. They paid barbers handsomely for this, and went about in exhibitionist groups that raised eyebrows, causing some ex-servicemen to declare the war wasn't fought to give birth to poofs. The media quickly found a more suitable name for them: Teddy boys, as per Teddy, otherwise remembered as King Edward the Seventh.

'Oh, it's just their way of showing off,' said Vi, 'and it doesn't hurt no-one.'

'It hurts my optics,' said Sammy, 'and a lot more than Philip's cowboy clobber.' He laughed. 'No, you're all right, Phil, only pulling your leg about gee-gees. Mind, would anybody here like to buy him 'one?'

'Sammy,' said Lizzy, 'if you don't stop all this funny stuff, I'll tell Philip about the time when you were ten and your school shorts fell down in Woolworths, and all the girls came from behind their counters to—'

'It's a porkic,' said Sammy.

'And the girls did what?' asked Susie.

'Helped him to pull them up,' said Lizzy, 'and Sammy, of course—'

'It's still a porkie,' said Sammy.

'He went red all over,' said Lizzy.

'And never showed himself in that Woolworths store again,' said Ned.

Chortles and titters ran around the garden table.

'Corblimey funny, I don't think,' said Sammy. 'And it's about time we invited Philip to sit down and tell us what he's been up to at his training camp.'

'Oh, just going steady,' said Philip, 'and getting to know how fighter planes work. Nothing like having my trousers fall down in the canteen.'

Phoebe laughed.

'D'you mind me saying they'd have a long way to fall?' she said.

'Aunt Susie,' said Philip, 'd'you mind if I get after Phoebe? She's been a bundle of sauce since she opened the door to me.'

'Help yourself,' smiled Susie, 'but treat her gently.'

Philip made his move. Phoebe, shrieking with laughter, hared up the garden, Philip in pursuit. It was hardly a close-run chase, since Philip's legs worked like a windmill in a strong wind. He caught her by the vegetable plot as she ran through the entrance gap in the hedge. She turned, her face alight with merriment.

'Watch it, cousin,' she said, 'if you tread all over Jimmy's up-and-coming potatoes, he'll bury you in his compost heap.'

Philip, looking into her laughing eyes, did what a natural impulse urged him to do, especially as the hedge hid him from the eyes of the adults. He kissed her. Phoebe stiffened, then quivered all over. Released, she smacked his face.

Philip stood back, expression wry.

Phoebe, face burning, went into reversal then, because of all kinds of strange emotions, and said, 'Oh, I'm sorry.'

'No, I deserved it,' said Philip, realizing how stupid he'd been in treating her like a flirtatious village girl of the kind who lived close to his training establishment. 'Yes, so sorry, Phoebe.'

Phoebe's burning flush receded somewhat.

'No, it's all right,' she said. She swallowed. 'But we're cousins,' she said.

'Not blood cousins,' said Philip.

'No, but –'

'What's going on up there?' That was Sammy's voice.

'Oh, we're just talking,' said Phoebe, and returned with Philip to rejoin the company. Susie glanced at her adopted daughter, and thought the girl slightly flushed. She smiled. Phoebe was at the age of discovery, and Philip at the age of helping a girl along that road.

Phoebe had been kissed, Susie felt sure, and

since she had no boyfriend yet, perhaps it had been her first memorable kiss, especially as Philip wasn't her natural cousin. Susie smiled again.

'Philip, stay to tea,' she said, 'I'm just about to put the kettle on and lay the table.'

'Yes, about time you honoured us at Sunday tea, me lad,' said Sammy.

'I'll help,' said Vi, rising from her chair.

'Well, thanks, Aunt Susie, I will stay,' said Philip.

'Crikey,' said Phoebe, 'we'll really be honoured.'

But she looks pleased, thought Susie.

'But I'll have to leave after tea,' said Philip, 'I promised Mum and Dad I'd call on Grandma and Grandpa Finch as well.'

'Bless me, Mum,' said Phoebe, 'the honour's only going to be a brief one.'

'Phoebe, you're a comic,' said Tommy.

'Sweet,' said Vi.

That can be said twice over, thought Philip.

No-one knew that Phoebe was still experiencing odd little vibrations, those of girlish innocence at the age of discovery.

Sometime after tea, when Philip and the other visitors had gone, and Sammy was motoring to Westerham to fetch Paula home, Susie put a pertinent question to Phoebe.

'What do you think of your cousin Philip?'

'Oh, quite nice,' said Phoebe, standing at the lounge window and looking at the garden. 'But cheeky.'

'Cheeky?' said Susie. 'How cheeky?'

'You'll never believe it, but he kissed me,' said

Phoebe, given like Paula and Jimmy to being frank with her parents.

'Well, I never,' said Susie, 'and that after not having seen you or any of us for at least a year.'

'I smacked his face,' confessed Phoebe. 'Well, I mean, he didn't even ask, he just did it. Of course, I was sorry afterwards because he looked sorry for himself. Mind, he's not actually my cousin, not actually, is he?'

'No, he isn't.' Susie smiled. 'Well, I suppose if he wants to take you out while he's on leave, just to make up for his cheek, me and your dad won't mind.'

'Take me out?' said Phoebe. 'Oh, I don't think he'll do that, he'll have lots of other things to do. Besides, I'll be at school every day.'

'There'll be the evenings,' said Susie.

'Mum, you're talking as if I'd like to have a date with him,' said Phoebe, 'and I really hardly know him.'

'Oh, well,' said Susie lightly, 'we'll see.'

Chapter Seven

Monday morning.

Chinese Lady, about to use the coffee percolator, answered the ringing phone.

'Yes, hello?'

'Hello. Excuse, but does Sir Edwin Finch live there?' It was a woman's voice. A foreign one, thought Chinese Lady, because of its accent.

'Yes, he lives here.'

'I would like to speak to him, if you please,' said Katje Galicia.

'Might I ask who you are?'

'I will tell him if he would come to the phone.'

'Well, I don't know, I'm sure,' said Chinese Lady, 'I'll have to ask him.'

She went to her husband's study. He glanced up, and although his silver hair was slightly ruffled, as if he'd been rubbing it with his pen, as he often did when going through his private papers, she thought how fit he looked for his age. It made her feel happy. She'd suffered grievous worry when he'd had a breakdown some years ago.

'Was that a phone call, Maisie?' he asked.

'Yes, it's a foreign woman that wants to speak to you,' said Chinese Lady.

'Foreign?' said Sir Edwin, coming to his feet.

Chinese Lady, who didn't hold with most foreigners, said, 'Well, that's what she sounded like.' A startling thought made her quiver. 'Lord, you don't think she's from a foreign newspaper, do you? We don't want to be read about in foreign newspapers, not when our own are bad enough.'

'I doubt if any foreign newspaper is interested in us, Maisie,' said Sir Edwin. 'I'll find out.'

'Yes, all right, Edwin, and I'll make the coffee.' Chinese Lady, still suspecting the caller did belong to a newspaper, was at least quite sure her husband would deal with the woman, and she returned to the kitchen.

Sir Edwin, reaching the hall phone, picked up the receiver and spoke. 'Hello?'

'Sir Edwin Finch?' said Katje Galicia, who had just put four extra pennies in the public phone's metal maw.

'Speaking,' said Sir Edwin. 'Who is that?'

'We met in Poland before the war, at the Polish army manoeuvres. I was then an officer, and you knew me as Major Katje Galicia.'

'Ah,' said Sir Edwin, remembering the pre-war manoeuvres. The vast plain, the columns of galloping Polish cavalry and the sad absence of tanks or any kind of armoured divisions. Inevitably, when war arrived and the colossal weight of German armour crossed the border, the ill-equipped Polish forces were destroyed all too quickly. And Katje Galicia, yes, he remembered her, a very handsome and extrovert woman officer who took a fancy to him and arranged for him to share her bed before he returned to London. He had discreetly vanished. He was long past that kind of liaison in his work as an agent. 'Ah,' hc said again, 'and to what, Madame Galicia, do I owe the pleasure of this phone call? And tell me, where are you speaking from? The People's Republic of Poland? Warsaw?'

He heard a husky little laugh.

'Dear man,' she said, 'as in Moscow, we don't have that kind of efficient phone system in Warsaw. Perhaps we should shoot some of the engineers. No, no, I'm here, in London, and wish to talk to you. I will come and see you. When can you receive me?'

'Dear lady,' said Sir Edwin, 'first tell me why you want to call.'

'On a matter of international Intelligence.'

'What has international Intelligence to do with me?'

'Come now; Sir Edwin, you are an old hand, as they say, and so am I now. The matter is important enough to interest you, I am sure, so when may I see you?'

'In my retirement,' said Sir Edwin, 'the only people who come to see me now are my relatives and friends.'

A whisper arrived in his ear.

'Your English relatives, Sir Edwin, or your German ones?'

Sir Edwin paused before answering. It wasn't the

first time he'd been up against this kind of damaging prospect. The secret of his German origins was known only to British Intelligence and to Boots, and he had a fixed intention to keep it so. There was, however, the fact that German Intelligence had a file on him, and now, somehow, this Polish woman had gained access to certain information. How long would it be, he wondered, before his English family finally found him out?

'Madame Galicia,' he said, 'I think you want something from me.'

'I assure you, my friend, nothing that will harm you,' said Katje.

'Very well,' said Sir Edwin, 'but I would prefer to meet you in town, not here.'

'That I understand,' said Katje. 'But when and where? Shall we say Hyde Park?'

No, thought Sir Edwin, no place of her own suggestion, not by any means.

'Outside the National Gallery at ten tomorrow morning,' he said.

'Ah, so?' said Katje. 'Good. Will you recognize me?'

'Have you changed much?'

'I am older, and a widow. My husband was among the Polish officers massacred in Katyn Forest. By the SS, it is said.'

'I'm sorry. But was it the SS? Fingers are pointing at the Russians.'

'Who knows? Have you changed yourself, Sir Edwin?'

'Like you, I am older.'

'Oh, I'm sure we'll know each other.'

'Very well. Tomorrow morning at ten, then.'

'I shall look forward to it,' said Katje, and rang off.

When Chinese Lady brought his coffee, she asked her husband, of course, what the foreign woman wanted.

'Oh, she's no journalist, Maisie, she's related to my old government department.' Sir Edwin used 'related' in a loose sense. 'I'm going up to town tomorrow morning for a meeting. Informal, of course. There are colleagues I still keep in touch with.'

'Well, it's a relief to know she wasn't from a foreign newspaper,' said Chinese Lady, content with that. 'And it'll be nice for you to see some of your old colleagues again.' She liked him to go up to town sometimes, and it was usually to have lunch with friends from the government department where he had worked for years. 'Will you be having lunch with them?'

'Not this time, I'll be back here for that, Maisie,' said Sir Edwin, refraining from correcting her assumption that old colleagues would be at the meeting.

Alas, Chinese Lady then put the cat among the pigeons by asking if the foreign woman was the wife of one of his old working friends. Sir Edwin coughed, considered what to do with the figurative cat, and got rid of it by saying no, the woman was an army widow. He always avoided coming out with what Sammy would have called an 'outright porkie'. Sir Walter Scott, Scotland's eminent writer, pointed out the trouble that could follow a lie with his immortal lines, 'O, what a tangled web we weave, when first we practise to deceive.' Sir Edwin was well aware of that warning.

'Oh, well, drink your coffee, love,' said Chinese Lady.

In their shared office on the first floor of the Labour Party's headquarters in Walworth, Lulu asked a question of Paul.

'What did your family think of us finally fixing a wedding date?'

'I only know what my parents thought,' said Paul, musing over a suggested programme of fund-raising events during the summer. 'Jolly good.'

'No, they didn't say that,' said Lulu. 'It's public school stuff. Your parents have got honest working-class roots. I bet that what they said was more like it was about time.'

'Same thing, in a way, as jolly good,' said Paul. 'They're happy to know you'll wear white. Oh, and will there be something blue, like a frilly garter?'

'Now you know that's not my style,' said Lulu. 'Frilly stuff is for frilly women.'

'What are frilly women?' asked Paul.

'Silly,' said Lulu, and looked at him over the top of her glasses. He smiled. She weakened. 'Still, if that's what you'd like?'

'You bct,' said Paul.

'Wait a minute,' said Lulu. 'Is it all going to be middle class? I mean, you're not going to wear a topper and tails, are you?'

'Well, knowing your opinions on middle-class customs,' said Paul, 'I thought you might like me to turn up in a sweater and jeans. My parents won't be blissful about it, especially Mum, and my Uncle Sammy will get close to falling down dead in his pew, but if it's what you—'

'Shut up,' said Lulu.

'Pardon?'

'I'll be frank,' said Lulu. 'I want to marry you, although I always told myself I didn't need to marry any bloke. But you've got to stop talking to me as if I'm some idiot female. Sweater and jeans my eye, what a load of piffle. You sound like one of the radio Goons. You'll wear a decent suit, d'you hear? Or there'll be no wedding. Understood?'

'Not half,' said Paul. 'A decent suit, right. Jacket, waistcoat and trousers. Well, a feller ought to show up in trousers on his wedding day. They're symbolic of his standing as a husband. You can ask my Uncle Sammy. All his married life he's fought to wear the trousers. Believe me, Lulu, that's common knowledge in our family.'

'More piffle, you mean,' said Lulu. 'Don't get old-fashioned ideas about that kind of thing. As I've told you before, ours is going to be a marriage of equal rights.'

'Now, Lulu, you're not going to let your politics interfere with the joys, are you?' said Paul.

'What joys?' asked Lulu with dark suspicion.

'The joys of conjugal rights,' said Paul, a solemn expression hiding his amusement. He was a hound at teasing Lulu. 'Equal rights, of course.'

Lulu actually went pink. She'd been thinking about that, naturally, and with the quivers of a virgin. However much she knew about politics and what a post-war world could offer women of independent outlook, she'd never had any kind of close relationship with a man. Until she fell in love with Paul, she'd thought men weren't an absolutely necessary sex. Well, not to career-minded women. So, at the advanced age of twenty-two, she was still a virgin. Accordingly, mention of conjugal rights made her quiver. Mind, the quivers had an element of feminine vibrations to them. Feminine. She was coming to accept that word, one she'd thought was on a par with feebleness. She'd actually come to like feminine wear, and even pretty lingerie. And why had she come to like such items? Because she was sure Paul would like them too.

She thought of her wedding night and her blush deepened. Her former world of strong resistance to a marital state was falling apart.

'Oh, help,' she breathed.

'Lulu?' said Paul. 'What's up? I mean, is that you blushing?'

'I'm not blushing,' she said. 'That's silly girlish stuff.'

'Suits you,' said Paul. 'Makes you look sweet.'

'Oh, really? D'you mind letting me got on with typing these letters for our boss?'

Their boss, the constituency's agent, put his head in at that moment.

'Have you worked out that programme yet, Paul?' he asked.

'Just finished,' said Paul.

The agent, a bluff bloke, stepped in and took it from him.

'How are you two lovebirds now you've fixed a date?' he asked.

'I'm on cloud nine,' said Paul.

'And it's sent him off his chump,' said Lulu.

'I'm not surprised,' said the agent, 'you're a winner, Lulu. That's a charming dress. Don't work too hard, but let me have those letters before lunch, if you can. Good luck.' He disappeared. Paul smiled. Lulu fixed him with a defiant look.

'You've got something else to say?' she asked.

'Yes,' said Paul.

'What, then?'

'Love you,' said Paul, 'and your charming dress.'

Lulu went over the top.

'Wait till you see my silver stockings on our wedding night,' she said.

'Eh?' said Paul.

'Oh, me Gawd,' breathed Lulu, 'what have I said?'

Paul smiled. It was almost unbelievable that a young lady who considered herself an ultra-modern woman could be so retiring about what, after all, was only her natural sex appeal. Let's be frank, he told himself, not many blokes marry a woman for her knowledge of maths or Karl Marx.

Monday evening.

By now, the latest news had flashed around the family.

Tommy and Vi's son Paul had at last fixed a date for his marriage to Lulu Saunders.

'Well, I don't know if he's doing the right thing,' said Chinese Lady over the phone to Lizzy. 'I can't say I've taken to her peculiar ways. Mind,

I don't mean unkind peculiar, as she seems to be respectable, and has come to dress nice.'

'Mum, I suppose we've got to face up to young women having different ideas these days,' said Lizzy. 'Look at Alice turning down that nice man from Scotland, Fergus MacAllister, because she wanted to work at her university instead of being a wife.'

'I just don't know what's got into some young women since the war,' said Chinese Lady, and went on about it all being the fault of that man Hitler and how he ought never to have been allowed to see the light of day. Then the war wouldn't have happened, and young women wouldn't have had to do soldiering and take on funny ideas. And so on.

'My gosh, Daniel,' said Patsy, when her husband arrived home, 'now your cousin Paul's hit a homer.'

'You mean a descendant of Homer the Greek?' said Daniel. 'If so, what made Paul hit him?'

'Daniel, you're showing off,' said Patsy, 'like you know your ancient history and I'm just a dumb chick. What I'm telling you is that Paul's going to marry Lulu at last.'

'I'll believe that when I hear it,' said Daniel.

'You're hearing it now,' said Patsy. 'From me. And I heard it from your Aunt Vi.'

'Well, I'll believe Aunt Vi,' said Daniel.

'Oh, great,' said Patsy. 'Why not me?'

'You make jokes,' said Daniel.

'Listen to who's talking,' said Patsy.

In another family home, Mrs Leah Somers,

Jewish wife of Edward, younger son of Lizzy and Ned, made her mark on her husband's ears.

'My life, Edward, Paul's done it at last!'

'Done what, might I ask?' enquired Edward, a serious-minded man, but nevertheless owning a sense of humour.

'Decided on a wedding date,' said Leah, twenty-five and, in the eyes of Edward, a replica of Elizabeth Taylor, the film star noted for her beauty.

'Good for Paul,' he said. 'And who's the privileged lady?'

'Who? Who? Why, Lulu Saunders, of course, who else? He's been engaged to her for ages, hasn't he?'

'I wish him luck as her future husband, then,' said Edward, 'especially if she arrives at the church wearing a gown made from the Red Flag.'

'Edward, we should think that?' said Leah, mother of five-year-old Eliza, named after Grandma Lizzy.

'It's a possibility,' said Edward.

'Of course not, you silly man,' said Leah. 'Lulu's not that kind of Socialist.'

'Well, you love, talk me into believing it,' said Edward.

That kind of dialogue went on between other members of Chinese Lady's family, in much the same way as when they had heard about her victorious confrontation with a thieving geezer, one Fred Summersby.

Chapter Eight

The following day.

At a couple of minutes before ten, a taxi pulled up outside the National Gallery in Trafalgar Square. There, Admiral Nelson looked down on London from a great height. During the war, Goering's bombers might have knocked him off his perch, but Nelson survived untouched and haughty, much as if he had regarded Goering's air force with disdain, or at least as far less menacing than Napoleon's navy.

The morning was cloudy but clear, and from the taxi Sir Edwin picked the woman out at once, tall and elegant in an oyster suit and a close-fitting hat. She was eyeing the cab. He opened the passenger door and beckoned. She glanced around, and then glided swiftly to the kerb. Sir Edwin moved back, she entered the taxi and pulled the door to. The cabbie set his vehicle in motion and filtered into the traffic.

'Good morning, my friend,' said Katje Galicia, and Sir Edwin, in a charcoal grey suit and light trilby hat, regarded her with interest. Yes, she was older, past fifty by now, but still handsome with her high cheekbones and her bold eyes, eyes as dark as violet. Her costume was faultless, a large cameo brooch pinned to her blouse.

'Good morning, madame,' he said, aware that he was under survey himself.

'I'm happy to see you again,' said Katje as the taxi entered the Strand, always a busy thoroughfare with its shops, theatres, restaurants and offices. Recovery from the damage inflicted by war was making its mark there too. 'You are very recognizable.'

'As a very elderly person?'

'My dear friend, you are no age,' said Katje, smile inviting confidences, 'and how could one see you as a mere person? It's the proletariat and the bourgeoisie who are mere persons.'

Sir Edwin thought of Chinese Lady and her extensive family.

'I belong to the bourgeoisie,' he said.

'You are still not a mere person,' said Katje. 'Tell me, where are we going?'

'To a quiet place,' said Sir Edwin. 'Are you working for the Communist government of Poland?'

'In the People's Republic of Poland, we are all loyal to the Government and its programme of reformation,' said Katje.

Sir Edwin took that with a pinch of salt. The taxi turned from Aldwych into Kingsway.

'During the few days I knew you,' he said, 'it never occurred to me you would opt for Communism.'

'Ah, so?' Katje shrugged. 'My friend, it was Hitler's plundering armies and his murderous SS that made every Pole, except a few dissidents, choose Communism as a way of life.'

'I see,' said Sir Edwin, watching the flow of traffic and the movements of people as the taxi took a right turn and came to a stop at Lincoln's Inn Fields. 'This is the place, madame,' he murmured, and they alighted. Sir Edwin, while paying the fare, took the opportunity to find out if they had been followed. It appeared not so. He tipped the cabbie handsomely. The man had carried out all his instructions without asking questions, much as if eccentric or questionable passengers were an everyday occurrence.

'Ta, guv, you're a sport.'

'My pleasure,' said Sir Edwin.

He escorted Katje into Lincoln's Inn Fields, a place patronized at lunchtime by City clerks and office girls, who strolled around the green expanses or sat on the benches to eat their sandwiches. Sometimes barristers appeared, discussing their briefs while they sauntered. At this time of day, however, there were only a few people about, and the atmosphere was one of undisturbed quiet. It was a peaceful oasis in the heart of busy, bustling London, a city still in the noisy throes of continuous reconstruction work.

The quietness was calming to the nerves, although some people might have said that neither Sir Edwin nor the Polish woman suffered uneasy pulse rates.

They walked at leisure.

'We can talk now?' said Katje.

'Of plots and plans?' said Sir Edwin drily.

'It's why we have met.'

'At your request, not mine.'

'True,' said Katje, who knew they had lost her shadower. She had advised Alexandrov of her arranged meeting with Sir Edwin. He had said that in turn he would arrange for a bodyguard to be on hand to ensure her safety. Bodyguard, thought Katje, was a very good word for one of Alexandrov's errand boys, and safety, of course, meant keeping her under observation. Like all senior KGB men, he left nothing to chance, nothing that would fail to keep him up to date with a situation. Well, the bodyguard had appeared and made himself known to her, but the taxi had swiftly taken her away, and Alexandrov must swallow failure this time. He would have to rely on her account of the meeting. 'Sir Edwin, you are no longer in the field, of course, but have spent many years on active service, first for your German masters, then for the British.'

'Obviously, you know more about me than most people,' said Sir Edwin. 'So what do you want from me?'

'During your later years, you would have known men in whom my principals are interested. Men who were active agents during the war, and some whose task was to find out all they could of Germany's programme of rocket propulsion and the creation of an atomic bomb.'

'Your principals, madame, if they're Russian, must know that their Soviet scientists now have the expertise to master the production of rocket-propelled machines, and that they've already provided the bomb.'

'My principals would still like names, Sir Edwin.'

Sir Edwin expressed himself firmly and to the effect that on no account would he name any names. Katje said that would be a pity, since it would mean the possibility of letting his English wife and family know all the details of his past.

'That possibility can blow in the wind,' said Sir Edwin. 'I repeat, I'll name no man or woman.'

'I admire you for that,' smiled Katje, 'it is the way of a true English gentleman, even if he was born a German. But come, let us sit down and talk some more.'

'It will do no good,' said Sir Edwin. 'I agreed to this meeting only to find out what you intended to ask of me.'

'I understand,' said Katje, 'but all the same, give me a few more minutes.'

'Very well,' said Sir Edwin, 'as long as you change your demands.'

He sat down with her.

They conversed quietly.

At the Camberwell offices of the family firm's parent company, Adams Enterprises Ltd, Rachel Goodman was talking to Sammy, he seated at his large oak desk, his solid business comfort for many years.

'Rachel, did you say you've received an offer?'

'Yes, Sammy, an offer of marriage. From Joseph Burns.'

'Otherwise known as Joe Burns the Walworth bookie?'

'That's the gentleman, Sammy.'

'Well, I admire his good taste, Rachel, but – um – ain't he a bit on the unfitful side for a female woman like you?'

'Unfitful?' said Rachel, looking splendid in a springtime dress of apricot.

'Er – a bit on the fat sidc?' said Sammy. He knew the gent, who had a paunch that even his winter coat with a fur collar couldn't hide. Mind, he was a nice enough bloke. He handed out pennies to kids and a beaming smile to his favourite punters. He was a widower, having lost his wife, a thin woman, some years ago. Sammy had suggested to Boots that bookie Joe had got on top of her once too often. Boots said tut tut, Sammy.

'A bit on the fat side, Sammy?' Rachel put that with a smile to show she wasn't offended.

'Well, looking at you, Rachel – no, half a mo, I'm treading on your toes, and me own as well,' said Sammy apologetically. 'And bookie Joe's. He's a kind bloke with a prosperous business, so what's a bit of extra weight?'

'A woman should worry about that?' Amusement showed in Rachel's luminous brown eyes. 'Well, she might if the extra had a promise of becoming extra extra.'

'Blind Amy,' said Sammy, 'extra extra don't bear thinking of, Rachel. It would mean he couldn't manage to—' He checked, and Rachel saw the little grin that came and went. 'No, me lips are sealed.'

'My life, Sammy,' said Rachel, 'does that mean you're incapable of speech for the first time ever?'

'I mean that what I was going to say is none of my business,' said Sammy. He looked up at her.

Rachel, standing on the other side of his desk, looked down at him. Eyes met, amusement in hers, a grin in his.

They both burst into laughter. Together they had hysterics.

When Rachel came to, she said, exultantly, 'Oh, the joys of life, Sammy, the joy of being alive.'

When Sammy came to, he said, soberly, 'I second that, Rachel.' He knew that to her, life was something that had been denied to millions of her kind in Europe, that only the Channel and the RAF had saved her and all other British Jews from being brutally eliminated. 'We're all lucky, Rachel,' he said, 'we all escaped Hitler and his Nazi gumboots.'

'Jackboots, Sammy.'

'Same thing,' said Sammy, 'except if Hitler had taken up gardening, a hell of a lot of people might still be alive. Anyway, what did you say in answer to bookie Joe?'

'I said he had paid me a great compliment, but that my memories of Benjamin were still too sensitive for me to think of marrying again.' It was not that, it was the fact that of all things she had no wish to change her prevailing circumstances, those that enabled her to enjoy a day-to-day relationship with Sammy. A business relationship, of course, but one that had its own pleasurable undercurrents and kept her contented, with no wish to be other than a free woman. Only Sammy had ever touched her deepest emotions, and only respect for her father and her faith had persuaded her to marry Benjamin Goodman those many years ago.

To her, Sammy was still the electric element of

the family and the business, Boots the guardian, Tommy the stalwart. If it had not been Sammy she had fallen in love with, it would have been Boots. Indeed, love would have come all too easily with any of Chinese Lady's three outstanding sons. What magic had existed between Danicl Adams, an army corporal, and Maisie Gibbs, a maidservant, that it created three such sons, and a daughter as endearing as Lizzy?

One thing governed Rachel's friendship with Sammy, that of never giving cause for worry to Susie, never. Sometimes, when she and Sammy were in close conference, either in her office or his, she longed to be kissed. She was nearly fifty-one, but there it was, the longing, and could it be helped? It could only be denied, and by herself.

'So that's it, Rachel?'

'Pardon? Oh, you mean about my answer to Mr Burns? Yes, that's it, Sammy, I shan't be marrying him. Should I even think of doing so?'

'Well, you're still a fine female woman of forty-odd –'

'Fifty, Sammy, but thank you.'

'– with a lot of years in front of you, but I've got feelings of relief that you're not going to spend 'em next to old Joe's outsize paunch, a decent bloke though he is.'

'One of my chief reasons for turning him down, Sammy, is that my father, like Polly's father and your stepfather, is in his seventies. Polly's father and your stepfather still have their caring wives. My father has only me, his daughter.'

'Well, Rachel me old friend,' said Sammy, 'I'll

bet more than me shirt tails that your dad considers himself a lucky bloke. So would anybody who's got you caring for them. Mind, I won't say Isaac doesn't deserve all you do for him. He financed my start in business, and that's something I ain't ever forgotten. Your dad's a genuine gent, Rachel, so give him my kind regards.'

'Sammy, what a very nice man you are,' said Rachel.

'Might a nice bloke now suggest we could think about doing a spot of work?' said Sammy. 'For instance, could you let me know if you're keeping a keen optic on our auditors? I mean, have they finished the audit for the last year yet?'

'They're working on it,' said Rachel, 'and I actually came in to tell you they can't find an invoice relating to an outlay from our bank of three hundred and fifty pounds.'

'Well, curses,' said Sammy, and asked Rachel if she knew something about it. Rachel said she'd referred the matter to the bookkeeper, and the bookkeeper had said Mr Sammy promised to come up with the invoice, and send it on to the auditors. 'Who was the payment to, Rachel?'

'You drew cash for it, Sammy.'

'Ruddy primroses,' said Sammy. 'I remember now. A payment to Charlie Mortimer for a large load of nylon when our factory ran short, and Charlie made a quick delivery for cash.'

'You're speaking of Mr Charles Mortimer, Camberwell's best-known spiv?' said Rachel.

'That's the geezer,' said Sammy, 'Cleverclogs Mortimer. Tell you what, get an invoice form printed in the name of C. Mortimer and Company, fill it in for goods supplied at an appropriate date and stamp it Paid, with a date that coincides with the date on the cheque-book stub, then let the auditors have it. Do a bit of folding and creasing first, and punch file holes in it.'

'I should take part in hiding a cash transaction with a black-marketeer Sammy? It's unlawful.'

'It hurts me too, Rachel,' said Sammy, 'so not a word to Susie, eh? I've mentioned before that she ain't in favour of the firm doing business with spivs. Why didn't we make out an invoice at the time?'

'I suppose we hadn't yet gone in for forgery, Sammy.'

'One thing we both ought to know by now,' said Sammy, 'is that you can't do reputable business without invoices, and this bit of business, Rachel, is just between you and me.'

Rachel smiled.

'Yes, Sammy, just you and me,' she said.

'Did you have a nice meeting, Edwin?' asked Chinese Lady when her husband arrived home at midday.

'An interesting one,' said Sir Edwin. 'All about old times, you might say.'

'Oh, old times always make nice conversation,' said Chinese Lady. 'I did say to myself after you'd gone that I hoped no-one was going to ask you to come out of retirement, not at your age. Well, I know the Government thought a lot of your work or you wouldn't have been honoured. Mind, not that we couldn't have done without it, and just stayed as Mr and Mrs Finch. I still don't know sometimes if it's me when a letter comes addressed to Lady Finch, like from my old insurance company. Still, I can't say I'm not proud about you being honoured . . .' She travelled on in her loquacious way. Sir Edwin, smiling, thought she often talked as much to herself as to her listeners.

Katje Galicia used a public phone to call a special number.

A man's voice said curtly, 'Room 123.'

'Good morning, Comrade Alexandrov –'

'State your code.' The exchanges were in Russian.

'KG51.' 51 was the year when she had offered her services to the Soviet Union, and been accepted.

'Continue.'

'My meeting with –'

'Your bodyguard lost track of it.'

'Only because our man did the unexpected.'

'You should not have entered the taxi. Your bodyguard was unable to maintain contact with you.'

'These things happen,' said Katje, 'particularly when dealing with such an expert operator as Edwin Finch, even at his age. However, we talked together in a place called Lincoln's Inn Fields.'

'We know it. State what came of your time with him.'

'Briefly, Comrade Alexandrov, I think he'll be willing to meet you, as long as Comrade Colonel Bukov is there too.' Colonel Bukov was Head of

KGB Political Intelligence in Britain, while posing as head of the Soviet Press Bureau in London. 'That is a condition.'

'I doubt if Bukov will consent.'

'Edwin Finch has names to offer and much information to give.'

'Information such as?'

'He refused to give any to me. Nor did he definitely promise a meeting, but I think he'll consider it if, as I said, Comrade Bukov is there too. He knows of both of you, and has a professional interest in a meeting.'

'He's a fool, then, if in his retirement he isn't growing cabbages.'

'He's no fool, Comrade Alexandrov, but I will contact him again and talk persuasively to him. He's aware he's under pressure because of his German roots, still unknown to his family.'

'Very well. Meet him again. I'll talk to Comrade Bukov. Keep in touch.'

'Of course,' said Katje, and Alexandrov rang off.

Chapter Nine

Wednesday.

One of the general office girls put her head into Jimmy's office. As the factory's personnel manager, he looked after the welfare of the machinists and seamstresses, a benevolent activity that his Uncle Tommy had passed onto him.

'Mister Jimmy?' That was in accord with custom, which meant there was Mister Tommy, Mister Sammy, Mister Jimmy and Mr Adams. The last was how Boots was addressed, as the eldest and the most imposing, whenever he appeared. Which got up Sammy's nose, of course.

'Yes, Sally?' said Jimmy.

'Someone wants to see you about a job.'

'What someone?'

'A young lady.'

'Oh, right, send her in.'

Moments later, Gertie Roper's granddaughter Clare entered, looking a well-arranged picture of feminine sex appeal. Her bright patterned dress with a flared skirt, beneath which frilly net danced, was a colourful example of the currently popular fashion.

Seeing Jimmy at his desk, she said, 'Oh, me goodness, it's you.' And she looked a little flustered, which she wasn't.

'Good afternoon and hello again,' said Jimmy, coming to his feet like a well-brought-up young gent, which he was.

'I didn't think – well, I just asked to see the manager about a job,' said Clare, 'and I didn't think it might be you.' Alas, that was a bit of a porkie, but when a young lady had made up her mind about her immediate future, she wasn't going to let a harmless porkie or two stand in her way.

'Dear oh dear,' said Jimmy, shaking his head, 'didn't I tell you at the retirement party that I'm the personnel manager?'

'Oh, help,' said Clare, thinking it utterly droll for a young man to come out with a term like 'dear oh dear'.

'Why d'you need help?' smiled Jimmy.

'I meant I must've forgot what you told me,' said Clare, who hadn't.

'Still, nice to see you again,' said Jimmy, thinking her a treat to the eye. 'Sit down, Clare.' Clare seated herself, and Jimmy plonked his manly frame on his desk chair. 'So you're after a job? As a machinist? Are you experienced?'

'As a machinist? Crikey, not likely,' said Clare. 'Me instincts told me not to go in for that kind of work, the kind me grandma was in all her working life, and starting in those horrible sweatshops. I did commercial lessons at school, so's I could do office work, which me grandma said would be more ladylike.'

Jimmy smiled. How often had he heard Grandma Finch talk about bringing girls up to be ladylike? More times than he could ever count. She'd once said that his late Aunt Emily, Uncle Boots's first wife, had been a proper young terror right up to the age of sixteen, when she then realized Boots preferred girls to be a bit ladylike, never mind how poor they were.

'Clare, you've worked in an office?' he said.

'Well, yes,' said Clare, nerves tingling because he was such an exciting feller. She'd gone right off Harry Dallimore. 'Yes, I work in an office now.'

'As a clerk?' said Jimmy, pleasantly encouraging.

'No, I'm in charge of the phone switchboard at Parsons Engineering fact'ry,' said Clare.

'You mean you're not actually unemployed?'

'Well, I will be when me notice expires,' said Clare.

'But why have you given notice?'

'I don't get on with the supervisor,' said Clare, which was true. 'Well, you ought to see her, talk about a bit of an old cow— oh, sorry, me tongue slipped.'

'So does mine, frequently,' said Jimmy, 'and it causes me pain and anguish.' Oh, the way he talks and the things he says, thought Clare. I could listen to him all day. 'So you don't get on with the old biddy, your supervisor, and you've given notice?' said Jimmy.

'Well, I will if your fact'ry can offer me a job,' said

Clare. 'I've taken the afternoon off so that I could come and see you – I mean whoever was the employment manager. So I'm going to be in more trouble with Miss Crawley.'

'Did you know we'll be losing our own switchboard operator in a few weeks?' asked Jimmy. 'She's getting married.'

'Well, I'm blessed,' said Clare, big eyes round with surprise, the artful girl. But who could blame her? She had already consigned Harry Dallimore to the dustbin of her personal history. 'Is that a fact? Oh, yes, I remember me grandma did mention something about that. Only in passing, mind, but don't you think it's like fate, you losing your switchboard operator and me being one meself?'

'It couldn't have happened to a nicer girl,' said Jimmy. 'We were going to advertise for a replacement in next week's local paper, but I tell you what, spend the rest of the afternoon with our present operator, Dodie – Dodie Woods – and she'll see how experienced you are.' While it would be a pleasure to have such an attractive girl around, Jimmy knew he couldn't simply give her the job without discovering if she really was able to handle a switchboard. It was his responsibility to ensure the firm didn't take on a beginner, even if she was adept enough to learn quickly. 'How's that?'

'Oh, thanks,' said Clare, 'you're a real sport.'

'Come on,' said Jimmy, 'I'll take you to our general office.' He came to his feet, smiled at Clare, and she followed him out, her frilly net rustling. He ushered her into the general office, where typists were busy at their machines, and a young woman, Dodie Woods, seated at the switchboard, was devouring a romantic novel while waiting to deal with calls.

Jimmy introduced Clare as the granddaughter of Gertie and Bert Roper, and as a possible replacement for Dodie. The girls gave her a welcome and Dodie said she'd be happy to hand over her job to any granddaughter of Gertie and Bert.

'Oh, that's ever so kind,' said Clare.

'Let her sit with you, Dodie,' said Jimmy. 'Give her some testing and see how she performs.'

'Mister Jimmy,' said Dodie, 'us girls don't perform here, not in the office. We—'

'Don't tell me,' said Jimmy, 'I'll get embarrassed.'

The girls shrieked.

'Oh, ain't you a one, Mister Jimmy?'

'Did I say something?' asked Jimmy.

'Yes, and we all noticed,' said Dodie. 'And what you didn't let me say was that us girls perform on a dance floor, not in the office.'

'On a dance floor?' said Jimmy. 'Well, believe me, Dodie, that's a shocker and even more embarrassing to a respectable feller. I'm going. Good luck, Clare. Look after her, Dodie.' He disappeared, leaving the general office noisy with more shrieks.

Twenty minutes later, his desk phone rang.

'Hello?'

'Mr Adams, there's a call for you, from a Mr Sylvester.' The voice belonged to Clare and it contained a note of well-versed tonsils. 'Shall I put the gentleman through?'

Jimmy grinned. So that was her switchboard voice. Highly creditable.

'Put him through, Clare.'

'There, you're connected, Mr Adams.'

Jimmy took the call. Ten minutes later, Dodie came to see him, to tell him Clare knew all there was to know about operating a switchboard.

'Right, send her in, Dodie, and thanks.'

Sex appeal entered a minute later, in the very attractive shape of Gertie and Bert's eldest granddaughter.

'Mr Adams, you going to give me the job?'

'Well, you've just received a handsome recommendation from Dodie,' said Jimmy, 'so yes, we'll take you on, starting three weeks from next Monday. Bring your insurance card and wear a pretty dress.'

'Beg pardon?' said Clare, happy but startled.

'I like our switchboard operator to look representative of our business, which is the manufacture of fashion wear,' said Jimmy with a straight face. He'd never made such a comment to Dodie, but then Dodie wasn't quite the eyeful that Clare was. 'It needn't be your best Sunday frock, just –'

'Mr Adams, you're doing it again, like at the party,' said Clare.

'Doing what again?' asked Jimmy.

'Having me on,' smiled Clare, keeping to herself the fact that she didn't mind what he said to her. Everything he did say was an entertainment. She wondered if, as the son of the main boss, Mr

Sammy Adams, he considered himself too – too what? – yes, too important to interest himself in an East End working-class girl. Mind, he didn't act or speak important, so she had hopes. He really was a lovely bloke. 'You are, ain't you, you are having me on?'

'Perish the thought,' said Jimmy. 'Would I do that to any of Gertie's granddaughters?'

'You're doing it to me, I just know you are,' she said.

'My own grandma would read me one of the Ten Commandments if I didn't give any young lady proper respect,' said Jimmy, neglecting his work for the moment, mainly because he enjoyed talking to this girl.

'Oh, go on, what Commandment?' asked Clare, fascinated.

'Well, isn't there one about honouring thy neighbour's granddaughter?'

Clare laughed, and her eyes sparkled.

'Mr Adams –'

'Businesswise, I'm Mister Jimmy.'

'Well, Mister Jimmy, me grandma's not your neighbour.'

'What's a few miles between Gertie and me?' said Jimmy. 'Look, I'm keeping you –'

'Oh, I'm not in no hurry,' said Clare, 'but I expect you've got work to do. Still, when you said about me wearing something pretty, could I ask if you like what I'm wearing now?' It was her best dress, and the old cow of a supervisor, Miss Crawley, had sniffed at it all through the morning.

She'd be spitting a bit now on account of her switchboard operator being absent without leave. 'I mean, is it – well, is it – ?'

'A bit of all right?' said Jimmy, noting the bright gleam of her nyloned legs. Well, he was as much of a leg man as most healthy blokes. His Uncle Boots had once told him that when legs, female, finally saw the light after the Great War, young men whistled joyfully and old men passed out. 'It's just what a doctor would order for the good of a bloke's peepers. Couldn't be prettier. Well, that's all, Clare. We'll be pleased to have you around.'

'Oh, before I go,' said Clare, 'could I ask what you'll pay me in wages?'

'What're you getting now?' asked Jimmy.

'Three pounds five a week,' said Clare.

'We'll up that to four pounds,' said Jimmy. It was what Dodie was earning. Post-war wages were better than pre-war. 'And you'll share in the bonuses which we pay twice a year.' Decent pay plus bonuses meant extra loyalty from the staff. Sammy had always believed in fair treatment of workers. Employers got a good return for that.

'Crikey, four pounds? Thanks,' said Clare, her eyes sparkling again. Now she could look forward to buying lots of appealing clothes, and to making sure Jimmy Adams really did like having her around.

'You're welcome,' said Jimmy, and saw her out.

'You've been ever so nice,' said Clare.

'It's been a pleasure,' said Jimmy. 'You can give

notice to your old biddy tomorrow, and we'll see you three weeks from next Monday.'

'Lor', I can hardly wait,' said Clare and left, feet dancing. I'm sure he likes me, or he wouldn't have spent all that time talking to me. Fancy him not having a girlfriend. Still, I'm glad he doesn't, I wouldn't be honest if I wasn't glad.

I could go for that girl, thought Jimmy. Pity she's got a bloke. What was his name? Ballymore? Had to be Irish, and probably with a large amount of blarney.

Clare called on her grandparents in Bow before going home. Gertie and Bert, enjoying a pot of tea in the kitchen, welcomed her affectionately. Clare was their favourite granddaughter, being the most caring. She exclaimed her news.

'Oh, what d'you think, I've got the job!'

'I said you would,' remarked Bert. 'Didn't I say so, Gertie?'

'Every five minutes till you got on me nerves,' said Gertie, dressed in her everyday blouse and skirt. Bert was in shirt, braces and trousers, his socked feet minus shoes.

'Got it off her own bat,' he said proudly, 'instead of asking us to speak for her.'

'Well, I'm pleased for her,' said Gertie. 'Sit down, Clare love, and I'll pour you a cup of tea.'

'Oh, ta, Gran,' said Clare, 'I could just do with a cup. Lor', I'm ever so happy.'

'Yes, you'll like working for Mister Sammy's firm,' said Gertie, pouring the tea. 'He's always been the best employer in the rag trade. Who did yer see, was it young Jimmy?'

'Yes, and he was so kind,' said Clare. 'Crikey, I never met a lovelier bloke.'

'Hello, hello,' said Bert, 'fancy 'im, do yer?'

'Me?' said Clare. 'Well, I like him, but I 'ardly know him.'

Bert winked. Clare affected not to notice.

'Grandpa, you're not wearing any shoes,' she said, changing tack.

'And why not, you might ask?' said Gertie. 'Because he's just come in from 'is allotment, and I ain't having 'im tread all over me floor in 'is gumboots, which he does whenever me back's turned. What did young Jimmy say they'd pay yer, Clare?'

'Four pounds a week and bonuses twice a year,' said Clare. 'Ain't that something? I'll be able to treat meself regularly to new clothes.'

'Don't forget you get special discount if you buy from the fact'ry showroom,' said Gertie.

Clare, sipping tea, took on a dreamy look.

'Oh, p'raps he'd show me round himself,' she murmured.

'Eh?' said Bert.

'Who?' said Gertie.

'Bet it won't be Harry Whatsismore,' grinned Bert.

'Grandpa, you know I've stopped seeing him,' said Clare.

'I could ask why,' said Bert, tickled.

'I don't suppose he can help it, poor bloke,' said Clare, 'but honest, he has got a bit boring.'

'Now I wonder when she found that out?' ruminated Bert.

'I never 'eard none of the girls say that about young Jimmy,' said Gertie, looking at Bert. Bert winked again.

'Ta for the information,' said Clare in throwaway fashion. Well, a young lady of eighteen simply couldn't admit she'd suffered a kind of schoolgirlish crush on a feller the first time she'd seen him and listened to him. But she did admit – to herself – that if any girl in the factory had ideas about making whoopee with Jimmy Adams, she'd give her a real hard time.

'Jimmy's like his dad,' said Gertie, 'he's got electrical waves.'

Crikey, no wonder I feel I've been electricated, thought Clare. If I go up in sparks in a minute, Grandma will think it's November the Fifth.

If Gertie and Bert's eldest granddaughter was suffering hitherto unknown pangs, so was Philip, grandson of Lizzy and Ned. For a few days he couldn't quite credit what had hit him. Then, correctly, he put it down to the fact that Phoebe had developed into a young beauty. So, he thought, where do I go from here? Absent without leave, probably.

'What's she up to?' asked Colonel Gregori Bukov. He and his team of KGB men, trained as journalists, occupied offices that were ostensibly given over to the Soviet Press Bureau. They actually existed to make contact with possible moles – men or women who could be persuaded to become agents of the KGB – but were compelled to proceed always with caution, since they did not have diplomatic immunity. 'Yes, what's Katje Galicia up to?'

'Snaring the man Finch,' said Lieutenant Colonel Boris Alexandrov.

'Do we trust her?'

'She's got a black mark. She helped her son to cross the border to the West. If we used that, she'd find herself under arrest as soon as she returned to Poland. She knows that. So I'm confident she'll get Finch to meet us and tell us exactly what he knows about British agents, such as Philby and Maclean, and others of the same brand who are working undercover for us.'

'You quarrel with the information they supply?' said Bukov, dark and cadaverous.

'I still suspect their motives,' said Alexandrov.

'Finch's demand is that he must meet both of us?'

'Apparently.'

'Is an old man with his kind of personal secrets able to make demands?' asked Bukov.

'A man as old as he is must own a store of varied secrets. That is, knowledge which, as an agent for many years, he keeps to himself by reason of a signed oath.'

'I'll think about both of us meeting him,' said Bukov. He got up, walked to the window and looked down at the scene. Taxis, always taxis. And cars, privately owned cars. Women well-dressed, girls in the bright apparel of summer. Drones, not workers. He made a gesture of disgust. 'If the

Soviet Union existed as close as this to the corruptive capitalism of London, we should have to fight and destroy it for fear of infection.'

'Well, here in London, you and I are fighting it together,' said Alexandrov.

They were a fearsome pair of operators, the kind of Russians Chinese Lady would have regarded as cut-throat Bolsheviks.

Chapter Ten

The following day.

Chinese Lady had been receiving letters from old friends and neighbours in Walworth, all about what they had read in newspapers concerning how she and Edwin had dealt with a burglar. This morning she received one from Mrs Brown, Susie's mother, who expressed the opinion that the burglar probably thought a titled couple would have any amount of money and jewellery waiting to fall into his hands. What a shame, wrote Mrs Brown, if the man thought that of you and your good husband when you've always been a nice modest couple.

A second letter came from Mrs Blake, an old neighbour.

'Dear Maisie . . .' That was crossed out and 'Dear Lady Finch,' inserted in place. 'I hope you still remember me and my husband George that used to drive a coal cart. I could hardly believe what he showed me in his newspaper that you'd had a burglar and that you and Sir Edwin gave him what for and handed him over to the police, we both feel very admiring of you. I made up my mind I'd write one day and let you know how we felt as we're still well and in good spirits in our old age and hope you and Mister Sir Edwin are too, yours sincerely Maud Blake.'

Chinese Lady, showing the letter to her husband, said, 'Well, I just don't know I want any more letters like this. Mrs Blake calling me Lady Finch and all, after knowing me for more years than I care to remember. Edwin, could you write to Buckingham Palace and ask if I could resign?'

'Resign, Maisie?'

'Yes, I just don't feel right being a Lady.'

'Maisie, you're a natural lady.'

'I mean titled. I don't suppose you're allowed to write to the Queen herself, but someone who's in charge, like the Keeper of the Keys. I've heard of him.'

'An officer of the Tower of London, Maisie.'

'Lord, don't write to him, Edwin, I don't want to end up there, just on the Buckingham Palace resigned list.'

'I doubt if that's possible, my dear, unless I could effectively disgrace myself and have my knighthood stripped from me. That would bring us back to plain Mr and Mrs Finch.'

'What? What, Edwin?'

'A home-made bomb thrown at the Palace sentry would be enough, I fancy. And I daresay Boots would help me put it together.'

'Lord above, don't talk like a Bolshevik, Edwin, you'll make me ill. Throw a bomb at the Queen's sentry? I can't believe my ears. I don't want you doing things like that, I just want to resign from being a Lady.'

'I'm afraid it can't be done without – um – the Palace finding grievous fault in me.'

'Well, I'm not going to let anyone at the Palace do that, I can tell you.'

'Then shall we forget about this resigning idea for the time being, Maisie? Why not go halfway towards a solution by signing all your letters simply as Maisie Finch? That will allow your old friends to infer your title hasn't changed you.'

'Well, if you think so, Edwin.'

'In any event, Maisie,' smiled Sir Edwin, 'nothing will ever change you. I'm happily sure you'll always be your very own self.'

As for my own self, he thought, a dark hand is knocking at my door.

He had a strange liking for Katje Galicia, but he did not trust her. He was waiting for her to contact him again.

'Well, it hasn't happened,' said Phoebe at supper that evening.

'What hasn't?' asked Jimmy. 'The end of the world?'

'It can't have,' said Paula, 'or we wouldn't all be sitting at table, and the house wouldn't be standing up.'

'Personally,' said Sammy, 'I'm not ready for the end of the world. I want fifty years notice.'

'Could some of us let Phoebe tell us what hasn't happened?' said Susie.

'I forget now what I was going to say,' said Phoebe, who was, of course, thinking of Philip.

'Talking about happenings, I'm up against a difficult one,' said Jimmy. 'It's these garden peas. They're fresh and sweet, but they keep falling off my fork. I think they're too round.'

Paula rolled her eyes.

Susie said, 'Oh, dear, what a shame, Jimmy, but never mind, I'll see if I can buy square ones next time I shop.'

'Well, I'm blessed, Mum's made a funny,' said Paula.

'By the way, Dad, did you know Paul and Lulu are going house-hunting over the weekend?' said Jimmy.

'No, I didn't, but thanks for informing me,' said Sammy. He looked at Susie as she slipped shining green peas into her mouth without any of them falling off her fork. She smiled and nodded. 'Well,' said Sammy, 'I'll see that the property company gives them a loan in the usual family fashion, and work out how much they can repay per month.'

'Plus interest,' said Jimmy.

'That's it, be hard-hearted,' said Paula.

'The property company's got to live,' said Jimmy.

'Yes, we don't want it falling down dead,' said Phoebe, 'especially as Dad's promised I can start work there when I leave school.' She placed her knife and fork down on her empty plate just as the phone rang. 'I'll go,' she said, rising like quicksilver from her chair. In the handsome hall of the well-designed house, she picked up the phone.

'Hello?'

'Good, it's you, Phoebe.' Philip was on the line. 'Are you busy?'

Bless me, thought Phoebe, it's happened at last, after half a week.

'Oh, I'm not busy right now,' she said, 'I've just finished my lamb chop, creamed potatoes and peas, with mint sauce.'

'Fascinating,' said Philip. 'What about afters?'

'Oh, jam roly-poly isn't on the table yet,' said Phoebe.

'Well, I won't keep you from that,' said Philip. 'I'll just ask if I could take you dancing. My leave finishes on Saturday, so if you're not doing anything on Friday evening –'

'How kind,' said Phoebe.

'But – ?'

'I accept,' said Phoebe. 'Well, if you're going to disappear for another year, we might as well see each other before you go. It's a kind of family obligation.'

'It's what?' said Philip.

'Never mind,' said Phoebe, 'what time will you call for me?'

'Seven?'

'How nice,' said Phoebe.

'Don't look at it as an obligation,' said Philip.

'Just bring yourself to our doorstep at seven,' said Phoebe, 'and we'll go dancing.'

'Pleasure, not half,' said Philip, 'and you can go and say hello to your jam roly-poly now.'

'My, my,' said Phoebe, 'how very kind we are this evening.'

'Saucebox,' said Philip.

'Same to you,' said Phoebe, and rang off.

When she acquainted her family with the news that Philip had made a date with her, no-one said this was a bit unusual for cousins. Everyone knew Philip and Phoebe had a loophole in that she was adopted.

Sammy and Susie, sensibly, had told her some time ago of the circumstances that led to her adoption, that her parents had died when she was a small child and an aunt had taken her in. What they did not tell her was that her mother and father had been cruelly murdered by a maniac. When the aunt died, well, said Susie, Sammy and me had the lovely good fortune to be given care of you, and of course we soon wanted you for our very own. So we adopted you because we loved you.

Phoebe did not have any bad moments about the facts. Like Rosie, adopted long ago by Boots and Emily, she was so attached to her adoptive parents, so happy as one of the family, that there was only a little pause before she spoke.

'Oh, if I was unlucky, losing my mum and dad, wasn't I really lucky finding you?'

It was said with the deep affection of a girl totally content with her existence. There were seemingly no worrying emotional problems, although Sammy and Susie both thought that one day she might reasonably want to know more about her natural parents.

In Chicago, Illinois, it was lunchtime, and many of its citizens were devouring hamburgers in diners, cafes and fast-food joints. In an exclusive residential area just south of the city, Mrs Bess Passmore, eldest daughter of Sammy and Susie, was lunching with husband Jeremy at his mother's palatial house. Bess, like Susie, was fair and blue-eyed, Jeremy dark and tanned. Bess had a calm outlook on life, Jeremy a philosophical one, which meant they were both disinclined to quarrel with people or with each other.

They had spent the last three weeks in America, travelling around to enable Bess to study the vastness of a land that seemed to have limitless horizons, especially in the Midwest. First, however, Jeremy had introduced her to his hometown, a city bustling and energetic, so much so that it left her a little dizzy. Buildings, high and enormous, took her breath away.

But she did discover the delights of American ice cream, which came in a score of different flavours, even peanut butter, and she also discovered, or at least she suspected, that the reason why Americans were on the whole large people was because they ate their way through hamburgers and hot dogs day by day. She liked the fact that Jeremy preferred better-balanced food, as did his widowed mother.

Jeremy was on fairly civilized terms with his maternal parent, a possessive woman who considered herself one of Chicago's elite, and carried herself around in the fashion of an aristocrat. This was supported by her claim to be a descendant of one of New England's Founding Fathers.

She was not enthusiastic about Jeremy's marriage to the young Englishwoman. While she could not dislike Bess, she did object to the rift the marriage had caused in her relationship with her only son. Mrs Passmore had wanted Jeremy to take up the reins of his late father's packaging empire on a permanent basis, and had intended to select his future wife for him, on the grounds that she knew better than he did what kind of a woman would be the most suitable. He had been a good catch for even the most eligible and high-born of Chicago's debutantes. It was a shock when he married an English girl she had only heard about, and handed control of the family business to his brother-in-law in order to buy and run a farm in England. She little suspected that her possessiveness played its part in Jeremy's decision. He knew she would attempt to dominate Bess.

At lunch this day, his mother's fine mouth was firmly set in the manner of a woman who had a quarrel with life. The open stand-up collar of her mustard-coloured dress revealed a choker of shining white pearls that exuded an air of aggression.

'Jeremy,' she said, 'I can't believe you're really flying back to England tomorrow. You've spent only a short time here at home, and you've been touring for the better part. Surely you and Bess can stay for two extra weeks so that I can see more of you?'

'So sorry, but it can't be done,' said Jeremy. 'I must get back to the farm.' He added gently, 'And I must point out my home is there now, Mother, not here.'

'Jeremy, of course this is your home, for I'm sure

you won't settle permanently in England.' Mrs Passmore senior glanced at Bess. 'Bess, you would know if that's his intention. If so, I do hope you can talk him out of it.'

'Mother-in-law,' said Bess with a conciliatory smile, 'I'm sure you could talk him out of it better than I could.'

Jeremy's mother sighed. Oh, dear, thought Bess, I think she's now going to play the part of a lonely and neglected widow. I'll let Jeremy handle that.

Jeremy did.

'I don't have any fixed plans for the future,' he said. 'Bess and I are happy with things as they are, which means there's always a possibility we'll opt for a change in a year or so.' That possibility was not in the forefront of his mind. The years he had spent with his English aunt and uncle in Kent immediately after the war had been years of content. He was not the kind of thrusting American who liked to be perpetually up and doing in the face of new challenges, even though he knew that that vigorous attitude had made America what it was today, the most powerful and dynamic nation in the world. If he found something that appealed to him, he stuck with it, however unexciting it might be to other men. He was, in fact, an undemanding man, much more like Boots than Sammy, two of his new English relatives.

Moreover, he adored Bess and her quiet Englishness, and he suspected the pace of life in the States, in Chicago particularly, would leave her bewildered. Further, she was three months pregnant with their first child, and he knew she wanted it to be born in England, as near to her English family as possible. He had discovered her family were like that, very close-knit within the tentacles of their matriarch, Bess's old-fashioned grandmother. So far, neither he nor Bess had told his mother a child was on the way. She would want to make plans for the infant to be born in Chicago.

'I feel upset,' said the aggrieved lady, pushing her plate aside, her meal only half-eaten. 'Is it too much to ask that you stay for two more weeks, Jeremy?'

'Mother, I repeat, I'm sorry,' said Jeremy, 'but I really must get back to the farm.'

'Much good your chosen way of life has done me,' she said, 'but I guess family sacrifices all come from a mother.'

'Oh, my brother Daniel, married to an American girl, would say that's what lovely mothers are for,' smiled Bess, 'that they put the happiness of their sons and daughters before their own. I think that's—'

'It's ridiculous,' said Mrs Passmore senior. A servant, a tall and hugely buxom woman, came in.

'Did you ring for dessert, ma'am?' she asked.

'No, I didn't. We aren't ready for it. Wait till I do ring.'

'I surely will, ma'am.' The servant disappeared like a sailing barge on heavy waters. Jeremy's mother turned to Bess.

'Did you say one of your brothers has an American wife?'

'Yes, Daniel,' said Bess, 'he met her during the

war when she was in England with her father, a radio newsman.'

'Oh, the war,' said Mrs Passmore senior, 'there were thousands of our American soldiers in England, I believe.'

'All over the United Kingdom,' said Bess, who thought Scotland, Wales and Northern Ireland ought to be included in any mention of the war.

'I'm not surprised there were some strange alliances formed,' said Jeremy's mother. Jeremy looked sorry for her in her prickly mood.

'Having met Bess's brother Daniel, and Patsy,' he said, 'I can assure you no strange alliance exists there. Daniel and Patsy are a delightful couple.'

'But what kind of future do they have?' said Mrs Passmore senior. 'I've heard and read that England is finished and in decline as a power.'

'Mother, all kinds of people have been saying that since the end of the war,' said Jeremy. 'There were weary years of austerity, yes, but the UK is now recovering. And it has what America should have, a health service with free treatment for all. Come along, ring for the dessert and let's enjoy it without any more argument.'

'I can't recall being argumentative myself,' said his mother, 'only disappointed that I'm going to lose you again, and so soon.' But she rang for the dessert, and the bulky servant waddled in with a huge dish of strawberry cheesecake and ice cream.

It set the tone for a more agreeable atmosphere.

Bess could understand her mother-in-law's discontent. No woman with such a lovable son as Jeremy would feel happy about him living so far away from her. Her real trouble, thought Bess, is that she doesn't like being a widow.

In bed that night, a whisper reached Jeremy's ear.

'Ask your sister and brother-in-law to go looking for a man who's looking for a woman like your mother.'

'Are you serious?'

'Very. He'll have to have character, of course, and a good presence.'

'Most guys with character and presence already have a woman. One each at least.'

'Your mother needs a marrying man. There must be some lovable middle-aged bachelor willing to share her life and her wealth.'

Jeremy indulged in muffled laughter.

'That's coming seriously from you of all people, Bess?'

'Why me of all people?'

'It's not your style, far from it.'

'Never mind that, ask your sister and brother-in-law.'

'By Jesus, perhaps I will, and before we leave tomorrow night.'

'There's a clever boy,' murmured Bess.

'By the way, I think we should tell my mother about your condition.'

'Yes, I think we should.'

They told her during breakfast. For a moment or two she looked animated, then, predictably, declared that if the child was a boy it rightly ought to be born here at home, in Chicago.

Since that had a note of the ridiculous to it, Jeremy did not respond at length.

He only said, 'We'll see.'

Bess said, 'I wonder if the time will come when doctors will be able to diagnose the sex of the unborn?'

'Mercy me,' said Jeremy's mother, 'I hope doctors will never be able to play God. Jeremy, see that you take care of Bess. Why, I'm not even sure women in her condition should cross the Atlantic in a plane.'

'Bess received reassurance from her doctor before we flew over here,' said Jeremy.

Later, when he and Bess visited his sister Louise, the suggestion that a new husband should be found for his mother was given an airing. His sister laughed and dismissed it as absurd.

'All the same, think about it,' said Jeremy.

'Yes, do,' said Bess.

'Crazy,' said Louise.

'You'll know the kind of guy who'll make the right impression,' said Jeremy.

'Civilized and cultured, yes,' said Louise, 'but a fortune-hunter, of course.'

'Mother will know how to handle him when the first flush has died down,' said Jeremy.

'Still crazy,' said Louise, 'but all right, I'll speak to Gough about it.' Gough was her husband.

'Tell him to go find the guy,' said Jeremy, as much amused as in favour.

It was close to midnight when he and Bess took the flight that brought them back to their English home in Kent. Bess immediately phoned Susie, her mother. The call lasted half an hour. Well, there was so much news to exchange while Jeremy did the unpacking.

When she finally put the phone down, Bess called up to him.

'Jeremy?'

'Hi there, Bess, delighted to hear you're with me again.'

'Come down, darling, I must tell you what happened to Grandma and Grandpa while we were away.'

So Jeremy became one more to hear how the old folk downed a burglar. He roared with laughter.

Chapter Eleven

Katje Galicia made an early morning phone call from a public booth. A man answered.

'Hello?'

Recognizing the voice, she slipped two pennies into the slot, and that connected her.

'Hello, my friend, a quick word, if you please.'

'I'm to listen to more absurdities?'

'I wish only to know if your wife is going shopping today.'

There was a pause before Sir Edwin said, 'Yes, at about ten this morning.'

'Good. I will call after I've seen her leave.'

'You need not bother.'

'Come, we are in this together.'

'Very well, I'll agree to another meeting, but it'll be the last,' said Sir Edwin.

'Your co-operation is a pleasure,' said Katje Galicia, and rang off. She left the phone box and walked to a bus stop. A hovering man followed. She smiled.

It was fifteen minutes to ten when she took up a watching brief in Red Post Hill, south of

Camberwell. She waited. It was not until five minutes past ten that Chinese Lady left her house to go shopping.

Katje knocked on the front door when the coast was quite clear. Sir Edwin answered her knock, hesitated for a moment, then let her in. Her hovering 'bodyguard' watched as the door closed behind her.

'Be brief,' said Sir Edwin.

'Of course,' said Katje.

What she had to say did not impress him. It was largely a repeat of what she had said before, and when she left he told her again that he could not be persuaded to give her names, and that she was welcome to do what she liked about that.

'My dear friend, I intend to.' Her smile could have meant anything. She left, taking a bus back to town. Her 'bodyguard' sat at a distance from her. Alexandrov was keeping a constant eye on her by way of this man, who at the moment looked darkly dissatisfied. She understood. He hadn't liked her disappearance when she entered the house. What did he think, then? That she would talk to Sir Edwin on his doorstep? An inward smile reached her lips.

Bess and Jeremy, now at home in Kent, were arranging to call on the family.

Patsy was looking forward to that.

'When we see them,' she said to Daniel, 'Bess's snapshots will give you a taste of what I'm going to show you when we go there in September.'

'Has she seen all of America, do you know?' said Daniel. 'Only it's pretty big, isn't it?'

'It sure is,' said Patsy, 'Jeremy couldn't have shown her more than a small part of it.'

'Right,' said Daniel, 'you do your best to show me and our kids all of it.'

'I'd need two years to do that, you kook, not two weeks,' said Patsy. 'We'll just do New England.'

'If Arabella and Andrew want to see some cowboys –'

'Nothing doing,' said Patsy, 'cowboys are way out West, so don't mention them to our children.'

'Patsy,' said Daniel, 'I hope the trip doesn't get you feeling homesick for Boston.'

'Daniel, you're my guy and this is my home,' said Patsy, 'so if I do get homesick it'll be for here. Right?'

'Patsy, I had my luckiest day when I met you.'

'Well, hold onto your luck, Daniel, I'm not fighting it.'

Boris Alexandrov received a phone call from agent KG51.

'Yes?'

'He'll co-operate,' said Katje.

'You saw him this morning.' It was a statement.

'You know that?' said Katje. 'Yes, of course you do.'

'What came of the interview?'

'As I've just said, he'll co-operate.'

'To what extent?'

'He'll give you written information on the British double agents that will tell you much more about their backgrounds than is on your files.'

'It will tell us they're likely to rat on Moscow?'

'And sell themselves to Mao Tse-tung and Red China? Or the American CIA? It's what you suspect, I know,' said Katje. There was little that KGB officers did not suspect. 'But Finch refused to give any details to me, and he still insists that both you and Comrade Bukov must meet him.'

'Why?'

'He has questions to ask Bukov.'

'Your man has retired. He can't be interested in answers.'

'He is still interested in our world, Comrade Alexandrov.'

'Find out when we can meet him and where.'

'Give me a little more time,' said Katje. 'He's not a man to be rushed.'

Paul called on his Aunt Polly and his Uncle Boots that evening, by arrangement. With twins Gemma and James upstairs in the games room taking turns to ride their rocking horse, he was able to talk without interruption to his aunt and uncle.

'It's like this,' he said.

'Go ahead,' said Boots.

'About my wedding day,' said Paul.

'Oh, yes, congratulations on fixing a date,' said Polly, and Paul thought how vital and alive she still was. Traces remained of what she'd been like as a Bright Young Thing in the Twenties, as one could discover in old photographs of her.

'Well, I had to wait until I had real prospects,' he said, 'which I do have now. Anyway, I need a best man. I could ask one of my cousins, but which one?'

'Any of them, I should think,' smiled Boots.

'Oh, I'm too sensitive to upset the rest,' said Paul, 'so I've come to ask if you'd do me the favour, Uncle Boots.'

'Paul old lad,' said Boots, 'I'm touched, but aren't I too old to be best man to you?'

'Too old?' said Paul. 'Uncle Boots, you're a spring chicken compared to some men, and you're a friend and help to everyone in the family. And I'm not forgetting you were best man to Tim and Bobby at their weddings. So come on, be a sport.'

'If you're sure –'

'I'll speak for our spring chicken, Paul,' said Polly, 'and say yes. Well, don't you see, old thing, as the wife of your best man I'll be entitled to a new outfit instead of making do with something fit only for an East End jumble sale.'

'I've heard some tall tales in my time,' said Boots, his long frame still in fine shape, 'and that's the tallest.'

'Aunt Polly,' said Paul, 'if any East End lady bought one of your outfits at a jumble sale and put it on there and then, she'd look as if she was ready to attend the Queen's coronation.'

King George the Sixth, the wartime monarch, had died last year, and his elder daughter was due to be officially crowned Queen Elizabeth the Second next month. London was preparing for a beanfeast of pageantry, and its cockneys for street parties and a knees-up.

Polly laughed.

'Would any of my old rags do that for a woman, Boots?' she asked.

'All your old rags still do everything for you, Polly,' said Boots.

Something crashed upstairs, followed by a yell from Gemma.

'What's that?' asked Paul.

'Oh, the rocking horse has fallen at a fence,' said Polly, 'with Gemma in the saddle. We'll soon know if there are any broken bones.'

James called down.

'Dad – Mum – Gemma tried to ride pillion behind me and made the rocking horse fall over again!'

'Anyone hurt?' called Boots.

'Only me,' shouted James. 'But it's all right, Dad, there's no blood.'

'Carry on,' called Boots.

Paul grinned. It was the kind of performance common to any of the Adams families with growing children.

'Well, I'm pleased to have you as best man, Uncle Boots,' he said.

'Happy days,' said Polly, 'we'll all need new outfits. How's Lulu, Paul?'

'She's definitely going to wear white,' said Paul, 'but I don't think she's going to include "obey" in her vows.'

'What, then?' asked Polly.

'Oh, I think it'll be something like, "I promise to love, honour and share equal rights,"' said Paul.

'Sounds ominous,' said Boots.

'It's all of that,' said Paul, 'so I might need your help.'

'Heigh-ho, life's a whizz, old dears,' said Polly.

* * *

The dance hall in Brixton was crowded with young people enjoying an end to their working week and a beginning of their weekend this Friday evening. They weren't dancing foxtrots or waltzes, not likely. That was long-gone stuff, man. They were jigging and jiving around to the music of what was called a skiffle band. It was a British craze, born of original minds wanting to get right away from what to the young were the tired sounds that hadn't altered since before the war. Skiffle was something crashingly new. A band's instruments consisted of a guitar, a washboard, and a bass made of a tea chest, broom handle and parachute cord. And sometimes other odds and ends. Weird was the sound to the ears of older generations, but to the young it was new and exciting music.

'It's on a par with dropping a tray of empty tin cans,' said Sammy Adams a week ago to Susie.

'Oh, it's still music,' said Susie. 'Of a kind.'

'Not my kind,' said Sammy. 'My kind is Harry Roy and "Tiger Rag".'

'That was in our day, love,' said Susie. 'Skiffle's a kind of new day for our young people.'

'Well, their new day sounds like an old mangle with loose bits,' said Sammy. 'Not much money in it, I should think,' he added as an afterthought.

Phoebe and Philip didn't have money on their minds as they jived around the crowded floor.

'This is fab,' said Phoebe, dressed in a skinny pink sweater and a flared skirt.

'Great,' said Philip, wearing shirt and jeans.

'Ever such a good idea of yours, bringing me here,' said Phoebe, face flushed, eyes alight, skirt swinging.

'I hope I'll have a lot more,' said Philip, lanky legs moving with the rhythm.

'A lot more good ideas?' said Phoebe.

'A bloke needs more than a few to make sure of a happy future,' said Philip.

'What's your kind of happy future?' asked Phoebe.

The noise of the band and the young revellers drowned that, so Philip said, 'What?'

'Yes, what?' asked Phoebe.

'What what?'

'Give over,' said Phoebe. 'I asked what your idea of a happy future was.'

'Oh, getting my wings and finding a smashing girlfriend,' said Philip.

'What things would she have to smash?' asked Phoebe, performing a swinging pirouette, with Philip holding her hand high and the bass thumping away.

'I didn't catch that,' said Philip.

'Still, it's great music,' said Phoebe, and lifted her voice. 'I asked what kind of things a smashing girlfriend would have to smash.'

'Watch it, cheeky chops.'

'I only asked,' said Phoebe. 'What's this band called?'

'Ross Durkin and his Mad Hatters,' said Philip.

'Great,' said Phoebe.

Her dad, familiar with titles that made sense, like

Jack Hylton and his Band, would have scratched his head at the meaning of Ross Durkin and his Mad Hatters. He little realized it was only the very beginning of a social revolution that would turn music upside down and offer the young the most bizarre titles for groups and bands.

The dance ended at the civilized time of ten thirty. Phoebe and Philip emerged from the hall into the lights of Brixton, noted over many years for its entertainments. They ran for a stationary bus that would carry them to Coldharbour Lane and Denmark Hill. Philip helped Phoebe to jump aboard. Before he could follow her, a Teddy boy beat him to it.

'G'night, tosh, I'll look after her,' he said, and put a restraining hand against Philip's face. Teddy boys weren't actually noted for being loutish, but this one was an exception. Unfortunately, he picked the wrong kind of bloke, very much so. Philip took hold of the saucy geezer's buttoned-up frock coat, yanked hard and stepped aside as the Ted tumbled off the platform and fell, and not without an outraged yell, either. Other young people, coming up fast to catch the bus, ran over him. One or two trod on him. By the time he was back on his feet, his frock coat bore footprints, his hair quiff was ruined, the bus was away, and he was too bruised and flabbergasted to run after it.

'You all right, mate?' asked an onlooker.

'Man, this ain't my scene,' said the Ted, 'it's a dump.'

Seated with Philip on the upper deck, Phoebe whispered, 'Well, goodness me, you're not just someone with lanky legs, are you?'

'Our training takes in a lot more than how to get a plane off the ground,' said Philip.

'How many have you got off the ground so far?' asked Phoebe.

'None yet,' he said. 'Flying instruction comes later.'

'Never mind,' murmured Phoebe, 'you got Teddy off the ground – I mean the bus.' She giggled. 'A pity he did a crash landing.'

'Let's hope it ruined his undercarriage,' said Philip.

He walked her home after they left the bus, and said hello to her parents, who were waiting up for her.

'Did you enjoy yourselves?' asked Susie, noting Phoebe was bubbly.

'Well, I did,' said Philip.

'We both did,' said Phoebe. 'Super skiffle.'

'Wasn't there any music?' asked Sammy.

'Now, Daddy,' said Phoebe, 'you know skiffle's our kind.'

'I've already told him that,' said Susie.

'I could still ask the same question,' said Sammy. 'By the way, would you two like a drink of some kind?'

'Thanks, but not for me, Uncle Sammy,' said Philip, 'I've still got some packing to do. I'm leaving in the morning.'

Sammy and Susie wished him luck and said

goodbye to him. Phoebe saw him to the front door.

She said, 'As I suppose we shan't see you for another year –'

'Don't be too sure,' said Philip.

'– you could at least write to me,' she finished.

'I'll do that,' said Philip. In the light of the hall, he saw brightness in her eyes, and a smile on her lips. My sainted aunt, what a poppet. He took the plunge. He kissed her.

Phoebe blinked.

'Cousin Philip –'

'We're not strictly cousins.'

'Oh, that's right, so we're not,' said Phoebe. 'Still, you shouldn't kiss me like that every time we meet.'

'Well, I'm not able to when we don't meet,' said Philip. 'Anyway, smashing evening, Phoebe. Thanks, and so long. Be good.'

'Bye, cowboy,' said Phoebe, and watched him disappear into the darkness before closing the door. She felt very pleased to have a cousin as dishy as he was, especially when he wasn't strictly a cousin.

In bed later, Sammy said, 'Well, Phoebe looked as if she enjoyed the dance.'

'And her time with Philip,' said Susie.

'Mind, it won't last,' said Sammy.

'What won't?' said Susie. 'Her friendship with Philip?'

'No, skiffle,' said Sammy. 'I've heard some of it on the radio. Give me Ambrose and his Band any day.'

In the United States, teenagers were into bebop, while a band called Bill Haley and the Comets was just about to create something called Rock 'n' Roll. When that hit Sammy, he'd probably think it was the end of civilization.

Chapter Twelve

Sunday morning.

Felicity, wife of Tim Adams, woke up. She had been dreaming of Scotland, Troon and 4 Commando. The dream had been crowded with the faces of men, dark faces, hatchet faces, fine and handsome faces, all against a background of green hills and cloudy sky. Every face came and went, for they were the faces of men moving, eyes squinting, and fixed, it seemed, on a target. The Troon Commando Group of nostalgic memory.

Felicity sighed. Those were the days. Days of dangerous endeavour for the men, rough, tough, bawdy, rowdy and as ruthless at the kill as hungry wolves. Days of excitement for the ATS personnel, and a sense of belonging to the Group. Sadness for the casualties of raids, gladness at the safe return of survivors, especially for her at the safe return of Tim.

All that was before she lost her eyesight during an air raid on London. Her one consolation was that she didn't lose Tim. He married her, became her lover, her chief reason for living, and then the father of her child, Jennifer, now eight.

How strange that in a dream the images were so visual to a person who, in reality, could not see a damned thing. She sighed again, and opened her eyes. The scars that marred them had gone. Tim assured her of that twelve months ago. It had taken ten years for them gradually to disappear, but blindness remained. Lying on her back, she looked upwards, although she knew bright mornings were as black as dark nights. There was nothing she could see. Yet she did see something, a dark grey cloudy blur.

A blur? A blur? What was it? Imagination, wishful thinking, or a deep fuzzy covering over the ceiling? Or the ceiling itself? She closed her eyes tightly, and kept them closed for long seconds, while Tim slept beside her.

Her eyelids parted, and she looked again at the ceiling. The dark fuzzy blur repeated itself. Her heart turned over, and her pulse rate leapt. It was the ceiling, it was, even if only a blurred expanse. She turned her head to look at where she knew the window would be letting in the morning light, the curtains always drawn back by Tim last thing at night. The blur was there, but just a shade lighter, surely. Dear God, even a blur was better than being totally blind. Her eyes travelled. The dressing table was a blur. So was the frontage of built-in wardrobes. So was the door to the bathroom. Each blur had a different shade, depending, of course, on individual colour.

Felicity drew a long breath. She closed her eyes again and lay in quietness, although her pulse rate was still agitated. Tim slept on. As it was Sunday, he would wake up at leisure. For several minutes she kept her eyes closed. Then she opened them once more.

Blackness greeted her like a long-established enemy. There were no grey blurs. Nothing. Her dream must have aroused her imagination to a deceitful extent. Again she closed her eyes, and again, after some thirty seconds, she opened them.

Nothing but the curse of total darkness. It took all her innermost strength not to weep.

Over breakfast with Tim and Jennifer, she said nothing about how her dream and her imagination had deceived her, how for a very brief measure of time she had experienced a wild hope that she might be experiencing partial return of her sight.

'Mummy,' said Jennifer, who, like her father, was often a guide to her mother, 'you're awf'lly quiet this morning.'

Felicity forced a smile.

'Not too awfully, I hope, darling,' she said.

'Are you all right, Puss?' asked Tim, her unfailing support.

'Oh, I'm fine,' said Felicity, 'I'm just thinking about the fact that this afternoon someone will have to describe to me what Bess and Jeremy's American snapshots are all about.'

'I'll do that, Mummy,' said Jennifer, 'especially if some show cowboys and Red Indians.'

They were among other members of the family who arrived at Susie and Sammy's house that afternoon, all for the purpose of celebrating the return from America of Bess and Jeremy, who were coming up from their Kentish farm for the occasion. Rosie and her husband Matthew arrived with their children, Giles and Emily. The two youngsters disappeared almost immediately, making for the garden with Boots's twins, all four in unspoken agreement that grown-ups did have a place in their lives, but not a huge crowd of them all at once.

Rosie, a golden blonde, was now thirty-eight and still the most striking of all the Adams women, her wide blue eyes always reflecting for Boots, her father, memories of her bright and effervescent young days. Their deep affection for each other was unchanging. Rosie, approaching Boots, gave him a hug, a kiss and a greeting.

'Hello, old sport.'

'Hello, poppet,' said Boots. That was his long-established endearment for her. 'Seems a long time since we last saw each other. How are the chickens?'

'Multiplying by the hundred,' said Rosie, her royal blue dress giving her an elegance equal to Polly's. She and Matthew, in partnership with Emma and Jonathan, ran a large poultry farm. At the moment, their foreman was in charge. 'And would you like to ask after the sheep?'

'I know little about sheep, except that they've got four legs and woolly coats,' said Boots.

'Well, you know so much about everything else, including people,' said Rosie, 'that I'll forgive your ignorance about sheep. Ours are thriving.'

'You look on equal terms with them,' said Boots.

'And you look as if you're never going to grow old,' said Rosie.

'I am old, I'm fifty-six,' said Boots, his smile lurking as always, his impaired left eye, damaged during the first battle of the Somme in 1916, almost useless. But his right one did the work for both. He was the first to understand Felicity's reaction to her sightless condition, since he had known blindness for years prior to a relieving operation.

'Daddy old love, fifty-six is no age in a man who's lived your kind of life,' said Rosie.

'And what's my kind of life?' asked Boots.

'Very varied,' said Rosie. 'Two wars, two wives and a French farmer's daughter as a lover, four children and me, many summers of garden cricket, and chief protector of the family.'

'You may think that's keeping me from growing old,' said Boots. 'I'm not so sure myself.'

'Uncle Boots, there you are.' Emma appeared. She hugged Boots, and remembered the happy days when she worked as his shorthand typist at the Camberwell offices. It was then that she really got to know him and his whimsical outlook on life and people. 'Lovely to see you. It's been over a month since you and Aunt Polly visited the farm.'

'At least we visit every month,' said Boots.

Annabelle and Nick arrived, in company with their daughter Linda. Linda, as distinct from her mother, was slim to the point of thinness, and since many of her contemporaries at school already had figures, she was desperately trying to catch up with them by eating mounds of potatoes and treacle puddings. Neither the potatoes nor the puddings were turning out to be helpful, and at the advanced age of fifteen she was having to live with the awful fact that a bra was surplus to her requirements.

However, after doing her social duty by saying hello to her titled grandparents, of whom she was proud, she went in search of Jimmy, her favourite cousin. She found him in the garden, seated at the patio table, watching the antics of Gemma, James, Giles and Emily.

'Hello, Jimmy.'

'Hi-ho, Linda, how's life treating you?'

'Well, you can see what it's doing to me,' said Linda. 'Not very much.'

'I can't say I see anything wrong,' said Jimmy.

'But I'm so skinny,' said Linda, sitting down.

'No, you're not,' said Jimmy, 'just a bit slim, that's all.' And the girl was nice-looking, with the same kind of shining chestnut hair as her mother's. 'Still, have you tried weight-lifting?'

'Weight-lifting?' said Linda.

'Cancel that suggestion,' said Jimmy, 'it'll only give you bulging muscles, and I don't suppose they're what you're after.'

'No, I don't want muscles,' said Linda. 'Look at me,' she commanded. Jimmy looked. Since she liked confiding in him, she said, 'I don't have any figure.' That camc out as a complaint as well as a confidence.

'Unfortunately,' said Jimmy, 'I'm not an expert on female development. I've always thought it's something that just happens.'

'Well, it's not happening to me,' gloomed Linda, and Jimmy thought, well, it's definitely happened to Bert and Gertie's granddaughter, Clare. She had an eye-catching figure. Funny how he kept thinking about her.

'Give it time, Linda,' he said.

Linda said cheerlessly, and with the unabashed frankness of a fifteen-year-old, 'But I'm flat.'

Jimmy's little cough kept a grin at bay.

'So am I,' he said.

'But you're man,' said Linda.

'True,' said Jimmy.

'Supposing I stay flat all my life?' said Linda. 'Think of that.'

'I can't, not without conjuring up images that would flummox me,' said Jimmy.

Linda found enough spirit to giggle.

'Jimmy, you're really nice,' she said. 'Why haven't you got a steady girlfriend?'

'Perhaps I'm too flat myself,' said Jimmy. 'Perhaps I'm the one who should do some weight-lifting and develop a few good-looking bulges. Do bulges on a bloke impress girls?'

'No, it's more what he's like,' said Linda. 'I mean, if he's kind and caring.'

An extra buzz of noise inside the house seemed to indicate that Bess and Jeremy had arrived. They had. So had Bobby and Helene, with their children, Estelle and Robert.

'Linda, before we go in and hear all about America,' said Jimmy, 'who's your favourite singer?'

'Frankie Laine,' said Linda. Frankie Laine was an American born of Italian stock in Chicago. He had giddy female fans all over the Western world, especially after his famous hit 'I Believe'.

'I thought so, I thought you'd mentioned that before,' said Jimmy. 'Well, did you know he's doing a tour over here, including an open-air concert at the Festival Gardens in Battersea Park next Saturday?'

The Festival Gardens were one of the showpieces of the Festival of Britain, organized by the Government not long after the war as a tribute to the people for their bravery and endurance.

'Crikey, is he really?' said Linda.

'Would you like me to take you?' asked Jimmy, thinking someone in the family ought to cheer her up.

'Would you, honest?' said Linda.

'Well, I'd like to go,' said Jimmy, 'so why not come with me?'

'Thanks ever so, I'd love to,' said Linda, blissed.

Out came Susie.

'Come on, Jimmy, your sister Bess is here, and wants to know where you are,' she said.

'Coming,' said Jimmy, rising. Linda went with him into the house.

They found Bess and Jeremy in the front room, furnished in modern lounge style but still referred to by Chinese Lady as Susie's parlour. The couple were entertaining a circle of relatives with descriptions of their American trip, Bess producing snapshots and handing them round.

'This one's all skyscrapers,' said Daniel.

'Oh, they're the first thing you'll see when we sail into New York harbour in September,' said Patsy.

'I've heard of the New York skyline,' said Emma.

'Pokes a hole in the Lord's kitchen, so I were told,' said Jonathan. Tanned from his outdoor work on the poultry farm, he looked the essence of a Sussex-born countryman, just as Matthew looked a prime Dorset-bred specimen.

Felicity eased herself out of the informal audience. For once her resilience and adaptability were failing her. There was nothing she could see, even if there had been a hundred snapshots passing around, and she was still suffering from having had imagination play a lousy trick on her.

A hand touched her arm, and a quiet baritone voice reached her ear. It belonged to Tim's father, Boots, a man she had never seen, but a man she instinctively liked a great deal.

'Need any help, Felicity?'

'Would you mind showing me where the garden is?' she asked. 'I need a little fresh air, and I've lost my bearings.'

'This way,' murmured Boots. He took her arm and guided her out of the crowded room and through to the garden by way of the kitchen. Felicity stepped out into light that was slightly subdued by a passing cloud. 'Here we are, fresh air unlimited,' said Boots, noting the twins and Rosie's children having fun at the top of the garden. 'Sit down, dear girl.'

She groped for a chair, found it and sat at the garden table. Boots seated himself opposite her. She heard the little sounds of his movements.

'It's just the two of us?' she said.

'If we can discount four lively kids at a distance,'

said Boots. 'Felicity, is there something on your mind?'

If Linda could confide in Jimmy, everyone in the family could confide in Boots. Felicity was no exception.

'Oh, something silly,' she said, and told him of how a dream and wishful thinking had made her imagine that the curtain of blackness had thinned to a grey blur for a minute or so. 'You were blind yourself once,' she said. 'During those years, did you ever imagine your sight was coming back?'

Boots studied her. She was without her dark glasses, and her eyes, unscarred now, looked clear, even if their expression seemed blank. He felt a deep sympathy for and an empathy with his handsome daughter-in-law. He also felt unfailing admiration for the way she had overcome so much of her disability. He could never come face to face with her without remembering how he himself had had to live with tormenting frustration. But his blindness had been a temporary one of four years. Hers was for the rest of her life.

'I think many people blinded by accident have moments when imagination deceives them,' he said.

Felicity responded to that.

'That's exactly how I felt, self-deceived,' she said.

'I can tell you I deceived myself more than once,' said Boots.

The sun sailed out of the cloud, and the garden filled with bright light. Felicity felt the sudden onset of extra warmth and turned her head in an instinctive attempt to visually catch its source, to urge the golden globe to make itself known to her eyes, even if only in the faintest way. But nothing broke through. She was still as blind as a bloody bat.

'There, you see, I'm still hoping the impossible will happen,' she said.

'Understandable,' said Boots, who hadn't missed the quick turn of her head.

'Wishful thinking has stayed with me since this morning.'

'What has Tim said?' asked Boots.

'I haven't told him,' said Felicity, 'I thought it would sound silly.'

'It doesn't sound so to me,' said Boots, 'and I'm sure Tim would always want you to talk things through with him.'

'Well, you dear man,' said Felicity, 'Tim has talked a thousand things through with me, and you know how much I've appreciated that. But there's a limit.'

'Is there?' said Boots, while the young boys and girls chased each other around. 'You've talked about your dream and imagination to me.'

'But not about a thousand other things,' said Felicity, 'just a few matters now and again.'

'I wish I could tell you imagination is the forerunner of reality,' said Boots. 'Perhaps it would be if an operation was possible. I understand it isn't for you.'

'That's been confirmed more than once,' said Felicity, 'so let's forget it. I'm hearing your twins, and that's something to enjoy.'

'You can enjoy yells and shrieks?' said Boots.

'You must know that hearing the sounds of life can be a consolation,' said Felicity.

'It always made me desperate to see what was happening,' said Boots.

Out came Jennifer.

'Mummy – Uncle Boots – tea's ready.'

'Can we have it out here?' smiled Boots.

'Oh, yes, there's too many for a proper sit-down tea,' said Jennifer, 'but you have to come and get it. I'll bring yours, Mummy.'

'Thank you, sweetie,' said Felicity.

'Yes, stay there, Felicity,' said Boots, fairly sure she did not want to return to the crush. 'I'll fetch Tim and Polly out as company for both of us.'

Felicity's hand reached out as she heard him rise. He took it. She pressed.

'You're always a dear man to talk to,' she murmured.

Chapter Thirteen

Two men, inconspicuously dressed in very ordinary serge suits, were walking the Embankment, the Polish woman, Katje Galicia, between them.

'So, you haven't seen Finch for several days?' said Gregori Bukov.

'You would know that, surely,' said Katje. It was an oblique reference to the man who constantly shadowed her.

'We ask for confirmation,' said Boris Alexandrov.

'I wish, naturally, that you would trust me,' said Katje, glancing at the flowing Thames. 'Or have I become suspect while being attached to the Company?' Company was the euphemism for the KGB.

'Not at all,' said Bukov, which amused Katje, since Bukov was well known for trusting nobody. It was rumoured that he did not completely trust himself, and accordingly never allowed anything to slip from his tongue that might count against him in the event of his appearance at one of the Central Committee's investigations into treason. True, such investigations were less frequent since the death of Stalin and the execution of his security chief, Beria. But they still happened, especially where Stalinites were concerned. Stalin, now dead, was being depopularized.

'If you weren't trusted, you know what would occur,' said Alexandrov. 'When do you next propose to see Finch?'

'I repeat, he's not a man to be rushed,' said Katje. 'Or frightened.'

'He has something to hide from his wife and family,' said Bukov.

'He knows that,' said Katje, 'and I've told you, he'll agree to a meeting, but only if both of you are present. You have questions to ask of him, and he has questions to ask of you.'

'What kind of questions?' enquired Bukov.

'He hasn't informed me,' said Katje, 'but I suspect they're to do with the disappearance of British agents who were his colleagues and friends during and after the war. He doesn't like to think that after Britain had been Russia's ally against Hitler, such disappearances were initiated by Stalin. He would consider that very ungrateful.'

'He has his own adopted countrymen, such as Burgess and Philby, to thank for that,' said Alexandrov.

Bukov was silent. He was taking time to make up his mind.

'Finch is an idiot if he doesn't know why such incidents occur,' he said eventually. 'Soviet agents have disappeared. Gratitude or ingratitude play no part in tit for tat. Finch should know that too. But, very well, arrange the required meeting. Not, however, at a place of his own choosing.'

'I understand,' said Katje.

'Proceed with care and caution,' said Alexandrov.

'Trust me,' said Katje.

The KGB officers departed then, giving her brief nods. She stopped, turned and advanced to the retaining wall of the Embankment, where she stayed for several minutes observing the Thames and the progress of the occasional river craft.

They trusted her. If not completely, then enough. That was a reward for being faithful to Communist ideology and its security system.

At nine thirty that evening, a man renting a prefabricated unit near the Elephant and Castle in Walworth answered the ringing phone.

'Hello?' His voice was quiet and cautious.

Pennies dropped into a public phone box. A woman's voice was heard.

'Stand by. That is all. Stand by.'

'I hear you.'

Phones were replaced.

Monday morning.

Sir Edwin Finch, waking up, wondered when the Polish woman would next contact him. Never, he hoped. Her demands represented sheer absurdity. She must know he would never name agents who had been colleagues. And what use, anyway, would they now be to her KGB friends? That did not mean he would name them. Would his refusal result in his wife and family receiving details of his German origins and activities? If so, it would mean a realization by Maisie that during the years he had spent as her lodger, he'd been a German agent in the service of Imperial Germany, and that he had kept this from her during all the time he had known her. Maisie had had an ingrained dislike and distrust of Germany and Germans since the time when the sabre-rattling Kaiser Wilhelm had strutted the stage in Berlin and allowed his army generals to plunge Europe into war in 1914, a war that became unimaginably ghastly. Later, during the rise of Hitler, she had constantly expressed her belief that the man was born to make trouble and that his Germans would follow him into another war, because that was the kind of people they were.

Perhaps he should have told her years ago of that which was known only to Boots, the most faithful of friends. Should he do so now? He wavered. Normally, he knew himself to be as clear-headed as any man could be, but the Polish woman had reduced him to what, in self-deprecation, he called a state of mental incompetence.

After breakfast, he made a phone call to Boots from his study, subsequent to which he spoke to his wife.

'Maisie, I'm having a light lunch with Boots today. Just a beer and a sandwich at his pub. Would you mind?'

'No, of course not, Edwin,' said Chinese Lady, 'it's something you and Boots enjoy, and it'll do you good to get out sociably instead of pottering away in the garden.' Chinese Lady, pleased for her husband, a man of kindness and integrity – a proper English gentleman, in short – did what she seldom did. She made a little joke, and with one of her rare smiles. 'Mind, don't let the barman know you've got a title, or he'll charge you double for the lunch.'

Sir Edwin laughed.

'I'll keep that to myself, I promise,' he said.

'It's best,' said Chinese Lady. 'I never speak my title in a shop in case they put extra on the bill. Well, I don't ever let anyone hear my title, anyway, it's not gracious to, it's more like showing off. I mean, Edwin, suppose I asked a bus conductor for a ticket to Walworth Road and told him I was Lady Finch? I should think only common people would do that. Well, I suppose some titled people can be common . . .' She trailed on.

Sir Edwin met Boots in the pub opposite the firm's offices near Camberwell Green. They found a corner table in the old-fashioned saloon, its atmosphere plushly Edwardian. Joe, the barman, was getting on a bit now, but still agile on his feet and receptive to customers, especially to long-standing ones like Boots. He took the order for beef sandwiches with mustard, and pints of dark ale. He began to slice the beef from a cold roast. Sandwiches in this pub were always made to order, and therefore came fresh to customers. It was traditional, and Joe's employer, the publican, took no notice of a post-war trend towards speed of service. As he said to his wife, people in a hurry reach their funeral all too quick.

'Well, Edwin, to what do I owe the pleasure of your company?' asked Boots. 'You did say over the phone that you wanted to talk to me.'

'So I do, Boots,' said Sir Edwin, and it was then that his mind cleared, and his first coherent thought was that his problem was entirely his own and not one he should ask Boots to share. It would put the man he most liked and admired into the impossible position of making a decision for him. A totally unfair responsibility. He knew now that he himself must be the sole arbiter.

He smiled.

'Oh, I simply thought, Boots, that it would be a pleasant change from pottering about to enjoy a light lunch and some conversation with you.'

'Oh, this is a whim, is it?' smiled Boots. 'Well, I favour it, since I mostly lunch by myself or with one of my acquaintances here.'

'I'm interested in the twins,' said Sir Edwin, 'and wanted to ask if you and Polly had discussed with them what kind of future they had in mind.'

'Is that what's on your mind, the careers of Gemma and James?' enquired Boots, just a little surprised.

'They're intelligent youngsters,' said Sir Edwin, 'and now that this country and Europe are well on the way to economic recovery, I fancy that by the time Gemma and James come of age the world will be wide open to them.'

'Don't you think their time at university will give them their own ideas about what they'd like to make of life?' said Boots. 'If, of course, they enter university.'

'That, in modern parlance, should be a doddle for Gemma and James,' said Sir Edwin, at which point Joe, grizzled and white-aproned, arrived with the lunch tray. He set down the platter of finely prepared beef sandwiches and the pint glasses of ale, together with plates, knives, napkins and a little pot of mustard if extra was required.

'There we are, Mr Adams,' he said.

'Thanks, Joe,' said Boots, 'see you later, on our way out.'

Joe knew he'd get a generous tip.

'Pleasure any time, Mr Adams,' he said, and returned to his white marble counter just as a beefy young bloke entered the saloon and made straight for the sandwich bar. A typical piece of dialogue followed.

'Ham sandwich, old cock, and a beer.'

'Five minutes,' said Joe.

'Eh? What d'yer mean, five minutes? I want it now. Pronto.'

'Sorry, sir. All sandwiches are prepared to order. Try the cafe by the Green for pronto service.'

'Sod that. Five minutes, then.'

Sir Edwin, after swallowing some rich ale, became quite brisk, suggesting in confident fashion to Boots that the prospects for young people in this post-war world were probably far better than anyone would have forecast in the chaos that obtained in 1945 and 1946. Such prospects were not immediately obvious, said Sir Edwin, but would be in a few more years. Boots listened, his expression one of whimsical interest. It was unusual for his stepfather to speak of and ask questions about the future of any of the family's school-aged children. Not that he was remote from them. He had always been able to identify with all the children, and to be an entertaining family figure. He could have been even more entertaining had he been in a position to tell them of his long and adventurous career, first as a German agent and then as a naturalized Briton in service with British Intelligence. He had always kept quiet about that, his German past in particular, and wisely, thought Boots, as he and his stepfather made a companionable meal of this light lunch.

'There's one prospect not so promising, Edwin,' he said.

'Which is?' said Sir Edwin, convinced he'd taken the right step in keeping his problem to himself.

'The bomb,' said Boots.

'The world's most infernal invention,' said Sir Edwin.

'Made even more infernal by what this damned Cold War could lead to,' said Boots, 'if one of the major powers lost its head.'

'If it does, Boots, it will be destroyed by whoever it attacked,' said Sir Edwin, 'since we can only be talking about the Soviet Union attacking America. The bomb is a preventive as much as it's a threat. Much more so, in fact. I prefer, by the way, to carry on our discussion concerning the future of Gemma and James.'

'I'm always inclined to look on and see how young people's lives develop,' said Boots, 'and chip in only when asked for advice or an opinion.'

'Your mother, Boots,' smiled Sir Edwin, 'would put that down to what she calls your airy-fairy attitude.'

'It's saved me from being labelled an interfering

old codger,' said Boots. 'I suppose it's inevitable that Gemma and James will make some mistakes, but Polly will tell you that that's all part of gaining a salutary experience of life, as long as they're not the kind of mistakes that can be destructive. If either of us thought the twins were heading for serious trouble, it's then that we'd step in with advice and warnings, and even try to put a stop to what was afoot.'

'It would be a parental responsibility to do so,' said Sir Edwin. 'Apart from that, I'd like to mention that if James wanted something a little more – ah, challenging – than a conventional career, I hope I'd still be around to help him.'

Boots smiled.

'So that's what you wanted to talk about,' he said. 'Helping James to latch onto a career with your old department in Whitehall. Edwin, that's a vocational career, suitable only for those with a natural instinct for it.'

'I mention it only as a thought,' said Sir Edwin. 'James is an adventurous lad.'

'Well, time will tell,' said Boots, 'so let's leave it at that.'

Sir Edwin was quite happy to do so. After all, he had only raised the subject as an excuse to cover up his original reason for meeting Boots. He had now left himself to make his own decision, and was back to waiting for the Polish woman to contact him again.

A day later, someone knocked on the door of Jimmy's office in the Bethnal Green factory. He heard the knock above the continuous buzz of the busy workshops.

'Come in.'

The door opened, and Gertie and Bert's eldest granddaughter showed herself. Not for the first time, Jimmy contemplated her sex appeal, which today was all nicely done up in a peach-coloured dress with a happily defining bodice, and jolly dishy nylon stockings. He did not know it, but not only was the dress new, she was also no more than an hour out of the hairdressers, and her springy auburn curls looked divine. Divine? I'm going weak in the head, thought Jimmy.

'Oh, hello,' she said.

'Hello yourself,' said Jimmy. 'But you're a bit early, aren't you? We weren't expecting you until next Monday fortnight.'

'Oh, Mister Adams – Mister Jimmy, I mean – you do tease a girl,' said Clare, carrying a square white cardboard box tied with pink ribbon. 'I 'aven't come to start me job, I bet you know that, I've come to give you something from me grandma.'

'My old friend Gertie?' said Jimmy, rising.

'Yes, me gran,' said Clare. 'Well, she was so pleased about you giving me the switchboard job that she said she just had to show proper appreciation. So I've brought you a present with her best wishes.'

'What a grand old lady is good old Gertie,' said Jimmy. He looked at the square box. 'Is it an alarm clock?'

'Now would me grandma give you an alarm clock?' said Clare.

'Well, she might if it's one that plays "Jingle Bells",' said Jimmy.

Oh, help, said Clare to herself, if I don't get him to take me serious, my romantic life will be ruined before it's started. The trouble was, she liked his nonsense.

'Mister Jimmy, stop having me on,' she said.

'You needn't call me Mister when you're on a friendly visit,' said Jimmy. 'Anyway, if it's not an alarm clock in that box, what is it, then?'

'It's a home-made fruit cake, which you can enjoy with your afternoon tea for as long as it lasts,' said Clare.

'A fruit cake, home-made?' said Jimmy. 'All for me? I'm blushing.'

'I bet,' said Clare, and placed the box on his desk. 'It's with me gran's compliments.' She didn't, however, mention that she had made it herself from one of her grandma's recipes. Well, it would look as if she wanted to be a bit special to him. Which she did. Not that she'd yet reached the state of calling it a labour of love. 'And with her kind regards, like.'

'And with pink ribbon?' said Jimmy. He undid it and opened the box to disclose the cake and its crusty-looking top. 'Well, I can see now it's not an alarm clock.' He caught the aroma of fruit cake fresh from an oven. 'Tell your grandma I'm chuffed up to my eyebrows, and that I'll do my best to make it last, which it won't if my Uncle Tommy and the office girls get a sniff of it. Thanks a million for bringing it, Clare.'

'Oh, you're ever so welcome,' said Clare.

'By the way, have you taken time off from your job again to bring the cake?' asked Jimmy.

'Well, no, I finished last week,' said Clare, 'because when I give me notice to the old – I mean Miss Crawley – she 'anded me me cards there and then. Still, it didn't upset me, knowing I'd got a new job here.'

The phone rang and Jimmy took the call. Clare supposed she ought to make an exit. Having found a good reason to show herself to Jimmy in her new outfit, well, she'd done that, and couldn't now hang about. But she was still in his office when he put the phone down.

'I think I'd better hide this cake, and the pink ribbon,' he said.

'Yes, and I'd best go,' she said, 'I'm sure you're busy. Still, when the weekend comes I expect you'll find time to go out with a girlfriend.'

'Well, I can tell you I'm taking a girl to the Frankie Laine concert at the Festival Gardens on Saturday,' said Jimmy.

Crikey, thought Clare, what girl?

'Oh, I'm going there meself,' she said, having taken only a second to declare war on whoever the girl was.

'We'll look out for you and your feller,' said Jimmy.

'No, I'm not going with any feller, just on me own,' said Clare.

'Then we'll definitely look out for you,' said Jimmy, which meant that when Clare left a minute later she was thinking he really must like me or he wouldn't want me butting in. Jimmy, seeing her out, expressed himself warmly again in acknowledgement of the cake. He also asked Clare not to forget to thank her grandma on his behalf.

Before the day was out, Gertie's eldest granddaughter had secured all the details of Frankie Laine's Saturday concert in Battersea Park.

Chapter Fourteen

Phoebe took an evening phone call.

'Hello, Pussycat. Philip here.'

'Who said you could call me Pussycat? And I thought you were going to write.'

'I'm phoning instead. I've got forty-eight hours leave the weekend after next. Well, we all have, and it's going to be regular. So I'm coming home each time. I'll hitch-hike.'

'On the back of a lorry?' asked Phoebe.

'In a Rolls-Royce, with luck,' said Philip. 'Drivers stop for blokes in uniform, so why not some lord?'

'My word, you do have fanciful ideas,' said Phoebe.

'I'm just hopeful,' said Philip. 'Anyway, how's your happy self, Phoebe?'

Phoebe said she'd be a lot happier if it was Christmas, because her dad had promised her a new bike and her old one was rattling like six tin kettles and Christmas was a light moon away and she was sure that her old machine would fall to pieces well before then and while she was riding it and she'd end up bruised all over and—

'Stop,' said Philip.

'Stop?' said Phoebe. 'What for?'

'You're breaking my heart,' said Philip.

'Oh, dear, what a shame,' said Phoebe.

'When I'm next home,' said Philip, 'shall we go dancing again?'

'Well, I think that's a very nice idea,' said Phoebe, 'as long as we go by bus and not on my old bike.'

'What a crackpot,' said Philip. 'If what you say about your old bike is only half true, it wouldn't carry the both of us for more than six yards before it fell to pieces.'

'Yes, that's what I mean, let's go by bus,' said Phoebe.

'Lucky for you that I'm here and you're there, monkey,' said Philip.

'Why, what would you do if you were here where I am?' asked Phoebe.

'I'm not sure,' said Philip, 'but I think you'd be yelling.'

'Crikey, what a brute,' said Phoebe, 'I'm having second thoughts about you, Philip Harrison.'

'What're your first thoughts, Phoebe Adams?'

'That you only appear once a year, and it ought to be twice at least,' said Phoebe.

'Well, now it looks as if it'll be once a fortnight,' said Philip.

'That's it, now overwhelm a girl,' said Phoebe.

Philip laughed.

'Phoebe, I like you,' he said.

'Oh, it's mutual,' said Phoebe. 'Would you like to buy me a new bike? Only Dad says it's got to be Christmas or not at all. It's not that he can't afford it, it's that he doesn't want to spoil me. He says.'

'If I had the right kind of money, I'd buy you one tomorrow,' said Philip.

'Philip, would you really? Why would you?'

'I simply can't think of a nice girl like you all tangled up with a collapsed collection of old iron without going grey,' said Philip.

'You must be very soft-hearted,' said Phoebe, hugely enjoying herself.

'No, it's just that I like you, full stop,' said Philip.

'Well, I like you too,' said Phoebe. 'Mind, I don't know about full stop, not when in a way we've only just met.'

'All right, Pussycat,' said Philip, 'I get the message, but when we do meet again I promise to take you to Brixton on a bus and not on your old bike.'

'Well, that's very kind, I must say,' said Phoebe.

They enjoyed a few more minutes of perky chat before Philip, up in the air about the delightful girl who wasn't strictly his cousin, said goodbye.

As Phoebe replaced the phone, Sammy appeared in the hall.

'Who was that you were talking to for half an hour, me pet?' he asked.

'Philip,' said Phoebe.

'What was he doing, telling you his life story?'

'Well, yes, in a way,' said Phoebe, 'and fascinating, of course. He'll be home again the weekend after next, and we'll be going dancing again.'

'I'll put that down in my diary,' said Sammy, 'and include it in my own life story.'

'Thrilling,' said Phoebe. 'Daddy,' she said

absently, 'do I have to wait until Christmas for a new bike?'

'Eh?' said Sammy.

'It's a long time away,' said Phoebe.

'You're losing me,' said Sammy, 'you had a new bike for your birthday months ago.'

'Did I?' said Phoebe. 'Oh, so I did. Crikey, I've been telling Philip I've still got my old one. I don't know what came over me.' She giggled. 'Oh, well, we all have our potty moments, don't we, Daddy?'

'Bucketfuls when we've got springtime fancies,' said Sammy, 'and you can get those any time of the year.'

'Don't look at me,' said Phoebe.

'No, all right, me pet,' said Sammy.

Phoebe laughed, and went dancing off to find her mum and talk to her about the cousin who wasn't strictly so.

Saturday morning.

Katje Galicia, walking from her flat in Bloomsbury, glimpsed the KGB's errand boy, the one to whom Boris Alexandrov gave the prestigious title of bodyguard. To Katje he was a dour, pudding-faced Russian lump, conditioned to obeying orders, however puerile, senseless or obscene, just as Himmler's SS had been. Robots, every one. That men could allow themselves to be turned into unthinking machines was a sad reflection on their capacity for surrendering their individualism.

She walked on until she reached and entered a public phone booth. She dialled a number, made the connection and slipped the required pennies into the slot.

'Hello?'

'Good, you're there,' she said, and conducted a conversation lasting a minute. When she left, she was shadowed, of course. The journey was short. It took her back to her flat.

At the RAF cadets' training unit in Wiltshire, a sergeant-instructor raised his voice.

'Cadet Harrison,' he bawled, 'what's up with you?'

'I'm feeling airborne, Sarge.'

'You're feeling what?'

'Up in the air.'

'Oh, is that so? Well, get your perishing feet back on the ground. You're not a fairy, are you?'

'No, I haven't got my wings yet, Sarge.'

'Gawd help old England when you do.'

That passed Philip by. He still had Phoebe on his mind, and his mind was kind of floating. What a girl.

Boris Alexandrov picked up the ringing phone.

'Yes?'

'KG51 here.'

'Proceed.'

'Finch will meet you and Comrade Bukov next Tuesday at three in the afternoon. You agree to this?'

'Where will he meet us?'

'At my flat,' said Katje. 'He demurred at first, suggesting Hyde Park. He wished, he said, not to feel crowded. However, I persuaded him that my flat would provide privacy.'

'He did not suspect that privacy would make him vulnerable?'

'To torture?' said Katje.

'Don't be impertinent. This is London, not Lubyanka. We proceed, therefore, on quiet feet and act with velvet gloves. But your man definitely agreed to using your flat?'

'Yes,' said Katje, 'but he'll give you nothing unless Comrade Bukov is with you.'

'You've made that all too plain more than once.'

'I'm sorry, of course, if you now find it irritating,' said Katje, 'but –'

'Never mind. We will come to your flat. Tuesday at three, you said?'

'Yes.'

'Very well.' Alexandrov rang off.

Katje put the phone back in place with the brisk gesture of a woman pleased and satisfied with what she had accomplished so far in this undertaking for the London representatives of the KGB. It was an undertaking she herself had suggested.

Battersea Park.

The Festival Gardens were bright in the afternoon sun, the funfair alive with young people clamouring to patronize its excitements, and its excitements aroused shrieks in girls on whirling machines. Skirts flew, exposed legs delighted male eyes, and although the shrieks mounted, it could not be said too many blushes were evident. In this era of the Fifties, young ladies, generally, were not as modest as their mothers or aunts had been. Changing with the times, and going along with social revolution, modern young women were more extrovert, more conscious that their place in life need not be governed by the formalities and conventions of yesteryear. The revolution might only be in its infancy, but it was still infectious enough to have its subconscious effect on teenage girls and young women. Blushes, therefore, were vanishing as fast as outgoing attitudes were growing. That is not to say every young lady was able to keep a pretty flush at bay. In fact, one very modern female by the name of Lulu Saunders, who believed women should be and could be more equal than men, had been known to turn a bright pink in the presence of one Paul Adams.

Very odd. But intriguing. Well, it tickled Paul.

In the sunshine, Clare Roper, a young lady of initiative, was presently bent on securing a happy place in the life of Paul's cousin Jimmy. Such a frank purpose was much in keeping with modern times, although as long ago as two thousand years, Queen Cleopatra had made no bones about grabbing Julius Caesar and then Mark Antony.

Clare was standing aside from the flowing stream of young people entering the concert arena, her big brown eyes focused on every oncoming couple. Saturday afternoon outfits were either informal or dressy, jeans and shirts for most of the fellers, sweaters and slacks for others, jeans and varied tops for some of their maidens, colourful dresses or the fashionable flared skirts and tops for others.

Clare herself looked a treat in a polka-dot

primrose dress with its skirt slightly flared, her dark auburn hair full of sunlit tints.

'Another new dress?' her mum had said.

'Oh, it ain't exactly new, Mum, I've had it for all of a week.'

'Seems to me you've been giving your savings a bit of a bashing lately,' said her dad.

'Oh, well, when I start me new job with Adams Fashions, I'll be getting fifteen bob a week more, and bonuses too. Jimmy Adams promised me.'

'Have I 'eard a lot of Jimmy Adams just recent?' asked her dad.

'I don't know, have you, Dad?'

'Bring 'im home and let's have a look at 'im,' said her mum.

Crikey, thought Clare, when that day arrives, I'll have bells ringing in me ears.

She watched the continuous stream of young people, all heading for the Frankie Laine concert. An unattached bloke with a bobbing Adam's apple stopped and spoke.

'Looking for someone like me, baby?'

'Not today,' said Clare, 'I've gone off everyone like you.'

'Girlie, I ain't everyone.'

'Never mind, keep going,' said Clare, and the bloke went on to cast around the arena for a more understanding piece of fluff.

Clare saw Jimmy then, in sports shirt and summer slacks. Out of feelings for his dad, he kept his distance from jeans. Clare also saw the girl with him. I don't believe it, she told herself. The girl was pretty enough, but real skinny, and no more than a young schoolgirl in her light frock. What's he up to, he's not a cradle-snatcher, is he?

Up they came, in line with Clare.

'Oh, hello,' she said.

'Hi-ho,' said Jimmy, very appreciative of her summary look, 'join in.'

'Oh, ta,' said Clare, and placed herself at his other side. 'I didn't really expect I'd see you.'

'Delighted you're here,' said Jimmy, as they moved along. 'Meet my cousin Linda.' Cousin? Young cousin? Clare experienced the relief of a young lady who didn't really want to go to war with a mere schoolgirl. 'Linda,' said Jimmy, 'meet someone's granddaughter, Clare Roper.'

'Oh, pleased, I'm sure,' said Linda, and the two girls, leaning, met eye to eye across Jimmy's chest. 'Here, what's he mean, someone's granddaughter?'

'I know, he's a joker,' said Clare.

'Linda, haven't you heard of our factory's Gertie Roper and her better half, Bert Roper?' asked Jimmy.

'Oh, yes, but only vaguely,' said Linda.

'Well, Clare's their happy granddaughter,' said Jimmy, 'and I'm pleased to formally announce she's going to be our new switchboard operator. So we can forget there's anything vague about her.'

Linda rolled her eyes and said to Clare, 'Jimmy talks out of the top of his head sometimes.'

'Oh, I'd better not say too much about that,' said Clare, 'he's going to be my boss when I start work at the fact'ry.'

'Come on,' said Jimmy. He put his arms around

their shoulders and shepherded them into the arena. Clare positively tingled at his touch. Oh, Lor', she thought, I can't hardly believe I've got it this bad already.

The open-air concert was a stand-up one for the audience, an overflowing multitude of fans. The arena was quivering under the impact of feet already jigging. There was some jostling, and although it was good-natured, Jimmy kept his arms around the girls. Linda felt comfy about it, Clare felt she was beginning to live an exciting life. Not that she hadn't enjoyed some lively moments with boyfriends, but all such fellers now seemed a bit stodgy.

Amid yells of delight, the members of an orchestra began to fill the open-air stage, and to tune their instruments. The voices of the young people, rising to the sky, caused Linda to say she was never going to hear herself think once Frankie Laine appeared. Jimmy said be of good cheer, infant, no-one was here to only think, they could listen as well, especially to Frankie Laine. Clare said she'd heard that in America the teenagers swooned.

'At what?' asked Jimmy.

'Well, like at Frank Sinatra,' said Clare.

'I've heard about that kind of carry-on myself,' said Jimmy, 'so listen, both of you. I don't want either of you swooning at Frankie Laine. I'm useless when it comes to knowing what to do to get swooning girls upright. Clare, that's a peach of a dress you're wearing.'

Clare went pink. (That was another modern

young lady not yet fully in tune with the revolution.)

'Oh, thanks,' she said.

'Yes, it's lovely,' said Linda, noting that the bodice was curved, not flat like her own. She sighed. 'Jimmy, we won't swoon.'

'Crikey, no,' said Clare, 'I can't think of anything more daft.'

'Will you two girls promise me one thing?' asked Jimmy above the noise of happy anticipation.

'What thing?' asked Linda.

'Enjoy yourselves,' said Jimmy, which made Linda think how nice he was. It made Clare think old-fashioned romantic thoughts, like walking hand in hand with him into the sunset. Oh, help, what's come over me?

A fat jolly bloke appeared on the stage, holding up his hands to enjoin silence, which took about a minute and a half in the climate of whoops and shrieks. He then announced it was his pleasure and privilege to introduce none other than the immortal and world-famous American singing star, Frankie Laine himself, over here in person to entertain his UK fans in a series of concerts, of which this one had been specially asked for by Frankie himself.

'Young ladies, young gentlemen, I give you the world's number one all-time vocalist, Frankie Laine!'

A pandemonium of welcome erupted as the star appeared. Dressed in navy blue trousers, blue shirt and white jacket, Frankie Laine had the dark good looks of a Latin and a great personality. His smile embraced the young people.

'Hiya, folks!'

'Hiya, Frankie!'

He turned to his musicians, smiled at them, nodded and they struck up the opening bars of 'Mule Train', creating a vociferous response from the audience.

'Oh, man,' groaned a young lady behind Clare.

Frankie sang. He had a strong rich voice and a hand-held microphone that helped to carry the song out into the open air. The young people of London were entranced, and that included Clare, Jimmy and Linda. To the electric atmosphere Frankie added his gift of melody, finishing 'Mule Train' to rapturous acclaim.

'Oh, man,' groaned the young lady behind Clare.

Frankie held up a hand, and the audience gradually curbed their enthusiasm to allow him to exercise his vibrant vocal cords in one of his new songs. He sang it with verve and without effort, and before the final notes had faded away, the crowded arena rang with yells of delight.

'Oh, man,' groaned the young lady behind Clare.

She's going to swoon, thought Clare. What's Jimmy going to do if she swoons on him? She glanced at him, liking his profile, that of a young man with firm features entirely pleasing. He returned the glance. He smiled and winked.

'Hope she doesn't ask me to pick her up,' he murmured.

Clare laughed. It was drowned by overwhelming applause as the orchestra let go with the opening bars of another of Frankie's popular hits, 'That Lucky Old Sun'.

Clare and Linda tapped their feet on flattened grass. Jimmy let his ears enjoy the rich voice. He was a fan of the new breed of songwriters, and the stars who delivered the goods at concerts, over the radio and on 78 gramophone records.

The susceptible young lady behind Clare swayed in happy delirium. Young blokes on either side of her held her upright.

'Oh, man,' she sighed.

Clare glanced at Jimmy again.

'Isn't it great?' she said.

'Too much for Linda,' he said, one arm around his cousin, 'she's gone swoony, after all.'

'No, I haven't,' said Linda, 'I just don't know what's happening to my knees, that's all.'

'Never mind your knees,' said Jimmy, 'enjoy yourself and you'll forget them.'

'Jimmy, I'm having a lovely time,' she said.

'Something to tell your schoolfriends,' said Jimmy.

Time went happily by for every fan as Frankie sang other popular hits such as 'Jezebel', and 'High Noon' from the film of that name. Eventually he delivered his greatest number, 'I Believe'.

The applause at the end of that song was touched with hysterical delight.

'Oh, gosh, great,' breathed Linda.

'Giddy,' breathed Clare.

'Hold up, girls,' said Jimmy.

'I need an arm,' sighed Clare, and Jimmy gave her one, around her ribcage. Oh, me pulses, she thought, what if I asked for a kiss as well? Would lightning strike?

Frankie encored a verse or two of 'I Believe', and that brought the concert to a rousing finale. Amid the delighted shrieks of girls, the mass of young people surged forward to mob the handsome star of song.

Clare would have been swept off her feet but for Jimmy's helpful arm. All the same, she was swept around him. Jimmy stood like a rock, his other arm holding Linda tightly and safely. Clare found herself up against him, bosom to chest in no uncertain way, which didn't cause her any embarrassment, but it did make her feel swoony.

'Oh, me feet,' she said, 'I think they're off the floor.'

What an armful, thought Jimmy.

'If you take off,' he said, 'I'll go up with you.'

Oh, bliss, thought Clare.

'Crikey, it's a riot,' said Linda.

'Hang on,' said Jimmy, as the excited crowd, surging forward from behind, peeled away on either side of the bunched trio. His firm body was warm against Clare's, and she thought hang on? Who wants to let go? I don't.

'Blessed elephants,' gasped Linda.

The musicians fled and Frankie Laine adroitly slipped away from the teeming female fans.

'All clear, girls,' said Jimmy moments later.

'You sure?' said Linda.

'Fairly sure,' said Jimmy, still in a clinch with Clare, who had her face in his shoulder. He felt quite happy about their close proximity, but wondered what Harry Ballymore would have said.

'Is it safe now?' asked Clare muffledly.

'Oh, yes,' said Linda, taking a look.

'Only I've got my eyes shut,' said Clare. 'Talk about charging loonies.'

'There's no-one near us now,' said Linda, 'and if you don't let Clare go, Jimmy, someone's going to start talking.'

Jimmy let go.

'Come on,' he said, 'let's find some refreshments, like tea and cake.'

Clare detached herself and smoothed her dress. She couldn't remember ever having this kind of fun with any of her boyfriends, all of whom were now consigned to the past. There had been some fun times, of course, but nothing memorable.

Both girls were arm in arm with Jimmy as he took them in search of the Festival Gardens cafe.

Chapter Fifteen

The cafe was crowded with young people still quivering and noisy. Jimmy collared the only vacant table.

'You girls sit yourselves down and keep off any trespassers,' he said. 'I'll get the tea and cake.'

Linda said she'd prefer Coke and a doughnut, and Jimmy took himself off to the self-service counter.

'Phew, what a lark,' said Linda.

'Great,' said Clare.

Up came a couple of young blokes in cowboy shirts and jeans.

'Hiya, dolls, can we do you a favour and join you?' suggested one.

'No, thanks,' said Linda.

'Company's good for the soul, y'know.'

'Well, our company's getting tea for us,' said Clare, 'our souls are a bit thirsty.'

'So push off,' said Linda.

'You could miss bliss, y'know, turning us down.'

'Is that your mum over there?' asked Clare witheringly.

'Eh?'

'Hoppit, there's good boys,' said Clare, and the young blokes departed with resigned grins. They'd just lost an encounter with a bird who hadn't fallen over backwards when invited to share bliss. Some birds were getting too choosy.

Jimmy came back with a tray of refreshments that added up to a Coke and a jam doughnut for Linda, and tea and cake for himself and Clare. He sat down, delivered the goodies, and they tucked in. Clare thought how much at ease he always was, which made him really good company. A girl just didn't have any awkward moments with him.

Sampling his slice of fruit cake, he said, 'Passable.'

'The cake?' said Clare.

'Yes, passable,' said Jimmy, 'but well below par compared to your granny's, Clare.'

'You really like it?' said Clare, who had made no attempt to outshine Linda by keeping Jimmy's attention mainly on herself. She didn't think she needed to, since it was obvious he and the schoolgirl were simply friendly cousins. 'I'm so pleased to know you're enjoying it – I mean, me grandma will be. Well, no,' she added in a free-thinking moment, 'actually I made it meself, from one of her recipes.'

'Did you?' said Jimmy, giving her a quizzical look, then a smile. 'Why didn't you say?'

'Oh, I didn't want you to think I was showing off,' said Clare.

'Listen, ladybird,' said Jimmy, 'any girl who can bake a cake as moreish as that is entitled to show off.'

'I'm in the dark,' said Linda.

'Well, come into the light,' said Jimmy. 'Clare baked me a cake to enjoy with my afternoon tea at the factory. Mind, I've got a problem. The office girls and Uncle Tommy are enjoying it too.' He smiled at Clare. 'They soon found out.'

'They're eating your cake?' said Linda, thinking Clare must have a soft spot for him. 'Blessed cheek.'

'Can't be helped,' said Jimmy. 'The fact is, Linda, it's the kind of cake de luxe I daresay Nell Gwynn served up to King Charlie as a welcome change from oranges. Was Nell Gwynn a good cook, d'you know, Linda?'

'It doesn't say so in our history books,' said Linda, 'more like she kept his bed warm.'

'Filled up his hot-water bottles, I suppose,' said Jimmy.

Clare laughed.

'Listen to him, Clare,' said Linda, 'talk about playing innocent. Even I know Nell Gwynn didn't go into the King's bedchamber just to fill his hot-water bottles.'

'Or to give him another orange,' said Clare.

'Here, wasn't Frankie Laine just great?' said Linda. 'Oh, d'you think I could have another doughnut, Jimmy?'

'Why not?' said Jimmy. 'Another slice of cake for you, Clare?'

'Well, yes, thanks ever so,' said Clare.

'Won't be a tick,' said Jimmy, and went to join the counter queue.

As casually as she could, Clare said to Linda,

'I suppose he's got a girlfriend. What's she like?'

'Oh, he doesn't have anyone special just now,' said Linda.

'No, go on?' said Clare, just as casually. 'I'm surprised. Well, I mean, I know some fellers a lot worse that are dating very heavy.'

'Jimmy did have a super girl once,' said Linda. 'So his sister Paula told me, but she went off to New York a few years ago and married an American.'

Far from casually, Clare said, 'Just like that? What a rotten thing to do. Well, I hope she ain't living happy ever after.'

'Oh, she and Jimmy weren't engaged, just going strong,' said Linda. 'Mind, his sister did say Jimmy was a bit cut up. Still, I'm sure he's over it by now, or he'd be all mopey.'

Crikey, I hope he's over it, thought Clare, I hope he hasn't turned into a woman-hater, like I've read about in pre-war novels. Mind, them novels are a bit soppy. I like modern ones best, where the heroines show woman-haters the front door.

'Well, I'm pleased he's going to be my boss, Linda,' she said, 'because I just know he'll treat me fair, and a lot better than the old – the old misery of a supervisor at my previous job.'

'Jimmy will probably spoil you,' said Linda artfully.

'Spoil me?' said Clare. 'Why would he do that?'

'It's your looks,' said Linda, 'and that gorgeous polka-dot dress.'

'Oh, go on,' said Clare, hiding pleasure.

Jimmy, at the counter now, guessed Linda was thinking doughnuts might do something for her underdevelopment, so he brought back two, with more cake for himself and Clare, who obviously didn't need doughnuts herself, since her development was well up to the mark. Lovely girl, really. Should he try competing with Harry Ballymore? No, that kind of stuff was for pushy blokes with no compunction about doing a girl's existing boyfriend in the eye while his back was turned. Of course, if he came face to face with the Irish-sounding feller, it might be fair enough to let him know he fancied Clare himself. If so, he'd probably have to watch out for Irish fists flying.

'Jimmy, you're really nice,' said Linda on receipt of the extras, and Clare thought that was so right. He was nice. He was kind of attentive and good-natured, with nice manners. She supposed he'd had a very good grammar-school education, especially as he spoke so well. Not that he was posh, and anyway, the war had pushed people together more, wherever they came from, although some working-class people still didn't want anything to do with the middle classes, which was silly.

'What're you thinking about, Clare?' asked Jimmy, who was going along with his own thoughts, those relating to his conviction that Gertie's eldest granddaughter was just about the best-looking and best-dressed young lady in this crowded cafe. 'Penny for 'em.'

'Oh, I was only thinking it was nice bumping into you and Linda,' she said. 'I know you mentioned you'd look out for me, but there were so many people I didn't think it would happen. Lor', suppose I'd been on me own in all that lot, I'd have had to run for me life.' She dropped an aitch or two, as she often did, which came from her cockney upbringing.

'Don't think about it,' said Jimmy, 'it's been a happy ending for all of us. Linda, you sure you can waffle both those doughnuts?'

'Easy,' said Linda, and giggled. 'Don't forget I'm a growing girl. Well, I'm trying to be.'

'Best of luck,' said Jimmy. 'Anyway, as soon as you've finished, we'll have to push off. I'm going out this evening with a mob of girls and fellers to see a Whitehall Theatre farce.'

'Can I come?' asked Linda.

'You could if I had a spare ticket,' said Jimmy. The girl was sweet. 'I'll include you when we do another theatre.'

Clare smothered an impulse to ask if she could be included too. She couldn't make herself as obvious and as forward as that. Even in modern novels, where heroines held their own with fellers, they still let the fellers take the initiative.

Finishing, they left the cafe and made their way out of the park and to a bus stop. There, when a bus for the East End arrived, Clare parted from Jimmy and Linda, but not before she declared she'd really enjoyed the afternoon.

'Considerably mutual,' said Jimmy, sounding like his dad.

'Ever so nice to have met you,' said Linda.

'Oh, that's mutual too,' said Clare from the platform, thinking it a shame that the schoolgirl was painfully thin.

'So long, bringer of cakes,' smiled Jimmy, and

Clare waved as the bus carried her away.

She sighed as she took her seat, knowing the rest of the day was going to be flat. Then she thought that perhaps she was being a bit silly. She was in the process of running after a bloke. She ought to have some pride. Only pride was sort of losing a battle with infatuation. Yes, that was what it was, infatuation, and by the time she'd been in her new job for a month, it was more than likely she'd have come to her senses.

But, at the moment, the memory of that brief blissful time she'd spent wrapped in his supportive arm didn't offer a lot of help.

On their own bus going home, Linda said, 'I think Clare's awf'lly nice, and isn't she pretty?'

'Near to lovely,' said Jimmy.

'Jimmy, why don't you ask her to be your girlfriend?' suggested Linda. 'I'm sure she likes you.'

'Unfortunately,' said Jimmy, 'and I admit I fancy her more than a bit, Clare's got a steady.'

'Has she really?' asked Linda. 'How d'you know, has she said so, then?'

'One of her cousins told me at Bert and Gertie Roper's retirement party,' said Jimmy. 'A bloke by the name of Harry Ballymore.'

'Harry who?'

'Harry Ballymore.'

'Ballymore?'

'Yes, a bit unusual,' said Jimmy. 'The name, I mean. I'm not personally acquainted with the bloke, I only know he sounds Irish.'

'Oh, well, hard luck, Jimmy,' said Linda, 'but there's got to be one super girl just waiting for you to meet her, and when you do I bet she won't complain.'

'What a sweet and gracious young lady you are,' said Jimmy. Linda giggled. 'Come round any time for Sunday tea, and I'll get Mum to include doughnuts with her jam tarts.'

'Jimmy, you're a great help,' said Linda.

Chapter Sixteen

In occupied West Germany, rageful complaints were coming from the Russian zone concerning several suspected Nazi war criminals who had escaped custody and crossed the border into the British zone. The British, complained the Soviet authorities, were refusing to send them back, although they were officially obliged to do so under the terms of a Four-Power agreement.

The people in question, Germans, were actually asking for political asylum, and were presently under interrogation in Brunswick.

At his desk, Colonel Lucas, husband of Eloise, Boots's French-born daughter, had dealt with three of the asylum-seekers, none of whom had been able to produce identity documents. They protested that their papers had been confiscated by the Russians. Colonel Lucas's interrogation, assisted by lists, descriptions and background data of known war criminals, plus helpful interventions by his wily sergeant, pointed him to conclusions of certainty. Two were ex-SS concentration camp guards, and the third a foolish anti-Communist political agitator, anathema to the Russians.

'They're bawling, sir,' said Sergeant Colley, tough, wiry and shrewd.

'In Moscow?' said Colonel Lucas, still a rugged and impressive military man, despite the loss of an arm.

'All over,' said Sergeant Colley. 'And as far as Siberia, so it sounds.'

'Well, I'm not rushing anything,' said Colonel Lucas, 'but it looks as if they can have two back at least. Who's next?'

'A regular innocent, sir.'

'One of those, eh?'

'Busting out all over with umbrage,' said Sergeant Colley.

'Well, sometimes the loud ones have got less to hide than the quiet ones,' said Colonel Lucas.

Sergeant Colley ushered the man in. Well-built, his good suit crumpled, his chin unshaven, his spectacles themselves seemed fiery with fury. His broad face, bearing a scar on the left side of his jaw, was flushed. In good English, he began a tirade of protests, and let go imprecations concerning Russian pigs.

'Shut up,' said Colonel Lucas, giving him a searching look.

'Eh? Eh?'

'Name?'

'Gerhard Weber. I—'

'Occupation?'

'Insurance broker of Leipzig. I demand a right to political asylum—'

'You'll get it if you qualify for it. At the moment, confine yourself to answering questions.' Colonel

Lucas was already making his first move, leafing through a huge album of photographs relating to known war criminals. That sometimes helped to cut short an interrogation. He glanced up, giving the man a second look. 'Take off your spectacles.'

'Why? Why? Damn and blast, I'm a man who has done no harm to anyone!'

'Sergeant Colley, remove his spectacles.'

Sergeant Colley, close to the man, whipped them off. The angry German became angrier, louder, and his scar turned livid. Colonel Lucas continued to leaf through pages of photographs.

'Give me your attention, I demand it!' shouted the German.

'You have all my attention, Herr Weber, I assure you,' said Colonel Lucas.

'Yes, calm down, sir,' said Sergeant Colley to the asylum-seeker, 'we don't go much on ructions. Best to stand on your dignity.'

'After what the Russian pigs did to me, you idiot, I expected to find—'

'Do be quiet, there's a good chap,' said Sergeant Colley.

Colonel Lucas stopped leafing. He looked up. Beneath the brim of his khaki cap, his blue eyes were glinting. Then he glanced down at a photograph. Following that, he consulted a list.

'Sergeant Colley,' he said, 'cap him. With C4.'

'Right, sir.' Sergeant Colley opened a cupboard, rummaged and brought forth the black cap of an SS officer. The German shouted with new fury as the cap was placed on his head. It was there for only five seconds before he snatched it off.

'This is intolerable, insulting—'

'Shut up,' said Colonel Lucas. He could be subtle in his interrogations, but had never been able to suffer fools or villains gladly. He looked once more at the photograph of a broad-faced man in the uniform of an SS officer. There was no scar to be seen. The scar on Herr Weber's jaw was very evident, very livid. Livid? Yes, of course. 'How did you come by that scar, Herr Weber?'

'Damn and blast, I was wounded serving with the Wehrmacht on the Russian Front! I had documents to prove it until the Russians confiscated them a few days ago. What those cursed pigs can do to beat a man's brains out—'

'Herr Weber, according to my records here, you are not who you say,' said Colonel Lucas. 'You are Maximilian Kurt Ziegler, once an SS officer. You were involved in the liquidation of the village of Lidice in Czechoslovakia and the extermination of its population. All the men, all the women, and all the children. Your scar is no more than four years old, and no doubt the wound was self-inflicted. I'm now informing you you'll be returned to the Russian sector—'

Almost at the speed of light, the German placed one hand on the desk and vaulted it, and as he landed beside Colonel Lucas's chair, he snatched up a heavy lead paperweight. He struck while issuing a spitting stream of obscene curses with such vocal violence that they might by themselves have reduced many a man to dumbfounded impotence. However, Colonel Lucas, an ex-commando born for action, reflexed instantaneously. His one arm shot up and his balled fist met the wrist of the hand that held the paperweight. The impact sent shudders through wrist and hand, while, with continuing fast movement, Colonel Lucas propelled himself backwards. He and his chair crashed to the floor. The German, savage, kicked him and lifted a booted foot to stamp on his thorax, a strike of lethal potential.

Sergeant Colley, shouting, hurled himself at this specimen indoctrinated by Himmler and knocked him sideways. The shout brought two British army MPs bursting in. Like a madman, ex-SS officer Maximilian Kurt Ziegler fought all three men. Sergeant Colley KO'd him with a violent blow to his scarred jaw. He went down poleaxed.

'Silly sod,' said Sergeant Colley, 'I told the bugger twice to stay quiet. You all right, sir?' he asked Colonel Lucas, helping him to his feet.

'Right enough,' said the colonel, 'but get rid of that paperweight, and I'll use a bunch of feathers in lieu.'

That evening, in the commandeered house that was the temporary home of his wife, his two children and himself, he described the events to Eloise.

'My God,' she said, 'you're still fighting a war. Resign and let's go home to England. Here we have no-one, except army personnel. In England we have families and friends. You have your parents, and I have my English father. I miss him. Luke, let us go home.'

'Damned if I won't think about it,' said Luke. 'This is no place for Charles and Pandora.'

Charles, aged six, and Pandora, aged two, were their children. 'West Germany is a nation of ghosts, shadows and ugly reminders of monsters and monstrosities.'

'And it's time you shook hands with civilization,' said Eloise. 'How many of those people will you advise the British authorities to deliver back to the Russians?'

'Five out of seven. The remaining two I'll recommend for consideration of asylum status.'

'Such problems and responsibilities you must give up,' said Eloise, 'and in favour of your responsibilities to your children and me. Luke, I am serious.'

'Well, so you should be,' said Luke, 'and you've made a hit. I'll talk to my superiors.'

'And you'll resign your commission and leave the army?' said Eloise.

'That's a different kettle of fish,' said Luke. 'I know only the army, and nothing of commerce.'

'Get a desk job in the War Office or whatever they call it now,' said Eloise.

'It's a place for failed army careerists and the infirm,' said Luke.

'I should like to point out that from what you've just told me, you could have been rendered infirm or even worse,' said Eloise. 'Ask for a posting back home, and then you'll have time to create a garden for your children.'

'Damn me,' said Luke, 'you're pointing me at a cabbage patch?'

'No, a peaceful life with me and the children, free of demanding orders,' said Eloise. 'And I must tell you that Charles and Pandora don't like cabbage. So grow lettuce, potatoes and runner beans. Oh, and plant an apple tree.'

Luke laughed, swept her inside his one arm and kissed her.

'You're still a precocious minx,' he said, 'but damned if I'd have you any other way.'

Evening in London.

Katje Galicia made another phone call.

'Hello?' A man's voice.

In went the pennies, and the connection was made.

'Good,' said Katje, 'you're there. Listen. It's to be Tuesday at three. Arrive at ten to. Ten to.'

'Right.'

'Don't forget your passport.'

'Of course not.'

'Don't forget it.'

'I heard you first time.'

'Just be sure. Goodbye.'

If there was one thing in this post-war world that made Felicity grit her teeth, it was television, the modern marvel of visual communication and entertainment. Understanding her frustrations, Tim had never made the slightest attempt to have a set installed. A modern radio, yes, that was a boon to the blind. A television set, no. And as far as he himself was concerned, what one never had one never missed. And that went for daughter Jennifer too.

Jennifer had reached the age of eight in close company with her mother's blindness, and accordingly was now a young girl with as much understanding as her father.

This evening, slipping into her bed, with Tim ready to tuck her in, she spoke to him.

'Daddy, we must never let one of those things into our house,' she said.

'One of which things, sweetheart?' asked Tim, who adored his sprightly daughter.

'A telly,' said Jennifer.

'Is that what little girls call a television set now?'

'It's what everyone calls them,' said Jennifer. 'But they're just an irritation to Mummy, so you must promise never to buy one.'

'I've never had any intention of doing so,' said Tim, a tall grey-eyed man close to thirty-two and very much like Boots, his father. 'We both know, don't we, that a – um – telly would make her throw a hammer at it. No, there'll be no set in our home, sweetheart, I promise.'

'Of course,' said Jennifer with a little girl's seriousness, 'you and Mummy could have a new radio, one for your bedroom. At school yesterday Lily Bessamy told me her parents had one with an alarm for waking up.'

'That's new,' said Tim.

'Yes, isn't it, Daddy? Crumbs, what's coming next?'

'A radio that cooks breakfast and does the washing-up, I shouldn't wonder,' said Tim.

'Daddy, it couldn't do that, could it?'

'It might come about,' said Tim. 'Some clever Dick might even invent one that does the Monday washing and hangs it out.'

Jennifer thought that very funny. She also thought it very satisfactory that he would never allow a telly to cross their doorstep and drive her blind mother potty.

As for the Monday washing, their maid of all work, Maggie Forbes, did that and hung it on the line too.

Tim, having tucked Jennifer in, kissed her good-night, switched off the bedroom light and went downstairs to spend the rest of the evening listening with Felicity to the Saturday evening play on the radio.

Felicity, curled up on a settee, had just caught a news flash.

'There's been some trouble in the British zone of West Germany,' she said. 'The Russians say that several war criminals due to stand trial managed to escape from a truck heading for Moscow. The truck broke down, apparently.'

'Soviet trucks do,' said Tim.

'The escapees crossed the border into the British zone,' said Felicity, 'and it seems the British are refusing to send them back, although they're legally obliged to do so.'

'They'll interrogate them first,' said Tim. 'What kind of war criminals are they?'

'German, according to the Russians,' said Felicity.

'Fanatical ex-Nazis, perhaps?' said Tim. 'Well, if the British prove that by interrogation, they'll return them to the Russians, or the Cold War will run a temperature and cause a blow-up. Incidentally, I believe Luke runs an interrogation unit close to the border with the Russian zone. I wonder if he's involved in this kerfuffle?'

'If he is,' said Felicity, who remembered Colonel Lucas and his uncompromising militarism when he was stationed with 4 Commando in Troon, 'any ex-Nazis he interrogates will wish they'd never joined. Come and sit, ducky, the play's just about to begin.'

The evening became typical of many they enjoyed in the quiet of their home. Such relaxing times made no demands on Felicity.

Chapter Seventeen

It was Sunday afternoon at Sammy and Susie's house.

Jimmy, just about to take a thriller into the garden for an hour's read, answered the ringing phone.

'Hold on,' he said, after a moment. He turned. 'Phoebeeee!' He sang the name and drew it out.

Phoebe responded from the kitchen.

'Jimmeeee?'

'You're wanted.'

'Where?'

'On the phone.'

'Who's calling?'

'Philip. Don't hang about or he might take off in a Spitfire in search of Marlene Dietrich.'

Phoebe appeared.

'He hasn't had flying instruction yet,' she said.

'No telling what an RAF cadet might get up to if Marlene Dietrich's not doing anything at the moment,' said Jimmy, and handed Phoebe the phone, as well as a broad grin.

'Philip?' said Phoebe.

'Hi there, Pussycat,' said Philip. 'I thought I'd

just ring and find out if your dad's relented and bought you a new bike, after all.'

'Well, fancy you asking,' said Phoebe. 'How kind. Yes, I do have a new bike, I expect it's because I'm one of my dad's loving daughters.' That quickly out of the way, she went on. 'Oh, Paula's home this weekend instead of at David and Kate's farm larking about with her Italian boyfriend. But he's coming here to tea, and we're expecting him any moment. So Paula's upstairs making herself look a Sunday afternoon dream.'

Philip asked if that was different from a Sunday morning dream, and Phoebe said well, a Sunday morning dream was a bit more holy, that's if she was going to church. Our vicar, she said, doesn't really go for unholy dreams unless they've come to repent.

'Might I ask how talk about a new bike turned into talk about Sunday dreams, holy or otherwise?' enquired Philip.

'Well, we talked a lot about bikes before,' said Phoebe, 'and we need a change. I once heard a radio programme which was a sort of discussion on what was called the art of dinner conversation, and one speaker said there was no art at all if someone stuck to the same subject all through dinner. Dad does that sometimes, usually about clever geezers who make a hole in his business overheads. Philip, could you recognize a geezer if you saw one?'

Philip said he supposed the bloke would be wearing a slicked moustache, a bowler hat and a loud tie. Phoebe said that was very educating to someone as ignorant about geezers as she was.

Well, spivs are geezers, said Philip, and you'd only get to know them if you bumped into one or two down a street market, where they'd be trying to sell pocketfuls of phoney watches. So you needn't worry about your ignorance, he said. Phoebe said she was surprised he knew so much about geezers himself, unless some were friends of his.

'What's happened to the art of conversation?' asked Philip. 'Let's talk about the art of dancing. Listen, if I manage to cop a hitch-hike on Friday evening, I could be home by ten and come round to have a chat with you by half past.'

'You'll be lucky,' said Phoebe. 'Mum won't let you in, because I'll be getting into bed by then, and she doesn't allow strange blokes to come up and chat while I'm in bed.'

'I'm not a strange bloke, I'm a relative,' said Philip.

'Yes, but you only turn up once a year,' said Phoebe, 'so you're as good as a stranger. Come to that, Mum doesn't allow any young men into my bedroom at any time. Nor does Dad. In fact, he'd flatten them with a club he keeps specially for that. What're you laughing at?'

'You,' said Philip.

'Listen,' said Phoebe, 'if you want to take me dancing regularly, you've got to treat me seriously.'

'I can't,' said Philip, 'you're too comical. Still, you're great as well— help, I've got to go. I'm using a forbidden phone and someone's coming. See you next weekend, you sugar baby.'

'Oh, goodbye, cowboy,' said Phoebe, and put the phone down.

Paula's Italian fancy, Enrico, arrived then, and Phoebe opened the door to him. On cue, Paula came swanning down the stairs to the hall in a kind of lilac gossamer.

'*Mama mia*,' said Enrico, Latin-dark and pop-eyed, 'is that your sister, Phoebe?'

'Yes, it's Paula,' said Phoebe, 'it's your Sunday afternoon dream, Rico.' And she left them to each other.

Paul and Lulu were in Brixton. Lately, they had been house-hunting. Tommy had said he'd make them a wedding present of enough money for a deposit on a mortgage.

'Pa, you're a good old dad,' said Paul.

'We're both grateful,' said Lulu.

'Oh, Tommy and me feel we'd like to give you young people a good start to your married life,' said Vi, much happier about Lulu now that she dressed in a more feminine way, even if she still had a few odd ideas.

This afternoon, by arrangement, Paul and Lulu were pointing themselves at Fairmount Road, off Brixton Hill. In this road, a house was up for sale which they hoped would suit them. They'd looked over properties in Kennington and Stockwell, without favouring any of them. Brixton, Lulu was saying as they walked up the hill, was as far south of real life as she was prepared to go. Anything beyond that, she insisted, was depressingly middle class.

'Shouldn't we just go for a house we like, even if it's in Streatham?' suggested Paul.

'Streatham? Streatham?' Lulu quivered. 'Paul, Streatham's full of bank managers and lace curtains. It's so middle class it ought to be emptied and filled with workers.'

'Sounds a bit hard on bank managers,' said Paul. 'Or at least on Mrs Bank Manager and her kids.'

'Oh, well,' said Lulu, 'perhaps my comment was a bit exaggerated.' Paul smiled. Lulu wasn't quite the uncompromising left-wing Socialist of former years. She made concessions. 'But I couldn't live in Streatham myself,' she went on. 'Not when my dad's an admired Labour MP who hardly had a pair of shoes to his name in his young days. As his daughter, I've got to keep faith with his honest working-class roots.'

Paul hid another smile. Her dad, known as Honest John, had told him a while ago that he now had invested savings. I know what a rainy day means, Paul me lad, he'd said, and I've turned thrifty. His second wife Sylvia, holding down a secretarial job, contributed to the kitty, so yes, he said, he did have a bit put by for their old age. But don't tell Lulu, he said, or she'll think I'm turning into a bloated capitalist.

The day was fine, if a little cloudy, and Brixton Hill, usually busy with people and traffic, basked in Sunday quiet. The owner of the house in question could only show prospective buyers around on Sundays, so the estate agent had arranged for him to let Paul and Lulu make their inspection this afternoon.

They turned into Fairmount Road, where the

terraced houses were typical of the Victorian residential development.

'Here we are,' said Paul, and they stopped outside Number 21. The first thing Lulu noticed were lace curtains ivory-yellow with age and in need of a wash. Well, at least they didn't look like middle-class curtains, just any old curtains.

Paul knocked on the front door. Its brown paint was peeling in places. A burly man in his forties appeared. In shirt, braces and trousers, he eyed them with a welcoming grin so wide that it split his rugged face in two.

'Hello, hello, you Mr Adams?' he said to Paul.

'That's me,' said Paul.

'Well, pleased to meet yer. I'm Gus Johnson. I've had me dinner, so come on, come in, and I'll show you and yer wife around.'

'The lady's my fiancée, Miss Saunders,' said Paul.

'How d'yer do, then, Miss Saunders, pleased to meet yer. Come in.'

Paul and Lulu entered a passage. A picture on the left, its dusty glass cracked, hung lopsidedly.

'Needs straightening,' said Paul, and in friendly fashion he attempted the gesture. The cord, dark with age, broke, and Paul caught the falling picture just in time. 'Sorry.'

'That's nobody's heirloom,' said Mr Johnson. It was a picture of an owl looking gloomy rather than wise. 'Ought to have dustbinned it years ago. Dump it on the floor against the wall, will yer, Mr Adams? That's it. Ta. This way.'

He led them into the parlour, which they immediately recognized as being in serious need of a non-stop twenty-four-hour spring clean. It smelled of dust, mould and neglect, and the tired-looking wallpaper, through which plaster showed in a multitude of places, needed stripping and burning.

'Not much lived in, is it?' said Paul.

'Well, I'm on me own, ain't I?' said Mr Johnson, a growl rumbling in his brawny throat. 'Come out of the bleedin' army, didn't I, at the end of the war. Yes, and where was me loving wife? Living it up with a Polish corporal in bloody Balham. I got her back, I tell yer, but she kept going off and went for good six year ago, but not before I put the bleedin' Pole in hospital. Know what the ruddy law did? Give me six months for assault and battery. So what with that and me trouble and strife doing me dirty, and me not having no kids, I ain't had the heart to be house-proud.' He glanced around questioningly, as if the parlour was a stranger to him. 'But don't let a bit of cracked paint put you off, friends. It's a house that'll still be standing up when I'm long gone. Me old dad bought it fifty year ago, and left it to me when he and me old mum turned their toes up halfway through the war. Come on, I'll show yer me bedroom now. It's where I mostly live, in me bedroom and kitchen.'

Paul looked at Lulu, and Lulu looked at him. He framed a few silent words.

'One of the suffering workers.'

They followed the man into the next room, a ground-floor bedroom. The bed wasn't made, the rumpled sheets looked grey and dingy, the mantelpiece was full of junk, and two empty beer bottles stood on the bedside table.

'There y'ar, friends,' said Mr Johnson, 'it ain't a royal bedchamber, I grant yer, but it's roomy and the fire draws up a treat in the winter. Not that I've lit one these last few winters. Well, yer don't bother much, do yer, when you're on your own and working like a carthorse at Plummer's Canning Fact'ry. Still, a young couple like you could spruce the place up with a bit of decorating, so don't take no notice of them beer bottles.'

'There's a few more just under the bed, Mr Johnson,' said Lulu.

'Yer don't say?' said Mr Johnson. He went down on one knee and rummaged about, testing one bottle after another by shaking them. 'Typical,' he grumbled, rising.

'Typical of what?' asked Paul.

'Of me perishing luck. They're all empty. Breaks yer heart, don't it? Oh, well, you only start worrying when you're dying, as me old sergeant used to say.' Mr Johnson indulged in a kind of gloomy laugh. 'He stopped worrying himself when he caught a nasty packet in Sicily. Blew his head off, and one of his legs went missing as well, poor old sarge. All done in here? Right, come on, then, and I'll show yer the kitchen.'

He did so, and Paul and Lulu wished he hadn't. The kitchen was another disaster area, with a mountain of unwashed crockery and utensils in the sink, a frying pan sitting next to a dinner plate and a beer bottle on the table, and the ceiling plaster showing ominous cracks. There was also a pungent odour.

Lulu inwardly groaned.

Paul said, 'Did you mention you mostly lived in here and the bedroom, Mr Johnson?'

'Well, I ain't one for wanting more than I've got,' said Mr Johnson, 'and I don't need more than I've got, not when I'm living on me own, and after what me wife did to me, I've gone off women and marrying again, which ain't said to offend you, Miss Saunders.'

'What's that smell?' asked Lulu.

'Eh? Smell?'

'Stink,' said Paul.

'Stink? Oh, half a tick.' Mr Johnson went to the sink, disturbed the unwashed mountain and sniffed. 'Bloody 'ell,' he said, 'sink's stopped up again. The bleedin' drain's blocked up again. I tell yer, everything unlucky happens to me. Still, it won't be your worry, I'll get someone in, and as you can see, it's got promise for a young couple, this kitchen. Just needs a bit of doing up. If I'd had the time I'd've done a bit of tidying before you come, like the estate agent suggested, but I just ain't found any time. Right, now I'll show yer the upstairs rooms and the lav and bathroom.'

'If you'll excuse us, Mr Johnson, I don't think we're interested,' said Paul, his sense of hygiene going spare at the thought of what the lav and bathroom would be like.

'Eh? What?'

'Sorry,' said Paul, 'but it's not the kind of house we're looking for.'

Mr Johnson didn't look disappointed. He looked disgusted.

'Might I ask why you've come here, then, and on me private Sunday afternoon, which I usually use for a kip?'

'We came to look it over, of course,' said Lulu.

'Well, you've only looked over half of it.'

'Sorry,' said Paul, 'but we've seen enough.'

'You mean you ain't going to make an offer?'

'Sorry,' said Paul again. 'We're not obliged to, Mr Johnson.'

'Well, you ought to be. What a bleedin' sauce, taking up me Sunday afternoon all for nothing.'

'Mr Johnson,' said Lulu, 'we—'

'I'll have the bloody law on you!' Mr Johnson was suddenly bawling and turning red. 'No, I won't. I'll do for the pair of you meself! Where's me old 303? I know, in the bleedin' larder.' He made a charge for the larder.

'Get going!' hissed Paul to Lulu, and they ran for the front door. Roars of rage sounded from the kitchen as Paul opened the door. He and Lulu hurled themselves out and hared away, making for Brixton Hill. A saucepan came whirling after them, followed by the frying pan. Both items fell short and clanged. Paul shot a backward glance. There he was, the barmy gorilla, out on his doorstep, shaking a fist and bellowing. What a character, thought Paul, no wonder his wife hopped the nest.

He and Lulu didn't stop running until they reached Brixton Hill, when they pulled up breathless.

'Poor bloke,' gasped Lulu. 'He's a victim of the war.'

'Off his wooden head,' said Paul. 'Lucky for us he didn't locate his 303 rifle. It was probably buried under a ton of junk. Ruddy earthquakes, the state of the place. Anyone who buys it would have to fork out for the cost of rebuilding it. I'll phone the estate agent tomorrow and let him know the bloke's a danger to prospective buyers.'

'He's just another worker of the world who's had a rotten deal under capitalism,' said Lulu. 'Still, he ought to have got his drain unblocked before we called.'

'He might have if he'd noticed the stink,' said Paul, 'but living like he does, I don't suppose he noticed at all. You all right, Lulu?'

'I'm alive,' said Lulu.

'Oh, good-oh,' said Paul, and they crossed the road to walk to a bus stop. A bus passed and pulled up at the stop some forty yards away, and at the same time they heard a bellowing roar. They looked back, and there was the burly, red-faced danger to life and limb, Mr Johnson. He was brandishing a saucepan as he careered off the pavement in pursuit of them. They began another flying run, towards the bus, reaching it just before it moved off. They leapt aboard, staying on the platform to watch the oncoming loony and his saucepan. The bus gathered speed and left him behind, still bellowing.

'He's ill, poor bloke,' said Lulu.

'So am I,' said Paul, 'with funk.'

'Well, we'll go home to my flat,' said Lulu. 'We can say our prayers of thanks there.'

'Let's say them on the bus,' said Paul, 'then when we get to your flat we can do something else, something that'll take our minds off Mr Johnson and his saucepans. That's it, something rapturous.'

His modern woman turned pink.

'Oh, no, you don't,' she said.

'Well, I'll be recovered enough to have a go,' said Paul.

'You'll run into one of my own saucepans,' said Lulu, who, to be frank, gulped every time she thought about what it was going to be like to lose her virginity on her wedding night. (Some modern women, it seemed, had similar flutterings to those experienced by coy Victorian maidens.)

'Off the platform, if you don't mind, and take your seats,' called the conductor from the interior. 'Standing on the platform ain't allowed in a moving bus.'

Nor is a hand on my bosom in my flat, thought Lulu, as she and Paul took their seats.

But Paul behaved himself, helping her to get Sunday tea for two on the table.

Strangely enough, her bosom felt disappointed.

Chapter Eighteen

Monday morning, and Sir Edwin, waking up, wondered again when Katje Galicia was next going to contact him in an attempt to force him into a corner. She was a creature of the time, the time of the Cold War, a conflict of ideologies between Communism and capitalism. Neither honour nor life was sacred to those engaging in the undercover war. Well, when the lady did make her next move, it was going to become a critical confrontation, for he was still determined to call her bluff.

Felicity had woken up much earlier. She wondered what the time was. She made an instinctive guess that dawn was just breaking. Most people would have known. Most people would have noticed early light fingering the window. All she knew was that she was awake, and so was her body, in a not unfamiliar way. Life was always a matter of coming to terms with its whims. She turned in the bed.

'Tim?' She touched him.

'Ur?' Tim came drowsily awake.

'Tim darling?' She touched him again.

Tim shot awake.

'Holy angels, Puss, mind my gear.'

'I need your gear. Make love to me.'

Tim, glancing at the illuminated dial of the alarm clock, breathed, 'At five o'clock in the morning?'

'There's got to be a first time for five o'clock in the morning,' whispered Felicity, and touched him yet again.

'Balls of fire,' breathed Tim, 'I haven't had my cornflakes yet, let alone my eggs and bacon, but all right, Puss, let's see if I'm working. You've asked for it.'

'I'm hoping I'll get it,' said Felicity.

They made love.

Felicity had none of Lulu's reservations.

Miss Clare Roper was walking in Victoria Park, close to her family's home in Bow, north-east of Bethnal Green.

Unemployed at the moment, she was restless. She was no friend of mental or physical inactivity. She traversed the paths almost irritably. Oh, blimey, she thought, it's still days and days away before I start my new job with Adams Fashions. I wouldn't be surprised if boredom didn't kill some girls. I think I'll go to the library and borrow a good book.

But she sat down instead, on a bench, and watched some old-age pensioners enjoying their daily constitutional.

A nice-looking plump woman came hurrying up. 'Oh, good, there you are, Clare,' she said.

'Oh, hello, Mum,' said Clare, 'I did tell you I was coming to the park.'

'Just as well you did, lovey,' said Mrs Edith Roper, daughter-in-law of Gertie and Bert Roper. 'A girl from the Adams fact'ry called with a note for you, saying someone name of Dodie had fell ill – look, here it is.'

Clare, instantly feeling she'd come to life, took the note and read it. It was from Jimmy Adams, and it said Dodie was away sick, that one of the office girls was operating the switchboard after a fashion, and was it possible for Clare, if she was free, to come in and do the honours until Dodie returned in a few days? If so, wrote Jimmy, my gratitude will know no bounds.

Clare, delighted, said, 'Oh, thanks for bringing the note, Mum, I'll go right away.' The time was coming up to ten thirty.

'You'd best come home first and I'll do you some sandwiches to take for your lunch,' said her motherly parent.

'No, you don't have to do that,' said Clare, 'they've got a staff canteen.'

'Oh, yes, course they have,' said Mrs Roper, 'I forgot in me hurry to come and find you.'

'Oh, but p'raps I will come home first and change into something more suitable,' said Clare, whose dress wasn't one of her best.

Later, it was a revitalized young lady who skipped off to Bethnal Green.

'Come in,' called Jimmy in response to a knock on his office door, and in came Clare, dressed in a white shirt-blouse, a little dark green bow tie and a short dark green skirt, pleated. It was an outfit she'd bought specially for her new job, along with alternatives.

'Mister Jimmy, here I am – thanks ever so much for your note – I'll be pleased to look after the switchboard till Dodie comes back – I'm not doing anything special at home except helping me mum a bit – or getting in her way.' Clare sounded a little breathless in her rush of words.

'Well, good morning, Miss Roper,' said Jimmy, thinking what excellent dress sense this young lady had. That was the kind of thing that went down well in a garments factory. 'Compliments on your outfit. Very attractive. And I'm delighted to see you in this hour of need. What a gracious girl you are to answer my call for help so quickly.'

Clare felt she was being mesmerized. She'd never ever had any feller talk to her like Jimmy Adams did. Mind, would some people call him a smoothie?

'Mister Jimmy, it's really nice of you to say so,' she said. 'Shall I start work now?'

'Pardon?' said Jimmy, frankly lost in his contemplation of this vital-looking young lady. Blowed if she isn't as stunning as I always felt Jenny Osborne was, if not more so.

'Mister Jimmy?'

'What?'

'I asked if you'd like me to start right away.'

'Oh, something must have screwed up my hearing,' said Jimmy, and came to his feet. The phone rang. He picked up the receiver. 'Yes? Pardon?

Sally, I've lost you.' He looked at the phone. 'Poor young Sally,' he said to Clare. 'She's trying, but she's cut me off, and the caller too, I daresay. Could you take over, Clare?'

'I'd be pleased to,' said Clare.

'What an obliging girl you are,' said Jimmy, giving her a very appreciative smile. Clare tingled. 'Come on, then.'

He took her into the general office, where the girls greeted her with whoops and glad cries.

'Welcome, Clare!'

'That switchboard's a beast.'

'Look after her,' said Jimmy, 'treat her as if she's a saviour, which she is. Good luck, Clare, and thanks.'

Clare took her place at the switchboard, and almost at once a call came through, and with it an impatient voice.

'Mr Carter here. What's going on? I've been cut off twice. What a shambles. Can I talk to Jimmy Adams or can't I?'

'Hold the line, Mr Carter,' said Clare in her purring switchboard voice. 'So sorry about our troubles at this end. I'm putting you through.' She rang Jimmy and established the connection smoothly.

She felt kind of richly happy.

Two well-spoken gentlemen sporting bowler hats had arrived in Brunswick, West Germany, to talk to Colonel Lucas. It was considered by London, they said, that the wisest course to take would be to return all seven escapees to the Soviet zone.

'Wisest?' said Colonel Lucas, not sure he liked

the officially correct demeanour of these messengers from the Foreign Office, an establishment well known as the citadel of bowler hats and self-infallibility. 'Wisest?'

'Ah – to avoid a diplomatic crisis.'

'The interrogation of all seven people has convinced everyone here that two of them are completely innocent of war crimes,' said Colonel Lucas. 'Accordingly, gentlemen, I'm not going to be responsible for returning them to the Russians.'

'Ah.' The bowler hats looked at each other.

'Ah what?' said Colonel Lucas, rarely in tune with the servants of politicians or politicians themselves, aside from Winston Churchill, the war leader who proved unafraid to make the boldest of decisions and damn all fainthearts. Unfortunately, the old boy, having expended so much effort on winning back his position as Prime Minister, was becoming too tired to exercise the kind of dynamic control that had been so much in evidence during the war.

'Colonel Lucas, our own responsibility is to point out to you that in the event of any – ah, shall we say understandable misapprehension or confusion regarding the suggested course of action, you will receive orders clarifying exactly what your duties are.'

'Whose orders?' asked Colonel Lucas, not given to being intimidated, particularly by any of Whitehall's bowler hats. 'The Prime Minister's?'

'We assure you, our authority is unimpeachable.'

'Then do me the favour of informing the unimpeachable that I am not, repeat not, going to send two innocent people back to the Soviet zone,' said Colonel Lucas, rugged frame as inflexible as his manner. 'The other five, yes, they'll be handed over at our border with the Soviet zone at the agreed time of five this afternoon.'

'Ah.'

'Yes?'

'Unfortunately, Colonel Lucas, that won't do. The Soviet ambassador in London has been informed that all seven will be handed over.'

'Unfortunately for whoever made that concession,' said Colonel Lucas, 'a representative of the Moscow Soviet has already accepted our offer to return only the five in question. Here on my desk I've a document and a signature.'

'Moscow agreed to this?'

'Yes, at noon today,' said Colonel Lucas. 'London has been signalled. Contact your principals for confirmation. You should have been recalled as soon as you arrived here. As to my own position at this point, since my authority was to be overruled, London must accept my resignation as the chief investigating officer in Brunswick.'

'Colonel Lucas, there's no need to resign.' The bowler hats looked dismayed, as if the situation was now of a personally damaging kind, the kind that could reduce their standing and even affect their pensions. Certainly, the mandarins at the Foreign Office would take no blame for Colonel Lucas's resignation. 'No need at all, we assure you.'

'Let me tell you there's every need as far as I'm concerned,' said Colonel Lucas, 'and let me also tell you I shan't go back on my decision.'

He was not too unhappy about that, for he knew Eloise would be delighted. It meant she could make plans for a definite return to England. The army would not deny him a transfer to some kind of home command.

The bowler hats were left with the hope that they could keep the news of the resignation from becoming public. Really, these army chaps were very touchy.

That evening, Clare's mum and dad asked her how she'd got on at the factory.

'Oh, marvellous,' she said. 'I didn't make no mistakes, even though it's a bigger switchboard than at Parsons Engineering. There's any amount of extensions.' She listed some. The overall manager, Mister Tommy Adams, his assistant, the canteen manageress, the workshops' supervisors, the maintenance foreman, the man in charge of the loading bays, and others. 'Oh, and Jimmy Adams too, of course,' she said.

'Thought you wouldn't forget him,' said her dad with a grin.

'Well, he's a lovely feller, Dad,' said Clare incautiously.

'Pretty?'

'Pretty? Don't be daft, Dad.'

'Well, I'll admit he didn't strike me as pretty when I saw him at your grandparents' retirement party.'

'So why'd you just ask if he was?'

'Forget meself,' said Mr Roper, who worked as a foreman at a lumber yard in Wapping, where extensive bomb damage was still being made good. There were many areas in London, particularly around its docklands, that still needed redevelopment. Churchill's Conservative government was hoping private investment would be interested enough to save hard-working taxpayers from forking out. 'Anyway, carry on, Clare.'

'About what?' asked Clare, now cautious. There was always this feeling that she simply had to keep her infatuation to herself, much as if disclosure would mean being laughed at. Well, young ladies going on for nineteen shouldn't suffer the kind of crushes that afflicted schoolgirls. And she sometimes supposed it was just a crush she had on Jimmy Adams, and that it would go away in time. 'Yes, about what, might I ask?'

'About Jimmy Adams,' smiled her mum.

'The lovely feller,' said her dad.

'Oh, I just remembered, I'm going round to see Daisy Hitchings this evening,' said Clare, and off she went. Daisy was surprised to see her, but made a very flattering comment about her outfit, saying the little bow tie was ever so catchy. Then she asked how Harry was.

'Harry?' said Clare.

'Harry Dallimore,' said Daisy.

'Oh, him,' said Clare.

'Does he still go on about football and John Wayne?' asked Daisy.

'I'm sure I don't know,' said Clare, 'I ain't seen him for weeks.'

'Lummy,' said Daisy, 'have you said a fond goodbye to him?'

'Well, he's just not much of a grown man yet,' said Clare.

'Well, he ought to be,' said Daisy, 'he's over twenty.'

'He's sort of lagging,' said Clare.

'Here, let's go up West,' said Daisy, 'and see if we can bump into real grown-up fellers. I'm going off blokes with adenoids meself.'

'I'll go up West with you, but not to get picked up,' said Clare. 'I'm not that kind. Let's look in dress-shop windows.'

'Me on my skimpy wage?' said Daisy. 'I can't even afford window-shopping.'

'All right, let's go to the pictures,' said Clare. 'I'll treat.' She'd had the kind of day that made her feel happy and expansive, especially as Jimmy had showered her with thanks and smiles when she left. In fact, he'd given her the impression that he really had got a very soft spot for her.

So she and Daisy went to a cinema, and they caught the extremely popular film *High Noon*, starring Gary Cooper. Clare sat through it in absorbed fashion, dreamily identifying Jimmy Adams with Gary Cooper. Oh, Lor', she said to herself at one point, I've got to grow up a bit myself or I'll get kind of unbalanced.

'Had something of a problem at the factory this morning, Dad,' said Jimmy over supper. Supper always took place in the panelled dining room, its pleasant family atmosphere inducing content in Susie, its central heating a boon in winter, and a framed enlargement of a wedding photograph of herself and Sammy hanging on one wall.

'Eh?' said Sammy. Problems were unwelcome, they could get out of hand and cause unprofitable hold-ups. 'Did your Uncle Tommy sort it out?'

'No, I did, with the help of Clare,' said Jimmy.

'Clare?' said Susie.

'Clare?' enquired Paula and Phoebe as one.

'Clare Roper, our forthcoming new switchboard operator,' said Jimmy, and recounted the details, including how Sally, one of the office girls, got her knickers in a twist with callers until Clare arrived.

'You're telling me a switchboard's a problem?' said Sammy. 'Jimmy me lad, that's only a fag-end.'

'Not for me,' said Jimmy, 'I'm responsible for an efficient general office, among other things, which include listening to heartbreaking recitations from some of the machinists who keep losing control of their private relationships. I'm getting careworn, Dad, in case you haven't noticed.'

'Oh, dear, what a shame,' said Paula.

'Is his hair falling out?' asked Phoebe.

'I hope not,' said Susie, 'or I won't be able to look Grandma Finch in the face. Grandma Finch prides herself that Adams men don't go bald, so don't you get to be different, Jimmy.'

'I must say Clare Roper's a bit of a stunner,' mused Jimmy over his helping of shepherd's pie.

'Like Jenny Osborne?' suggested Paula.

'Yes, like Jenny,' said Jimmy.

'Has she got a boyfriend?' asked Phoebe.

'Yup,' said Jimmy. 'Still, I think Joyce Nightingale is starting to favour me.' Joyce Nightingale was a neighbour's daughter and one of a crowd of friends who enjoyed the social scene together.

'Jimmy, she's drippy,' said Paula.

'Pretty, though,' said Jimmy.

'Crikey, I'll get sick if something happens,' said Phoebe.

'What something?' asked Susie.

'Something like me waking up one day to find Joyce Nightingale is my sister-in-law,' said Phoebe.

'Oh, I get you,' said Paula. 'Mum, what's for afters?'

'Peaches and ice cream,' said Susie.

'Tinned peaches?' said Sammy.

'Fresh imported,' said Susie. 'Our greengrocer's getting to be ever so sweet to me.'

'Watch him, Dad,' said Jimmy.

'I ain't too bothered,' said Sammy, 'he's got no teeth and can't even suck his own lemons.'

'Mum, if it's really fresh peaches and ice cream,' said Phoebe, 'I won't feel so sick about what might happen with Joyce Nightingale. Well, in any case, I'm sure our Jimmy wouldn't ever be as careless as that.'

'Oh, I see,' said Jimmy, 'it would be an act of carelessness, would it, if I married Joyce?'

'Yes, like slipping on a banana skin,' said Phoebe.

Sammy roared with laughter, the girls went hilarious, Jimmy grinned good-naturedly, and Susie, smiling, went to fetch the dish of peaches and the ice cream.

* * *

Boots and Polly switched on their television set to catch the BBC's nine o'clock news broadcast. Nothing dramatic was happening on the home front, apart from the threat of another strike by the coal miners.

'If any workers have a genuine grievance, it has to be the miners,' said Polly. 'Imagine working down a black hellhole to earn one's daily bread.'

'A coal-black hellhole, Polly,' said Boots.

'Parliament needs blowing up to be woken up,' said Polly. 'Come back, Guy Fawkes.' Except for those of a statesmanlike kind, such as Clement Attlee and Winston Churchill, Polly had very little time for politicians, of whom she thought there were far too many in Westminster, since she knew that the USA, with a much greater population, made do with about half the number. Because of the Tommies she had known during the Great War, Polly always identified far more with the common man than politicians. 'Even if I were capable enough with a pick and shovel,' she said, 'I'd not work down a mine for all the gold in the Bank of England. The men who do should be paid a decent wage, and a lot more on top of that, if you'll excuse my hot blood.'

'Help yourself to a soapbox, and I'll hand you a megaphone,' said Boots. 'It's a sad fact that men born in a mining village can see no other way of life open to them. That's the curse of being trapped from birth.'

'How right you are,' said Polly.

Then they sat up, for the announcer reported that the crisis in West Germany was over, that the

Soviet Union, after its representative's negotiations with the British army unit in Brunswick, had accepted the return of five suspected war criminals out of the seven people who had crossed into the British zone. The transfer had taken place at five o'clock, although not without an internal disagreement at the British army headquarters, which had resulted in the resignation of the officer in charge, Colonel William Lucas, an ex-commando war veteran who had conducted the negotiations.

There was a glimpse of Colonel Lucas leaving headquarters, and brief though the glimpse was, he looked a formidable figure. He refused brusquely to be interviewed by the BBC's man on the spot.

'Well, I'm damned,' said Boots, 'Luke's made the headlines.'

'I fancy, Boots old sport, that someone mucked him about,' said Polly. 'Hence his resignation. Eloise will be up in arms and very ready to be interviewed herself. Oh, joy, she'll spit.'

'Judging by her letters to us,' said Boots, 'I'd say she'll now concentrate on persuading Luke to ask for a transfer back home.'

'That will please you?' said Polly.

'I'd like to see her again,' said Boots, 'and Luke and the children.'

'You old darling,' smiled Polly, 'you're as much of an old-fashioned family man as Tommy and Sammy are. You all get it from your mother. But from where or whom, I wonder, did you get that which she calls your airy-fairy self?'

'I probably picked it up on a tram in my young

days,' said Boots. 'You could pick up anything on a crowded tram, including measles, sniffles and orange peel.'

'I'm a happy woman, old love, knowing you survived,' said Polly. 'And Luke and Eloise will survive this kerfuffle.'

She and Boots weren't the only members of the family who caught that particular news item. So did Tommy and Vi, Sammy and Susie, Lizzy and Ned, Daniel and Patsy, Bobby and Helene, as well as Jeremy and Bess, down in Kent, and Rosie and Matthew up in their Woldingham poultry farm. Nor did Chinese Lady and Sir Edwin miss it. Felicity and Tim caught it on their radio. Family phones began to ring. As always when the unusual affected them, the family buzzed like bees carrying the news of a new source of honey to their hives.

Chapter Nineteen

When Clare woke up on Tuesday morning she felt quite relaxed, so much so that she was able to tell herself she'd come to her senses, that her silly crush on Jimmy Adams had gone. Yes, I think I can see him as just another feller. What a relief. Fancy me at my age going about like a droopy schoolgirl.

On arrival at the factory she entered the general office and said hello to the girls already there.

'Morning, Clare.'

'There's that troublesome old switchboard, Clare.'

'It's all yours, Clare.'

The switchboard burped. Office 4 showed up. The office of the personnel manager, Mister Jimmy.

She answered.

'Yes, Mister Jimmy?'

'Glad you're here again, Clare. Pop into my office for a tick, will you?'

'Of course, Mister Jimmy.'

Clare went in, feeling quite in charge of herself.

'Good morning, young lady,' said Jimmy, bright and breezy. 'With the approval of the girls, I picked up a bunch of flowers on my way here. They're for you. Gesture of gratitude for coming to our rescue so quickly yesterday. Put 'em in a bucket of water until you leave at the end of the day.'

'Beg pardon?' Clare looked at the large bouquet of irises and then at him. He smiled. Her pulse rate jumped, and everything she thought she'd left behind came back into being. 'Oh,' she said. 'Oh,' she said again.

'Oh-oh?' said Jimmy. 'Is that what flowers do to you?'

'No, I just feel a bit overcome,' said Clare. In her very attractive outfit of yesterday, she looked to Jimmy like a welcome return of yesterday. 'Well, I mean, all them flowers – I mean – Mister Jimmy, I don't know what to say.'

'Have a banana,' said Jimmy.

'Pardon?' said Clare.

'That's always good for a laugh,' said Jimmy. 'Come on, take the flowers and plop them in a bucket of water. You deserve 'em.'

'Oh, thanks ever so much,' said Clare.

'You're welcome,' said Jimmy.

Clare began another happy day, and decided not to bother about trying to fight her feelings. Feelings were natural, but for the sake of your pride you had to make sure they didn't escape and run about for everyone to see.

Jimmy was trying very much to fight his own feelings, while hoping Harry Ballymore would buzz off back to Ireland, if that was where he came from.

* * *

At twelve minutes to three that afternoon, a taxi pulled up outside a three-storeyed house in Bloomsbury. Out stepped a tall man in a well-fitting dark grey suit and a light trilby hat. Silver-grey hair was visible. He paid the driver, took a few leisurely strides to the house and studied the nameplates of tenants. He pressed the button of an electric bell. After about twenty seconds the door was opened by Katje Galicia. She smiled at the visitor.

'So, you're here, Sir Edwin,' she said. 'Please come in.'

Her visitor entered and she closed the door.

From a point fifty yards away, Bukov and Alexandrov discussed what they had witnessed.

'Well, she was right,' said Alexandrov, 'she's brought him to us.'

'One might say in a little while that she's brought us to him,' murmured Bukov, ever a man of suspicion.

'You don't intend we should pass up the opportunity of meeting Finch, do you?' said Alexandrov.

'I wouldn't be here if I intended that,' said Bukov. 'He may still have enough useful contacts for us to turn him into a mole. I suggest we make our move now, minutes in advance of our appointed time.'

In her ground-floor flat, Katje was addressing her visitor.

'Everything is ready, everything. They're down the street, and we can be sure their back-up man isn't far away. You're quite ready yourself?'

'Ready and willing.'

'Good,' said Katje. 'Don't show yourself until I call.'

The bell rang only seconds later.

Katje opened it.

'You're very punctual,' she said.

'Where is he?' asked Bukov.

'Come with me,' said Katje, closing the door. She led the two KGB officers to her sparsely furnished living room, its only item of any value being a large square of patterned red carpet, on which stood a plain table. The room was adjacent to her kitchen.

Since no-one was present, Bukov, eyes darting, repeated his question.

'Where is he?'

'Oh, he's here, Comrade Colonel,' said Katje, 'and I'm sure you noted his arrival. First, however, I must say something to both of you.'

'Be quick, then,' said Alexandrov, 'we aren't here for a gossip.'

'First,' said Katje, 'I wish to refer to the murder of two thousand Polish officers at Katyn. Their bodies, you remember, were uncovered by the Nazis in 1943.'

'They uncovered the work of their own barbaric deed,' said Alexandrov.

'Which has nothing to do with this meeting,' said Bukov.

'Bear with me,' said Katje. 'You aren't the only KGB officers I know. I also know one who defected.'

'What the devil are you on about, woman?' rasped Bukov. 'It's well known that KGB officers don't defect. We're too careful about the characters of those we enlist.'

'Even so, a few have defected,' said Katje. 'This one did, and when speaking to him of the Katyn massacre he informed me he had seen documents in a special section of the main Soviet Archives that prove the massacre was initiated by Beria, once your undisputed chief. He also informed me that you two, along with other KGB officers, were at Katyn where, on orders from Beria, you took part in the cold-blooded murder of these Polish officers.'

'Katje Galicia, you are out of your mind!' hissed Bukov.

'Among the murdered officers were my husband and brother,' said Katje.

'Drivel!' spat Alexandrov. 'A Nazi act, I tell you. In any event, a lot you cared for your husband, since we know you were constantly unfaithful to him.'

'Not constantly, occasionally,' said Katje. 'Nevertheless, I had affection for him. As my husband, he was also the father of my son.'

'A son whose escape from the Republic of Poland to the West you contrived,' said Bukov. 'That will go against you. Now, have done with your ravings and let us meet the man Finch.'

'Very well, I don't intend to disappoint you.' Katje lifted her voice. 'Sir Edwin, please to come in.'

An inner door opened and in from the kitchen came the tall man in the dark grey suit and light grey trilby hat. He walked straight up to Bukov, and a revolver, with a thick black silencer attached, appeared lightning-fast. Its snout pushed into Bukov's chest, and with both KGB men momentarily transfixed, despite their training, experience and their still active reflexes, Bukov received a point-blank bullet in his heart. The sound was merely that of a muffled phutt. Bukov dropped, face ghastly, eyes turning upwards in his death throes.

Alexandrov choked on a paroxysm of rage. His hand darted inside his jacket. A second bullet was fired. It buried itself in his burly chest, and a third followed as he staggered. He collapsed across the body of Bukov. For a split second his eyes glared up at Katje. Then he shuddered and died.

'Well, Mama?' said Jan Lukic, a man of thirty. Lukic was his father's name. His mother, an officer in the Polish army before and during the war, used her maiden name.

'Very well indeed, my good and obedient son,' said Katje. 'Yes, all over in seconds, and without a sound, except for a gurgle from Boris Alexandrov. Now perhaps the bones of your father and your Uncle Peter will rest in peace.'

'It's been a long time, Mama,' said Jan, his slim and straight-backed figure not unlike that of Sir Edwin Finch.

'Twelve years,' said Katje, 'but I feel it's taken me a hundred to catch up with these KGB pigs. Jan, tidy up while I find out where their pudding-faced errand boy is. Be ready.'

Jan removed his hat, jacket and a silver-grey wig.

He rolled up his shirtsleeves. Tidying up meant the removal of all extraneous bloodstains. Katje went to the front door of the house. She opened it and showed herself. She smiled. There he was, the lump of a man said by Alexandrov to be her protector and bodyguard. He was lurking in a doorway across the street. She waited until two pedestrians were out of the way and the street was clear. Then she beckoned. The KGB errand boy hesitated before he walked across and arrived at the door. Katje gently drew him in. She closed the door while the street was still clear.

'You have instructions for me?' he said.

'I have none myself,' said Katje, listening for the sound of footsteps that would tell her a tenant was coming down the stairs. 'It's our Comrade Colonel who has. It's to do with a message he wishes you to deliver. Yes, you may come through. I'll lead the way.'

He followed her into the living room. He stopped, his jaw sagged and his eyes popped at the sight of the dead men. He stared in paralysed disbelief at the Polish woman. From behind the door stepped her son. The KGB junior officer turned, and received a phutting discharge from the revolver. Another followed.

He was the third KGB man to die in Katje's Bloomsbury flat, the one flat that was on the ground floor.

She and her son went quickly to work. They moved the table, rolled back the large square of carpet, and lifted floorboards already loosened.

Katje was no beginner in matters of life and death, and she had every Pole's thirst for revenge, when revenge was a demanding concept.

The floorboards, placed aside, revealed deep gaps between widely spaced joists. Mother and son worked quickly, but without any sign of worry. There was no phone to disturb them. A phone, Katje knew, would have been bugged, and so she used public facilities.

One by one they lowered the corpses into the gaps. Each was a dead weight, but Jan was a man of vigour and Katje was strong.

'Mama,' said Jan, 'one could almost say these gaps had been made for them.'

'Well, they fit very nicely,' said Katje, breathing a little fast from her exertions. 'Now, my son, let us put the lids on their coffins.'

The floorboards were carefully replaced, and so were the nails, which Jan drove home with some gentle, muffled taps of a hammer with its head covered by baize. Katje produced a dustpan. It contained the dust she had swept up early this morning. She spilled it lightly over the replaced floorboards, and those that surrounded the 'coffin lids'.

Finally, Jan rolled back the carpet and put the table back in place.

'The devil will give them a welcome,' he said.

'The devil received them years ago,' said Katje. Neither she nor her son showed regret for their deed. She advised him she had given her landlord a week's notice four days ago, telling him she was returning to Poland. Therefore, her departure would not be unexpected. Jan said that the unexpected would be the sudden disappearance of three KGB officers.

'A balloon will go up,' he said.

'Oh, the Soviet ambassador, after a day or so, will demand to see Britain's Foreign Minister and accuse him of being responsible for the illegal detention of three Soviet journalists from their Press Bureau,' said Katje. 'There will be one more diplomatic crisis, and the Iron Curtain will rattle and shudder. We shall not be here.'

'When do we leave?' asked Jan. He and his mother were standing beside the carpet-covered tombs of the dead.

She looked at her watch.

'In twenty minutes,' she said.

'Are we taking a taxi to London Airport?'

'I am taking a ride on the Underground to Ealing Broadway, and you are taking a bus there,' said Katje. 'I'll wait for you, and when you arrive, then we shall use taxis, you in one, while I travel in another. At the airport, we will board separately. Here is your ticket. Jan, you have your visa?'

'I have it, Mama, and all else I need.'

'Good. We shall begin a new life in America, where freedom is prized above all other privileges. You will takc up your post as a doctor in Vermont, and I will find myself a rich American husband.'

'I wish you luck,' said Jan, 'but must point out you're no longer quite as young as you were.'

'I'm young enough for a rich American of sixty,' said Katje. 'That reminds me, I have a letter to post when I leave.'

'A letter to a rich American?' said Jan.

'To an English gentleman, Sir Edwin Finch.'

'Finch? Finch? But he was once –'

'A German?' Katje smiled. 'He was born a German, yes, but he's a natural English gentleman, and a man I'd seek to marry if he didn't have a wife.'

'Great God,' said Jan, 'I have it from your own lips that he's well over seventy.'

'There are some men who, at any age, are preferable to most others,' said Katje. 'I saw Sir Edwin only twice during the time I was planning to bring Bukov and Alexandrov to this flat, although they believed I had several meetings with him. I blush for the worry I gave him.'

'I'm to believe that?' said Jan.

'Of course,' said Katje. 'Blushes don't always show. Now, one last look around, and then you will leave by the back way. I'll lock the door after you, and use the front door myself when the street is clear. We must sow confusion among any KGB investigators who poke their noses into this flat. Don't forget that before you take your bus ride, you must pick up your suitcase at the Marylebone railway station. I'll pick my own up a little later. You have the left-luggage ticket?'

'Don't fuss,' said Jan. 'I told you, I have all I need.'

'One can't be too careful when one has just sent three KGB officers to the devil,' said Katje. 'Now, this last look around.'

They made a careful sweep of the flat, satisfying

themselves that they had left nothing to indicate three men lay dead and buried here.

Then they left, Katje first seeing Jan out by way of the back door, and locking it after him. A minute later, she herself departed, posting a letter on her way to the Marylebone railway station.

The empty flat was silent.

Chapter Twenty

By evening of that day, the undercover element of the Soviet Press Bureau was in a ferment about the disappearance of the three KGB officers. The first assumption was that someone had blown their cover, and that they had been picked up by British Security men. That was dismissed almost at once, since their ambassador had received no official notification of any arrest.

'Well, would you believe it,' said Clare's fond mum when her daughter arrived home with a huge bouquet of irises, 'I never saw such a big bunch of flowers. Your dad's never come home with a bunch like that. Did Harry meet you from work and give them to you?'

'Mum, I've told you and Dad more than once that I'm not seeing Harry no more,' said Clare. If that was a kind of complaint, she didn't look the part. She looked glowing. As Jimmy had noted, she had a rich colouring, not unlike his cousins Annabelle and Emma, daughters of Aunt Lizzy and Uncle Ned.

'Oh, sorry, love,' said Mrs Roper. 'Did you buy them yourself for the house?'

'No, Jimmy Adams gave them to me.' Clare smiled reminiscently. 'In what he said was a gesture of gratitude for me gracious appearance as a stand-in for Dodie.'

'He said what?' asked Mrs Roper, busy in her kitchen with supper preparations.

'Well, something like that,' said Clare, unwrapping the blooms. 'He's ever so good at using words.'

'If I remember right,' said her mum, 'your grandma once told me all the Adamses can use words like most other people never could. They must've been born of talking machines.'

'No, it's not like that, Mum,' said Clare, hunting for a suitable vase on the top shelf of the kitchen cupboard. 'Jimmy doesn't natter on. He says what he has to say, then it's your turn. And he listens, which makes a talk with him really pleasing.'

'And it was him that gave you all them irises?'

'Yes, for helping out with the switchboard.'

'My, my,' said Mrs Roper, whipping a saucepan of hot custard into creamy perfection.

Clare, arranging the irises to form a spreading galaxy in the decorative glazed vase, said, 'What d'you mean, my, my?'

'Oh, nothing much, love,' said her mum, pouring the custard into a jug, 'except, well, I can't say me and your dad are too upset that you're not seeing Harry no more. Your dad was saying you've got the kind of looks that ought to interest some young man that's got a lot more to offer than Harry ever will. Mind, it wasn't said unkindly.'

Clare, deciding not to pursue the topic, and knowing her mum was thinking of Jimmy Adams, said, 'There, don't the flowers look lovely in this vase? I'll put them in the parlour and then go upstairs to tidy up after me day at the switchboard – oh, that reminds me, Jimmy's Uncle Tommy, the fact'ry manager, came in to talk to me. Ain't he a handsome man? He was really nice to me. I feel I'm really going to like working at his fact'ry. Oh, well, here goes.' She took the vase of irises into the parlour, and then went up to her room.

Sitting at the dressing table, she gazed at herself in the mirror. She lapsed into a daydream. It's all come back again. I can't help meself. I'm never going to feel – what's the word? Oh, yes, I've read it in books. Fulfilled. Yes, I'm never going to feel fulfilled unless I get to be Mrs Jimmy Adams. Help.

Clare came to and laughed at herself.

At home, Jimmy was taking a shower and musing on what was currently most pleasing to his optics.

Clare Roper, of course. A colourful cockney girl with a natural dress sense, a rattling fine figure, gorgeous brown eyes, and a super pair of legs. Well, I'll be frank with myself, he thought, I'm like Dad, I first of all favour feminine females. I find an eyeful like Clare a lot more visionary to a bloke than a fat woman smoking a pipe. Wait a minute, have I ever seen a fat woman smoking a pipe? Yes, once. In an old Western. A fat Red Indian woman having a powwow with Buffalo Bill in her wigwam, him sitting cross-legged, and her letting smoke rings rise from her pipe. What was the dialogue now?

'You heap dirty paleface with crooked tongue.'

'Aw, no, I'm a good friend of Chief Running Cloud.'

'You still heap dirty paleface with crooked tongue. Why you crying?'

'I guess it's all this smoke.'

Have a banana.

I'm going sideways, and I know who's doing it to me. Gertie and Bert's eldest granddaughter. In conjunction with Harry Ballymore. Why did he have to enter her life before I did? Luck of the Irish, I suppose.

'Jimmy!' That was Paula, keen on an Italian bloke. Talk about a cosmopolitan world closing in on the family.

'Yup?'

'Is that you in the shower?'

'Is it? Half a mo, I'll have a look. Yes, it's nobody else, Sis, it's me.'

'Ha ha, Funnycuts. Well, supper's nearly on the table, and Mum says if you're not down in five minutes, you'll only get dry bread.'

'Have a heart, Paula, I haven't scrubbed my back yet, and inside five minutes I'll still be all wet.'

'Oh, damp hard luck,' said Paula. 'You'll have to put up with dripping all over your chair.'

Down the stairs she went, singing.

There was nothing in the evening's news bulletins about three Russians who'd gone absent from their work with the London section of the Soviet Press Bureau. There had, however, been a great deal of discreet investigation after the British Foreign Office had assured a Soviet Embassy official that no members of their staff were suspected of being persona non grata. Therefore, no-one was being held for questioning.

In Lubyanka, Moscow, the impregnable fortress of the KGB, with its underground torture chambers so soundproof that the screams of the victims never disturbed the ears of anyone above, the news that two senior officers and a junior had disappeared in London had not yet arrived. The London section was hoping it would not have cause to send it.

Chapter Twenty-One

Wednesday morning.

Chinese Lady received a letter from Susie's mother, Mrs Brown, an old friend.

Sir Edwin received two letters, one from his insurance company concerning the renewal of his house and contents policy, the other a brief one from Katje Galicia.

> 'Dear Sir Edwin,
>
> 'Your troubles are over. You need have no more worries. You must believe me when I tell you I never intended to harm you in any way. In this world there are very few real gentlemen. You are one of them.
>
> 'I send you my love and respect. May you exist in happiness. Goodbye. Katje Galicia.'

There was no address.

With Chinese Lady absorbed in her own correspondence, Sir Edwin allowed himself a little sigh of relief. How right he had been not to burden Boots with his worries. This letter convinced him, if he needed convincing, that he was also right to hold fast to the secret of those years before and during the Great War, the war that had ravaged France and Flanders.

He sipped his breakfast tea. Tea, English tea. How many cups had Maisie served him in their time together? Thousands. Unobtrusively, he slipped Katje Galicia's letter into his pocket.

He had never trusted her. But he liked her, and that liking, by reason of her letter, seemed to be based on sound instinct. Silently, he wished her well.

'Maisie?'

'Yes, Edwin?' Chinese Lady looked up from Mrs Brown's chatty letter.

'It's a fine day,' said Sir Edwin. 'How about a leisurely drive into the countryside and finding a place that will serve us an appetizing lunch?'

'Well, that would be nice,' said Chinese Lady. 'You sure you can manage a long drive?'

'True, I'm a little ancient, my dear, and so is our banger, but –'

'Banger?' said Chinese Lady, refilling their teacups.

'Um – that, I believe, is how certain people have referred for years to cars as old as ours,' said Sir Edwin. 'However, I'm sure that our ancient automobile and myself will be able to convey us as far as we care to go, especially as the garage filled the tank yesterday.'

'Well, if you're sure, Edwin,' said Chinese Lady. A thought struck. 'Why don't we go and visit that boarding school where you were educated?'

Sir Edwin looked rueful. Occasionally, awkward

reminders of words spoken to camouflage the truth arrived two or three at a time.

'Unfortunately, Maisie, it's long been closed.' It had never existed. At least, not in England. 'And even if it weren't, the journey would be too long. Shall we simply go where the car takes us?'

'I don't mind, Edwin,' said Chinese Lady. 'Except I will if it takes us into somewhere we won't like. Like a field of cows. As a little girl on country holidays, I never got on with cows.'

'Well, you're not a little girl now, Maisie,' smiled Sir Edwin. 'All the same, I promise to avoid any that might be lying in wait for us.'

'You're a kind man, Edwin,' said Chinese Lady.

'Paul,' said Lulu, 'we've got to come out in positive favour of Ho Chi Minh.'

Ho Chi Minh of Vietnam was leading the rebellion of his people against their colonial masters, the French.

'We?' said Paul, busy on behalf of the constituency's agent.

'The Labour Party,' said Lulu.

'Oh, good,' said Paul, 'I thought you meant you and me, and I'm busy right now.'

'Don't be futile,' said Lulu.

'Listen,' said Paul, 'Ho Chi Minh is a raving Communist, and the Party can't give positive support to a Red fanatic without losing a hell of a lot of votes.'

'Well, we can't support French oppression,' said Lulu, with the spirited defiance of her kind.

'And further,' said Paul, 'as your prospective husband I want some respect from you.'

'Oh, kiss me quick, I don't think,' said Lulu.

'I'm not an aggressive bloke,' said Paul, 'but I'm having to think seriously about turning you upside down and spanking you. Not here, of course. In your flat, say.'

'Like to see you try,' said Lulu. 'You'd end up dead.'

'All the same, watch out, Lulu,' said Paul.

'Typical of a man, resorting to brute force,' said Lulu. 'But you wouldn't, would you?'

'At the moment, I'm only thinking about it,' said Paul.

'Well, get this,' said Lulu. 'I'm doing some thinking myself. About not being daft enough to marry a man who'd assault me.'

A woman, secretary to Mr Allen, the agent, came in.

'Hello, lovebirds,' she said. 'Happy days, eh? Memo for you, Paul, from Mr Allen.'

'I've already got six in front of me,' said Paul, taking it, 'but what's one more?'

'Yes, what?' said the woman. 'Anyway, a good time's coming, Paul. Lulu will tickle your fancy, won't you, Lulu?'

'I refuse to comment on that puerile remark,' said Lulu.

'Don't be like that, ducky,' said the woman and went back to where she came from.

'What vulgarity,' said Lulu.

'Cheer up, love,' said Paul. 'Let's be friends again, shall we? I don't want to miss out.'

'On what?' asked Lulu.

'Having you tickle my fancy,' said Paul.

Lulu surprised him then. She shrieked with laughter.

Chinese Lady and Sir Edwin were travelling south on the A233 road. A signpost caught her eye.

'Edwin, look, we're near Westerham,' she said, 'that's where David and Kate have their farm.'

'True, Maisie, we are near,' said Sir Edwin.

'Well, we ought to call in,' said Chinese Lady. 'I don't know what they might think if we just drove past without seeing them.'

Sir Edwin smiled. The attraction of any place belonging to a relative was of the kind his wife could never resist. She would, in any case, consider it a family duty to drop in.

'Very well, Maisie,' he said. 'I think there's a turning leading to their farm a few miles on.'

'Yes, I remember it from before,' said Chinese Lady.

'On the left,' said Sir Edwin.

'It's a shame David and Kate don't have any children yet,' said Chinese Lady, who thought any married couple without issue were sadly deprived.

'They're still young,' said Sir Edwin, who, in his days of cloak-and-dagger adventurism, had known women, but had never had children of his own.

He took the turning to the farm, a country lane of gentle descent. The hedgerows were prolific with early summer growth, and wild primroses peeped at the passing car. Halfway down to a bend, Sir Edwin lightly pressed the footbrake. Nothing happened. The car ran on, beginning to gather speed. Sir Edwin applied his foot more firmly. No response. He pulled on the handbrake. Nothing happened to slow the car down.

'Edwin,' said Chinese Lady, 'you're going a bit fast, love.'

Inside the bend was a gate. It was open. Outside, a milk churn stood on a raised thick plank of wood. Sir Edwin did the only thing he could think of before he lost complete control of the car. He swung the steering wheel wide. The car rushed over the verge, bumping and shaking, and through the open gate.

'Edwin!'

The car travelled on over the lumpy grassy field. The heads of a herd of cows lifted, and brown bovine eyes watched the bumping metal intruder while jaws chewed. Fortunately, the field sloped slightly upward and that, together with the rough going, brought the car to a stop.

'Prayers answered,' said Sir Edwin throatily. He was frankly shaking with relief at the avoidance of disaster and death.

Chinese Lady, appalled by what she considered criminally reckless driving, gasped, 'Edwin, don't you ever do anything like that again. I was never more shocked or frightened in all my life. We didn't have to get to the farm as quick as that.'

'Are you all right, Maisie?' That was Sir Edwin's one concern at the moment.

'I'm not hurt, if that's what you mean,' said Chinese Lady, quite pale, 'but I don't know when my legs are going to stop shaking. What made you start driving like a – yes, like a lunatic gone off his head?'

'Alas, Maisie –'

'Don't give me no alas,' said Chinese Lady, cross and suffering.

'To be frank, Maisie, the brakes failed.'

'What d'you mean?'

'They failed to work. Perhaps our ancient chariot is too ancient.'

'Oh,' said Chinese Lady. 'Oh, I'm sorry I spoke so angry. Edwin, we could have been killed. You did wonderful, turning like you did into this field – oh, my goodness, look at all them cows!'

'And look at someone coming,' said Sir Edwin.

A young man, having entered the field by a gate at the far end, was running towards them. His feet flew over the ground. He rushed up to the car.

'Excuse, no cars, please. Cows don't-a like cars. Also, this field is private.'

Sir Edwin wound the window down and spoke.

'Good morning, Enrico.'

Enrico Cellino, a dark, sinewy Italian in his twenties, stared, blinked and then let his teeth show in a gleaming smile.

'Ah, Signor Finch, yes? And I see, yes, Signora Finch also.' He knew them both, having met them when they visited the farm in company with Tommy and Vi on two occasions. 'Welcome, signora, how fine you look. But I ask, signor, why do you drive into this field? The farmhouse is more down the lane.'

Sir Edwin opened the door and detached himself from his old banger.

'I'm delighted to see you, Enrico,' he said, 'and the reason why we're precisely where we are is the result of brake failure.'

'Signor?'

While Chinese Lady stayed in the car to avoid any close encounters with the cud-chewing cows, Sir Edwin explained. Enrico, a demonstrative Latin, rolled his eyes in horror at what might have befallen this elderly couple, the grandparents of a young lady he was courting with hope and enthusiasm, Paula Adams.

'The signora, she isn't hurt?' he said, bending to peer in concern at Chinese Lady.

'I'm just a bit shaky, but all right, Mr Chello,' she said.

'We were lucky to find that gate open,' said Sir Edwin.

Enrico, large of heart, declared himself overwhelmed with gladness that, for once, he had carelessly left it open. He had only come back to the field, he said, because he remembered his mistake.

'But how glad I am that I did leave it open,' he said. He begged them to stay where they were while he went to fetch Signor David's car. He would ask him to phone a garage for help.

'Thank you, Enrico,' said Sir Edwin.

'I go,' said Enrico.

'Wait,' called Chinese Lady in nervous apprehension, 'the cows are coming.'

The whole herd of beasts was on the move, heading in curiosity towards the car.

'Not to worry, signora, they are very friendly,' said Enrico, and off he went at a run.

'Edwin,' breathed Chinese Lady, 'get back in the car or they'll run you over – oh, Lor', I never did know a time like this.'

Sir Edwin, although not greatly worried himself, got back into the car and closed the door. That eased her nerves to some extent. The enquiring cows lumbered up and surrounded the car, and here and there large red tongues licked at it.

'Yes, they are friendly, Maisie,' smiled Sir Edwin.

'Edwin, you sure some of them aren't bulls?'

'Quite sure, my dear.'

'Well, I wish they weren't so big – Edwin, there's one looking right at me.'

'Wind your window down and give it a pat, Maisie.'

'Edwin, I hope you're not trying to be comical at a time like this.'

Chinese Lady felt herself besieged. In her book, cows were far more intimidating than burglars.

It was David himself who came to their rescue. He arrived at the closed gate in his car. He jumped out, opened the gate, and half a minute later his car rolled in, its horn hooting. The startled cows lumbered back to their pasture. Not long after that he was driving his grandparents to the farmhouse, while listening to what Sir Edwin had to say about the incident of failed brakes, and what Chinese Lady had to say about finishing up in the middle of hundreds of cows.

'Not quite as many as that, Gran,' said David, a robust man of twenty-seven living the kind of open-air life to which he had become addicted during his years as a wartime evacuee in Devon. He still kept in regular touch with Jake and Beth Goodworthy, the kind-hearted couple who had looked after him, together with his sister Alice and his brother Paul. It was Jake who had taught him so much about farming, including the subtle way of keeping cows contented, and Beth who had endeared her hospitable self to him. 'By the way, Grandpa,' he said, 'I've phoned a local garage, and they'll send a breakdown truck to pick up your car and tow it in for an examination of your braking system. You and Grandma can stay and have lunch with us.'

'Oh, we don't want to be no inconvenience, David,' said Chinese Lady.

'You won't be,' said David, pulling up beside the attractive farmhouse.

Inside, they met Kate, also twenty-seven and as robust in her own way as David after her years on the farm. Her work in the dairy had contributed to that.

Irrepressible in her vitality and personality, and a reminder to all the family of David's late Aunt Emily because of her rich dark auburn hair and her green eyes, she greeted Chinese Lady and Sir Edwin exuberantly as they entered her large, airy kitchen.

'Grandma! Grandpa! Lovely to see you. Ever so sorry about your rotten brakes, Grandpa, but ever so glad you didn't suffer no harm.' Kate had never let go of her cockney roots, and had once told David that she didn't think her late good old dad, a trade unionist, would have approved of her marrying a middle-class bloke. David had said well, if he did his best to be more like her and her good old dad, would that help? Oh, all right, said Kate, but of course she really liked him as he was.

She hugged David's grandparents in frank affection.

'Tell them, Kate,' said David, 'let them be the first in the family to know.'

Kate smiled.

'Well,' she said, 'I went to see me doctor this morning, and I only got back a bit ago. Grandma, Grandpa, I'm going to have a baby at last. What d'you think, ain't that lovely?'

'Oh, what a blessing,' said Chinese Lady, a rare beam lighting up her face. 'Kate, I was never more pleased for you and David.'

'Oh, thanks,' said Kate. 'Of course, David thinks it's all his own work. Talk about the way husbands kid themselves.'

'I'm sure it was a mutual accomplishment,' smiled Sir Edwin.

'Mind, I was beginning to think I might end up as an old maid,' said Kate.

'Kate, an old maid is an elderly spinster,' said David.

'Oh, you know what I mean,' said Kate. 'Grandma, would you and Grandpa like David to show you round a bit of the farm while I start doing the lunch?'

'Well, a little walk would be nice,' said Chinese Lady, so David, giving work a miss until after lunch, took them on a leisurely stroll to the dairy, Kate's own daily habitat. There they met Joyce Hope, a fat and jolly woman taken on by David a year ago. Joyce, fat though she was, had a rare capacity for work and a happy enjoyment of it. David and Enrico did most of the outdoor work. Their herd of cows increased year by year, and David was waiting to acquire extra land.

On cue, Sir Edwin said, 'Weren't you and Kate going to combine with Rosie and Matthew and farm a larger area?'

'We're having to wait until the owners of the adjacent farm decide to sell,' said David. 'We've made an offer and they're considering it, but have asked for another year to make up their minds. For a merger with Rosie and Matthew, and Emma and Jonathan as well, we need land three times our present size, especially as Rosie wants to continue poultry farming. If we get it, then we'll really be in business, although it might bring my wrinkles on early.'

In the end, Chinese Lady and Sir Edwin spent the day there, and very happily. At five, the garage brought the car back, its bald brakes fully relined and the brake fluid renewed. The car had also been given a service. Sir Edwin paid the bill on the spot.

David and Kate came out to see the grandparents off, and to say how great it had been to have them.

'Grandma,' said David, 'I'm sure Kate and I can leave it to you to spread the glad news, and save us the trouble.'

'Well, David,' said Chinese Lady, missing the twinkle in his eye, 'I'll be downright pleasured to tell all the family.'

'Ta and thanks, Gran,' said Kate, and kissed her goodbye.

There were no incidents or alarms on the way home, which meant that later in the evening Chinese Lady was in fine enough fettle to begin informing her family by phone that Kate was expecting at last, what a blessing.

Chapter Twenty-Two

At seven in the evening on Thursday, Boots answered the ringing doorbell. In the drive stood a Daimler limousine. On the step stood a willowy woman, a brunette of fine, if sultry, looks. He judged her to be in her late thirties. Beside her was a young girl in a gingham school dress, dark hair fashioned in what could be termed an old-style bob that curved over her cheeks, reminding him of the Colleen Moore style favoured by Polly all through the Twenties and Thirties. Wide hazel eyes were bright with young life.

'Hello,' he said with a smile, 'what can I do for you, little lady and escort?'

The woman, dreamy eyes regarding him with frank approval, said, 'Forgive this unannounced call, but are you Mr Adams?'

'I am,' said Boots.

'I'm Mrs Davidson of Woodwarde Road.' That was in the exclusive heart of Dulwich Village. 'This is my daughter Cathy.'

'Hello,' said Cathy a little shyly.

'Hello yourself, Cathy,' said Boots.

'Do you have a son called James?' asked Mrs Davidson.

'I do,' said Boots.

'Cathy would like to see him.'

'Yes, Mummy's brought me so that I can ask if James could come to my birthday party on Saturday,' said Cathy, engagingly precise.

'Well, lucky young James,' said Boots. 'Come in, both of you, and I'll call him.'

'Thank you,' said Mrs Davidson, entering the wide hall with her daughter.

'James?' called Boots.

James called back from the study, in which he was allowed to do his homework without distractions.

'What's up, Dad?'

'You've a visitor,' said Boots.

'Me?' James's boyish voice, floating out, was edged with surprise. 'I can't remember I've ever had a visitor.'

'Well, you have one now,' said Boots, 'so show yourself.'

Out came James, a boy in his twelfth year, with his father's deep brown hair, grey eyes and firm features, his slim, supple body showing signs that he was likely to become as tall as Boots. He was attending Alleyn's, Dulwich's famous public school. At the moment he was in his school shirt and trousers, the shirt unbuttoned at the neck, his tie loose and his hair rumpled. It was that kind of appearance which often made Polly think of the rumbustious hero of the 'Just William' stories by

Richmal Crompton, but she always refrained from telling James to brush his hair or do up his shoelaces. The image was too endearing.

'Here's your visitor, old lad,' said Boots.

James, seeing Cathy, stopped. His eyes opened wide.

'Gosh,' he said. He had the same kind of ready smile as Boots, and it came into being. 'That's not a visitor, Dad, that's Cathy, a friend of mine. Hello, Cathy, you're looking nice.'

Cathy blushed a little, just a little. She didn't know that blushes were supposed to be going out of fashion.

'Oh, you don't mind my mother bringing me to see you?' she said.

'Of course not,' said James, taking an interested look at the dark attractive lady. 'How d'you do, Mrs Davidson, pleased to meet you.'

'How d'you do, James,' said the lady.

'James, I've actually come to ask if you can be at my eleventh birthday party on Saturday,' said Cathy.

'Eleventh?' said James, no more prone to youthful inhibitions than Boots had been at his age. 'Well, isn't eleven supposed to be a turning point for girls, or is it twelve? Is it twelve, Dad?'

Boots, fascinated by this development, said, 'It's twelve that puts a girl on the way to her teens.'

'Oh, well, Cathy's only got a year to go,' said James.

'Yes, just a year,' said Mrs Davidson, who seemed more taken with Boots than with his outgoing son.

'Still,' said Boots, 'even if it's only her eleventh,

I'd certainly go to her party, if I were you, old chap.'

'Well, I will,' said James, 'thanks very much, Cathy.'

The delicious young lady looked blissful.

'It starts at four o'clock,' she said. 'Saturday,' she added, as if she needed to make sure James wouldn't arrive on Sunday.

'Where did these two meet?' asked Boots of Mrs Davidson.

'On their way home from school, I believe,' she said.

James said yes, on his way home from school about a month ago, when the heel of Cathy's shoe had come off, and he'd banged it in for her on the pavement. Then they walked home together, and he'd met her several times since.

'Yes, James was a wizard with my shoe,' said Cathy. 'Mind, the heel came off again, but not till I was home.'

Gemma came down the stairs at that moment, looking like a young version of her mother. She eyed Cathy with interest.

'Hello, where did you come from?'

'She's James's friend, Miss Cathy Davidson,' said Boots. 'Cathy, this is Gemma, James's sister.'

'Oh, hello,' said Cathy with a friendly smile, 'James has told me about you.'

'He hasn't told me about you,' said Gemma, who regarded her brother as her own property, but had learned from parental homilies that he wasn't a teddy bear she could keep to herself and lock away when other girls were around. So her possessiveness had mellowed. 'Still, I don't mind.'

'Gemma,' said Boots, 'this lady is Cathy's mother, Mrs Davidson.'

'Oh, hello,' said Gemma, just as uninhibited as James, 'isn't it nice we've all got mothers?'

'Dear child,' said Mrs Davidson, a slight drawl to her voice, 'it's nature's way.'

'Bless me, Daddy's never told me that,' said Gemma, and turned to Cathy. 'Listen,' she said with sisterly mischievousness, 'did you know James bites?'

'Oh, what does he bite?' asked Cathy. 'I mean, he hasn't bitten me.'

'What a relief,' said Gemma, 'he's bitten all kinds.'

'All kinds of what?' asked Cathy, glancing at James. He rolled his eyes.

'Chicken legs and lamb chops,' he said, and Cathy laughed. Her mother looked at Boots. They exchanged smiles, hers of a winning kind, his of an easy kind.

'Well, I'm jolly glad I'm not a chicken leg or lamb chop,' said Cathy.

Boots said, 'Would you and Cathy like to stay a while, Mrs Davidson, and meet my wife?'

Mrs Davidson looked at her watch.

'Thank you, Mr Adams, but we do have to get back home for dinner now,' she said. 'I'm delighted to have met you and your children. Perhaps we'll have the pleasure of meeting again. Goodbye.'

'So long, Cathy,' said James.

'Oh, goodbye, James, don't forget Saturday,' said Cathy, and Boots saw mother and daughter out. Mrs Davidson gave him another smile, then returned with Cathy to her gleaming limousine.

'I could have walked Cathy home actually,' said James. 'That's if you could have finished my homework for me while I was gone, Dad.'

'Could you have lived with a refusal?' said Boots. 'I'll help with your homework at any time, old lad, but I'm on my honour as a parent not to actually do it.'

'I just can't believe all this,' said Gemma, 'specially about James walking girls home at his age. I don't get boys walking me home, and I don't expect I will until I'm at least –' She paused for thought. 'At least twelve.'

Polly appeared.

'What's been going on out here?' she asked.

'Gosh, Mummy,' said Gemma, 'what d'you think? James has started to walk girls home.'

'Have you, James?' said Polly, showing a smile.

James explained how he had come to meet Cathy, that as he had been brought up not to pass by old ladies in trouble or girls with the heel of a shoe off, well, what else could he do but fix the heel and then walk her safely home? He'd bumped into her several times since.

'Well, she's a nice girl,' he said.

'I see,' said Polly, 'so is there a problem?'

'Not at all,' said Boots, 'the little lady is so impressed that she called to invite James to her eleventh birthday party on Saturday.'

'Well, I'm blessed,' said Gemma, 'no-one told me.'

'Her mother brought her along,' said Boots.

'I suppose she thought that right and proper,' said Polly, 'I'm not sure I've ever been too right and proper myself. It's fuss-making.'

'Oh, Cathy's mum wasn't a bit fussy,' said Gemma. 'She was sort of dreamy and slinky.'

'Slinky?' said Polly. 'Now I'm on my guard. If she calls again, don't anyone let her in. Remember our watchword. Nothing slinky must ever cross our doorstep.'

'Is than an old watchword?' asked Boots.

'No, brand new,' said Polly. 'What was this slinky woman's name?'

'Mrs Davidson,' said Boots.

Gemma and James went open-mouthed as their elegant mum gave a little yell.

'Never!' she cried theatrically.

'Something tickling you?' said Boots.

'I know that woman,' said Polly. 'I met her at one of Stepmama's charity functions.' Her stepmother, Lady Simms, although now seventy-two, still involved herself in the field of good causes. 'Slinky indeed. She's a man-eater.' Polly went on to say the woman's grandparents were Russian aristocrats who escaped the Bolsheviks and settled here with their daughter, who married an Englishman. She produced a daughter in turn, who married a man called Davidson and became a widow when he lost his life during the battles in Italy.

'You managed to find out the family history at a charity do?' said Boots, smile lurking.

'The information came from Stepmama,' said Polly. 'Children, bolt all doors, put barbed wire around the house and lock up your father somewhere safe. Anastasia Davidson is on the prowl.'

Boots looked highly amused, James looked disbelieving.

'Anastasia?' he said.

'It's a Russian name,' informed Gemma. 'Mummy, d'you mean Cathy's mother is Mrs Anastasia Davidson?'

'I do,' said Polly.

'Gosh,' said James, 'what a mouthful. Still, she seemed quite nice.'

'She isn't,' said Polly, 'and I despair at having to tell you and Gemma that your father is in mortal danger.'

'Crikey,' breathed Gemma.

James hid a grin. It wasn't the first time he'd heard his entrancing mother being a bit dramatic with and about his dad. She was a real yell on those occasions, and could easily have done Lady Macbeth at the Old Vic. Of course, his dad hardly turned a hair, even though he always had a kind of front-row seat.

His dad coughed.

'Might I point out, Polly, that the lady and I had never set eyes on each other until a short while ago?' he said.

'She's seen you somewhere and asked about you,' said Polly. 'That's why she turned up with Cathy, who could easily have walked here by herself.'

'Ah,' said Boots. 'H'm,' he said. 'James,' he said, 'perhaps you and Gemma had better get busy with the barbed wire.'

Gemma and James looked at each other, then at

their parents. Then everyone looked at everyone else. Gemma began to giggle, James began to splutter, and Boots coughed again. It was too much for Polly. She began to laugh.

Moments later, they were all laughing.

Colonel Bukov and Lieutenant Colonel Alexandrov had left very little in the way of notes. In the typically secretive fashion of all senior KGB officers, they kept details of their activities to an absolute minimum until such time as any one particular commission was successfully completed, when that success would be recorded, and so add further credit to their diligence and efficiency on behalf of the Soviet Union.

However, by the time a top KGB man arrived from Moscow at noon on Friday, underlings had at least discovered that Bukov and Alexandrov had been engaged in some kind of operation with the Polish agent, Katje Galicia, and a man called Finch. They had also just discovered the Polish agent's address.

Midway through the afternoon, the important man from Moscow, accompanied by four junior officers, went to Bloomsbury, an area forever associated with the late Virginia Woolf, to confront Katje Galicia. She was not at home. At least, she did not answer the door of the house in which her flat was situated.

The man from Moscow, bulky and beetle-browed Lieutenant General Kersch, ordered the door to be opened without smashing it down, since he didn't want other tenants or passers-by poking their noses in and sending for the police. Members of the London section of the Soviet Press Bureau had no authority from the British Foreign Office to smash down doors, only to gather news for the interest of the Russian people.

The door was eventually opened by a key, one of a large bunch, and the five men poured silently into the hall. Again a key unlocked a door, and they entered the Polish agent's flat. An exhaustive search began. It was a search for anything that would offer a clue to the whereabouts of Katje Galicia and the three missing KGB officers, as well as a revelation of the identity of a person called Finch.

The place was ransacked. Every kind of receptacle, every drawer and every possible hiding place was searched, but of papers, letters and documents there was a complete absence. A small table standing on a large square of carpet in the living room was turned upside down without revealing a thing. The carpet itself was turned back. Carpets often covered secrets.

This one covered a grisly secret, but not of the kind Lieutenant General Kersch was looking for, or even thought of looking for. His prevailing suspicion was that the missing men and the Polish agent, seduced by the fleshpots, the shops, night life and entertainments of recovering post-war London, had defected. It might be an unbelievable possibility, but the suspicion existed.

'Nothing?' he said, when the carpet was rolled

back into place in consideration of leaving everything tidy. 'Nothing?'

'Nothing, Comrade General.'

'Impossible.'

'She has flown, Comrade General, and left her cupboards bare.'

'The fireplaces?'

'Empty. Not even a single ash.'

'Some of you will pay for not keeping a closer eye on Bukov. Did none of you at any time suspect all three officers were showing signs of embracing the decadence of this corrupt city?'

Before any denials came, a key turned in the lock of the door. The five KGB officers alerted in anticipation of seeing Katje Galicia. Ah, here she is, thought Kersch, as into the living room walked a handsome woman accompanied by a portly man.

He seized the moment to say, in Russian, 'So, here you are, Katje Galicia.'

The handsome woman said to her companion, 'What's he saying, for God's sake, and what are all these men doing here? You told me this flat was vacant.'

Kersch, understanding English and missing the gestures of an underling who had once met Katje Galicia, said, 'I won't be fooled.'

'You won't what?' said the portly man, bristling. 'I don't know who the hell you are, but I'm George Fisher, the owner of this house, and this lady is the prospective tenant of this flat. What the devil are you and these other men doing here, and how did you get in?'

Lieutenant General Kersch, too experienced

not to recognize what was genuine and what was bluff, sighed.

'I must apologize,' he said politely. 'We came looking for a friend –'

'All five of you?'

'We are all her friends, close friends. And I assure you, we did not force an entry, no, no. The door was not locked.'

'If you're talking about the woman you mentioned, Miss Galicia, she gave up her tenancy three days ago, on Tuesday,' said the landlord. He made a quick survey of the men. None was carrying a case or holdall. Not that there was anything of real value to be stolen, except the carpet, which Miss Galicia had bought herself, and, apparently, had either forgotten to take with her or had left as a gift. 'I demand you leave, all of you, or I'll call the police.'

'Again, my apologies,' said Lieutenant General Kersch, and he left quietly, with the junior officers. Halfway down the street, he spoke raspingly of inefficiency and dereliction of duty, which did the underlings no good at all. 'This person Finch,' he said. 'Consult a London telephone directory and make phone calls until you alight on the obvious.'

'How are we to know the obvious?'

'Tell the person who answers that you have a message from Katje Galicia to deliver. An affirmative or guarded response will tell you you've found the man or woman she was in touch with. Unless –' He checked. 'Unless that man or woman has defected too.'

'Defected? You are speaking of all of them?'

'That must be considered.'

'In respect of Comrade Bukov and Alexandrov, Comrade General, we can hardly believe defection was ever in the minds of such officers.'

'It must be considered.'

'Very well, Comrade General.'

Chapter Twenty-Three

Saturday morning was eventful. To begin with, RAF Cadet Philip Harrison, having arrived home late Friday night for his weekend leave, phoned Phoebe after breakfast.

'Hello, Pussycat, Philip here.'

'My, how thrilling,' said Phoebe, 'but do I know you?'

'Yes, I'm the feller who's taking you dancing tonight.'

'Oh, you're that Philip,' said Phoebe.

'Is there another one, then?'

'Goodness, yes, not half,' said Phoebe, 'there's Philips all over the country, and I daresay in Australia too.'

'Cheeky chops, watch your saucy self. Anyway, how are you this morning?'

'Oh, just a day older than I was yesterday,' said Phoebe. 'Actually, so's everyone. Mum says that's one of the blessed nuisances of life, that you're always older tomorrow than the day before.'

'I'm learning to live with it,' said Philip. 'Best thing, y'know, Phoebe.'

'Wow, aren't you comforting,' said Phoebe.

They chatted away, and at the end Philip promised to call for Phoebe at seven to take her dancing again.

Then there was Clare, who had found overnight that her wages envelope from Jimmy contained three pounds ten shillings for her four days at the switchboard. Seeing her weekly wage was four pounds, which was sixteen shillings a day, she'd been overpaid by six shillings. It gave her an excuse to phone him this Saturday morning. She could, of course, have waited until Monday, as it seemed unlikely that Dodie would be back by then. But she didn't wait.

It was Jimmy himself who answered the phone.

'Hello?'

'Oh, hello, it's Clare here, Clare Roper.'

'What a pleasure,' said Jimmy.

'Pardon?'

'Nice to hear from you,' said Jimmy.

'Thanks, Mister Jimmy,' said Clare.

'It's Jimmy out of office hours, Clare.'

'Oh, friendly, like,' said Clare, pleased.

'That's it,' said Jimmy, wondering just how friendly she was with Barry Hallymore. Eh? What am I talking about, it's Harry Ballymore. Still, I can't help hating the bloke, whatever his name is.

'I hope you don't mind me phoning you on a Saturday morning,' said Clare.

'You can phone me any time,' said Jimmy, always a very agreeable young man. 'I'm just in from the garden, having done some planting and now hoping for a coffee break.'

'Oh, d'you like gardening?' asked Clare.

'It's a hobby of mine,' said Jimmy. 'It used to be Daniel's, my brother, but I took over from him with some help from my dad after Daniel got married. He had other things to do then. You could almost see his label.'

'What label?' asked Clare.

'The "Just Married" one,' said Jimmy, and heard her laugh.

'Jimmy, you're really funny,' she said.

'I'll get over it,' said Jimmy, 'and I still like gardening.'

'So do I,' said Clare, although her experience was limited to using a watering can. 'Except we've only got a small garden.'

'Well, we've got a large one,' said Jimmy, 'so you can come and help me put in some runner bean seedlings this afternoon, as well as a lot of bedding plants in our herbaceous borders.'

'Help you?' said Clare, who had been thinking about spending the afternoon with her friend Daisy.

'Only joking,' said Jimmy.

'Oh, but I'd like to,' she said impulsively.

'You're offering?' said Jimmy.

'Well, I'm not busy this afternoon,' said Clare.

'It's a long way for you to come,' said Jimmy.

'But I don't have to walk,' said Clare. 'There's trams and buses.'

'What a rattling good idea,' said Jimmy. 'You're

a thinking girl, Clare, like my mother. She's always thinking up how to stop my dad talking in his sleep.'

'Oh, some people do that, talk in their sleep, don't they?' said Clare. 'What does your dad talk about?'

'Business overheads,' said Jimmy.

'He doesn't, does he?' said Clare.

'All the time, except when he's muttering about what taxes are doing to him,' said Jimmy. 'Or except when Mum puts one of his socks in his mouth. That was something she thought up. One morning Dad said his left sock was missing. Mum told him he'd eaten it in the night.'

'Oh, crikey, you'll give me hysterics in a minute,' gasped Clare, a newly entertained young lady.

'Anyway, if you're serious about it, come up this afternoon,' said Jimmy, delighted at the thought of seeing her. He told her to make for the Elephant and Castle and to catch a bus there for Denmark Hill. Did she know where his home was?

'Yes, it's in our phone direct'ry,' said Clare, who had looked up his dad's number before ringing.

'Better bring your gumboots,' said Jimmy.

'What?' said Clare.

'No, never mind, you can use Mum's,' said Jimmy. 'She's got pretty feet, just like yours.'

'Jimmy, you've never seen me feet,' said Clare.

'I'm a good guesser,' said Jimmy. 'So long now until this afternoon.'

Clare, who simply couldn't wait, said, 'I'm sure I'll get there.'

As soon as she put the receiver down she remembered she hadn't told him her reason for phoning, and he hadn't asked. Did that mean she didn't need a reason, that she could phone him whenever she liked? Actually, he'd said so.

A little later her mum said, 'Clare, you're walking about in a dream.'

'Oh, I think I'll go and help Dad in the garden,' said Clare.

'Your dad's not in the garden,' said her mum, 'he's down at the 'ardware shop.'

'Fancy not being in the garden on a nice morning like this,' said Clare.

'Don't worry,' smiled her mum, 'he'll be there this afternoon, in a deckchair.'

'Oh, I'll be at Jimmy Adams's home,' said Clare.

'Where?'

'Well, he spoke to me on the phone and invited me,' said Clare.

'Jimmy Adams did?'

'Yes, Mum.'

'Well, I'm blessed,' said Mrs Roper. 'How did that come about, might I ask? Clare?' Clare had disappeared. 'Now where's she gone? I never saw a more restless girl just lately.'

There was another event, that of Chinese Lady and Sir Edwin now on the way to Devon with Polly's parents, Sir Henry Simms and Lady Dorothy Simms, in a chauffeur-driven car. The holiday had been arranged some time ago.

On an incidental note, Sir Edwin had made a

phone call to his old department the previous evening.

At the offices of the Soviet Press Bureau, two English-speaking KGB officers of junior rank had begun the grinding chore ordered by Lieutenant General Kersch, that of trying to make phone contact with a certain person called Finch. One man quoted phone numbers from the London directory, and the other dialled each relevant subscriber in turn. Saturday favoured the chore, for most people were more likely to be at home than at work.

A connection brought the following statement and question from the caller.

'Good morning, Mr Finch, I have a message from Katje Galicia to deliver to you in person. When can I arrange to let you have it?'

Exchanges were on the following lines.

'Eh? What?'

'You know Katje Galicia?'

'What's that, a Christmas fairy? Get off the line.'

Or, 'Excuse me, what are you talking about and who are you?'

'A friend.'

'I think you've got the wrong number.'

'Let us talk about Katje Galicia.'

'You can. I've got other things to do. Goodbye.'

Or, 'I'm afraid you've got the wrong number.'

'Permit me to ask if you can put me in touch with the lady.'

'What lady?'

'Katje Galicia.'

'She's a lady, is she? Sounds more like a tropical plant to me. Hang up, you're wasting my time.'

And so on. Additional questions to the subscribers only irked them. It became impossible to alight on what Lieutenant General Kersch had called the obvious.

Dogged application was the name of the game. Failure allied with an accusation that they had been remiss in not keeping a closer watch on the missing trio could mean ending up in a Siberian Gulag.

Two other junior officers had been sent to Bloomsbury to ask discreet questions of people who might have known Katje Galicia. Some, given her description, thought they might have seen her, but never with a companion. No-one who actually knew her was found. That spoke of an efficient agent who wisely kept to herself.

Meanwhile, Lieutenant General Kersch was making a minute study of files he had brought with him from Moscow. These were the thick files on Bukov and Alexandrov, and the thinner files of Katje Galicia and Lieutenant Maxim Kirov, the man who had shadowed the Polish woman and disappeared along with the two senior men. Files could be informative if studied with keen concentration.

Kersch was not to know it, but there was nothing he would find in the file on Katje Galicia that would tell him she was now in the State of Vermont, New England.

* * *

Over lunch, Jimmy said, 'I'll be putting in your bedding plants this afternoon, Mum, as well as the runner bean seedlings.'

'Well, thank you, Jimmy,' said Susie, and thought, as she often did, of her years as a young girl, in Peabody's Buildings in Brandon Street, Walworth, when one had to go to Ruskin Park to see what flowers looked like when they were actually growing. That she had ended up in this handsome house on Denmark Hill, with a large and lovely garden, sometimes caused her a moment of disbelief. 'I expect your dad will help you.'

'Unfortunate, like,' said Sammy. 'I'll be –'

'Watching cricket on the television,' said Phoebe.

'Well, my feet need a rest, I grant,' said Sammy, 'they've had a long week.'

'You watch cricket, Dad,' said Jimmy. 'I've got someone's granddaughter coming to help.'

'I'm someone's granddaughter,' said Phoebe, 'but I'm going out to the shops with Mum.'

'Come on, Jimmy,' said Susie, 'whose granddaughter is she?'

'Good old Gertie Roper's eldest,' said Jimmy. 'Clare Roper.'

'Goodness me, fancy going all round the mulberry bush to tell us her name,' said Phoebe. 'Dad, this points to something kind of fateful.'

'Does it?' grinned Sammy. 'How fateful?'

'Forget it,' said Jimmy, 'I've told you all, Clare Roper's got a feller.'

'Well, I just don't know,' said Susie.

Sammy, enjoying one of Susie's light Saturday lunches of Kennedy's Scotch eggs with salad and tomatoes, said, 'Don't know what?'

'How our Jimmy managed to get someone else's girlfriend to help him in the garden, and on a Saturday afternoon too,' said Susie.

'Yes, fancy,' said Phoebe. She was looking forward to telling Paula of this new development. Her sister was at David and Kate's farm, making hay with Enrico, Phoebe presumed. 'Yes, how did you, Jimmy?'

'Oh, we simply got round to it on the phone,' said Jimmy. 'Don't let it give any of you hidden thoughts.'

'Hidden thoughts?' said Phoebe to her Scotch egg. 'He gets worse, poor old thing.'

'I'll be a sport,' said Sammy, 'I'll watch the cricket, Jimmy.'

'Your turn to mow the lawn sometime this weekend, Dad old sport,' said Jimmy.

'I'll find time sometime,' said Sammy.

With Chinese Lady and Sir Edwin well on the way to Devon, the phone rang in their empty house. It rang unanswered for a while, then stopped.

'Try again later,' said the KGB man who was reading numbers from the London phone directory.

'That means more than a few for later,' said the man making the calls.

'Can't be helped, comrade. Here's the next one.'

*　*　*

Clare arrived at two thirty. Wearing a light summer dress of bright apricot, she presented herself as a picture to Jimmy when he opened the door to her.

'Hello,' he said.

'Hello,' said Clare.

Dressed in an old sports shirt and well-worn slacks himself, Jimmy said, 'I was actually expecting a lady gardener.'

'I know,' said Clare, 'it's me.'

'Well, good-oh,' said Jimmy, 'but I must say you look like young Lady Marigold on her way to a royal garden party.'

'Oh, go on,' said Clare. 'Who's Lady Marigold?'

'Oh, just some figment of my imagination,' said Jimmy. 'Come on, step into the family shack and make yourself at home.'

'Thanks,' said Clare, and stepped in. She blinked at the spaciousness of the hall, which suggested here lived a family that had money in the bank. 'Crikey,' she said in typical cockney reaction.

'Anything wrong?' enquired Jimmy.

'Some shack,' said Clare, and laughed. She was impressed, but not overawed. She wasn't given, in any case, to letting someone's posh house knock her dizzy. What she most liked at the moment was a feeling that she and Jimmy were getting closer, close enough, perhaps, for him to start taking her out. She'd just love to go jiving with him.

Susie might have offered to show Clare around the house. Jimmy didn't even think about it.

'My sister Phoebe's out shopping with Mum, and Dad's watching cricket on the television,' he said. 'So it's just you and me for the garden, Clare.'

Bliss, thought Clare.

'Oh, I don't mind,' she said.

'You're a girl with a future,' smiled Jimmy.

'How'd you know that?' she asked.

'Any girl who can come all the way from Bow to help a bloke with his gardening on a Saturday afternoon is bound to be blessed,' said Jimmy.

'I just don't know where you get all your funny ideas from,' said Clare, which echoed the kind of comments that Patsy, an all-American girl, had made to Jimmy's brother Daniel when she first knew him.

'Let me know whenever I talk too much,' said Jimmy. 'This way to the garden, Clare.' Although he hadn't shown her over the house, on the way to the kitchen he did point to a door and tell her there were the ground-floor offices. Clare guessed what he meant. He led her to the kitchen, which also impressed her, then through to the garden.

Clare blinked again. It was lovely, a large green lawn, colourful flower beds on either side, a hedge at the top and a gap that led to the vegetable plot, beyond which she could see the green branches of fruit trees.

'Help,' she said.

'No, I'm the one asking for help,' said Jimmy, 'but you'd better take your shoes off. Hold on, and I'll fetch Mum's gumboots.'

Back into the kitchen he went, and returned with the boots. Down he went on one knee as Clare slipped off a shining new white leather shoe. She hitched her dress a little as he pushed the short gumboot over her foot. It was his turn to blink.

Gertie's eldest granddaughter had gorgeous legs, made the more so by her nylon stockings. Not that Clare didn't know it.

'Oh, good, it fits,' she said when the boot was in place.

'My pleasure,' said Jimmy, which it was. He knew what a feller's optics could appreciate. On went the other boot, and Clare, hitching her dress just a little higher, looked down at herself. Jimmy blinked again. Bless my living peepers, he said to himself, no wonder that Irish leprechaun has staked his claim, curse him.

'Jimmy, I don't think gumboots go with me dress,' said Clare.

Jimmy, straightening up, said, 'Well, as I see it, what would go best of all are Cinderella's party slippers. But you couldn't garden in those, either. Can you settle for Mum's gumboots?'

'Yes, course I can,' said Clare. 'What d'you want me to do?'

And so began an afternoon in which Clare, the complete novice, cleverly avoided all embarrassments by simply doing as Jimmy asked her to. She wasn't short of sense, nor of an aptitude for learning, as long as learning was a pleasure and not a bore. Wearing Susie's gardening gloves, she used the hose to soak a long stretch of earth at the edge of each herbaceous border, and a watering can to soak trays of bedding plants. To Jimmy's instructions, she subsequently lifted each plant out of its pot and handed it to him. She watched as he used a trowel to dig into the wet soil and then to drop the plants in and tamp them down. The polyanthus and impatiens began to make a lovely, colourful border.

'How we doing?' asked Jimmy at one point.

'Jimmy, I'm just loving it.'

On his knees, Jimmy looked up at her. The sunlight was on her glowing face and tinting her dark auburn hair. Her wide eyes were alight. Unless the sun's getting at me, I think I'm in love, he told himself. Shoot Harry Ballymore. I know one thing, I was never quite like this about Jenny Osborne, stunning though she was. Live happy ever after, Jenny, I'll just keep hoping that this Irish bloke takes a trip to Paris and falls off the top of the Eiffel Tower.

'Let's have another plant, Clare,' he said.

Out came Sammy.

'Hello, hello,' he called, 'Gertie's granddaughter is here, then, Jimmy.'

'Did we wake you up?' smiled Jimmy.

'No, just thought I'd pop out into all this sunshine and see what was going on,' said Sammy, still a fine physical specimen in a tailored open-neck shirt and light summer slacks. 'How's your busy self, Clare? Glad to see you've got our Jimmy down on his knees.'

'Oh, Jimmy's doing great, Mister Sammy,' said Clare. 'Look at all these lovely plants.'

'Well, his mother's going to like them,' said Sammy, 'but I like your dress more. Do I recognize one of Lilian's designs?' Lilian Chapman (née Hyams) was his high-class designer.

'Mister Sammy, I bought it from the fact'ry saleroom yesterday lunchtime,' said Clare.

'That's what I call loyalty and good taste,' said Sammy. 'Hope you got your discount.'

'Oh, yes,' said Clare.

'Dad, kindly remember it's Saturday and tomorrow's Sunday,' said Jimmy. 'It's against the house rules and, more important, against Mum's rules, to talk business during weekends.'

'Message received and understood, Jimmy my lad,' said Sammy.

'That's it, back to cricket,' said Jimmy.

Sammy disappeared, smiling broadly. Clare might be going steady with some bloke, but there she was with Jimmy and in a new dress well above the average price. Some girls would have turned up in jeans and a top when a spot of gardening was on their minds.

'Your dad's a nice man, Jimmy,' said Clare.

'Three's a crowd,' murmured Jimmy to his trowel.

'Beg pardon?' said Clare. 'I didn't catch that.'

'Pass another plant, Clare. No, half a mo, how about an ice-cream cornet? There's ice cream in the fridge and cornets in the larder. I'll make us two.'

'Lovely,' said Clare.

'Mum will make a pot of tea for all of us when she gets back from the shops,' said Jimmy, at which point Clare's light dress was smacked by a breeze against her body to outline her figure.

'Oops,' she said. Then, 'Jimmy, you're giving me a really nice afternoon.'

That, thought Jimmy, is nothing to what you're giving me, a shocking urge to kiss you quick and so on. I wonder, would a cold shower be better for me than an ice-cream cornet?

The phone rang again in the empty house on Red Post Hill, off Denmark Hill. It remained unanswered. It stopped ringing.

Chapter Twenty-Four

When Susie and Phoebe arrived back, Jimmy and Clare couldn't be seen, but the long rows of newly planted polyanthus and impatiens could. They looked brilliant with colour. Susie said what a lovely display, Jimmy and Clare deserved tea and cake for all that work. Phoebe said yes, but where were they? In the garden shed? Perhaps they're watching cricket with Sammy, said Susie.

'I bet,' said Phoebe.

They heard Clare then. Her sudden burst of laughter sailed up over the hedge.

'They're by the vegetable plot,' said Susie. 'Go and tell them I'm making a pot of tea, Phoebe love.'

Up went Phoebe, over the lawn and through the gap in the hedge. She found Jimmy down on his knees on a path dividing two plots. Clare was standing beside him, handing him sturdy runner bean seedlings.

Wow, thought Phoebe, so that's someone's granddaughter. She's lovely. Now I really am sorry for Jimmy, seeing she's going steady with some other young man.

'Hello,' she said.

Clare turned her head and Jimmy looked up.

'Clare, meet my sister Phoebe,' he said.

'Oh, hello,' said Clare.

'Nice to meet you,' said Phoebe. 'I hope Jimmy's grateful for your help.'

'I'm breathless with gratitude, you bet,' said Jimmy.

'Jolly good,' said Phoebe. 'Mum's making a pot of tea, so come and have it when I call. Bring Clare with you, don't leave her standing about up here.' She smiled at Clare and went back to the house.

'Well, isn't she pretty?' said Clare.

'And cheeky,' said Jimmy, dropping one more runner bean seedling into soil watered by his helpmate of the moment.

'How old is she?' asked Clare, freeing another seedling from a deep tray.

'Sixteen, and into her school-leaving exams,' said Jimmy, taking the seedling.

'It seems ages since I left school,' said Clare. 'Well, I'm nearly nineteen.' Perhaps that came out as a hint to Jimmy that she was at a very eligible age.

'Fascinating,' said Jimmy to the seedling.

'Pardon?' said Clare.

'What did I say?' asked Jimmy, planting the seedling.

'I said I was nearly nineteen and you said fascinating.'

'Well, yes,' said Jimmy, finding it increasingly difficult not to give Harry Ballymore some serious competition. Get stuck in, his feelings told him. Don't be a stinker, his principles argued, the Irish bloke's never done you any harm. 'I meant you're not an old lady yet.'

'Crikey, that's fascinating, me not being an old lady yet?' said Clare, enjoying the happiest afternoon of her life.

'Old age can be worrying, y'know,' said Jimmy, receiving the last of the seedlings from the fair hand of the gorgeous girl from Bow. One ignored the fact that it was gloved. 'It goes with false teeth, backache, bronchitis, arthritis and being permanently under the doctor. It's a happy thing that you're light years away from false teeth, Clare. Yes, definitely fascinating.'

Clare shrieked with laughter.

Phoebe called from the open kitchen door.

'Jimmeeee! Teeeea!'

'Phoebeee! Coming!' called Jimmy.

Susie served it on the garden table to Sammy, Phoebe, Clare, Jimmy and herself. She made a point of being very welcoming to Clare, not failing to notice just how lovely the girl was. She'd met her only in passing at Gertie and Bert's retirement party. Now, seeing her close to, she thought what a well-matched couple she and Jimmy would make. Jimmy was the kindest of young men, and as easy-going as his Uncle Boots. Susie supposed that Clare's present admirer must be even more of a catch than Jimmy.

Clare, drinking tea and eating Susie's home-made cake, thought what a nice family Jimmy had, everyone so natural in their talk, and always bringing her into the conversation.

'Let's see,' said Sammy, 'how's things with

your grandparents, Clare, now they're retired?'

'Oh, Granny's enjoying giving her feet a rest,' said Clare, 'and Grandpa's enjoying hisself on his allotment.'

'Give 'em me kind regards,' said Sammy.

'Oh, thanks,' said Clare.

'I believe you've been working the factory switchboard this week,' said Susie.

'I been doing me best,' said Clare.

'Not half,' said Jimmy. 'Believe me, Dad, the firm's found a treasure. No, correction, we didn't find her. I could say she appeared out of a golden cloud one day and dropped in front of my desk like Fantonia.'

Clare suppressed an involuntary giggle. Well, she was nearly nineteen, and going along with being modern, which meant no giggling.

'Oh, good grief,' said Phoebe, rolling her eyes, 'what a performance. Jimmy's gone right over the top, Mum.'

'Jimmy, who's Fantonia?' asked Susie.

'Some fairy queen, isn't she?' said Jimmy.

Laughter ran round the table.

'Do I conclude we've got a fairy queen taking tea with us?' enquired Sammy, winking at Clare.

'More like Max Miller, Mr Adams,' said Clare.

'Our Jimmy, you mean?' said Sammy.

'More like Max Miller gone bonkers,' said Phoebe.

'Clare, would you like to stay for supper?' asked Susie.

'Oh, thanks ever so, Mrs Adams,' said Clare. Then her face dropped. 'Oh, no, I can't, I'm going out this evening.' She had promised to go to a dance hall with Daisy. She couldn't phone her to call it off. Daisy's family, like others in the East End, didn't have a phone, and she didn't feel she could let her friend down, anyway. 'I'm ever so sorry I can't stay. In fact, I'd better go in a minute.'

'Understood, Clare,' said Sammy. They all understood. A date with her boyfriend on a Saturday evening was a natural. 'I'll drive you down to the Camberwell Green bus stop. That'll give you a good start.'

Sammy did that after Clare had said goodbye to the others and had let them know how much she'd enjoyed the afternoon. Jimmy told her what a great help she'd been, and an entertainment too. But he didn't ask if he could take her out, even though she was sure he really did like her. Perhaps there was someone else, after all. If so, talk about me having a future, like he said. I'll go sick, she thought.

Felicity was in the kitchen, doing her limited best, as usual, to help her housemaid, Maggie Forbes, in the preparation of supper. Felicity never failed to exercise feel and touch in a ceaseless attempt to increase her usefulness. She knew by now exactly how to prepare vegetables, extract required food from the fridge and the right condiments from the larder. She knew how to fill a kettle, boil it and fill the teapot without any risk of scalding herself. She also knew exactly how to find her way around the house, to direct herself to the phone, and to choose which clothes she wanted from her wardrobe, and which underwear from a drawer of her dressing table. Her dressing table, of course, was a laugh. At least, its mirror was. But she could apply her make-up quite skilfully now.

'Here we are, Maggie,' she said, and Maggie took a dish of prepared carrots from her.

'Oh, you've done these very nice, Mrs Adams,' said Maggie, buxom, good-natured and wholly in tune with the mistress's blindness.

'Sheer expertise, Maggie old thing,' said Felicity.

Tim and Jennifer were in the garden. She heard Jennifer shouting with the uninhibited laughter of the young. She heard Tim respond.

'Right, monkey, I'm after you.'

Felicity walked to the open kitchen door and out onto the paved rectangle fronting the lawn. The bright sun, descending, smacked into her eyes. She blinked. A golden blur appeared. Her heart jumped. It was there, yes, a golden blur. She shut it out for a moment, clamping her lids tightly. She lifted them after a few moments. The blur disappeared. Her eyes closed, opened, closed and opened again. A sun-heated blankness was all that greeted her.

She used the language of her time at Troon.

'Oh, sod it!' It came out in a whispered rush, and she returned to the kitchen, bitter with acute disillusionment at the tricks of scurvy fate.

Chapter Twenty-Five

The dance hall in Brixton was packed with young people, the floor rumbling beneath beating feet. Flared skirts and flared dresses of swinging girls produced a picture of dancing clouds of colour, and in the vernacular of the times, nyloned legs were fab. Not that cockney girls of other times didn't show a famous leg or two while doing Mother Brown's knees-up.

Enthusiasm was at a peak, for on the stage was the teenage prodigy, young Tommy Steele, who, although yet to make his professional debut at a public concert, was already known to dance-hall teenagers as one of the first British exponents of America's up-and-coming craze, rock and roll. Tommy and his guitar were backed by a skiffle group.

'Wow oh wow,' gasped Phoebe in delight.

'Swing it, man,' said Philip.

'Don't be daft,' said Phoebe, rocking.

'In modern music, man embraces woman,' said Philip, rolling.

'Who said?'

'Louis Armstrong.'

Phoebe took up the gauntlet.

'He's jazz, man, New Orleans, man. Come on, man, go, go.'

They were shouting to make themselves heard, and they'd been performing for over an hour.

'How about a breather at the coffee bar?' suggested Philip.

'What?' said Phoebe.

Philip repeated himself in shouting fashion.

'You asking me, feller?' said a girl at his elbow.

'No, me,' said Phoebe, and took Philip away. 'Don't do that again,' she said when they'd seated themselves.

'Don't do what?' asked Philip, flushed and hot.

'Make up to other girls when you're with me,' said Phoebe, also flushed, but looking a cool number in her skinny sweater and flared skirt.

'Believe me, Phoebe,' said Philip, 'I'm not even conscious of other girls when I'm with you.'

'Well, you said that quite nicely,' said Phoebe. 'Are you going to get the coffee? If so, I'll have a Coca-Cola.'

'Got you, man,' said Philip.

'Oh, goody,' said Phoebe, 'pop along, then.'

'Cheeky chops,' said Philip, and off he went to the self-service counter.

Precisely at this time, Cathy Davidson's birthday party had come to a close, and guests were departing. Up came Mrs Anastasia Davidson, silk dress gliding around her moving body, to check the exit of Cathy's best-liked guest. Best-liked by Cathy, that is, especially as he'd given her a super present, a little silver filigree brooch. The silver content was disputable, but it still looked very nice. James had paid for it, and Polly had helped him choose it.

'James,' said Mrs Davidson, 'I'll drive you home.'

'Oh, I can walk, Mrs Davidson,' said James. 'It's not all that far.'

'No, I insist, dear boy,' said Mrs Davidson in her engaging drawl.

'Oh, well, thanks,' said James. 'Goodnight, Cathy, smashing party. Er?'

Young Cathy had lifted her face for a kiss. Oh, I might as well, thought James, and kissed her rosebud lips, her mother looking on with a smile.

'Ever so glad you came,' said eleven-year-old Cathy. 'Let's meet after school next week, shall we?'

'I'll look out for you, Cathy.'

'Come along, James,' said Mrs Davidson, and he followed her out to her sleek car.

She drove him home, talking pleasantly to him on the way. In the drive of his parents' house, she said she'd see him to his front door. James said he really could manage that by himself, but she insisted, so he went round the car to open the driver's door for her. She eased herself out with a sinuous movement of limbs and body. Her dress slithered up, and her legs gleamed from her ankles to just above her knees.

James's optics popped. Well, he thought, I don't know if I'll ever get my eyesight back in the same condition as before. Unless I have an operation.

She went to the front door with him and rang the bell. Boots appeared. Mrs Davidson smiled.

'Mr Adams, Cathy's party is over and here's James,' she purred.

Boots, seeing the Daimler, said, 'You've driven him home?'

'Of course,' said Mrs Davidson, 'he's a charming boy.'

'But has he broken a leg?' asked Boots.

'No, I'm all present and correct, Dad,' said James. 'Mrs Davidson gave me a lift, that's all.' She'd also given him an eyeful, but of course a feller didn't have to mention that.

'Well, my thanks, Mrs Davidson, for bringing him home,' said Boots.

'Oh, a pleasure,' said the lady, moving closer.

Help, thought James, and trod on his dad's foot as a warning not to invite her in. Mother Dear had said she was never to cross the doorstep.

Boots's easy smile surfaced. The lady softly sighed.

'Thanks again, Mrs Davidson,' he said. 'Goodnight.'

She looked willing to linger, to accept an invitation, but drawled, 'Goodnight, Mr Adams. Goodnight, James.' She departed to her car, her silk dress shiningly embracing her. Boots closed the door.

'Well, James?' he said.

'That was a narrow squeak, Dad,' said James, 'she almost had one foot inside the door. Still, I won't tell Mum that, I'll tell her you guarded our threshold like a sturdy oak of old England.'

'I'm obliged, old chap,' said Boots.

Polly and Gemma appeared.

'James, you're back,' said Polly. 'What was Cathy's party like?'

'Fun,' said James.

'Kissing games?' said Gemma.

'No, fun,' said James.

'Well, come and tell us all about it, young sport,' said Polly.

James glanced at his dad. Boots winked, which told James that there was no need to mention the lady man-eater had almost crossed the threshold. Mother Dear hadn't been aware that she'd turned up. Nor had Gemma. Just as well. Gemma could always start a riot, and often did.

James, for all his youth, understood more clearly now why his mum thought his dad was in mortal danger.

The two junior KGB officers, after well-needed breaks at midday and early evening, were still at their chore.

For a third time, Sir Edwin's phone rang.

For a third time it rang unanswered.

'Try again tomorrow.'

'Tomorrow's Sunday.'

'So?'

'An English Sunday.'

'So?'

'They take their Sundays seriously.'

'And we take Kersch's orders seriously, or get chopped, so ring again tomorrow. The number's one of the few left.'

Lieutenant General Kersch had also experienced a blank day. So far Bukov's file had given him no clue. Nor had Alexandrov's. He must go through them again tomorrow. Both files were too faultless.

In Moscow, he hadn't thought of looking for a file on a person called Finch. But then he hadn't heard the name mentioned until he arrived in London. Even then, he didn't think about a file. The name and the connection with Katje Galicia were too abstract. But wait, what if the Polish woman had seen Finch as a prospective mole? That was the main purpose of the Soviet Press Bureau, to recruit moles. Gathering news for home consumption was secondary, but necessary, of course. It allowed them to obtain their work permits.

On those thoughts, Kersch downed a large vodka and went to bed. It was one of the few occasions when, mentally drained, he needed an early night. It was ten o'clock, very early for him.

At ten thirty, the dance hall closed and Phoebe and Philip left soon after to make for the bus stop along with other teenagers.

'Wasn't Tommy Steele fab?' said Phoebe.

'Great,' said Philip.

'He's only sixteen,' said Phoebe.

'Think of all the time he's got to make a name for himself,' said Philip.

'So have you,' said Phoebe.

'Only if there was another Battle of Britain, and I could fly a new kind of Hurricane or Spitfire against the foe,' said Philip.

'Crikey, we don't want another war just for you to make a name for yourself,' said Phoebe, as they joined the bus queue. 'I meant couldn't you do something like swimming the Channel in record time?'

'Not without sinking halfway,' said Philip.

Up came a bus, and as soon as it stopped the queue began to jostle forward. Philip put an arm around Phoebe's waist. She liked that protective gesture. For all her sense of fun and her whimsies, Phoebe was a romantic who favoured gallantries.

She and Philip found a vacant seat on the upper deck. Her smooth rounded knees peeped from her short skirt. What a darling girl, thought Philip.

He saw her home, to her front door, and there he embraced her, selected his target and made his aim. His lips landed on her dewy mouth, which was pretty good going considering he was a bit cross-eyed at the moment.

Phoebe came out of the kiss with pulses fluttering.

'Stop,' she said huskily.

'Phoebe, I'm not doing anything.'

'Yes, you are, you're kissing me.'

'Only the once.'

'Oh, really? Well, all right, you can do it again, then.'

So he kissed her again. Oh, the cheeky devil, thought Phoebe, which was hardly a rational reaction.

She pushed him off, just in case he went a bit too far. What was a bit too far?

'Phoebe, you're a great girl.'

'Well, yes, perhaps I am, but I don't want to get

a reputation for letting boys kiss me on my doorstep.'

'We could go inside.'

'Not likely. Still, d'you want to come in for a drink?'

'Well, thanks, Phoebe, but it's late and I'm off whisky and gin, anyway. Actually, I'm not on them yet.'

'Oh, funny ha ha, I don't think. Still, it's been a fab evening, and I think I could soon get to like you.'

'Well, that's something to live for.'

'I'm not doing anything special tomorrow afternoon, by the way.'

'Great. I'll come round and take you to the park.'

'Goodness, what a thrill for a girl,' said Phoebe.

At Lulu's flat in Kennington, she and Paul had been discussing whether or not to make an offer for a house they'd looked over in Brixton during the afternoon. It was a well-kept property of good old solid Victorian construction, its interior modernized to some extent. There was a modest-sized garden, a shed and an ancient timber-framed greenhouse harbouring a host of spiders' webs and their eight-legged inhabitants. The garden appealed to Paul, the spiders made Lulu shudder. No problem, said Paul, I'll soon make friends of them. Over my dead body you will, said Lulu. OK, I'll clear them out if we take the place, said Paul.

At the end of their discussion, they'd come to an

agreement. They'd make an offer. The sale price was seven hundred and fifty pounds. They'd offer seven hundred as a starter.

'Come and have Sunday dinner with my family,' said Paul, 'and then we'll pop along to see Uncle Sammy and find out if he'll keep to a promise he made me. To loan us what we'll need on top of my dad's gift of a deposit.'

'Well, that sounds fine,' said Lulu. 'I'm not one to turn my nose up at kindness from capitalists. Actually, it's a way of helping them to be humanitarian.' She frowned at herself. 'No, that was petty. Black mark, Lulu Saunders.'

'Somehow,' mused Paul, 'I never see my dad or my uncles as capitalists. I've heard too much about their years in Walworth. Sometimes my lovely old granny never even had a penny for the gas, but she managed. They all did, Aunt Lizzy as well, and they climbed out of poverty and patchwork clothes to better themselves by hard work and sound ideas. And inspired marriages. I love them all, Lulu.'

It was now eleven o'clock. They were sitting side by side on Lulu's old settee that had creaking springs. Lulu looked quite touched.

'Paul, I like you for that,' she said.

'Did I strike a chord? Good,' he said, 'and now I'd better be on my way.'

'And I'd better be in my bed,' said Lulu, her attractive green dress symbolizing that which she considered her descent into a weak woman's role.

'Goodnight, then,' said Paul. He slipped an arm around her and kissed her smack on the lips. Her glasses, dislodged, travelled down her nose. Paul took them off and placed them on the arm of the settee. He kissed her again. Unlike Phoebe, Lulu didn't go swoony. She stiffened. Sometimes, this kind of intimacy embarrassed her, as it did now when she felt his hand touch her knees and sneak a little way upwards under her dress and slip. Tiny sparks emanated from her nylon stockings. God, what a swine.

'What d'you think you're up to?' she demanded.

'Nowhere yet, but let's see –' His hand went further upwards. So did her dress and slip. Nylon stockings gleamed. No doubt about it, thought Paul, women were the photogenic sex, although it was said that Liberace, the American entertainer, ran them close.

Lulu jumped up, took hold of a women's magazine containing an article on how to succeed in a man's world, rolled it up and went for Paul. Paul, laughing, made a running exit from the flat.

Lulu stood breathing hard, her face flushed.

She had trouble in getting to sleep. Much against her will, she kept having thoughts about Paul.

Thoughts definitely embarrassing. And the wedding wasn't until September. What should she say to him next time he visited her flat?

'All right, I'll give in. Now.'

Could she, would she, really do that?

Chapter Twenty-Six

Sunday midday.

Bobby and his French wife, Helene, arrived to spend the day with Lizzy and Ned, bringing their children, Estelle and Robert, with them. Estelle, six, was named after Helene's mother. Robert, four, was named after Boots.

Lizzy gave them all her usual open-hearted welcome, producing a sweet for each of the children.

'How's Pa?' asked Bobby.

'Pottering in the garden,' said Lizzy.

'I'll go and potter with him,' said Bobby, and out he went to talk to his ageing dad. Ned was troubled by hardening arteries, much more than by his tin leg, a constant aid and support since the 1914–18 war. His hair was grey and thin, his face drawn, but a smile came at once as Bobby arrived at his side. 'How are you, Dad old feller?'

'Still on my feet,' said Ned.

'Take it easy and stay that way,' said Bobby. 'The garden looks fine.'

'Thanks to you and Helene,' said Ned. His son and daughter-in-law had an arrangement that relieved him of all heavy work. They came on most Saturday mornings during spring, summer and autumn, Bobby hoeing, weeding, and mowing the lawn, while Helene, the robust daughter of a farmer, assiduously cultivated the vegetable plot. Ned only needed to lightly potter, which he did regularly to get himself out of doors now that he was retired.

Aged fifty-eight, and contemporary with Boots, fifty-six, Ned looked far older than his brother-in-law. He complained to Boots that in another year or two he'd look like his dad. Ned old lad, said Boots, right now we both look like everybody's grandfathers.

Out came Helene and the children, Helene to give Ned a hug and a fond kiss, and the children to make a fuss of their English granddad. Helene loved Lizzy and Ned for all the kindness and affection they had given her from the moment Bobby brought her to them, just after Dunkirk, which first represented a shambolic defeat, and then a triumph of evacuation. It was she who kept Bobby rigidly to the gardening arrangement.

'We shall never fail your papa, never,' she once said. 'He is like my own papa, a good and kind man.'

'I'm not arguing, my French firework,' said Bobby.

'Then be quick and put your gardening clothes on, or I shall blow up in your face,' said Helene.

'That'll get rid of my face,' said Bobby, 'and my need of a razor.'

'Ah, what an idiot you are with your terrible

jokes,' said Helene for about the five-hundredth time. 'But never mind, you're my own idiot and better than most others. Shoo now, shoo.'

Ned's grey, drawn look worried her. She drew Lizzy aside after the Sunday dinner.

'Helene?' said Lizzy, now buxom. It was an unwanted development, but she was living with it.

'Mama, I cannot help it, I'm worried about how ill Papa looks. Does his doctor call?'

'Often,' said Lizzy. She winced. 'I'm worried too, my dear.'

'Should he have an operation?'

'I believe there's not an operation for hardening arteries,' said Lizzy. 'Ned can only take life quietly, and I make sure he does.'

'Well, Mama, I don't want to tread on toes, but I think I shall ask my own doctor. Would you mind?'

'No, of course not,' said Lizzy, 'but Ned has seen specialists.'

'Then I shall ask some other specialist,' said Helene.

'Bless us,' said Lizzy, 'you're such a caring daughter-in-law, lovey.'

'I like to feel I'm your daughter, not an in-law,' said Helene. 'I love you all, and see how lucky I was to find Bobby before some other woman did. And see how fortunate I was to have his children, as well as you and Papa. There, I have said everything that is important to me.'

Lizzy, all of old-fashioned and sentimental, touched Helene's hand.

'Thank you, lovey,' she said, her brown eyes quite misty. 'Ned and me, we've been lucky too.'

* * *

Sir Edwin's phone rang for the second time that day. As with the first call, there was no answer.

'Are you thinking as I'm thinking?' said one KGB man to the other.

'What are you thinking, then?'

'Comrade Kersch suspects defection, so is it possible the person Finch has gone with Katje Galicia? If a man, perhaps he's in love with her.'

'She's an old woman, according to the file Comrade Kersch showed us.'

'And perhaps Finch is an old man.'

'Well, we have to visit the homes of all subscribers who haven't answered our calls. Their addresses are in that directory in which you've had your nose for two days.'

'Leave my nose out of it. Yours is longer.'

'A lie. By the way, I still don't believe that Bukov and Alexandrov defected. They are not the kind, and never have been.'

'I agree.'

'It's very fishy.'

'Yes, I can smell it.'

'That's your nose again.'

Sometime after Sunday dinner with Tommy and Vi, Paul and Lulu called on Sammy and Susie. There they had a private word with Sammy about their prospective purchase of a house in Chaucer Road, Brixton.

'Chaucer Road, eh?' said Sammy. 'Yes, I know it.'

'It's not far from the working-class market,' said Lulu, looking a credit to her sex in a light costume and blouse. She had long given up sending Paul spare by wearing masculine rig. 'Paul and I still identify with the workers and their problems, Mr Adams.'

'Good, I'm one of them meself, and so's Paul's dad,' said Sammy. 'And as for problems, if my highly regarded personal assistant, Mrs Rachel Goodman, and yours truly hadn't worked our brains off to get an import licence, the family business would've fallen down dead and we'd all be on the dole.'

'Well,' said Lulu, not to be outdone, 'you'd at least be benefiting from the increased dole brought about by a Labour government, Mr Adams.'

Sammy smiled. You had to hand it to Lulu, she always stood her ground.

'Anyway,' he said, 'you both like this house enough to make a happy family home of it?'

'That's the idea, Uncle Sammy,' said Paul.

Help, thought Lulu, what about my career and my life as an independent woman? A family? I'll lose my equality if I get to be a housebound mum. I'd better read Marie Stopes on family planning.

'The owners are asking seven hundred and fifty pounds, Mr Adams,' she said, 'and we've offered seven hundred.'

'Well, whatever,' said Sammy, 'the property company will make you a loan of what you need. How's that?'

'Maximum generosity, Uncle Sammy,' said Paul.

Lulu, spectacles reflecting the light of earnest

appreciation, said, 'You're a very nice man, Mr Adams.'

'Don't mention it,' said Sammy, pretty sure she was forgiving him for being a capitalist. 'You're more than welcome. What's our most profitable asset in the country, eh? Our young people. And there's a lot of 'em in the Adams family, which is a pleasure to your grandma, Paul, even if she loses count now and again.'

'Well, we've got a new asset in Lulu and her gift for arithmetic,' said Paul. 'Once she's part of the family, she'll always help Grandma to do some family counting.'

'Ha ha,' said Lulu, but she smiled.

Lulu had mellowed.

Phoebe and Philip were sauntering around the paths of Ruskin Park, Phoebe in her best Sunday dress, Philip in the uniform of an RAF cadet, which Phoebe thought a compliment to her. Mind, she wasn't too keen on the glances he drew from the occasional girl.

'If you pass your exams and get your Matric,' said Philip, 'will you go on and try for a university place?'

'Goodness gracious me,' said Phoebe, coming on fast as a versatile exponent of the English language, 'what a question. I'm going into my dad's business. I don't have any intention of spending years at a university so that I can devote the rest of my life to something like teaching, or grubbing about in ancient ruins with a lot of crusty old archaeologists.'

'Blimey,' said Philip, 'can you spell it as well?'

'Spell what?' said Phoebe, putting her nose in the air as a couple of impeccably dressed Teddy boys gave her the eye.

'Archaeologists,' said Philip.

'Easily. A – r – c –'

'Don't bother, Pussycat, I believe you.'

'I'm not sure you ought to call me Pussycat.'

'Pussy Willow, then?'

'That sounds worse, especially as I don't feel fully recovered from my awful experience on my own doorstep last night.'

'What awful experience?' asked Philip, getting a come-on look from a slightly plump but hopeful young lady. She had every right to be hopeful, because a kind aunt had assured her she was plump in all the right places. Also, she thought the girl walking with the lanky cadet could be his sister. Well, they weren't arm in arm or hand in hand. 'Come on, what awful experience?' asked Philip.

'It's all gone blank,' said Phoebe, 'and that shows just how awful it was. It happens, you know. Dad said so once. He said if you get knocked sideways by something like an awful profit and loss account, your mind goes blank for a week, and you can't eat or sleep, either.'

'Did you sleep last night?' asked Philip.

'I had to, I had to shut it all out,' said Phoebe. 'Oh, and I ate a good breakfast too. Mum always gives us a good breakfast on Sunday mornings.'

'So after your awful experience, you had a sound sleep and a hearty breakfast?' said Philip.

'Well,' said Phoebe thoughtfully, 'I suppose I'm

made of sterner stuff than poor old Dad. He might look healthy and tough, but he's got a weak will.'

'A weak will?' said Philip. 'Your dad? My Uncle Sammy? You're asking me to believe that?'

'Of course,' said Phoebe, admiring some well-groomed flower beds. 'After all, I should know. His business competitors know it too, and take callous advantage.'

'Say that again.'

'I'm sure you heard,' said Phoebe.

'Phoebe, hearing isn't always believing.'

'You can believe me,' said Phoebe. 'Dad's business competitors keep getting the better of his weak will and dealing him the kind of blows that send him mentally blank for a week, and by the time he comes to, all is lost.'

'I can just see your dad in an all-is-lost state,' said Philip.

'Yes, I almost felt like that on my doorstep last night,' said Phoebe. 'I kept thinking oh help, what's he going to do to me next?'

'I can't believe this,' grinned Philip. 'What a lot of old codswallop.'

'Language, language,' chided Phoebe.

'And all over a couple of kisses,' said Philip. 'Cheeky chops, wait till I get you home and behind your garden hedge.'

'You'll be lucky,' said Phoebe. Then, fifty yards further on, 'Well, I suppose we'd better go home now.'

Philip took her home. A little later, behind the hedge, where Daniel and Patsy had once enjoyed some larky moments, Cheeky-chops Phoebe

Adams, a large-leafed stick of plucked rhubarb in her hand, was hitting Philip with it.

'Blessed sauce, kissing me in Jimmy's spring cabbage plot. Take that. Yes, and that as well, and stop laughing.'

Phoebe was in the happy process of establishing herself as Philip's major interest in life. Some girls of sixteen were already clever enough to know that slapping a young man with a stick of rhubarb had the right kind of psychological effect.

Clare was with her granddad on his allotment. She wasn't doing anything, just watching him using twigs to support his growing garden peas.

'So you had a good time helping Jimmy Adams with a bit of gardening yesterday, did yer, Clare?' said Bert.

'Lovely,' said Clare.

'First time I've known you take an interest in gardening,' said Bert.

'All right, Grandpa, you don't have to be sly,' said Clare. 'I know I'm daft.'

'Not you, love,' said Bert, a hale and hearty figure in his shirt, trousers and boots. 'I won't say me other granddaughters ain't a bit that way, bless 'em, but not you. You're well grown-up, so what's yer problem?'

'Me feelings,' said Clare.

'Well, we've all got feelings,' said Bert. 'Of course, there's ordin'ry feelings, funny feelings and special feelings. What's yours?'

'Mixed-up,' said Clare, 'and I want to know why. I mean, I'm not a schoolgirl, I've got a decent job coming up for good next Monday, and I'm independent in me prospects and me spirit, so why can't I act more intelligent when –' She stopped.

Bert, who had a good idea of what was bothering her, said, 'When what?'

'When Jimmy Adams is looking at me and talking to me,' said Clare. 'Grandpa, I just lose all me sense and all me intelligence. Don't you think that's real daft?'

'Well, I got to admit that does sound like a problem,' said Bert, 'but I tell you one thing, pet, don't let go of your intelligence, nor your independence. If – well, let's face it, if you've got a genuine fancy for Jimmy Adams –'

'Grandpa, oh, Lor', I think I'm in love.' Clare was unburdening herself to her kind and worldly old grandfather.

'Well, then,' said Bert, straightening up and giving her a sympathetic pat, 'you just make sure you look like the Queen of Sheba, and don't do no more than that. It's the fellers that 'ave got to do the running and chasing, and there ain't many of 'em that won't start running after the Queen of Sheba. Wasn't it King Solomon that tripped over his carpet and fell flat on his hooter the first time he saw her?'

Clare managed a smile at that, but said she didn't think she could look like the Queen of Sheba, so Bert said she could easily look like Sheba's nearest female relative, and get young Jimmy Adams knocking on her door once every day and twice on Sundays. Clare said just once on a Saturday evening would be enough to start with.

Bert said Saturday evenings sounded highly romantic, seeing that was when Jimmy could take her waltzing. Grandpa, said Clare, it's only middle-aged couples that go waltzing these days. All right, love, said Bert, what do young couples do, then? Jiving, said Clare. Bert said what's that, then? All the rage, said Clare. Yes, said Bert, but what is it? Modern dancing, said Clare. You've lost me, said Bert, but if you want some of it, you make sure it's Jimmy that asks you, not the other way about.

'Well, I hope he asks before I'm forty,' said Clare.

Philip returned to his unit that evening, and when Phoebe went to bed later, she felt there was something quite nice about the recurring reminder that they weren't strictly cousins. Well, when a girl was enjoying the attentions of her very first boyfriend, she didn't want a barrier to get in the way.

Chapter Twenty-Seven

Dodie turned up at mid-morning on Monday to tell Jimmy she was well enough to get back to the switchboard, especially as she wanted to work out her notice for the week. It was only fair, she said. So she took over from Clare, who went to see Jimmy in his office to say she'd be back next Monday to start permanently.

'Clare, you've been a godsend, standing in for Dodie,' said Jimmy, 'and let's see, we must pay you something for coming in this morning.'

'Oh, that's all right, Mister Jimmy,' said Clare, determined to exercise sense in his presence and not let it run away from her. 'Oh, and I forgot when I phoned you at the weekend to tell you you over-paid me on Friday. You gave me three pounds ten when it should only have been three pounds four, sixteen shillings a day.'

'Let's say the extra was a deserved bonus,' said Jimmy, regarding her very pretty dress out of slightly bemused optics. What a picture she was. What would happen if he kissed her goodbye until next Monday? Probably a smack round his chops and a complaint to her mum and dad, or even her steady. That might bring Harry Ballymore to the factory to land him an Irish one smack on his kisser. 'Yes, call it a bonus, Clare, with the compliments of the firm, even if it's only six bob.'

'But you haven't even charged me for me insurance stamp,' said Clare.

'Never mind, the wages clerk has stamped your card,' said Jimmy, who had actually paid her out of petty cash. 'We'll keep the card. Now you can go off to Ascot.'

'Ascot?' said Clare.

'Yes, join all the other lovely young ladies there,' said Jimmy. 'You're dressed for it, providing you buy yourself a birdcage on the way.'

'A birdcage?' Clare was losing it on account of being numbered among the lovely young ladies of Ascot.

'Don't all Ascot hats look like birdcages?' said Jimmy. 'No, hold on, I don't think it's Ascot week, it's Coronation week. Well, enjoy yourself at someone's garden party.'

'Mister Jimmy, you're having me on all the time,' said Clare. Oh, me Gawd, she thought, here I go again, talking like a schoolgirl. She pulled herself together. 'Aren't you ever serious?'

'Permanently,' said Jimmy, who had work to do but was compulsively delaying it. 'I've got managerial responsibilities that never stop being serious.'

'Well, Mister Jimmy,' said Clare, rising above her problems, 'all I can say is that you've got a funny way of being serious.'

Well, you darling, thought Jimmy, I'm serious

about you, and if I make jokes it's to hide my aching heart.

'Oh, funny ways can't be helped in my family,' he said, and came to his feet. 'Clare, thanks again for being a great help – yes, and with the gardening too. We'll see you next Monday, when you take over permanently from Dodie. So long now.' He put out a hand. Clare took it. His grasp was firm and warm, pleasing her. 'Wait, half a mo, Clare.' He leaned over his desk, opened its main drawer, and lifted out the petty-cash box.

'No,' said Clare.

'But we must pay you something for this morning,' said Jimmy.

'Mister Jimmy, everyone's been so good to me here that I really don't want anything for the little time I spent at the switchboard this morning.' Clare spoke all that with admirable decisiveness.

'Fair enough,' said Jimmy. 'If it wasn't taking advantage of your good nature, and if you weren't doing anything, I'd ask you to come up again next Sunday and help me plant some more vegetable seedlings, like tomato plants.'

'Oh, I –' Clare checked. She mustn't show too eager. 'Well, I'm not sure I –'

'Understood,' said Jimmy, 'not to worry.'

Clare failed herself.

'Oh, now I come to think, yes, I could manage Sunday afternoon,' she said. 'It's only Saturday evenings when I always go out.'

With her Irish bloke and his fiddle, I suppose, thought Jimmy. He smiled. Clare tingled.

'Well, good on you, Clare, see you at home next

Sunday, then, if that's not upsetting anyone,' said Jimmy. He meant her steady date, the lucky old Irish feller, of course.

'Oh, it won't upset me,' said Clare. 'Well, I mean, tomato plants and all, they're kind of –' She thought of a word. 'Exotic, like.'

'Yup,' said Jimmy, and saw her out.

Clare left on dancing feet. Inviting her to his home again was almost as good as asking her for a date.

Jimmy, back at his desk, asked himself a question.

'How long did it take me to say goodbye to her this time?'

Ten minutes? Half an hour?

Do some work, mate, and stop thinking about Harry Ballymore falling off a ferry and drowning in the Irish Sea.

The world-famous star of silent films, Charlie Chaplin, had arrived in London to do a nostalgic tour of the cockney area in which he had been born and brought up, before going on with his wife and many children to a new home in Switzerland. He had left Hollywood following accusations that he had Communist leanings. His accuser was Senator Joseph McCarthy, a fanatical witch-hunter of 'Commies' high and low. He was compulsively committed to burning them at the stake.

Charlie Chaplin, refusing on principle to be subjected to McCarthy's infamous bullying, departed in dignified contempt, not only of the witch-hunter but of a Senate that allowed such a bigot to conduct what were virtually trials in the Land of the Free. In London, he was mobbed by cheering crowds.

Patsy was furious about what had driven him from the USA. Never had she thought she would have to apologize for the country of her birth, a country noted for its breadth of vision and its championing of the individual.

'Daniel, I'm mad, real mad,' she fumed.

'Oh, I wouldn't say that, Patsy,' said Daniel. 'Just a bit touched at times, that's all, but nowhere near qualifying for a loony bin.'

'Not that kind of mad, you kook,' said Patsy. 'Hopping mad.'

'Oh, right,' said Daniel. 'About what? Or who with?'

'That lousy skunk McCarthy,' said Patsy, breathing fire and fury. It activated her nicely constructed bosom, which rose and fell, as in pre-war novels heavily romantic. 'Imagine America giving birth to a creep, a Himmler. It's humiliating.'

'Not your fault, Patsy love,' said Daniel. 'It could have been the result of a couple of Nazi creeps, one male and one female, meeting in the murky swamps of Mississippi and doing something to pass the time. If you know what I mean.'

'Oh, shoot that stuff,' said Patsy, able to let herself go because the children were in bed. 'I'm seriously hopping mad. I need to strike out, so don't get in my way.'

'Patsy, if it'll make you feel better, try kicking a door down,' said Daniel.

'I'd do that if I knew it would fall on McCarthy and turn him into a pancake,' said Patsy. 'He's a lousy blot on the fair face of America.'

'He may be,' said Daniel, 'but think of everything about America you can be proud of. And look, when we go over in September, I'll help you find some way of getting at McCarthy.'

'Oh, yes?' said Patsy. 'Like hiring a hood to chuck a bomb at the stinker?'

'How much would that cost?'

'Daniel, how would you like a death blow?'

'Not much,' said Daniel. 'Come on, cheer up, Patsy, it's a public holiday tomorrow, remember. Think how the kids will enjoy seeing the Coronation procession.'

June had arrived and so had a change in the weather. It was cool and cloudy. But the country was happily geared up for the official crowning of Queen Elizabeth the Second. Kings and queens, Heads of State, Prime Ministers and ambassadors were in town to add international flavour to the spectacle.

The great day dawned to overcast skies. A little rain fell early in the morning. But huge crowds were rolling up hours before the celebrations began. Young Queen Liz was a highly popular monarch, and countless newspaper headlines enthused about a new Elizabethan age. Old people who could remember the days of Queen Victoria hoped that Elizabeth would carpet her Prime Ministers as firmly as Victoria carpeted hers. Or frighten them to death as Good Queen Bess had. Prime Ministers were apt to see themselves as more important than their monarchs.

London's cockneys turned up in their thousands, along with their Pearly Kings and Queens. Waving Union Jacks were everywhere, creating a moving tide of colour. Cheerful bobbies marshalled the growing influx of excited families and foreign visitors. An event that gave extra lustre to Elizabeth's great day was the news that Everest had at last been conquered by a team of the Empire's leading mountaineers, New Zealander Edmund Hillary being the first to reach the top in company with a Sherpa guide called Tenzing.

The procession to Westminster Abbey was headed by members of the Royal Family, followed by foreign royals and the international eminences, all in open carriages, despite the occasional light shower and the threat of persistent rain. The noise from the welcoming crowds was huge.

'I'm going deaf,' said fifteen-year-old Maureen, daughter of Freddy and Cassie Brown.

'I can't hear nothing,' said her thirteen-year-old brother, Lewis.

'What's that?' asked Cassie, now thirty-seven but still as perky as she ever was.

'I can't hear nothing!' bawled Lewis.

'Don't worry about what you can't hear,' said his dad Freddy, younger brother of Susie, and a bemedalled veteran of the Burma campaign. 'It's what you can see that counts on a day like this, laddie.'

'I can't see nothing!' bawled Lewis. 'There's a fat woman in me way!'

'Bloody 'ard luck,' said the fat woman, turning round, 'and mind yer manners. Oh, all right, then, come on, Sonny Jim.' Using a beefy arm, she brought him forward. His feet left the ground, but found it again as she plonked him beside her.

'Crikey, you a weight-lifter, missus?' asked Lewis.

'No, I'm yer kind aunt, so don't fidget or holler, just look.'

Worth a good look was Queen Salote of Tonga as she rode by in a carriage. Brown, big and beaming, her smile was huge and dazzling, and every wave to the crowds was greeted with roars of delight. Falling rain did not dampen any aspect of her tremendous enjoyment of the occasion. Salote of Tonga became the favourite celebrity of the day.

In the forefront of one section of massed spectators, Daniel had Arabella perched on his shoulders, and Patsy had little Andrew lifted high.

'Look, look!' Arabella kept shrieking at the horse and carriage procession, and Patsy forgot about the lousy American witch-hunter in her open-eyed admiration of traditional pomp and circumstance at its most spectacular.

'Oh, my stars, Daniel, aren't you proud of all this?' she said.

'I'm prouder of you and our cherubs, Patsy,' said Daniel.

'Well, I like that, Daniel, I really do,' said Patsy.

Scattered around were other members of the Adams families, such as Tommy and Vi, Edward and Leah, Bobby and Helene with Estelle and Robert, Sammy and Susie with Paula and Phoebe, and Polly and Boots with their twins. Lizzy and Ned stayed home to watch it all on television. Also among the crowds was Paul, and beside him was Lulu.

'God knows why I'm here,' said Lulu, 'it's all so archaic.'

'It's still spectacular,' said Paul, 'and Liz herself will be coming along in ten minutes or so.'

'Don't let me down by telling me you're a monarchist,' said Lulu. 'Think of the cost of this medieval circus, and how the workers could benefit if the money were used to ease their lot.'

'I think most of London's workers are here waving their flags,' said Paul.

'Poor deluded people,' said Lulu.

She and Paul were among the crowds thickly lining the Mall as the Queen in the gilded coach drawn by six horses came out through the gates of Buckingham Palace to be acclaimed by thousands of uplifted voices. With her consort Philip beside her, she began her ride to Westminster Abbey. A young woman of twenty-seven, she had inherited the throne following the abdication of her dilettante uncle, now the Duke of Windsor, and the death of her father.

Immense enthusiasm greeted her progress, an enthusiasm so atmospheric and infectious that as her great lumbering coach travelled down the Mall, an earnest female Socialist actually joined in the acclaim.

Lulu's reservations had flown away. At least for the moment.

The Queen was officially crowned in the

splendour of Westminster Abbey, watched by her ermine-clad lords, spiritual and temporal, and all the important personages from home and abroad.

A light rain fell on her way back to the Palace, but no-one cared, and Queen Salote's already famous beam symbolized the happiness of the day.

'Well, gee whizz,' said Patsy, on her way home with Daniel and the children, 'that was something special.'

'Glad you enjoyed it,' said Daniel.

Patsy smiled.

'Blimey, not 'alf, mate,' she said in perfect cockney lingo.

The Coronation, in fact, was of such international interest that America, the last country to interest itself in monarchs and monarchies, covered the whole proceedings through television and radio. When Patsy found that out in the evening, she forgave her country for allowing the abominable Joseph McCarthy a platform for his bigotry.

The multitude of foreign newsmen who had sent reports back home included members of the Soviet Press Bureau. All their reporting work for Moscow's news agencies covered their underground search for potential moles.

They were still after the person called Finch.

Chapter Twenty-Eight

The following day.

'We'll call this evening,' said one KGB man to the other.

'Agreed,' said the other. All their phone calls to the person they only knew as Finch had been unanswered. 'If he's there at all, it'll be in the evening.'

'He?'

'Yes. I'm inclined to believe, along with Comrade Kersch, that we're dealing with a man, the possible lover of Katje Galicia.'

'Do you also believe, then, that our lieutenant general is right in suspecting Galicia has defected and that her lover has gone with her?'

'Yes, that is believable.'

'So what's the point of calling on Finch's house?'

'To help us make sure. And because that's what Comrade Kersch has ordered.'

'Comrade Kersch will be out of favour with Moscow if he can't lay his hands on Bukov and Alexandrov.'

'No, we shall get the blame and a journey to Siberia. And no pension. So let us at least find

Finch, or some kind of information that will lead us to his whereabouts.'

'This evening, then.'

Boots and Polly received a letter from Eloise, in which she expressed her delight that husband Luke, following his resignation due to the events in Brunswick, had been offered the command of a training camp in Aldershot. They were coming home with their children next week.

> 'I am longing to see you all, and have told Luke never to accept another overseas posting or I'll divorce him for cruelty. Luke said that would be a fate worse than falling on his sword, but of course he's always saying something dramatic. I send my love to both of you and to the twins, and Luke sends his regards.'

Polly, smiling, said, 'So, your dramatic daughter has a dramatic husband, Boots.'

'It should make for lively theatre sometimes,' said Boots, 'and I wonder, who takes the most curtain calls?'

'Who else but Eloise?' said Polly. 'She's more dramatic than Sybil Thorndike, and we can look forward to a tophole performance when we see her.'

'Not the kind that will bring the house down, I hope,' said Boots.

He drove to his mother's house that evening to check that everything was as it should be, and to water her indoor potted plants, as he had promised.

He noted a car parked a little way down. That was a mere insignificance compared to what greeted him when he let himself into the hall. Two men at once emerged from his stepfather's study. One was chunky and square-faced, the other lean and bony. Both wore blue suits and grey trilby hats.

Boots tensed on the balls of his feet.

'Can you explain yourselves?' It was a calm enquiry.

'I ask you, are you Finch?' The question shot out, but its aggressive note did not disguise a thick accent. Boots's mental processes worked overtime. He took in the appearance of the speaker, the chunky man. A foreigner from his accent, undoubtedly, but from where? Because of his square jaw and narrow eyes, Boots made a guess. Russia. The Soviet Union was a nation wholly suspicious of the West, a nation known to have planted its agents worldwide. And Edwin, a versatile and experienced agent for Britain from 1918 until the end of the war against Hitler, had probably encountered Russians. Boots had encountered them himself following Germany's defeat.

The question came again.

'Are you Finch?'

'What if I am?' said Boots. 'And who's asking?'

'Friends,' said the bony man, his accent less pronounced. 'Yes, you will come to understand we are friends.'

And the chunky man said, 'I now ask you where is Katje Galicia, also a friend of ours?'

Boots did some more quick thinking. Would Edwin recognize such a name? Did he know its owner?

'Well, friends of Katje Galicia,' he said, 'first show me what you've been doing in the study.'

'Ah, you will co-operate?' said Bony.

'I'll think about it, as long as you haven't turned the study upside down,' said Boots. 'If you have, I'll promise only reservations.'

'Nothing has been smashed,' said Chunky, and went back with his colleague into the study, followed by Boots, who closed the door and stood with his back to it.

Desk drawers were out and on the floor, their contents strewn. Bookshelves had been swept clear, the books scattered over the floor. Sir Edwin's small filing cabinet had not yet been touched. That, perhaps, was of no account anyway, thought Boots, since he knew his stepfather kept nothing which, after his death, would reveal details of his German origins. His one fixed wish was to keep these details from the family for all time. He may have been treading on thin ice for years, but hadn't broken it so far. Boots had helped him in his footsteps.

'Clear up this mess,' he said. 'I'm a tidy man, and I take offence not only at your intrusion, but your ransacking of this study. Clear it up.'

'It is not important, surely,' said Bony.

'It is to me,' said Boots, 'so earn my co-operation.'

Chunky growled, and Bony looked disgusted at such a finicky reaction. However, they both began a clearing-up process, since a quiet and discreet response was obligatory, even if the time might come within the next half-hour to be less amenable.

Silently, slowly, and with one hand behind his back, Boots drew the key from the door lock. The moment came when both intruders were down on their knees, piling papers and books. Boots, still with his back to the door, eased it open a foot or two. It made no sound. Creaking doors were unknown in any house run by Chinese Lady.

He slipped out swiftly, pulled the door to, inserted the key and turned it. Then he went straight to the phone, dialled the number of the local police station, only half a mile away, and was put through to the desk sergeant, by which time the locked-in men were thumping on the study door.

Curses, which he was sure were shouted in Russian, reached his ears as he informed the sergeant of the situation brought about by intruders.

'Right, sir. You are Mr Adams, you say?'

'My name is Adams, yes, and this is the home of my parents. Don't hang about, get here fast.'

'I'll get men there quick as a shot, Mr Adams. Don't try tackling the men yourself.' The police sergeant rang off.

The study door was being battered. Boots decided they would not break it down, if indeed they were able to, since in a moment or two they would, of course, realize the study window offered an easier exit. Pulling a stout walking stick from the hallstand, he slipped out of the house. He sped round to the side to cover such an exit. Sure enough, after a few moments, the window was opened, a hand visible. Boots struck it heavily with the walking stick. That brought forth a yelling curse, and made Boots think of Chinese Lady using this selfsame weapon to bash burglar Fred Summersby. He permitted himself an inward smile and struck again as a chunky leg mounted the window ledge. The leg vanished amid a shout of pain, and he heard its owner take a bruising fall to the study floor.

Boots slammed the window shut. It opened again, and the bony man, hatless, thrust out his head and shoulders. Boots dealt the right shoulder a discouraging blow. Bony hissed like a tortured prisoner of the KGB suffering a sharp turn of the wheel, and his head and shoulders withdrew.

Boots, hearing a violent noise, chanced a look through the open window. Bony was sitting up, rubbing his bruised shoulder. Chunky was aiming kicks at the study door, which was vibrating but unyielding. Every door in the place was as solid as the house itself, its general construction another example of Victorian devotion to durability.

'Don't do that,' he called, 'you're wasting your time.'

Chunky whipped round.

'You will let us out,' he said, 'or I will shoot you.'

'Don't do that, either,' said Boots, 'talk instead. I'm willing to listen, and to find out exactly what you want of me. Then perhaps I'll let you out.'

Chunky came to the window.'

'We want to know where Katje Galicia is.'

'Ah,' said Boots, and rubbed his chin.

'Also, what you can tell us of her association with three friends of ours.' The thick accent was laden not with venom, but persuasiveness. He knew he and his KGB colleague were in a fix, close to breaking a paramount injunction, that of never allowing a discreet meeting with a potential mole to become the kind of incident that would attract the interest of the police, a certain consequence if he shot this man Finch. The sound was likely to arouse his immediate neighbours and cause them to come to their doors or windows. He and his fellow KGB officer might well be seen running to their car and driving it away. Cars had number plates. 'There is no need for any fuss.'

'There'll be a hell of a fuss if you shoot me,' said Boots. Playing for time, he went on. 'You say you are friends. Entering a man's house and turning it into a rubbish dump isn't my idea of friendship.'

'Come inside and let us talk,' said Chunky.

'I'm not going to risk you climbing out of this window and disappearing before I know exactly why you're here and why you wish to know where a certain lady is.' Taking up more time, Boots added, 'So far, you've said very little about yourselves or about the lady, so I'm naturally suspicious.'

'The lady, Katje Galicia, is an associate of ours,' said Bony.

'An associate, not a friend?' said Boots.

'Associate and friend.'

'I'll be frank,' said Boots, 'I'm never too disposed to talk about a lady behind her back.'

'Ah, I see,' said Chunky.

'What do you see?' asked Chinese Lady's time-wasting son.

'That you're her lover.'

'Am I?'

'It's obvious, and what we suspected,' said Bony.

'You're from Moscow, of course,' said Boots, flying a kite.

'You would know that, yes? So tell us where Katje Galicia is, and if she has won your allegiance.'

'Allegiance?' said Boots. 'That's something else.' He heard the hum of a speeding car. 'Very well, I'll come inside and talk to you.'

'Good, that is a reasonable suggestion,' said Chunky.

Boots walked round to the front door as a police vehicle pulled up next to his own car. He lifted a hand and gestured. Out of the car slipped two uniformed constables. Boots opened the front door. The policemen hurried up the drive.

'Mr Adams?'

'They're in the study,' said Boots. 'I recommend one of you to cover the window at that side of the house, to your right, while I unlock the study door.'

It was a dramatic confrontation, that of the two KGB men coming face to face with the English police constables, one having climbed in through the open window. Both Russians made a desperate and violent attempt to escape. Boots, however, blocked the door. Truncheons had to be used before handcuffs could be snapped on and the men charged with illegal entrance and resisting arrest. They were then hustled away.

Boots, left alone, stood contemplating the meaning of the incident, then tidied up the study and watered his mother's pot plants. Following which, he drove home. Polly remarked that he'd taken over an hour to water the plants. Boots said he'd explain later, and did so when the twins were in bed. First, he served Polly with a gin and tonic, and helped himself to a finger of whisky.

'Well, come on, old sport,' said Polly, 'what's the mystery? Or is it a calamity? Have the plants died a scorched-earth death?'

Boots recounted the events, up to a point.

'You think the men were Russians?' said Polly.

'I'm fairly sure,' said Boots.

Polly said, 'And their excuse for being in the house was that they were looking for a woman called – what did you say her name was?'

'They didn't spell it out for me,' said Boots, 'but I took it to be Katje Galicia.'

'That sounds Russian,' said Polly, 'but why on earth should they think they might find her in your stepfather's study? Balls of fire, old lad, is Edwin having an affair at his age? If so, could the Russian johnnies have been her relatives?'

'I doubt it,' said Boots. 'In fact, it's more likely that they encountered the previous break-in merchant, Fred Summersby, in prison, and that, by way of having his own back on Edwin and Chinese Lady, he drew for them a tempting picture of a house worth stripping.'

'And their tale of looking for a woman was a fairy story?' said Polly. 'Well, to conjure up a name like Katje Galicia on the spur of the moment earns them a medal for fast thinking. But look here, Horatio, to tackle the pair on the spot as you did wasn't up to your usual level of intelligence. Kindly bear in mind, if anything like this happens again, that you've a wife and family.'

'Oh, I simply kept the infidels locked up in the study and called the police,' said Boots.

'Shades of the recent past,' said Polly, 'didn't your mother lock up her burglar after downing him with that walking stick? Could history repeat itself so quickly?'

'It could, if the men really were tipped off by Summersby,' said Boots, who thought that if they were definitely Russian, and they hadn't denied they were from Moscow, the hearing could well be in camera. Because of the aspects of the Cold War, Russians caught in suspicious circumstances were treated as visitors of hostile political intent. 'Yes, it's possible, Polly.'

'Will you let Edwin know there's been another break-in?' asked Polly.

It occurred to Boots then that there had been no signs of a break-in, that all doors and windows were intact. That could mean entry by a key, something in keeping with the tools carried by agents of espionage.

'Yes, I'll let him know, but not until he gets back from Devon.'

'I suppose you'll be called as a witness at the hearing,' said Polly. 'Your mother won't like it if the local paper publishes a report with a headline that Sir Edwin and Lady Finch have suffered another break-in.'

'I'll tell her to make herself a pot of consoling tea,' said Boots.

'You're a cool customer, you old darling,' said Polly.

Chapter Twenty-Nine

June was deplorably indifferent to what was expected of it, blue skies, sunshine and warmth. It was cool, cloudy and wet. Down in Kent, on David and Kate's farm, the rain was falling there as elsewhere. It was Saturday afternoon, and the Italian farmhand, Enrico Cellino, had just attended to the needs of a bawling cow by reuniting it with its misplaced and bemused calf. He entered the barn, took off his rain cape and shook it. Drops flew.

'Thanks,' said Sammy and Susie's daughter Paula, shaking her own rainwear. 'That went over me.' She had been out there with Enrico, who was her chief reason for spending most of her spring and summer weekends at the farm.

'So sorry,' said Enrico. He sat down on a bale of hay and stared silently at the falling rain.

'Rico, what's wrong?' asked Paula, shapely and as fair as her mother.

'I have no real money,' said Enrico.

'Well, neither have I,' said Paula, 'but I'm not glooming about it.'

'I have savings of only two hundred pounds,' said Enrico, elbows on his knees, hands cupping his chin, and eyes now contemplating the straw-strewn floor of the barn.

'That's about a hundred and sixty pounds more than I've got in my savings bank,' said Paula.

'It's different for you, Paula, see? You're not a man in love.'

Paula eyed him with a smile.

'Who are you in love with?'

'That I must not say. David would not like me to.'

'Why wouldn't he?'

'He would tell me what I know, that I can't afford to be in love, so go and talk to the cows.'

'Rico, it doesn't cost anything to be in love.'

'It costs much to –' Enrico stopped. He gloomed again, giving an expressive Italian sigh.

'What costs much?' asked Paula, and sat down beside him on the bale of hay.

'No, no, I can't say, Paula.'

'Yes, you can,' said Paula, 'but first tell me who you're in love with.'

'To you I can say Little Lucille.'

'Little Lucille?' Paula laughed. 'That's the biggest cow, you silly man.'

'But dear to my heart.'

'Rico, you're hedging.'

'Hedging?'

'Yes, you're dodging the question.'

'What question, Paula?'

'Who are you in love with? If you don't tell me, I'll make trouble.'

'But I think you know.'

'Never mind what you think. Tell me.'

'It's you, isn't it?'

'Well, it had better not be some other girl,' said Paula.

Enrico lifted his head and looked at her. Her smile sparkled in the gloom that the clouds and the rain brought to the barn, matching the Italian's mood. That is, until now. Paula's smile lifted him into an arena of tropical brightness, in a manner of speaking.

'You like it that I love you?' he said.

'Well, I haven't been coming here all this time because I'm crazy about the cows,' said Paula. 'Rico, you can kiss me now.' Happily, Enrico kissed her. Paula kissed him back, and for the next few minutes they kissed each other, very happily. Also, the rejuvenated Italian did what came naturally. He caressed her. Paula's virgin bosom stirred. Well, she thought of it as virginal. The sensations, however, didn't alarm her. Far from it. All the same, she said, 'Well, really, I didn't ask you to take liberties with my person.'

'Ah, your person is pretty nice, Paula, not half,' said Enrico. Then he sighed again. 'But how can I marry you?' he asked. 'I have so little, and your family, they have much.'

'You won't be marrying my family, just me,' said Paula. 'And you've got a really roomy flat above the stables. We can both live there and work here, because I know Cousin David will give me a job, especially when he buys the farm next door.'

'David will tell me I can't afford to marry you,' said Enrico.

'Well, I'm fond of David,' said Paula, 'but I shall

tell him you've made up your mind, and so have I.'

'David is good to me, like a brother,' said Enrico.

'So he should be, you work your head off for him,' said Paula. 'Besides, when Kate has her baby, someone will have to take over her farm work. I will. Rico, when shall we marry?'

'Perhaps next Easter?' suggested Enrico.

'Easter next year?' said Paula. 'Next year? That's famous, I don't think. We'll be getting on a bit by next year, you know.' Thus spoke an eighteen-year-old girl to a young man of twenty-three, but of course the heart often caused the head to flip a bit in such circumstances. 'Is Little Lucille dearer to you than I am?'

'No-one is dearer than you,' said Enrico with Italian fervour.

'I like you saying so,' said Paula blissfully, and suggested that as her cousin Paul was getting married in September, a double wedding could be arranged. Enrico said that would make him very happy. 'Oh, wait,' said Paula, 'you're Roman Catholic and you can't marry in my kind of church, can you?'

'Well, lovely young lady,' said Enrico, who hadn't been to Mass for two years and had almost lapsed, 'it's true the Pope won't recognize the marriage, but what the hell, eh? He won't be there, no, and I won't tell him, will I?'

So they agreed on a September wedding that would coincide with that of Paul and Lulu. In the rain and wrapped in her raincoat, Paula went up to the farmhouse to tell David and Kate. David was using the opportunity of the sodden day to do his accounts and to fill in the forms required by the Ministry and its civil servants.

'I knew it would happen,' he said.

'I knew it ages ago,' said Kate.

'I didn't know it until an hour ago,' said Paula.

'Well, now you and Rico have made up your minds, we're happy for you,' said David, not in the least discouraging, after all, although he wondered if Uncle Sammy and Aunt Susie would be wholly in favour.

Paula phoned her parents that evening. Susie, answering, received the glad tidings from her bubbling daughter.

'Well, isn't that exciting, Paula love, but goodness, what's come over the families?' she said. 'Americans, French and now Italians, like we've often talked about.'

'Only one Italian, Mum,' said Paula.

'Your dad will probably say that one is only the start,' said Susie. 'My, what a mixed lot we're getting to be.'

'But you're happy about me and Rico?' said Paula.

'Yes, of course, lovey, your dad and me have been wondering these last few months just when it would come about,' said Susie. 'Rico's such a nice young man, and we couldn't be more pleased for you. Hold on, I know your dad will want to talk to you.' She called. 'Sammy, come and talk to our Paula.'

Sammy arrived at the phone, to be told by Susie

that Paula had something exciting to say to him.

'She's found a gold mine on the farm?' said Sammy.

'Forget pots of gold, just talk to her,' said Susie.

So Sammy received the news, to which he responded like a fond but cautious dad.

'Well, bless you, me pet,' he said, 'but has Rico got decent prospects?'

'Not half he has,' said Paula, 'he's got me.'

'He couldn't do better,' said Sammy. 'But can he keep you in style? I like to think me daughters don't have to patronize jumble sales once they're married.'

'Give over, Dad,' said Paula, 'I won't need ball gowns or mink coats on the farm. Dungarees will do.'

'Eh? Dungarees? All day every day?' Sammy held onto the phone to stop himself tottering. 'Don't give me earache, me pet. Tell you what I'll do. Take you to our Oxford Street shop just before the wedding, and let you choose a trunkful of our best high-class creations, and also get Lilian to design and make your wedding dress. I further offer to charge the cost of everything to our overheads. What's a hole in our profit and loss account if it'll make you look like Lili Marlene?'

'Dad, you're a darling,' said Paula. 'I'm not going to say no to all that, even if I'd just as soon look like myself as Lili Marlene. What does she look like, anyway?'

'Search me,' said Sammy, 'I've only heard about her. Didn't she float about the desert in see-through pink muslin during the war, giving the troops the kind of eyefuls that took their minds off their skin rash?'

Paula laughed.

'Well, I'm not going to float about the farm in anything see-through myself,' she said.

'That's the stuff,' said Sammy. 'Your grandma ain't in favour of anything improper. Nor's your mum. Mind, I must admit that if Lili Marlene floated by our front garden, I'd likely go looking for a camera. Anyway, me pet, I'm gladsome for you and Rico, and you can tell him so.'

'Thanks, Dad, you're one of the best, and Mum's lovely too,' said Paula.

Susie began to circulate the news that evening, of course.

Clare arrived on Sunday afternoon with a bunch of flowers for Susie, which Susie thought very sweet of her. Jimmy thought her a danger to his peace of mind, for with a pretty flared skirt she was wearing a canary-coloured sweater. It clung so revealingly that he was sure it was going to be too much for his eyesight before the afternoon was out. I call it unfair, he told himself. I'd be better off if she'd kept her mackintosh on. While there was no rain, the clouds looked as if they meant to empty gallons from a low height.

Along with the flowers, Clare had brought blue jeans.

'I thought I'd best change into them for me bit of gardening,' she said.

'Don't worry about them on my account,' said Sammy.

'Beg pardon, Mr Adams?' said Clare, hair burnished to a dark auburn glow.

'Oh, Dad's got a thing about jeans,' said Phoebe, 'but we're gradually curing him.'

'Phoebe, take Clare up to your room and she can change there,' said Susie.

'Come on,' said Phoebe, and Clare followed her out of the lounge – parlour to Sammy – and up the stairs.

'Jimmy, she really is a lovely girl,' said Susie. There was no lack of feminine appeal in the Adams family, but Susie did think Clare a bit special. 'Really lovely.'

'Granted,' said Jimmy.

'What happened to your initiative that you let someone else beat you to Clare?' asked Sammy.

'Someone else knew her before I did,' said Jimmy. His smile, if rueful, was typical of his good nature. 'Just one of those things.'

'Get some competition in if you fancy her,' said Sammy.

'Against my principles,' said Jimmy.

'Jimmy me lad,' said Sammy, 'we've all got principles, but no-one has to treat 'em like the Twelve Commandments.'

'Ten,' said Jimmy. 'You're thinking of the twelve disciples. Look, when Clare comes down, tell her I'm up at the plot sorting out the tomato seedlings.' Off he went.

Susie smiled.

'I think our Jimmy's wrestling with his principles,' she said.

'Well, there's no halfway,' said Sammy, 'it's either win or lose.'

Jimmy had thirty tomato seedlings, all looking sturdy in their pots. He'd prepared a long strip of fertilized ground, and was marking it out. He could, of course, have done the planting easily enough by himself, and he knew it. But there it was, he'd given in to the temptation of inviting Clare to help him. Would it do him any good? No, it was much more likely to increase his frustrations.

'Jimmy, here I am.'

Clare came up, dressed now in her sweater and jeans, plus Susie's gumboots. Well, the jeans will do, thought Jimmy, but I'm not sure I'm going to stick with the tomatoes if her sweater gets too close to my shirt. I'm only human.

'I'm ready for you, Clare,' he said, which was true in more ways than one.

'Shall I fill the watering can?' asked Clare.

'No need,' said Jimmy, studying the prepared ground like a man who needed a distraction, even if it was only the look of Mother Earth. 'It's been raining, the soil's nicely moist and I've had the tomato plants out, so they're moist too. I'll start creating some favourable holes, while you lift the plants out of the pots one by one, just as you did with the bedding plants last week. Nice of you to come all the way from Bow again. What an obliging girl you are.'

'Oh, I like being a help and learning things,' said Clare. 'As I mentioned to me parents this morning, there's always something you can learn on your way through life, and the more you get to know, the more you improve yourself, don't you?'

'Well, I suppose getting to know about gardening improves your chance of being creative when you have a garden of your own,' said Jimmy, and went down on one knee to put distance between himself and her sweater.

'When I get married, you mean?' said Clare, happy that she was with him again.

If there's one thing I don't want to think about, said Jimmy to himself, it's her and Harry Ballymore getting together on their wedding night.

'Are you engaged, then?' he asked.

'Oh, no, nothing like that, not yet,' said Clare.

So, thought Jimmy, the Irish bloke hasn't popped the question yet.

'Well, I daresay you've got a happy home and garden in mind,' he said, using a dibber to make a hole for the first plant.

Crikey, not half I have, thought Clare, and I know who with.

'Well, that's what a lot of young people think about,' she said. 'I mean, it's natural.'

'Hand me one,' said Jimmy.

'One what?'

'One plant.'

'Oh. Oh, of course.' Clare picked up a seedling pot and lifted the plant out. Jimmy took it from her and dropped it in. That was the first of thirty, and their partnership took on a flourishing note. After a while, Clare, in her jeans, went down on her knees beside the young man who made her cuddle her pillow at nights and think thoughts that were blush-making. She didn't know it, but Jimmy had similar thoughts day and night, all on her account. The only difference was that they weren't blush-making to him.

In went one seedling after another, with Jimmy taking his time and trying to rise above what the proximity of her colourful sweater was doing to him. Any day now, he thought, I'm going to dynamite my principles and blow them up. If I don't, I'll get repressed, turn into a furtive sex maniac and follow her about with foul intent.

That reflection made him break into a laugh.

'Jimmy?' said Clare.

'Oh, just some silly thoughts,' said Jimmy.

'How silly?' asked Clare, freeing one more plant from its pot.

'Well, when is a tomato not a tomato?'

'I don't know,' said Clare.

'Nor do I,' said Jimmy, 'that's what's silly about it.'

It was Clare's turn to laugh. Her sweater seemed to join in. Jimmy turned his thoughts to rowing a boat on a choppy Serpentine. Did the Serpentine get choppy?

They continued with their work. The clouds lifted a little and the afternoon brightened.

'I'm starting permanent at the fact'ry tomorrow,' said Clare.

'So you are,' said Jimmy, feeling he'd be safe with two doors and a corridor between him and the general office switchboard. 'You'll be an asset. An asset is highly popular with my dad, he equates it with a credit balance.'

'D'you mean that every time he comes to the fact'ry he'll see me as a credit balance on the firm's bank account?' asked Clare, tickled.

'Well, he won't see a better-looking one,' said Jimmy, letting his guard drop.

'Oh, I bet a credit balance has never been more complimented,' said Clare, delighted.

'There, that's the lot,' said Jimmy, firming down the last plant. 'Now, seeing the weather's a bit cool, and probably cold at night, we'll use cloches to cover the plants.'

'Cloches?' said Clare. 'D'you mean cloche hats? Crikey, you don't put a cloche hat over every plant, do you, Jimmy?'

'Only old ones left over from my Aunt Polly's flapper days,' said Jimmy. 'And only if I had any, which I don't. No, I use those glass cloches.' He pointed and Clare saw them, sheets of glass fixed by triangular metal frames. 'They'll protect the plants from any chilly winds and help to bring them on. Tomato seedlings don't like chilly winds. It retards them.'

'I think I'm really learning things,' said Clare.

All I'm learning, thought Jimmy, is how to stick to being a decent bloke in highly difficult circumstances. What a peach, what a ray of sunshine when she smiles, and what a good-natured girl. There must be something on the debit side, but blowed if I can spot it. Well, they say love is blind.

Together they covered the long row of plants,

using nine cloches in all. Eight would have been enough, but Clare dropped one, breaking glass.

'Oh, help, sorry,' she said.

Now I wonder, thought Jimmy, have I found a fault, is she clumsy?

'Don't worry, no problem,' he said, 'we've got spares.'

'Jimmy, I'll pay for a new one, honest.'

'Well, that's sweet,' said Jimmy, 'but what's one cloche compared to the pleasure of having a working partner on this old vegetable plot? No, let's go and have tea and cake now.'

'Lovely,' said Clare.

Susie served the tea and cake around the kitchen table, and Clare, having changed back into her skirt, found favour in Sammy's fashion-conscious optics. He was currently complaining to Rachel Goodman about the Paris designer who'd thought up trouser suits for women. That could lead to dressing them in boiler suits and sending them down the mines. Rachel kept assuring him she wouldn't be one of them.

Over the tea and cake, Clare thought the atmosphere informal and homely, especially as Jimmy's parents never attempted to hide their cockney roots, even though their house and its furnishings were all of posh. She liked them a lot, and Jimmy's pretty sister, Phoebe, as well. And Jimmy, of course, except it was more than liking in his case.

When she said goodbye later, Jimmy told her he was looking forward to seeing her at the factory tomorrow, Phoebe said they'd name the tomato plants after her, and Susie said what a pleasure it was to have her. Sammy again drove her to a bus stop. All the way home she kept thinking that if Jimmy didn't ask her for a date soon, she'd begin to believe there really was someone else. That would mean scratching someone else's face and ruining her looks. I'm only human, she told herself.

Chapter Thirty

The East Dulwich police, finding the two arrested men were not only Russian, but highly suspect, contacted Scotland Yard. CID men from the Yard arrived to put their own questions to the Russians, and that led to MI5 taking an interest in them.

Boots, having received no call from the local police to attend as a witness in the case of the arrested men, let sleeping dogs lie.

Meanwhile Sir Edwin and Chinese Lady were enjoying a quiet and relaxing time in Devon with Sir Henry and Lady Simms.

At the end of her day on the switchboard, Clare put her head into Jimmy's office to say goodnight. She'd seen very little of him, morning or afternoon. Fortunately, she'd been too busy to get depressed.

'I'm going now, Mister Jimmy.' She wasn't keen on addressing him in that way. It sounded silly. 'Goodnight.'

'Goodnight, Clare,' said Jimmy, who'd dreamt last night that he was being chased up a hill by a huge hairy Irishman wielding a Scottish claymore. His running feet became heavier and heavier, but much to his relief he woke up just as the swinging claymore was about to slice his head off. Jesus, he thought at the time, now Gertie and Bert's eldest granddaughter is indirectly giving me nightmares. 'Off you go, then, see you again tomorrow, we're a lucky lot here for having you with us permanently.'

'I'm thrilled about that,' said Clare.

'I include the switchboard,' said Jimmy.

'Oh, ta,' said Clare, 'including the switchboard is a real compliment.' And she departed with a smile on account of getting the last word in. A young lady couldn't always do that with Jimmy Adams, so he must be weakening.

Clare had no idea he was nearly a pushover. But then, she also had no idea he thought she was going steady with an Irish bloke.

Boots and Polly were playing Monopoly with Gemma and James in the evening. Polly was coining it, having houses on Mayfair and Bond Street, and Boots had just landed on Mayfair.

'Pay up, old sport,' she said.

'You're in terrible trouble, Daddy,' said Gemma.

'I'm done for,' said Boots.

'I'm in jail,' said James.

The phone rang.

'I'll go, Boots,' said Polly, 'while you sort out your cash problems.'

Answering the phone, she said, 'Hello?'

'Oh, good evening, it's Mrs Davidson here.'

'Here, it's Mrs Adams,' said Polly coolly.

'Is Mr Adams there?'

'He's busy with money problems,' said Polly.

'I'm sorry to hear that,' the languid voice drawled.

'Not as sorry as he is,' said Polly.

'Mrs Adams, do I know you?'

'We met at one of my stepmother's charity functions,' said Polly. 'She's Lady Simms.'

'Oh, such a splendid lady. I really am sorry about your husband's financial difficulties –'

'Don't be,' said Polly, 'I know him well enough to be certain he's wriggling out of them. What can I do for you?'

'My daughter Cathy would like to talk to your son James.'

So why, thought Polly, did you ask if Boots was available? I know, of course. You're stalking him.

'I'll call James,' she said, and did so. Out he came. 'James, Cathy Davidson wants to talk to you.'

'Again?' said James. 'She talked to me on our way home from school, and yesterday as well. And the day before. I'm getting the feeling that she'll talk me into my grave before my next birthday.'

'Romance is wearing off?' smiled Polly, hand over the mouth of the phone.

'Oh, she's quite nice,' said James, 'but I think her tongue needs an operation. Poor child,' he murmured. 'Oh, well, let's be kind.' He took the phone from Polly, and Polly left him to it.

Returning to the living room, she said, 'Cathy Davidson, the sweet child, is trying to make a pet of James, and her dear mother, Anastasia Davidson, has definite designs on you, Boots.'

'Oh, help, do we lock all the doors, Mummy, like you said?' asked Gemma, but with a giggle.

'Yes, and raise the drawbridge and fill the moat with sharks,' said Polly. 'Now, have you paid up, Boots old chum?'

'I'm broke and out of the game,' said Boots.

'Frightfully rotten luck,' said Polly, 'but never mind, you're now free to go and hide yourself in the attic. Bolt the door after you.'

'I don't favour that,' said Boots, 'let's leave danger woman to the sharks.'

'Still, we ought to give her a warning,' said Gemma, 'like putting up a notice that says "Mind the fishes".'

James came back, eyes rolling.

'You'll never believe this,' he said.

'What won't we?' asked Gemma.

'Cathy's been talking to me,' he said. 'As usual,' he added, with a grin. 'She told me she and her mother are going to the South of France in July. They've got a villa there, and we're all invited to join them. What d'you think of that?'

'Very little,' said Polly.

'But, Mummy, the South of France,' said Gemma, eyes huge.

'Just the place for your father to fall into the clutches of a harpy and disappear under a midnight sky,' said Polly.

'Oh, I think Dad could always fight his way out,' said James.

'He won't be given the chance to,' said Polly, 'we won't be going.'

'Is that official, Mum?' asked James.

'Official, full stop,' said Polly.

'Cathy mentioned we can have time to think about it,' said James, 'but I'm not sure I want to be talked to in the South of France for a whole fortnight.'

'Fortunately,' said Boots, 'we've already booked our usual fortnight in Cornwall, and can therefore decline the invitation without having to tell a porkie. Will you be seeing Cathy on your way home from school tomorrow, James?'

'She's always waiting for me,' said James.

'Golly,' said Gemma, 'next thing we know she'll be waiting at the church door for him.'

'I totally forbid you to turn up, James,' said Polly. 'Great calamities, that Russian dragonfly as your mother-in-law? Never.'

'James, tell Cathy our summer holiday is already arranged,' said Boots.

'And next year's as well,' said Polly.

'All the same, Mummy,' said Gemma, 'I suppose we'd still best keep Daddy locked up in the attic.'

'Well, we'll finish our game first, darling,' said Polly, 'and then you and James can take him up.'

'I've a feeling,' said Boots, 'that as well as being bankrupted by Monopoly, I'm going to forfeit my liberty.'

'Hard luck, Dad,' said James, 'but that's better than having you disappear at midnight.'

'Not half,' said Gemma. She thought. 'Yes, not half, full stop.'

Sammy, who visited the Bethnal Green factory once a week to confer with Tommy on any problems affecting production, supplies of raw materials or staff, was on his way the following day, Rachel accompanying him as his personal assistant. She was also the company secretary, as well as a director and shareholder. Sammy liked to keep her up to date with all that concerned the factory. Rachel had a business instinct that could sometimes help to double the anticipated profit on a completed contract.

The weather was warm, but rolling clouds were thundery.

'We'll call on old Eli first,' said Sammy.

'Mr Greenberg?' said Rachel.

'My old friend and business comrade,' said Sammy, and drove into Mr Greenberg's Camberwell yard. He and Rachel alighted, and out of his office, a green-painted shed that needed a new coat, came Eli Greenberg, almost as ancient as his round black hat that looked as if it was being overtaken by moss. His hair and beard were flecked with white. He was seventy-two, but unfailing.

'Well, how's yourself, Eli old cock?' said Sammy.

'Vhy, vhat a pleasure, Sammy, ain't it?' beamed Mr Greenberg. 'And don't I see Rachel there? Vhat a treat for my old eyes.'

'Shalom, Eli,' smiled Rachel, 'haven't you retired yet?'

'So I have, Rachel, so I have,' said the old rag and bone merchant, known all over South London. 'Don't my Michal and Jacob run the business now?' Michal and Jacob, his stepsons, had returned from a two-year stint in an Israeli kibbutz to relieve him of his toil.

'So why are you here?' asked Rachel.

'Vell, Rachel my dear, it's like this, ain't it?' said Mr Greenberg. 'At home, Hannah is alvays a busy voman.' Hannah was his wife. 'And vhat do I do vhen I'm there all day? Get under her feet. So I come here and do the business books and answer the phone, don't I? Especially vhen Michal and Jacob are out with the cart doing a house clearance, like today. See vhat a fine collection of valuable goods ve have.'

Behind him, in the covered area of the yard, was something familiar to Sammy, a mountain of every kind of household furniture and domestic equipment, all on offer to customers looking for second-hand bargains.

'Some things don't change, Eli, which pleases me,' said Sammy. 'I ain't too taken with what Boots calls galloping social revolution.'

'Evolution, I think he said, Sammy,' smiled Rachel.

'Same thing, Rachel,' said Sammy, with which many people would have agreed, particularly Chinese Lady and her contemporaries. 'Eli old mate, what I'm here for is to inform you that me daughter Paula is getting married on the first Saturday in September, and so is Tommy and Vi's son, Paul, me nephew.'

'Vell, ain't I happy for them, Sammy?' said Mr Greenberg.

'Point is,' said Sammy, 'can the family call on you and your pony and cart, as per custom that goes back to the wedding of Boots and Emily?'

'Ah, Emily,' sighed Mr Greenberg sorrowfully,

'never vas there a sadder day than vhen a devil's bomb took her life. But other lives, vell, they must go on. Sammy, ain't I in pleasure to be asked to cart the brides to the church as per custom?'

A tremendous flash of lightning struck, followed by a huge roll of thunder. The yard seemed to tremble, and from the top of a stack of chairs one toppled and fell.

Rachel shouted.

'Eli!'

Mr Greenberg, closest to the stack and with his back to it, turned. The falling chair, made of pine, struck him on his head, crushing his ancient hat. He staggered and fell.

'Christ!' breathed Sammy, and rushed to kneel beside his old and faithful friend. 'Eli?' Mr Greenberg was on his back, hat off, bearded face grey. 'Eli?' Mr Greenberg lay still, his breathing hoarse but faint. Sammy noted, thankfully, that there was no blood oozing from the bushy head of hair, but he spoke urgently to Rachel. 'Phone for an ambulance, Rachel, quick!'

Rachel darted into the office shed, grabbed the phone and dialled for help. The response was speedy.

'Ambulance service, please,' she said.

She was put through. She stated the necessary details, and received a promise of immediate help. She came out of the shed. Sammy had taken off his jacket and placed it over the unconscious rag and bone man. Mr Greenberg, as ever, was wearing his old coat with its capacious pockets, but Sammy, despite knowing little of first aid, felt sure an injured person needed to be kept as warm as possible.

Thunder was still rolling, and the sky was darkening.

'My God, Sammy,' said Rachel, 'what do we do if rain starts sheeting down on him? We daren't move him.'

'Keep an eye on him, Rachel, while I look for some waterproof covers.'

'My God,' breathed Rachel, 'don't look for them in that stack or the whole lot might come down on you.'

Sammy rummaged around the stack and the yard, feeling sick at heart for a man who, in his understanding of how demoralizing poverty could be, had done a thousand good turns during his many years in London.

'Vhy, missus,' he would say to a housewife striving to keep her family going, 'you vant only sixpence for that vase? I ain't letting you cheat yourself vhen it's vorth a shilling.'

He would get a Sunday market trader to sell the vase for one and sixpence, and he and the trader would pocket threepence each, a fair return for a good deed.

The thunder rolled away, the dark clouds lightened, and Sammy's search for waterproof covering and Rachel's vigil beside Mr Greenberg came to a close on the arrival of an ambulance. The medics took over at once as Sammy explained what had happened.

'It looks serious for the old lad,' he said. 'Is it?'

One medic, making the required examination,

opened Mr Greenberg's closed eyes and noted cloudiness.

'Concussion at least,' he said.

The stretcher had been brought from the ambulance, and the medics eased Mr Greenberg onto it with care and expertise. Sammy and Rachel followed them and watched as they slid the stretcher into the ambulance.

'Which hospital, please?' asked Rachel.

'St Thomas's.'

'When can we phone to ask about his condition?' enquired Sammy anxiously.

'Couple of hours, say.'

'Thanks.' Sammy and Rachel watched the ambulance depart, its bell ringing. 'God, I feel for old Eli, Rachel.'

'My life, don't both of us, Sammy?' said Rachel. 'I'm praying it's only concussion.'

'That corblimey chair hit him a hell of a crack. His hat and his hair might have softened the blow, but I've got to hope his head was hard enough not to get seriously damaged.'

'Sammy, how do we let his sons know?'

'We can't at the moment,' said Sammy, 'they're out on a house clearance.' He was fond of Eli's sturdy and pleasant stepsons. They had once been a great help to him in seeing off the Fat Man's heavies at a time when Fatty was coming it like an American gangster. 'No, wait a bit, I wonder if there's anything in the office that'll tell us which house and where, and if there's a phone number?'

Rachel searched the office desk, and Sammy searched an old wooden filing cabinet. They had no luck until Rachel found a diary in one of the desk's drawers. She opened it. It was full of business entries. She turned to the page covering today's details.

'Sammy, look!'

There it was.

'Clearance. 9.30. Matthews. 103 Brancaster Lane, Purley. Uplands 3066.'

The handwriting was Eli's own.

'Got you, Rachel,' said Sammy. The time now was a little after ten thirty. He dialled the number. A lady answered.

'Mrs Matthews speaking.'

'Good morning to you, Mrs Matthews,' said Sammy politely, 'is your house being cleared of furniture and effects today?'

'Indeed it is. Who are you?'

'My name is Adams, and I'm a friend of the men doing the job. Would you mind if I spoke to one of them?'

'I hope it's not to take them off their work.'

'No, it concerns their father,' said Sammy.

'Very well. Hold on, Mr Adams.'

It was Michal, the elder son, who came to the phone.

'Who's calling?' he asked.

'Sammy Adams.'

'What's cooking, Mr Adams? Mrs Matthews mentioned my father.'

Sammy didn't make a long or dramatic rigmarole of the details. He was quick and concise, and didn't mention his suspicion that Eli might have suffered a fractured skull. Michal struggled with emotion. He and his brother Jacob had a genuine affection for their enduring stepfather and his little eccentricities.

'He's been taken to St Thomas's Hospital,' said Sammy at the close of his account.

'I'll go there with Jacob. Poor old Papa. No, I'd better phone Mama first.'

'Yes, do that,' said Sammy, 'and explain to Mrs Matthews.'

'I'll have to,' said Michal, 'since I'll be driving the van to St Thomas's with a fair amount of her furniture already loaded.'

'Well, I'm not going to keep you,' said Sammy, 'but did you say van and not the old horse and cart?'

'The old horse and cart are in retirement, Mr Adams, along with the little cart. Look, I must ring off now.'

'Michal, you go ahead,' said Sammy, 'I'll be phoning the hospital in about an hour or so to find out how your dad is.'

He put the phone down. He looked at Rachel. Her brown eyes were dark with concern, and he felt that she too suspected a fractured skull, not the best thing by a long chalk to happen to a man of seventy-two.

'How did Michal take it?' she asked.

'He was shocked but sensible,' said Sammy. 'He's going to phone his mother and then motor off with Jacob to St Thomas's.'

'And what are you and I going to do, Sammy?'

Someone entered the yard then, a man in a suit and bowler.

'Anyone at home?' he hollered.

Sammy and Rachel emerged from the shed.

'Can I help?' asked Sammy.

'Well, I bleedin' hope so, chummy, I've called to pick up a crate of kitchen utensils. Where is it?'

Sammy looked around, and spotted an open wooden crate on the far side of the shed. It was full of knives, forks, spoons and ladles. A corkscrew with a bamboo handle and a nutmeg grater were also visible. Stuck on one side of the crate was a label, marked 'Higson, five shillings'.

'What's your monicker, mate?' he asked.

'Higson, and is that me job lot?'

'Looks like it,' said Sammy. 'At five bob.'

'Hold on, cully, I ain't putting me mitt into me pocket for someone I ain't seen here before.'

'Take a good look at me and this lady,' said Sammy, 'and if you see a couple of fly operators, you need a new pair of mince pies. Eli Greenberg's had an accident, and we're looking after his yard for him.'

'An accident?'

'A serious one,' said Rachel. She pointed. 'That chair fell on his head and sent him to hospital. We should take advantage of that? Not on your life.'

'Hang around for another hour or so, and you can listen to me phoning St Thomas's,' said Sammy.

'Blimey, that ruddy chair downed poor old Eli? I got to believe that?'

'Up to you,' said Sammy.

'Good enough, chummy. Here's the five bob and give me best wishes to Eli.'

The exchange was made and the customer went off with the crate, shaking his head in sympathetic disbelief that the wily old rag and bone merchant could be in the wrong place at the wrong moment. It wasn't like him to make that kind of mistake.

James informed Cathy that as he and his family were booked for a Cornish holiday, they couldn't accept the invitation to the South of France. It was regretful, of course, but couldn't be helped. Cathy said she and her mother would be ever so disappointed. James said everyone had to swallow a bit of disappointment at times, so could she swallow this bit?

'I'll have to,' said Cathy, 'but it'll hurt going down. James, Mummy thinks your dad's awfully nice.'

'Yes, that's why we've got him locked up.'

'What?'

'Just a joke,' said James.

But it was no joke to Mother Dear.

Chapter Thirty-One

Minutes passed.

'What do we do, Sammy?' asked Rachel.

'We could shut the place up if we had the keys to the shed and the gate padlock,' said Sammy, 'but we don't have 'em, which is another headache. Well, I'll phone the factory to let Tommy know what's holding us up, then I'll stick around, see to any other customers that come hollering in, and get through to St Thomas's later. Rachel, you can go back to the office. D'you mind the walk?'

'Sammy, I'd prefer to stay and see things through with you,' said Rachel. 'My life, I should leave you here worrying about Eli by yourself? I should say not. Let's worry together. That might earn us good news.'

'Well, I've got old friends, more than a few of them,' said Sammy, 'but some are special, like you and Eli. I'll phone Tommy now, then we'll put Eli's kettle on and see if there's some coffee in his cupboard, eh? He's not the kind of bloke to spend his retirement in that shed without having tea and coffee to keep him company.'

'I'm a believer too, Sammy.'

* * *

Sammy and Rachel had to deal with two more customers, both of whom wanted to talk to Michal and Jacob about their stocks of items suitable for selling on market stalls. Both accepted the suggestion of calling at some other time.

At midday, Sammy phoned the hospital. He was told that Mr Eli Greenberg had a hairline fracture of the skull, and was suffering the effects of severe concussion. There were no immediate complications, however, and his condition was stable.

'The old lad will recover?' said Sammy.

'We hope so, Mr Adams. You may phone again tomorrow.'

'Thanks,' said Sammy. 'D'you know if his sons are there?'

'They left five minutes ago, but Mrs Greenberg is with the patient.'

'Right,' said Sammy, 'thanks again.'

He informed Rachel of Eli's condition.

'I hope that's good news,' she said.

'Don't we all?' said Sammy. He and Rachel stayed, guarding the yard and Eli's petty-cash box. The old lad might call himself retired, but he was obviously still keeping an eye on the business.

At one o'clock, Michal phoned. He was back with Jacob at the house in Purley to complete the clearance job for Mr and Mrs Matthews. His dad, he said, had a hairline fracture of the skull. Sammy said yes, he'd received the news from the hospital, and hoped a recovery was on its way.

'Incidentally, Michal, I'm still at your yard with

Rachel Goodman. It's open to all comers. We can't close it, we don't have the keys.'

'Well, it's good of you to be keeping an eye on it, Mr Adams,' said Michal, 'but I can't expect you to stay until me and Jacob get back. There's spare keys in the bottom drawer of the filing cabinet. Use those to lock the shed and the gate padlock. And thanks for everything.'

'Right,' said Sammy. 'By the way, a bloke name of Higson called to collect the crate of cutlery. He paid up and his five bob is in the petty-cash box.'

'My thanks,' said Michal. 'Shalom, Mr Adams.'

'Shalom,' said Sammy, and hung up.

'Well?' said Rachel.

'We can lock up now,' said Sammy, 'there's spare keys at the bottom of the filing cabinet. I'll phone Tommy first, and let him know we're leaving. I'll ask him to have a word with the canteen manageress about finding some lunch for us, as long as it's not leftovers.'

'Sammy, you're still a thinking man,' smiled Rachel, happy to be a free woman able to enjoy a continuing relationship with him, even if it was permanently platonic.

On arrival at the factory, Sammy and Rachel put Tommy fully in the picture regarding the morning's events. Tommy shook his head.

'What a piece of howling bad luck for old Eli,' he said. 'Some people might deserve a chronic bash on the head, but not Eli. Let's fancy his chances, let's hope his fracture will mend. Anyway, there's some lunch for both of you in the canteen, so do some work on it with a knife and fork, and I'll see you afterwards.'

'Right,' said Sammy.

'Pleasure,' said Rachel.

Afterwards she went to see Lilian, the designer, and Sammy had a chat with Tommy about prices. Competitors were active. Not that there was anything like an economic boom, just a slow progressive relaxing of some restrictions on the importation of certain consumer goods and raw materials for factories. It was enough to make Tommy and Sammy keep a wary eye on competitors sharp enough to attempt an undercutting of their wholesale prices. Sammy suggested that as the firm's overall financial situation was as healthy as Rosie and Matthew's chickens and David and Kate's cows, they'd do some undercutting themselves, the kind that would put their chief competitors in a state of fatal ruination.

'That's your suggestion?' said Tommy.

'Well, you know me,' said Sammy, 'I can't tell a porkie. Boots came up with it before I left the office this morning.'

'Well, if it comes from Boots –'

'Don't tell me anything about the family's mastermind that I don't already know,' said Sammy.

The phone rang. That was for the third time since they had begun their conference. It seemed that much of Tommy's time was spent talking to customers. While he was talking to this one, Sammy, never able to simply stand by, went to the general office to see Clare.

The office girls' greeting was a chorus.

'Hello, Mister Sammy, how's yourself?'

'Waiting for Christmas,' said Sammy. 'How's the switchboard, Clare?'

'Trying to beat me, Mister Sammy,' said Clare, all delightful sex appeal in a pretty shirt-blouse and a maroon skirt. Well, thought Sammy, no wonder Jimmy's going about like an absent-minded circus act that's just fallen off the high wire and given himself a serious headache.

'You'll win, Clare.'

'Well, I hope so,' said Clare, 'or Mister Jimmy will lose his good opinion of me talents.'

Sammy smiled, quite sure it wasn't her switchboard talents that were flummoxing Jimmy.

He rejoined Tommy, and they worked out the extent of a price cut that would make their competitors emigrate while they still had enough lolly for the fare to Australia, land of the jumping kangaroos.

MI5, concluding its interrogation of the two Germans whose papers were those of journalists attached to the Soviet Press Bureau, had no hesitation in deciding they were working as undercover agents of the KGB, not an unusual occupation for so-called Communist journalists in the capitals of Western democracies. MI5 accordingly informed the Foreign Office. There, by coincidence, it was Sir Edwin's step-grandson Bobby who drafted the usual kind of note for delivery to the Soviet ambassador. The note defined two Soviet citizens, Igor Koppe and Vasily Dubenny, as personae non grata, and therefore to be deported.

No attempt had been made by MI5 to contact the owner of the house in which the men had been arrested. The owner, Sir Edwin Finch, was known. Further, he had made a phone call to his old department before going on holiday.

The woman now occupying the Bloomsbury flat vacated by Katje Galicia was the proprietress of an employment agency that specialized in finding shorthand typists and secretaries for businesses in need. She used the table in the living room as a desk. She sat at it most evenings, attending to work she had brought from her office, her feet resting on the carpet.

She had no idea that the chair and table, along with her feet, were resting on a makeshift coffin.

As for Kersch, he was at his lowest ebb. Being no nearer to solving the mystery of the disappearance of three KGB officers, he was now having to ask Moscow to send two of its most experienced KGB investigators to track down the missing trio. His own unsuccessful efforts were doing him no good at all, especially when he thought about the possibility of failure being recorded in his file. However, if the investigators themselves failed, he could only hope it would be their files in which black marks were subsequently recorded.

On top of that worry, he had to face the fact that two other officers, Dubenny and Koppe, had committed the idiotic indiscretion of getting themselves arrested.

No wonder he was off his food.

Clare, finishing her duties, went to say goodnight to Jimmy. She had seen more of him today.

'Goodnight, Mister Jimmy.'

'Goodnight, Clare,' said Jimmy. 'By the way,' he said, thinking it was time to get a positive picture of the opposition, 'how's Harry?'

'Harry?' said Clare.

'Harry Ballymore.'

'Who?' Clare looked lost for a moment. 'Oh, you mean Harry Dallimore.'

'Is that his name?' said Jimmy, who had a feeling he was marooned on a desert island, with nothing to cheer him up except coconuts. And when you've had coconuts for a week, you're already longing for something as basic as fishcakes. 'One of your cousins mentioned him at your grandparents' retirement party. I thought she said Ballymore. It's Dallimore, is it?'

'Yes, Harry Dallimore,' said Clare, 'but why did you ask after him?'

'He's your steady date, isn't he?' said Jimmy.

'Who told you that?' She threw the question at him almost indignantly.

'Your cousin, the elder one,' said Jimmy, and Clare had a sudden feeling he wasn't in favour of Harry, no, not a bit. Her pulse rate jumped.

'Jimmy, no. No, he isn't.' Her words came a little emotionally. 'I haven't seen him for ages. I don't have a steady, specially not Harry Dallimore. Or anyone else.'

'Say that again,' said Jimmy, coming to his feet.

'There's no-one,' breathed Clare. 'I ain't— I'm not dating any feller.'

'Well, talk about suffering cats,' said Jimmy. 'Clare, come right in and shut that door.'

'Jimmy?' Clare spoke his name faintly.

Jimmy walked over to her, closed the door and said, 'You darling.'

'Jimmy?' she breathed again, wondering if he had actually said that.

'Have you any idea how many times I've thought up a way of making some Irish bloke disappear in a Tipperary bog?'

'What d'you mean? Jimmy, what d'you mean?'

'All right, so he's not Irish,' said Jimmy. 'What do I care? Even if his grandmother's as much as the Pearly Queen of Bethnal Green, that doesn't bother me, either. All I care about is whether or not I can take you out every Saturday night, and round Victoria Park on Sundays. Any chance, Miss Roper?'

'You're asking?' murmured Clare. 'Jimmy, you're really asking?'

'You bet I am,' said Jimmy, 'and I'd like an answer in the affirmative.'

'Oh, how could I say no?'

'Well, you could,' said Jimmy, 'but I hope you won't.'

'Jimmy, d'you mean you – ?'

'Not half I do, you darling,' said Jimmy.

Despite the warning from her grandpa not to throw herself at any feller, Clare threw herself at Jimmy and landed in his ready arms. Thrilling kisses took place. Jimmy hadn't closed the door just to talk about the switchboard or how the tomato seedlings were doing.

'Oh, I'm going giddy,' gasped Clare. 'And I don't know what to say, except I think I'm in love.'

'I know I am,' said Jimmy, 'let's make a twosome in a garden.'

'Mum! Dad!' Clare bounced into her mum's kitchen. 'What d'you think?'

'Search me,' said her dad.

'What's happened?' asked her mum.

'We're in love,' said Clare.

'Who, you and the milkman?' said her dad. 'I ain't having that.'

'Don't be daft, Dad, you know I mean me and Jimmy. Jimmy Adams. Lor', I never met a lovelier bloke. Mum, I think he's going to ask me to marry him, he's taking me dancing on Saturday.' Clare was glowing.

'Well, that's really nice, love,' said her mum.

'Nice? It's a lot more than nice,' said Clare, 'it's me wildest dream.'

'If he's taking you waltzing,' said her dad, 'you could be right about a proposal.'

'Waltzing? Dad, it's 1953, not 1933,' said Clare. 'I'm going to put me best glad rags on.'

'Here, I hope that don't include anything too short,' said her dad.

'But Clare's got nice legs,' said her mum.

Clare laughed and danced.

What a wonderful world.

That evening, Jimmy received a phone call from his young cousin Linda.

'Jimmy?'

'Hello, hello,' he said cheerfully. Well, he was in a fine state of health and feelings. 'What can I do for you, Linda?'

'Oh, I just wanted to tell you something,' said Linda.

'And what's something?'

'Jimmy, I've started growing!'

'Didn't you start in your pram?'

'I mean now. Jimmy, I'm shaping up.'

'You mean – ?'

'Yes. Gosh, isn't it a relief I'm going to be normal? I've been eating doughnuts, and I'm sure they're what's doing it for me.'

Jimmy smiled.

'Is this conversation confidential?' he asked.

'Oh, yes, just between you and me,' said Linda.

'Right, I'll keep it to myself,' said Jimmy, 'until everyone starts noticing.'

'Oh, you're nice,' said Linda. 'Have you seen that girl Clare lately?'

'I saw her today, at the factory,' said Jimmy, 'and I'm going to marry her.'

'Jimmy, you're what?'

'That's if she says yes. If so, that'll be between me, you and everybody else in the family.'

'Oh, golly,' said Linda. 'Well, I bet she won't say no.'

'You can wish me luck, then,' said Jimmy.

The Soviet ambassador received the note from the Foreign Office on Friday, and, as protocol demanded, he made the usual official protest but perforce had to agree to the return of the named men to Moscow.

Saturday morning.

Sir Edwin and Chinese Lady were on their way back from Devon, in company with Sir Henry and Lady Simms. They'd all enjoyed a quiet and relaxing holiday, with regular leisurely walks around the lush green countryside, but Chinese Lady was now looking forward to a return to the familiar, where she could get up to date with the latest family news.

Chapter Thirty-Two

Saturday evening.

Philip was on the phone to Phoebe again, and Phoebe was verbally tying him up again. Jimmy was getting ready to go to Bow and pick up Clare for their evening out. Clare was selecting an outfit which she hoped would knock him for six, and at the same time encourage him to pop the question. She might see herself as part of the modern young people's scene, with a thoughtful interest in contemporary novels, but she still couldn't think of anything she wanted more than marriage to Jimmy.

And Jimmy couldn't think of anything more to his liking than Gertie and Bert's eldest granddaughter, a cockney Bow belle with a bucketful of sex appeal.

'He's gone out in his best suit,' said Susie to Sammy.

'Our Jimmy?' said Sammy. 'So I noticed. Well, he's going dancing with Clare.'

'Sammy, not many young men go dancing in a

suit these days,' said Susie. 'More like a shirt and jeans.'

'Let's see,' mused Sammy. 'His best suit, and he's borrowed the car. Sounds to me as if he's going to duck a dance hall and take Clare for a ride in the moonlight. Well, I tell you, Susie, I'm approving of a best suit, a car ride, no jeans and a spot of moonlight. Not that I'm old-fashioned.'

'Yes, you are,' said Susie, 'you're all old-fashioned, you, Lizzy, Boots and Tommy. Still, so am I. Sammy, I suppose you realize we're having to face the prospect of Jimmy getting married, as well as Paula.'

'Talk about lambs flying the coop,' said Sammy.

'That's pigeons, Sammy.'

'Blimey,' said Sammy, 'and there's Phoebe still on the phone to Philip, and probably talking like a bride-to-be about what they're going to do on their honeymoon. As if she didn't know. They all know these days. Me, I only guessed.'

'Guessed?' said Susie. 'Not much you didn't. I nearly thought of going back home to Mum and Dad. There must be a good reason why I didn't. I'll remember what it was one day. And you needn't worry about losing Phoebe just yet. She's only sixteen.'

'I'm hanging onto Phoebe,' said Sammy.

'Until when ?' asked Susie.

'Till she's forty, say,' said Sammy.

'You'll be lucky if you think she's going to stay and nurse you in your old age,' said Susie. 'Well, we'll see what happens between Jimmy and Clare tonight.'

Jimmy had changed his mind about taking Clare to a dance hall. He was aiming to surprise her by driving her to a West End restaurant. He'd booked a cosy table for two.

It was nearly eleven when a car pulled up outside a house in Bow. The driver, a young man, alighted, went round to the passenger door and opened it. A young lady in a flowery print dress with a flared skirt, and sporting a delightful ponytail hairdo, emerged to enchant the young man's eyes in the light of a street lamp.

'Lovely,' he said. Jimmy was quite sure that this visionary girl of London's East End owned a dress sense any debutante would have envied.

'You really like my dress, Jimmy?' said Clare.

'Love it,' said Jimmy, 'and everything else about you.'

'You're going to come in, aren't you?' said Clare.

'I think I'd better,' said Jimmy, 'in case your dad is an old-time parent and expects me to ask him for permission to marry you.'

'Jimmy, no, he's not like that,' said Clare, 'you only have to tell him and Mum you've got my permission. That's all the permission you need. Jimmy, I'm so happy, I never ever thought I'd get proposed to in a restaurant up West, and by someone like you. Jimmy, I love you ever so much.'

'What a coincidence, so do I,' said Jimmy.

'Beg pardon?'

'I mean I've got exactly the same feelings about you, you lovely girl,' said Jimmy. 'Um, permission to kiss you on your doorstep?'

'My doorstep doesn't need kissing, so could you just kiss me?' said Gertie and Bert's eldest granddaughter.

Sunday evening.

The June weather was improving, the day had been brighter and warmer. Felicity was in her bedroom, changing into something loose and comfortable. Tim and Jennifer were downstairs, and she could hear the girl laughing. It was a happy sound.

She groped inside her wardrobe, her touch her guide, her wish always to do what she could for herself. Her touch enabled her to find what she wanted, a soft dress of lemon crêpe de Chine. Well, Tim had said it was lemon when they'd bought it. He was always with her whenever she went shopping for clothes. On Saturday shopping for groceries, either he or Jennifer accompanied her, and sometimes both.

She drew the dress out and released it from its hanger. Her touch was sure.

A blur suddenly appeared in front of her, a faint and delicate blur. She stared, knowing she was looking at the dress. Oh, no, was it her damned imagination again, or simply wishful thinking?

Still holding the dress, she closed her eyes and kept them closed for a full minute. When she opened them again, tentatively, the blur was like a furry patch of faint colour. Lemon colour, lemon? Her breath almost stopped, for the image didn't go away, it stayed. In a kind of demented rush, she crossed to where she knew the window was. The

June evening was bright, although a few white clouds were running across the blue sky. She saw nothing of the clouds or the sky, but she did see a blur of light, a wide blur.

With her heart beating so fast it was almost painful, Felicity moved from the window and tried to steady herself. She did something of an everyday kind. She stepped into her dress, and as she drew it upwards she was visually conscious of a faint, pale shimmer. Keeping her eyes open, she brought the garment up over her tense body and slipped her arms into the sleeves. The pale shimmer did not recede. She reached around her back and zipped the dress, then tugged at it until she was sure there were no creases. That done, she moved to her dressing table, and tried to locate the mirror with her eyes. She found it, and it reflected the faint blur.

'Dear God,' she breathed, and stood there, unmoving and looking for two or three minutes. Slowly the pale image faded away until everything was invisible once more. But this time there was no bitter reaction, no disillusion, for she was now certain it was not imagination or self-deception she had suffered twice before. It was real. She was also certain it would happen again, and more frequently, perhaps, with the blur becoming brighter and clearer, until –

Until a miracle occurred?

'Felicity?' Tim was calling. 'Are you all right?'

Dear Tim. Always her chief support, always in care of her. She left the bedroom, still a blind woman. But with the geography of the house so familiar, and her body alive, she began a sure descent of the stairs.

'Felicity?'

'Coming, darling.'

This time she was going to tell him.

THE END

THE GHOST OF WHITECHAPEL
by Mary Jane Staples

When fiery Bridget Cummings advertised for a lodger, she did not expect a policeman to apply for the room. She wasn't fond of the coppers, believing them to be traitors to the poor of Whitechapel, but her younger brother and sister moved P.C. Fred Billings in the moment Bridget's back was turned, and she seemed to have little say in the matter. Still, she had to admit that she was glad of Fred's company in the walk back from her late-night washing up job, particularly when a young girl was found in a nearby street with her throat cut.

The discovery of the body of Maureen Flanagan who was, the neighbours believed, a respectable woman, naturally stirred memories of Jack the Ripper. His horrific crimes had shocked the neighbourhood only twelve years before, but Chief Inspector Dobbs of the City of London Police was convinced, like most other police officers, that the Ripper was dead. But when a second body was discovered, and Bridget noticed a strange man following her, the neighbourhood was alert to the possibility that the terror had returned . . .

0 552 14548 3